Jezebel

A Novel by K. Larsen

D1365078

Other K. Larsen Books

30 Days ~ FREE
Committed

Bloodlines Series
All can be read as stand-alone books.

Tug of War ~ FREE
Objective
Resistance
Target 84

Stand Alones
Dating Delaney
Saving Caroline

Prologue

Her recently manicured nails bit marks into her palms. She fought the urge to squirm under the acidic looks currently directed at her. "Annabelle Fortin, you will listen to your father," her mother snapped, hands planted on her hips. Annabelle stood defiantly before her parents, desperately wishing her life was someone else's — anyone else's.

"You don't need to punish me more," she retaliated. "I know how bad this is, and how bad it *looks*." Her relationship with her parents was strained, at best. Gavin and Monica Fortin wanted their child to live a life of decadence. However, with that lifestyle came endless opportunities for experimentation. And experiment she had.

Recently eighteen, Annabelle had already dabbled in sex, drugs, and other extra-curricular activities of the sordid variety. And she now had a police record to prove it. The DUI had been an extremely unfortunate event. She had been terrified sitting in the car, waiting for the police officer to arrive at her window. The blue lights had created a blurry strobe effect in her rearview. *Madison is going to kill me,* she'd thought. Not her parents — she had been worried her best friend would look down on her. Her parents only felt shamed by fellow country clubbers, and as a result Annabelle's life was being scrutinized.

Part of her punishment: a six-month court-ordered volunteer gig. She was pissed that she didn't even get a say in where she would volunteer. She'd been assigned to Glenview. Four hours a day, once a week, for six *long* months, at an assisted living facility for people with early onset dementia. She disliked old people in general . . . *Great, old people who don't even know they're old.* She snickered at her own jab.

"Annabelle, your phone. *Now,*" her father barked. His hand stretched out. Palm flat, waiting expectantly, his eyes boring into hers in that deep, intense way only a father's could.

She forked over her phone with a pout and scowled. Annabelle's friends joked that her dad was hot enough to be a GQ model even at fifty-four. She hated the way they giggled at his slight accent—at *anything* he said—and ogled him. It was lame and disgusting. He was old fashioned and didn't parent the way other kids' parents did. He said it was how *he* was raised, but she hated it. When she was little, she'd thought it was cool that her dad was foreign—but now, she wished he'd accept the way things were done in the U.S. and leave his European parenting skills behind.

"I hardly think losing your phone is worth all the dramatics, Belle."

Annabelle said nothing as she stewed in anger. "Your mother and I have talked, and we've decided that for the duration of your probation your curfew is six p.m. You're to be home for dinner every night. And no friends are allowed over."

She threw her hands up in the air. "Six months? I drove drunk! I didn't *kill* anyone. You've been letting me drink at home since I was fifteen—"

"Enough!" her father roared. He raked a hand through his hair, gripping the back of his head in frustration. Annabelle cowered slightly at his booming voice. "You got lucky. You were driving *my* car. Using *my* money to buy alcohol, and hanging out with that degenerate boyfriend of yours—not studying at Madison's house as you led us to believe."

"I'm eighteen, Daddy . . . I could just leave." She crossed her arms over her chest. Her father's face descended into an unusual shade of red. The back of his hand pressed to his mouth as he stifled his first train of thought. She thought for a moment that steam might start billowing out from his ears like they did in the cartoons she used to watch as a child. His breathing was ragged and his nostrils flared. Her resolve faltered slightly.

"You wouldn't even know how to begin to support yourself. We've spoiled you your entire life. But if you want to go—" he gestured to the door, "you know the way out." His tone was venomous.

A wave of guilt engulfed her. Annabelle *was* spoiled, she had to admit. She didn't have a clue what she'd do if she walked out of the house. She had no car, had never worked, had never paid a bill of her own . . . and—outside of her trust fund—had no accessible money until, ironically, her twenty-first birthday.

Her parents owned her.

She turned and stomped to her room, feeling helpless and irritated. School would be over in three months. She'd graduate and spend her entire summer before college confined to the house. This house. The toxic display case *they* called a home. Her life officially sucked more than it had before, which was a feat.

She had known she was too buzzed that night to drive but quite frankly, she just hadn't cared enough to *not* do it. It was a rash decision. It never should have happened. Throwing herself onto her bed, she flipped onto her back and then reached toward her pocket, only to remember that she didn't have her phone. She rolled onto her stomach, stuck her face into her pillow and screamed so loud and hard her voice finally gave out. Tears of frustration and bitterness still flowed long after.

Hours passed. She got bored. She tried reading. After a chapter she gave up. She couldn't concentrate. Restless, she tried listening to music. After that failed to calm her she tried watching TV, but she only managed to endlessly flip through the channels. She tried on all the clothes in her closet. Nothing distracted her. Nothing held her interest. She hated feeling emotions. She did whatever it took to avoid facing the issues that plagued her. Her apathy for her home life bordered on acute hatred. For years now she had buried herself with distractions. She did anything to keep her head in the sand. It was easier *not* to feel. It was easier to get up every morning and ignore the disappointment, the aloofness. Finally, she trudged downstairs to beg her mother for her laptop back. She'd need it for school, anyhow. They couldn't take away *everything*.

"Mom."

"Belle," her mother answered absently and glanced at the clock on the stove. *Typical*, Annabelle thought, look anywhere but at her very own daughter.

"Can I have my laptop back? I need it for schoolwork."

"I will talk with your father about it." Annabelle's shoulders sagged at the response.

"Please," she tried. Her mother turned to face her and her eyes softened.

"One hour. Bring it downstairs with you when you come down for dinner."

Annabelle didn't dare utter a word for fear her mom would change her mind. She quietly waited while her mom unlocked a drawer and pulled her laptop out.

"Thanks," she said quietly as she took it from her mother's hands. Quickly racing up to her room, she smiled before she plunked down on her bed and fired up the machine.

After messaging Damon, her boyfriend, and Madison on Facebook to let them know she would see them tomorrow at school and what her punishment was, she Googled the assisted living facility where she'd be volunteering. She was not looking forward to working with these old people; they smelled funny and their wrinkled, loose skin made her gag.

"We pride ourselves on being an assisted living community that promotes living life to its fullest. By providing a wide range of activities, amenities, and events, we encourage our residents to enjoy the greatness life has to offer. We encourage independence while offering safety and support. When you live at Glenview, you are more than a resident. You are family."

She sighed and shut the laptop lid. *Family.* She laughed at the notion. Nothing good seemed to come from family. She glanced at the picture on her nightstand. Smiling faces. Hair blowing in the salty wind, the beach and ocean behind them. It had been an amazing vacation. It had been the last time she remembered family as something *good*.

~***~

Annabelle's first day at Glenview was chaotic. She'd barely had time to make the bus from school to the facility. Change would come, she thought. Maybe not today. But it would come. It *had* too. Annabelle had to believe. She closed her eyes, and pictured a different world. Where people were fearless and unified. Free. Healed and cheerful. A place where nothing hurt. She drew in a deep breath and stepped off the bus in the direction of Glenview. Tuesday, the day she was to volunteer. Her time would be dictated by the staff and spent in the kitchen or sitting in a recreation room with senile senior citizens. Neither option appealed to her at all.

She was a ball of raw nerves. She hadn't volunteered before. She had never been in *real* trouble before. She pushed through the doors of the facility and stopped short. It smelled funny. It smelled like punishment. It was days like these she felt like the world was against her, that everyone around her seemed mean. And ugly. There were times she burned with antipathy. In those moments, she was repulsive too. She didn't want to hate. Annabelle wanted to be kindhearted. But she had a difficult time executing her wants as of late.

"Can I help you?" A dirty blonde haired woman looked her up and down and Annabelle stiffened.

"Annabelle Fortin. I'm here to volunteer." Her voice wasn't her own. It sounded meek and pathetic even to her.

"Ah yes." The woman smoothed an errant tendril of her hair, eyes locked on Annabelle. "We're short-staffed in the kitchen today. Follow me."

Annabelle wanted to find a dark corner and hide there. *The kitchen?* She knew nothing about cooking or serving food. Life was beginning to look like a bad dream. She inhaled sharply, put one foot in front of the other and followed the dishwater blonde down the kitchen where she was promptly handed a hairnet and a pair of plastic gloves. *Ugh*, she thought. This was so much worse than she imagined.

Chapter 1

Annabelle

"I gave you all that I could give. My soul, my heart, my mind."

~ L'ame Immortelle — Betrayal

Tuesday. Again.

Annabelle had been dreading Tuesday for a week now. After last week's kitchen duty she was sure her life *was* a nightmare. She'd left Glenview smelling like pureed spinach, bad breath and old people. It was a disaster. Her four hours had felt like ten.

As she walked down the brightly lit corridor toward the recreation room, a ruckus came from suite 208. She slowed her pace, eavesdropping. Her purple Converse sneakers squeaked on the sterile linoleum floor. She hated it here. She hated what volunteering represented in her life. Visit number two, and she was already willing away the next twenty-three, mandated volunteer days.

"I'm not riled up, you fools!" A woman swatted attendants' hands away from her. "I'm bored. This place is like hell," she huffed, resigning and settling down in the overstuffed chair behind her. The sight of this woman, scarcely as old as her own parents, struck her. Her skin was soft looking, her eyes clear and her posture self-assured.

"I'll sit with you," Annabelle boldly suggested from the doorway.

The woman's weathered but clear hazel eyes shot to hers, and she smiled ruefully.

"Can you be trusted?" the woman asked, eyes narrowed.

What a strange question. Maybe this hellish punishment wouldn't be so bad, after all.

Annabelle shrugged. "Sure."

"And who, my dear, are you?" the woman asked.

Annabelle took the woman in now. Really took her in. She was tall, slender, and quite pretty despite being her parents' age. Her salt and pepper hair was swept up into a French twist. She thought what a shame it was when dementia hit this young. Ten years in a nursing home seemed like torturous eons to her, but having to endure these sterile places for nearly half a lifetime was just cruel. It was depressing knowing that this was the last stop. When a person was out in the world anything was still possible but once they moved into a place like Glenview there was only one way they would move out.

She straightened her shoulders. "I'm

Annabelle Fortin."

"Well, Annabelle Fortin, why on earth do you want to sit with a bumbling middle-aged fart like myself?"

"I don't know, you seem kind of . . . spirited to me. Maybe you'll have something interesting to say." Annabelle peeled her eyes from the woman and glanced out the window near the woman's bed while absently tucking her hair behind one ear.

"Oh, posh. You pity me. Think I'm lonely." The woman huffed. "I'm not, you know. One can never be bored with a mind full of memories. I had quite the life before this." Her hands splayed wide and gestured to the cold, eggshell-colored room. The attendants that lingered seemed to warm to the idea of Annabelle placating the woman. "Is it alright that I sit with her instead of working in the kitchen?" she asked the nursing assistant.

"I'll check but as far as I'm concerned you're a godsend. If she gives you any trouble, holler. She's a mean bird," the nursing assistant stated as he exited the room. Annabelle wrinkled her nose at him.

Moving across the sterile room toward the chair opposite the lady, Annabelle cracked her knuckles then sat. Unlike the other rooms she'd passed in the hallway, this woman's was cold.

Not homey at all. No pictures or decorations hung on the walls, no trinkets sat on shelves.

"So, am I allowed to stay?" she asked scratching her arm that didn't even itch.

"I suppose." The woman looked her up and down, weariness pulling heavily at her features.

"What's your name?" Annabelle finally asked, desperate to break the silence between them.

"Wouldn't you like to know?" the woman answered with a smart-ass grin. The corners of Annabelle's mouth kicked up into a smile. She chuckled and tucked her legs up under herself in her chair.

"I could probably just ask someone," she returned.

"Where's the fun in that?" the woman answered, a sour expression on her face as if she had just bitten into a lemon. Annabelle shrugged. "How old are you?"

"Eighteen," she answered. The woman's eyes lit up like sparklers.

"Eighteen was grand! You must be having the time of your life." The woman clapped her hands together excitedly.

Annabelle frowned. She was definitely *not* having the time of her life. "It's been less than awesome," she answered dryly.

"Bullshit!" the woman squawked.

Annabelle started at the curse from the woman before noting the huge smile on her face. "Eighteen will be the best year. You'll see. You'll look back when you're sitting in some home somewhere, like me, and think, *damn*, eighteen was fabulous."

"I sure hope so," she answered, frowning.

"You have quite the pout, you know that? It twists up your features and makes you ugly."

"That's not very nice." Annabelle scowled. She eyed the old woman, a sudden wave of insecurity rushing through her.

"It's not meant to be nice. It's the truth. Truths are often ugly." Annabelle blinked, unsure how to respond.

"Child, are you always this . . . this boring?" the woman asked.

"I'm not boring!" she squawked crossing her arms and pursing her lips in irritation.

"Well you're not exactly *riveting* either, are you?" the woman volleyed back, revealing a half smile.

"What do you want from me?" Annabelle asked irritated. This woman was crazy but definitely not boring. She might actually enjoy some of her time if she got to sit with this mystery woman each week.

"Well, Annabelle Fortin, *eighteen*, let's start with something easy."

"Okay." she answered.

"Why are you here?" the woman asked while pulling a blanket from the back of her chair and placing it over lap. Annabelle looked at the woman's sock clad feet. For the first time since her DUI she felt ashamed to admit why she was here. "This isn't rocket science love, just spit it out," pushed the woman after a pause of silence.

"I don't have a choice. It was volunteer for six months or serve jail time. I chose this." she answered lifting her chin and meeting the woman's gaze.

"A rebel. I like it. What'd you do?"

"I got pulled over for driving drunk," Annabelle explained.

"Was anyone hurt?"

"Only my pride." Her tone was laced with sarcasm.

"Oh posh, scandals and alcohol go together like peanut butter and jelly. That's not all that exciting," the woman *tsked*. Annabelle felt her face wrinkle in confusion. "There must be more to it . . ."

"Nope. Grounded until I leave for college. No phone. Limited computer use. No friends over and stuck here once a week for four hours."

Stifling a snort the woman said, "Dear God, you mean that I'm to be your *only* source of entertainment for the next six months?" She slapped a hand to her chest dramatically. Annabelle cocked her head and stared at the nut job, hard. "Your life is *definitely* worse than mine," the woman concluded with a roll of her hazel eyes.

Bubbles formed in Annabelle's gut. Her rib cage started to shake and finally, she laughed. A loud, hearty laugh. A laugh that startled her. A laugh the likes of which was so genuine that she couldn't remember the last time it had happened. The mystery woman promptly joined in, giggling right alongside her. It put her at ease. Her heart felt lighter.

"So tell me, do you have a boyfriend?" the woman asked as their laughter died down.

"Do you have a name?" she responded with a smart-ass smile.

"Touché, tiger, touché." The woman grinned a dazzling smile revealing a row of straight white teeth.

"So, are you going to tell me?" she pushed.

"Not today," the woman answered simply.

"You are strange. *Very* strange. And you don't seem to be confused at all. Why are you here?"

"Ahh, life's great mysteries. *Confused* – is that what you think dementia is?" the woman asked.

"Well, mostly. Forgetful and confused." She shrugged.

"And does that come and go?" the woman pushed.

"Sure, like you're fine for a while and then not. That's why you need to live somewhere like this."

"I think based on your definition I would be delirious. Dementia affects memory, thinking, language, behavior. Delirium is more of a sudden unexpected severe confusion and rapid change in the brain's ability to function."

Annabelle rolled her eyes. "How are those different?" Annabelle asked. She was struggling a bit to keep up with the woman. Her brows were knit together as she tried to work out what the woman was getting at.

"Exactly my dear! How *are* they different?" Annabelle huffed and shook her head in frustration. Having a real conversation with this woman proved difficult and tiring.

"Okay, I give up. New topic? You said you had quite the life before this. Will you tell me about it?" she asked.

"That depends."

"On what?" she sighed. *Maybe the kitchen crew would be better.*

"Whether or not you like love stories."

Annabelle half-shrugged. "Sure. I usually like a little suspense or mystery with my romance but a love story could be alright."

"Oh but my dear, every great love story has a twist. If there's no twist, how does one ever know if their love can endure?"

"Endure what?" she questioned as she pulled at imaginary threads on her sleeve.

"Anything," the woman answered as if that were the only answer.

Annabelle thought about her words for a moment. Let them sink into her brain. Did her parents' love story have a twist? Surely not one that she'd heard about. Or could a twist be a tragic event? If that was the case then her family, her parents, had endured a twist and survived it together, even if just barely. Either way, she wanted to corral the woman into a singular train of thought.

"Okay. Tell me your story," she answered.

"It might upset you, or perhaps I have no story to tell. We have six months! Let's start with someone far more interesting. Celeste Fontaine."

Annabelle's face scrunched up. "Who the heck is Celeste Fontaine?"

"Oh, she was a girl I knew. A caretaker for a large chateau just outside of Paris. She had everything she ever imagined in life: blissfully happy parents who spoiled her rotten, friends she adored, and a man that made every woman on the planet jealous of her. But let's go back to the very start shall we?"

The woman had a mischievous gleam in her eye. Annabelle would be lying if she said she wasn't a little bit curious about *any* story this woman might tell. She was a character for sure, and that meant she probably hung out with some interesting people before she ended up at Glenview. She probably had lots of good stories to tell. Hell, it beat wearing a hairnet and latex gloves in the kitchen. She shivered at the thought of cafeteria food, trays and dirty silverware. And hairnets.

"Are you cold?" the woman asked, head cocked to the side.

"No," she answered, shrugging away the kitchen visual.

"Are you ready to pay attention?"

Annabelle nodded. "Excellent. If you don't pay attention, you'll miss things. *Important* things." Annabelle cocked her head to the side and wondered what the woman was yammering on about. "Make sure you listen carefully, and try not to jump to conclusions until I'm finished telling you everything. What happens from here on out isn't my responsibility. It's yours, so take notice." Annabelle scrunched up her nose in confusion and shrugged. The woman stared a moment longer at her before she nodded saying, "Alright then. Remember kid, the devil is in the details. Paris. Nineteen eighty-four."

Chapter 2

Celeste

Paris 1984

Celeste smoothed the fabric of her dress. Her gown hugged her body in all the right places. The silk felt luscious against her skin. The gardens twinkled under the strand lighting as she walked through row after row of flowers, taking in their unique smells and blossoms. Her hair was massed on top of her head with a select few tendrils hanging down, framing her face. She had spent the better part of the afternoon at the salon with Mara perfecting their looks. Celeste felt like a princess at these affairs no matter how much she loathed wasting an entire night with the stiff crowds of the upper crust. She was used to it, yes, but that didn't mean she wouldn't rather be elsewhere.

At twenty years old, she wanted to be at a pub with Matteo and Mara, singing karaoke and not caring if her shoulders were squared, which utensil to use or whether or not she was behaving in a ladylike manner. She wanted to live in the moment. Be whoever she felt like that evening. Instead, she was here, at the Garden Gala, where her parents were raising money for new pharmaceutical research. FogPharm was one of the leading research facilities in the world. Her parents, both scientists, were passionate about their work and their company. She had been required to attend these lavish parties since she'd turned sixteen.

She was thinking about her teenage years when he walked into the gala like he was walking the red carpet. Every woman in the room stopped and noticed him, no doubt hoping they'd be the one to catch his eye. Just the sight of him across the open space sent Celeste's heart beating rapid-fire. He flashed a smile here and there as he walked. Smirking, showing a dimple, he shook hands with all the right people.

Then, just five minutes later, she watched as he grabbed a champagne flute and chugged the contents in an empty corner of the garden. Suddenly, he looked miserable. She read his tension in the tight, bunched line of his shoulders. Although she wanted to be out with friends having a good time rather than here because it was expected of her, she wondered how anyone choosing to be here could be tense at this event eluded her. Lights twinkled. Music played. Drinks flowed. It was magical here. Late spring in Paris offered nothing less.

Celeste was not short by any standard, but from what she could tell the man stood at least six inches taller than her five-foot-eight-in-heels height. His broad shoulders were encased in an expensive dove gray suit that tapered down to narrow hips. His dirty blond hair hung mussed, tucked behind his ears. Tan and lean and athletic, his body looked damn near perfect with clothes on. She could only wonder what it looked like without them. Wealth, authority and virility rolled off him in great waves. His strong jaw added to the overall appeal. Green eyes landed on hers and she froze in her spot. The light captured them, making them appear to twinkle. Her breath faltered and heat warmed her cheeks. She darted her eyes to the floor quickly after she realized she was blatantly staring at the handsome stranger.

"He's a looker," Mara pretend-panted in her ear. Celeste jumped at the sudden break in the spell of the evening. "Didn't mean to scare you, Cece." Mara's arm linked through Celeste's at the elbow as she laughed.

"I was just . . ."

"Fantasizing. Like every other straight gal in this place," Mara cut her off. Celeste slumped her shoulders as the truth of her friend's statement washed over her. She was pretty, but there were far more attractive women here tonight to catch his eye. Plus, she wasn't looking. She had two more years left at university and a career to map out.

"Who is he?" Celeste asked.

"That happens to be *the* Gabriel Fontaine," Mara answered.

"The biochemist?" she squeaked. She'd wondered about him. Her parents had made him an offer to work for them upon his finishing graduate school. They were still waiting on an answer three months later. He was one of the most coveted up-and-comers in the biochemistry field.

"The very one."

"I thought he'd look older and less hot. Aren't biochemists supposed to be extra nerdy and unattractive?" Celeste joked.

"They are. He defies logic." Mara laughed. "Come on, we need drinks!" Mara tugged on Celeste until she finally moved her feet. The hairs on the back of her neck stood at attention as they made their way to the bar. She felt as if she was being watched and she blushed thinking about whom it might be. She could feel his green-eyed gaze burning into her back.

"How're your parents?" Mara asked. The two of them had been friends since high school. The best of friends. Mara came from an affluent background like she did. The pressures *and* perks were understood without words. Mara's penchant for being somewhat of a wild child irked her parents but without her, Celeste would have drowned under the pressure of life long ago. Her parents loved her. They did, but the world they existed in was wrought with discipline, expectations and beliefs that were ironclad from years of breeding. They showered her with love and encouragement, yet that encouragement always seemed to come with a price.

"At table six," Celeste said.

"Ahh, so are mine." Mara nodded.

"You'd better behave, Mara. They'll never let you room with me if you cause a scene again."

Mara's last stunt had sent both sets of parents over the edge. She'd streaked through campus last semester drunk. Her parents had threatened pulling her from school until she could learn how to behave appropriately. Her response to the situation hadn't helped any: 'If by behave, you mean find myself a suitable husband, then no thank you.' They'd laughed and laughed, huddled in their dorm room together over their reaction. Their blood-drained faces, her mother's gasp, her father's look of disdain. It had shaken them both, and over the summer Mara had been nothing short of a model of finance-driven breeding. She had no choice.

"Oh, shut it, Cece. I'll behave." Mara lifted her wine glass and drained it as Celeste shook her head and giggled. "Where is Matteo?" Mara asked, drawing out his name to make a point. Celeste blushed, knowing that in another life, maybe Matteo and she would be free to explore their budding feelings for each other.

"He's there," she answered, pointing across the dance floor. Matteo, tall dark and brutally handsome, made his way through the crowd, offering appetizers. She sighed at the unfairness of life. How some could be viewed as inconsequential simply because of their bank balance. How the world was built on dreams and iron and greed. Matteo was brilliant, handsome and going to make a name for himself. She knew it. She had unwavering faith in him.

"If you're not going to take advantage of that fine work of art, I will." Mara giggled. Matteo was absolutely beautiful. She slapped Mara's arm playfully and laughed alongside her friend. The three of them were like three peas in a pod. It was rare that they spent longer than a day or two without seeing each other.

"He's too important to me to do that. Have at it," Celeste said. Above all else, she valued Matteo's friendship. They'd met in their Intro to Horticulture class in their freshman year of university and instantly formed a bond, a bond that neither of them seemed willing to take further than friendship. It was odd in a way. They held hands when they explored the campus, he picked her up from parties when she'd had too much to drink, and sometimes they shared a bed, to sleep only, simply to ward off anyone else from doing so. They talked about their dreams, their goals, and their differences. He dated and she dated and there was no jealousy harbored between them. It just . . . was what it was. There was an understanding.

She looked to him now. His nose was perfectly straight, and his jaw was well defined. His lips were perfection. Mara winked at Matteo from across the floor and they both laughed when he dramatically winked back.

"Excuse me. What are you drinking?" It was a deep, *lush* male voice. Mara's head whipped around and her jaw dropped. Using her index finger, Celeste pushed Mara's chin up until her mouth closed again and suppressed a chuckle. Turning, she noticed the body behind the voice.

The biochemist.

Gabriel Fontaine.

"Who were you directing that question to?" she asked. Mara snorted and started to back away. Celeste grabbed Mara's wrist to hold her in place.

"I think your friend is quite observant." He laughed as Mara released herself from Celeste's grip and moved another step away.

"Me then?" she asked, smiling as heat warmed her body from her belly up.

"Yes. You," he confirmed.

"White wine spritzer. But, as you can see, my glass is half full."

"Witty." He grinned, flashing her a row of dazzling white teeth.

"Perhaps." She felt a flutter in her belly. What was his angle here? She tried to work it out as he took a step closer to her.

"I'm not sure we've met. Gabriel," he said.

"The biochemist with the inflated ego," she returned coyly. His reputation was no secret. He was said to be brilliant in his field and popular with the ladies, and was modest about neither. A bachelor at heart.

"Ah, so you've heard of me," he laughed. It was a deep, carefree sound that resonated. She instantly liked it.

"Celeste Fogarty." She extended her free hand to him. He took it, gently but firmly, and turned it over before placing a kiss on the inside of her wrist. A small move, bold in its intimacy, but not outright inappropriate. If she could stop the damn butterflies demanding to break free from her belly she could analyze the moment.

"Fogarty . . ." he murmured. "Julian and Roberta's daughter?"

"The very one," she answered. He let his eyes roam her form—top to toe. His perusal made her squirm. She'd never been so blatantly stared at before. His gaze was appreciative though, not critical.

"I can see it now," he said finally.

Celeste laughed. She truly looked nothing like her parents. Her mother's blond hair and blue eyes were a far cry from her auburn locks and hazel eyes. Her mother was petite, while she was more athletically built. Her father, also blond, albeit a darker shade than her mother's, was fit, but stocky. They loved to say she got her height, hazel eyes and brunette coloring from her grandparents. Celeste couldn't be sure though, as she'd never met either set. Both were deceased by the time she was six and had never bothered to come to France from the States to visit.

"I hate it when people say that."

"It was rather lame." He shrugged. He looked to table six, where her parents were seated, and then back to her. "And, I suppose, not exactly true." Celeste shook her head and grinned at him.

"So, Gabriel, what can I do for you?" she asked, feeling bold. From the corner of her eye she caught Mara and Matteo watching her. Suddenly she felt as if she were betraying them somehow. Leaving them out. They would bombard her with questions later tonight, no doubt.

"Épouse-moi," *Marry me,* he said. Celeste felt

her brows lift and her eyes grow wide.

"Very funny. I've only just met you!" she laughed. *What a strange thing to say,* she thought.

"What does that have to do with anything?" He grinned at her.

"Everything!" she replied, raising her hands in the air. His grin widened. She couldn't help but be swept up in his dimpled smile. His carefree expressions were mesmerizing. Hell, everything thus far was mesmerizing about him.

"I'll ask you every day until I wear you down and the only logical answer becomes yes."

"You're crazy," she answered, snorting. She slapped a hand over her mouth and nose, embarrassed that she'd snorted out loud. Gabriel didn't seem to notice or mind as he continued on.

"I'm many things. Taken by you. Frappe." *Smitten.* The French word rolled off his tongue the way calm water lapped a shoreline. *Provocatively.* She loved the way the language here sounded. She loved listening to it. Matteo teased her love of languages by speaking his native Italian to her. Mara always joked that anytime a man spoke a foreign language, Celeste became putty their hands. Mostly, it was true. She could close her eyes and get lost in the gentle lilts and smooth sounding words of either French or Italian.

"That's bold," she scoffed, trying to remain unaffected by his words.

"Maybe."

"No. Definitely," she stated, chin raised.

"Okay, it is, but I know what I want." Such conviction. Such allure. Curiosity to know if he was serious bloomed in her.

"What about next month? Next year? Twenty years from now?" she quizzed, deciding to play along. Her parents, still at their table, caught her eye, nodding their approval. *Of course.*

"Je vous veux." *I'll want you,* he answered. The conviction in his voice made her heart slam against her ribs.

"I can't take you seriously right now, this is preposterous." She laughed at the handsome stranger before stepping backward a step. He caught her wrist, stopping her movement. The rugged pad of his thumb grazed the delicate underside of her skin. Fire bloomed in her belly, swelling upward through her chest, warming her cheeks and surely staining them an obvious pink. Her eyes snapped to his.

"Settle for a dance with me then?" His eyes, stormy and serious, captivated her, kept her rooted in her spot. "Celeste, s'il vous plaît, juste une danse?" *Just one dance.* That damned French again, so fluid. So deceptively seductive. Her name sounded exotic they way he drew out the ending. She nodded her permission. He smiled a wolf-like grin, full of victory and blatant desire.

Sweeping her effortlessly into his arms and on to the dance floor, he promptly began to waltz. Looking back, that was probably the very moment he captured her heart.

His hand rested just above her rear, low on the small of her back. He was dangerously skirting that invisible line between gentlemanly and lewd. His other hand kept her right palm captured and pressed to his shoulder. They were molded together, touching from chest to hip as he led her to the rhythm of the music. The quartet played flawlessly, and Celeste found herself entranced. The warmth of his embrace, the music a soundtrack to their moment, his grace and ease on the dance floor, she felt swept away. Lost in a moment of fairy lights, blooming fragrant plants, a stunning man and music.

"So, Celeste," her name again drawn out, lustfully, "what are you studying?"

She tipped her head back to look him in the eye and smiled. The stars sparkled above against the navy velvet-looking sky.

"Horticulture." It sounded so unbelievably pathetic. Not an ounce of sex appeal could be found in a word like horticulture.

"Ah, my girl likes flowers."

"I don't know anything about *your* girl, but

most do." Her comeback brought a devilish smile from Gabriel.

"You are quick. I'll give you that." He laughed. It was throaty and deep and it made her pulse race. The music slowed and finally stopped.

"Why, thank you," she answered, grinning. She pried herself from his embrace and took a step backward.

"Where are you going?" he asked, stepping towards her.

"My dance card is rather full and your girl is probably waiting." She took another step away and watched as his eyes grew large with understanding. She was leaving him on the dance floor. "Also," she said with a smirk, "I don't much like flowers; they die. I prefer perennials."

Celeste turned and, she hoped, sashayed seductively away from Gabriel Fontaine.

"That was either the most amazing thing you've ever done, or the absolute stupidest," Mara said as Celeste returned to her two friends.

"I vote most amazing," Matteo said, and laughed. "Leaves him to do the chasing. Leaves him wondering if you're the *one* woman here tonight who wouldn't go home with him."

"Thank you, thank you," she laughed and curtsied dramatically for her friends.

"How did it feel?" Mara asked.

"Huh?"

"Being pressed up against him. I mean, the man is a god. Look at him!"

"Hey!" Matteo chuckled and ruffled Mara's hair. "I thought I was a god?"

"Shhh! We'll discuss *you* later tonight." Mara batted his hand away and kept her drooling, star-struck expression glued to Celeste.

"He's dreamy," she sighed.

"Dreamy?" Matteo barked out a laugh. Celeste bristled at his mocking.

"He was. It was. I mean, look around us. This place is magical tonight. He is handsome and smooth and yeah, dreamy, alright?" Matteo's hand encircled her waist and he tugged her close. He kissed her temple. Her irritation waned.

"Aww, fiore mio, scusa." *My flower, I'm sorry.* The Italian somehow made everything easier to hear. Easier to forgive. His nickname for her, flower, always made it impossible to stay mad at him.

"Yeah, yeah." She nudged him. "I don't rain on your parades. So be nice."

"Celeste, if the man makes you happy, then I'm happy."

"It was just a dance. And don't you have work to do?" She *tsked.*

Matteo gave her his best shocked-by-her-rudeness face before kissing her again on the temple and then kissing Mara's cheek. "Sì. I do. Can't lose this job. Veterinary school won't pay for itself." Celeste frowned at the truth in his statement as he strode away.

"Man, those pants sure look good on him," Mara joked. Celeste rolled her eyes and smiled at her best friend.

"So, your glass is empty and I don't even have a glass. Let's rectify that, shall we?" she suggested with a wink. Mara nodded and hooked her arm through Celeste's as they walked.

"Holy hell, he's watching you," Mara whispered.

"Oh, please."

"Look!"

Celeste turned her head a fraction toward Mara. Gabriel's gaze was on her, and he smiled when he caught her looking in his direction. Heat bloomed and reddened her cheeks. A striking blonde patted his arm to get his attention, but Gabriel didn't break eye contact with Celeste. He winked. She smirked and shook her head. Mara moved them along the perimeter of the dance floor until they reached the bar. Snapping fingers drew her head back in the right direction.

"You are *so* hooked." Mara laughed.

Celeste wasn't sure what to think. He intrigued her, sure. He was easy to look at, yes. Was he interested in more than a fling? She didn't know. She couldn't know. All she was sure of was that she didn't function that way. A few dates here and there were fine, but she wasn't the type to jump into bed with a man after the third date just because. Celeste was a relationship girl.

"He's a ladies man. Look, he has three women surrounding him as we speak," she said.

"He looks trapped. You should rescue him." Mara nodded in his direction.

"Not my style," she said.

"No, you're right; you, Celeste, are a true lady. Make him beg you for a date."

"Begging seems a little harsh, don't you think?" she asked.

"To a man like him? No. I think he likes the game."

"I think maybe you're wrong. I think he's used to the game, the chase, but that isn't what he truly wants."

"Here we go." Mara laughed. Celeste had a tendency to do that often, to look deeper. To dig deeper into people and see past what they project all the way down to what secrets they harbor deep in their soul. Matteo said it was what drew people to her, that she beckoned all those with something to share to her like a siren's call. He said she should be a psychology major, that it suited her more than plants. But Celeste loved plants. Flowers that bloom vibrant rich colors, shrubs that can be artfully arranged to create a labyrinth, the sight, the smell of a well-planned and maintained garden. It truly brought joy to her. Her parents didn't understand it, they wanted her in a biology or chemistry field so she could carry on the family business someday, but she'd never had the interest. "We need two champagnes, please," Mara told the bartender.

Three glasses later, Celeste was feeling lightheaded and warm. Her parents and Mara's had stopped by the girls' table to say their goodnights thirty minutes ago. Mara and Matteo were chatting near the bar as the party wound down. Celeste walked—shoes in hand, now that her parents were gone—through the dewy grass toward her friends. A large, warm hand clutched her elbow and spun her around.

"I got it," Gabriel said.

"I'm sorry?"

"Perennial. I'm not great with plants. It took me a while to get your joke."

"I'm still not following you." She cocked her head sideways.

"You said my girl probably likes flowers, but

you like perennials . . . as in you're the sort of girl who prefers relationships to flings. Something that comes back year after year."

"You got all that from my nerdy joke? You remember I'm a horticulture major, right?" Celeste laughed hard at the look on his fallen face. She hadn't meant anything deeper by her comment earlier, but she was pleased that he'd been dissecting it the entire night looking for meaning. "Aww, don't look so sad. I'm sorry." She watched as he rubbed the back of his neck with one hand. His other still clasped her elbow.

"Tell me, *si ce n'est pas indiscret*, do you have a boyfriend? Did I step on someone's toes tonight?" he asked. *If it's not too personal a question.* Celeste willed herself *not* to melt at his use of French.

"Why do you ask?" She bit her lip to keep from smiling like a ridiculous schoolgirl.

"By the looks of you, you should have someone, but—" he smirked and plucked the straps of her shoes from her hand "—you're tired and ready to leave." He leaned in, placing his face next to her ear. "And by the looks of your friends, they're not. A boyfriend would have surely noticed already that it's time to bring you home." His breath was warm and sent shivers down her spine. "May *I* give you a ride home?"

Spurred on by the thought of giving into this

man for a single evening, Celeste nodded her head. Matteo and Mara were watching her when she finally found the will to look away from Gabriel. She waved twice and winked at them, the trio's signal for: "all is right." Mara's face blossomed into a great grin and Matteo smiled, looking a little worried too. Celeste would speak with him later. He had to stop worrying over her so much. In some ways it prohibited him from living his own life to the fullest. She never wanted to become a burden to him.

Gabriel's hand came to rest at the small of her back — such an benign area on the body. It never really got any attention, yet when a man's hand rested casually there, it could cause the entire body to go on high alert. A simple gesture. A boring part of the body. He still clung to the straps of her shoes, carrying them for her. She smiled at the chivalry of it all. Her heart stuttered and in that moment she didn't care where they went or what they would do, just as long as she was with him.

He stopped short at the entrance to the gardens. Kneeling, he cupped her left calf and brought it to rest on his thigh. Celeste shooed him off, telling him she could manage putting her own shoes on, but he wouldn't relent. His fingers buckled the straps at her ankle. The rough pads of his fingers set her smooth skin on fire in the most impossible way. He repeated the process on her right foot before standing again.

She stared at him in awe. *Who does that?*

He took her hand, threaded their fingers together and gently tugged. Her feet moved on their own, wanting to stay next to the Adonis-like man holding her hand. Walking along-side him she realized there probably weren't many women who didn't give at least a passing thought to the idea of him in their bed. It was a quality some men exuded that promised he knew where to linger and what to do.

Stopping at his car, he opened the door for her. Gabriel turned to face her. There was a magnetic energy between them growing in intensity that sent a tremble quivering through Celeste. Gabriel cupped her face, and his eyes softened while his thumbs stroked back and forth over her cheeks. His green eyes bore into hers. His hands swept into her hair and weaved through the strands—a primal, masculine move.

"I'm going to kiss you now, Celeste Fogarty."

Celeste didn't move. She didn't speak. She was afraid to break the magical spell of the moment. She licked her lips in anticipation. He swallowed and took a breath, his Adam's apple bobbing up and down. Then, he did the simplest thing in the world. He leaned in and his lips met hers, softly, tenderly at first, and she swore the skies cracked open and swallowed the both of them whole. He tasted of champagne, wild nights and reckless desire. She relaxed into him and let impulse and passion fuel her. Celeste's heart thumped, kicking her ribs. Their lips, mouths, tongues . . . danced together. Time was lost. The spring air blew over them as he pressed soft kisses to the corners of her lips with reverence. Celeste had been kissed many times before, but none compared to the way Gabriel's laid claim to her.

Chapter 3

Annabelle

"You took all that you could get from me. Until the final day."

~ L'ame Immortelle — Betrayal

The woman's voice tapered off. She looked lost in thought, or maybe memory. Wistful.

"That seems like a fine stopping point, don't you think?"

Annabelle shrugged. "Sure."

"Do you have questions?"

She had a million things she wanted to ask but she wasn't sure where to start. "Why'd Celeste understand other languages?" Annabelle asked.

"The private school she attended demanded the students be as fluent as possible in the local language and one other. She took Italian."

"Are you Mara?" Annabelle's question made the woman gasp and laugh loudly.

"No ladybug, I'm most definitely *not* Mara." The woman smiled a wolfish grin.

"How do you know this Celeste lady's story so well, then?" she asked.

"Questions for another visit, I suppose. It's

almost dinner time." The woman waved her hand through the air dismissively.

"Okay," Annabelle responded. Pushing herself to a standing position, she faced the woman awkwardly, unsure how to leave.

"What is it child?" she pursed her lips in irritation.

"Bye, I guess," Annabelle answered meekly.

"Don't ever say *bye*. It sounds juvenile. Use something more exciting or concrete," the woman said with a pointed look.

Annabelle shook her head. She wondered if the woman was someone important or famous. She seemed so exotic yet demure and eccentric compared to anyone else she knew.

"See you next week then," she said, and half lifted her hand in a wave.

"Better, but lacks enthusiasm." A playful edge laced the woman's tone. Annabelle chuckled and turned away from the strange woman.

She stopped just outside of room 208. The name card read: Jezebel. No last name. She turned and checked the name card across the hall. *Milly*. Maybe the names are just to help the patients remember, not the staff. She'd been lost in all the commotion earlier and hadn't bothered to look.

Later, after checking in at the office making

sure they recorded that she had indeed been there today, she trotted out the double doors and into the evening air. The sun was just starting its descent and the sky shone with fabulous shades of pinks and oranges. She loved sunsets. They were magical. If the sky could produce such a show it seemed as though life could do the same. That anything was possible. As she walked toward the bus, she realized her four hours had passed rather quickly. It was definitely better than hanging out in the common room or helping in the kitchen.

~***~

Dinner was dry. Her mother's attempts at cooking always ended in bland food that made you want to swallow your own tongue. Her father smiled tightly as he chewed. *Fake smiles for fake parents,* she thought.

"How was Glenview?" he asked without looking up from his plate.

"Fine," she answered shoving chunks of chicken around on her plate.

"Just fine?" he pushed.

Annabelle swallowed her bite and rolled her eyes. Of course they'd want details. She was their only source of distraction these days—if and when they chose to acknowledge her at all. Sorrow moved through her chest. It hadn't always been this way between them. She could not suppress the wave of sadness that overcame her as she recalled how her family used to be. Once upon a time the house was warm and messy and lived in. Now it was an immaculate prison that smelled like Pledge and Pine Sol, no longer occupied by people, but ghosts. An empty shell really.

"I made a friend. Jezebel." She stabbed a dry hunk of chicken and forced it into her mouth. She wasn't really hungry.

"You aren't there to make friends, Annabelle," her mother clucked her disapproval.

Her mother's blonde hair shone under the bright dining room lighting. Annabelle had her mother's skin, alabaster white and blemish free, and her father's hair, wavy and thick but hers was darker. A deep brunette color to his sandy blonde. Her eyes were a deep blue and her lips tinted naturally red. Damon liked to joke that her lips were meant to be kissed. Her father's hair was cut short now, but she'd seen pictures from her parents' wedding, when it was longer. It suited him short, though. It was stern looking, like his personality.

Her mother was lithe, a real beauty. When she was little she wanted to look just like her. Now though, Annabelle noticed fine lines around her eyes and mouth from years of twisting her face into a hard pinched look, or scowling in general. Her mother was bitter, but she didn't know why. They lived well. Her father provided his family with endless opportunities, but still, her mother never seemed satisfied. Maybe that was only in the last eight years. She didn't really remember too much of how her parents interacted *before*. She was only ten. If someone had told her to pay attention, to notice the details, she would have, but no one did and this was her life now, the third wheel of a family stuck somewhere between anger and grief with a little pinch of denial mixed in.

"She's a resident there," she explained after chugging water to wash down the dried out chicken.

"What did you two do?"

"Nothing. I let her talk." Annabelle shrugged, wishing they could go back to silence. Sometimes the idea of something was better than the real thing. Interacting with them was painful. A painful reminder of how they were no longer a family.

Her mother nodded and her father pushed food around his plate. The rest of their dinner was spent in tense silence. She couldn't remember the last time she'd heard her parents actually have a conversation together. One that mattered anyway. One that wasn't completely superficial.

Annabelle rolled her shoulders to relieve the tension before excusing herself from the table. The hopeless weight she carried around with her seemed to get even heavier in that moment. After she'd cleared her plate she lazily walked to her room to finish her homework and hopefully sneak in a little messaging time with Damon before her Internet time was revoked for the night.

Annabelle's week sped by despite being stuck at home. She finally managed to read the books that had been stacked on the floor beside her bed. Her teachers were impressed that her assignments had been turned in on time. Every dinner with her parents since her first day volunteering had been bland and awkward. They hadn't spent this much time together in eight years and it was very evident. All parties fumbled their way through simple conversation.

~***~

Hello, Jezebel," she greeted the woman from the doorway.

"Ah, so the girl does have a brain. I'd wondered how long it'd take you to get my name."

Annabelle ignored the woman's jab and wandered toward the window. A beautiful potted plant bloomed generously. It hadn't been there last week.

"That's pretty. What is it?" she asked Jezebel.

"Gloxinia. It represents love at first sight."

"You got a boyfriend in here?" She raised an eyebrow at the woman. It would be hilarious to hear about that romance.

"Darling, I have a *man*, there is no *boy* in him." She winked.

Annabelle found herself blushing at Jezebel's words.

"Are you going to tell me more of your story today?"

"Possibly, but first, let's talk about you. I hardly know a thing!"

"There isn't much to tell. I live here in town. I'm due to graduate in May and hopefully head off to college after that."

"You literally could be any one of thousands of girls. Nothing personal was shared." Jezebel frowned.

"I guess there isn't much more worth sharing?"

"What makes you tick, Annabelle? What are your parents like? Are you in love with your boyfriend? What are you going to do with your life? Are you musical, artistic, book smart?"

Annabelle looked out the window and fiddled with the cuffs of her shirt sleeves. "My family sucks. My parents hardly speak. Damon is fun but I'm eighteen, how should I know if it's true love? And frankly, my biggest goal is to get the hell out of this town, *state,* and start over somewhere."

"You're awfully bitter." Jezebel said tartly.

"Am I?" she asked turning her focus back to Jezebel.

"I'd say. You're far too young to sound so . . . jaded. You've only just started your life. Why do you say your family sucks?"

Annabelle sighed. She wasn't interested in talking about her family and their issues, but Jezebel seemed fixated on the topic.

"Well, we're wealthy enough. My mom never seems pleased by anything. The house is filled with silence. It has been for years. It's just . . . depressing."

"Was it always that way?" Jezebel's face pulled tight. Annabelle couldn't discern if it was genuine concern or something else.

"No." She sighed. "No, it wasn't. For a while I remember them being happy. All of us being happy. When I was little they made their entire lives about us. The house was full, or it felt full. Lively, even."

"Ah, so something has changed since then?"

"Yes," she said twisting a strand of hair around her index finger.

"Are you going to share?" Jezebel arched a challenging brow at her.

"I don't like talking about it."

"We all have chapters we'd rather keep unpublished, tiger. But how can you ever forgive if you don't put it all out there?"

Annabelle tensed and looked away. "Forgive?"

"It's obvious that you resent them. Hold them accountable for your unhappiness. It's written on your face, in your body language and bad attitude."

"They'd have to admit fault for me to forgive," she returned.

"Ah, but you're wrong, darling. Forgiveness doesn't make them right, it only sets *you* free."

Annabelle huffed and sat down in the chair adjacent to Jezebel. "I'd like to hear more of your story."

"On one condition." Jezebel held up one perfectly elegant finger. Annabelle looked at her own hands. There was nothing remotely noticeable about them.

"What?"

"Tonight, at dinner, you ask your parent's one question about each of their days *and* listen to the answers they give."

Annabelle rolled her eyes. "Why?"

"Because, dear, what defines a person is how well they rise after falling down."

"You talk in riddles," she complained.

"And you don't *listen* hard enough," Jezebel scolded.

"Fine. I'll ask them each a question and *listen* to their answers tonight, okay?" she agreed.

"Brava, darling! You'll see . . . things will settle into place. Just trust me."

Annabelle stared at the woman. She was stunning, really. She thought she could have been a model when she was young. Her salt and pepper hair was still more pepper than salt, and her olive-tinted skin gave her an exotic look somehow. She was almost always smiling and had an aura about her, like she came from castles and grace and beauty. Annabelle wanted to glom on to all the woman offered. No one had bothered to *talk* to her, to ask her questions about her life, in so long, and that sudden interest reminded her that she *had* a life. She felt she was fading away into invisibility like her parents. Didn't she need someone to notice her and to care? It surprised her that she missed a mother-like connection so much. It surprised her that she was finding a small piece of that in the stranger seated across from her.

"Could you tell me more now?" she asked.

"Absolutely. Where were we?"

"Celeste and Gabriel's first kiss," she answered quickly.

"Ah, yes. The epic first kiss." Jezebel giggled, then ran a hand through her long hair. She watched as the woman shifted her gaze to the window. The afternoon sun streamed in and you could see all the tiny flecks of dust floating in the light beams. "Paris, nineteen eighty-four."

Chapter 4

Celeste

Paris 1984

Celeste found it impossible to calm her racing heart. Gabriel had driven her to her dorm and asked for her number before wrapping her up in his strong arms and kissing her goodnight. She was giddy with anticipation, but also felt a slight hesitation in her joy. Could she truly be so lucky to meet someone so intriguing, so handsome and so intelligent who might also feel so lucky to meet her?

She dropped onto her bed and thought about the *way* he had kissed her. *Twice.* Some of the greatest things in life were moments you collected with your eyes closed, like dreaming or kissing. Celeste had always preferred collecting moments over things, and Gabriel was another moment added to her mental arsenal. The moment had been worth cherishing, tucking aside for a rainy day long in the future to pull her out of a mood.

Mara rolled and grunted something inaudible from her bed. Celeste quietly laughed at her friend. *Would he call?* she wondered. He was nothing like what her parents had described.

She noted that she hadn't felt a pull this strong toward a man since she met Matteo. She was besotted. Questions burned in her mind. Her heart raced and her blush persisted as she tried to get comfortable in her bed.

Gabriel Fontaine had worked her into a hormonal frenzy.

~***~

You have to eat," Mara pushed giving her a pointed look.

"What if he calls?"

"Exactly." Mara said.

"Huh?" She raised her eyebrows confused.

"So what if he does, Cece? You can't sit here all day because he kissed you."

"Twice," she clarified with a smile.

"My God, I've never seen you this . . . worked up." Celeste bit her lip to stifle the grin on her face.

"It would be really, extra lame to sit here wouldn't it?" Celeste finally gave in. She knew it was foolish to sit by the phone waiting for a man to call, but the anticipation made it hard to risk missing hearing his voice.

"It would. It would also be very un-Celeste-like." She thought about Mara's statement. She was absolutely correct. She stood before slipping her feet into flats.

"You're right. Breakfast."

"Crepes or croissants this morning?" Mara asked, looping an arm through hers.

"Crepes. Always crepes."

"Let's stop and grab Matteo too," Mara suggested.

"I wouldn't dream of leaving him out."

At four o'clock, Celeste had nearly tricked herself into forgetting that Gabriel may call her. Brunch had been delicious and packed with witty banter from her two favorite people. She was thick-in-the-thrall of her studying when the phone rang. She jumped, clutched her chest and tried to calm her breathing. Mara, unaffected by the intrusive noise, picked up the phone.

"Bonjour," she giggled. Mara only answered the phone in French when she was trying to be funny. Celeste shook her head in amusement. "Hmm, I'm not sure, let me check." Mara grinned at Celeste.

Celeste shot her a look that begged to know who her friend was talking to.

"Aw, yes. Celeste *is* here, but she's studying, because she gave up hope that the handsome prince from last night would actually call."

She jumped from her desk chair and snatched the phone from Mara's hand. "Hello?" she answered breathless.

"Cheri, your friend thinks she's witty."

Gabriel's deep baritone vibrated through the receiver and straight to her core.

"True. She does. Sometimes she even *is*." She laughed, but glared at her friend.

"Did I really keep you waiting?" he asked. Celeste drew in a breath, not wanting to answer. "Je suis tellement désolé, cheri," *I'm so sorry, darling.* She puddled on the floor at his words.

"I was plenty busy today," she finally spat out.

"I'm sure. Listen, I'd like to take you out, tomorrow." Bold. Straight to the point. Celeste appreciated those qualities.

"I'm sure that can be arranged."

"Is there someone else I should arrange it with? Please don't tell me Mara is your keeper. I think that one would torture me for fun." He chuckled.

Celeste let out a laugh before answering. "I might like to see that, actually."

"S'il vous plaît, pas de," *Please, no,* he groaned.

"What did you have in mind? Sundays I try to get home for dinner with my parents."

"I will pick you up at eight tomorrow morning, then. We'll be outside mostly, so dress for that."

"And my parents' dinner?" she hedged.

"Tell them you can't make it. We'll be late."

Celeste twisted the phone cord around a finger. "That's bold. What makes you think I won't tire of you by dinner time?"

"Mon instinct." *My gut.* He seemed to have an answer for everything.

"Are you always this demanding?" she asked playfully.

"When I want something," he answered. Celeste's breath hitched.

"And you want . . ." she flirted.

"Don't fish for compliments. It's beneath you, Cheri," he answered in a curt tone.

Celeste pulled the phone from her ear and stared at it as if it had just slapped her. Her heart sank into her stomach at his rudeness. Mara raised her brows in silent question. She let out a groan, hoping to indicate her irritation.

"Celeste," he called. She put the receiver back to her ear. "I'm sorry. That sounded harsh. Please, tomorrow, let me show you what I want. How much I want it."

She thought about his request, swallowing the knot in her throat. "Please," he repeated.

"Alright," she answered, brow furrowed, feeling hesitant.

"I promise, you'll have the *best* time."

"Right. Well . . ." her voice faded.

"Au revoir," he said.

Celeste mimicked his goodbye and hung up the phone, feeling perplexed.

"What in the . . . what was all that about?" Mara asked. "You looked like the phone sank its fangs into you!"

"I don't know. He asked me out. I thought I was just flirting, but he snapped at me. It was weird."

"So don't go," Mara said with a shrug.

"He apologized. It just seemed . . . *odd*. I'm sure I'm making more of it then necessary."

"You? The sensitive one?" Mara giggled with sarcasm.

Celeste picked a pillow up from her bed and chucked it at Mara's head. She *was* sensitive. It was one of the things that people said they loved about her. She wondered briefly, as a pillow shot through the air at her face, if Gabriel would be one of those people.

"What the hell is going on here?" Matteo laughed as he stepped into their room. Mara and Celeste looked between each other and burst into a fit of laughter. Both of them lifted their pillows and chucked them at Matteo.

"Celeste was just asked out by Gabriel." Mara drew out his name for emphasis.

Matteo picked up the pillows and carried them to Celeste's bed. "Fiore mio, do tell." He sat, pillows clutched to his chest on the edge of her mattress.

"There's nothing to tell. He called and asked to take me out tomorrow." She bit her lip as her imagination took off.

"She's blowing her parents' dinner off," Mara interjected.

"Skipping family dinner? *Tsk, tsk.*" Matteo shook his head at her and cracked his knuckles. He grabbed a cigarette and lit it, letting it dangle between his lips. Mara fanned the air in front of her and scowled at him. Celeste moved to the bed and sat next to Matteo. He swung an arm around her shoulders and pulled her close. She looked up into his dark eyes and smiled, happy to see him. He pulled her tighter to his side and kissed her hair as she melted comfortably into his side.

"I hope you have fun," Matteo stated simply.

Celeste nodded and snuggled into the crook of his arm more. Mara jumped onto the bed, plucked the cigarette from his mouth and stubbed it out in the lid of a mason jar on the bedside table.

"Are we going to chat about this all night or can we put on Hill Street Blues?" Mara asked, smirking.

"HSB!" Matteo and Celeste shouted in unison.

The morning came much too quickly in Celeste's opinion. She tip-toed around the room, gathering her shower things. She didn't want wake Mara. Butterflies stormed around her stomach. She was excited and nervous for her day-long date with Gabriel.

She took her time getting ready. She carefully applied just the right amount of make-up, not so much to come across as *easy*, but not too little to seem prudish either. She wanted to look just right. She twisted her long brown hair loosely into a French twist, leaving little wisps down framing her face. She paired her jeans with an ultra-soft T-shirt that hung off one shoulder. At eight, she took one more long, hard look in the mirror, adjusted her shirt just so and tucked a stray piece of hair behind her ear before grabbing her coat and heading down stairs.

Gabriel Fontaine was leaning against a light pole, looking tall, muscular, and strong. She approached slowly, letting herself drink in his features. His hair was tied back in a low ponytail, his jacket open, exposing the tautness of his T-shirt, the firm physique hidden beneath. Long, jean-clad legs led to sensible sneakers. She wondered where he was taking her. Truly, it didn't matter; just being near him made her stomach drop and her heart flutter frantically.

His arms opened wide when she stopped before of him. He pulled her into a warm embrace, and she wanted to be lost in the smell and sight and feel of him forever. His cologne lingered in her nose as she pressed her face into his chest. His touch was warm and electric. She felt his lips touch her hair before she pulled away. She liked that.

A smile tugged at her lips. "Hello, Gabriel," she said.

"Celeste . . ." He drew her name out. "How are you?"

"I'm . . ." she started. "I'm good. Excited for what you have planned." Her smile was large and genuine.

"As am I. On y va ?" *Ready?* he asked.

A spring wind whipped around them. Strands of hair blew across her face, sticking to her lips. He reached out and swept the hair aside with the lightest touch of his finger, tucking it behind her ear. Celeste was dazzled by the small but not insignificant gesture. His fingers trailed down, from behind her ear, tracing her exposed neck, collarbone and shoulder before running softly down her jacketed arm until their hands met. He laced their fingers together and smiled at her. She felt a stirring in her stomach; a nervous riot of butterflies taking flight. She mentally gained composure before speaking.

"So, where are you taking me?" she finally asked.

"I thought we could explore Buttes Chaumont today. Have a picnic and star gaze later." His voice was satin—crimson satin—a dark, deep seductive sound. Celeste shuddered at the tingle traveling through her body.

"That sounds perfect, but I'll never make it through the day without coffee first."

"That can be arranged. Let's stop up the street, have breakfast and get you your much needed caffeine before we head over." He squeezed her hand briefly, causing a smile to bloom on her face.

The morning was nothing short of a quintessential late spring morning. Sun filtered through the clouds, coating everything in a pale pink. The clouds looked like brushstrokes flicked downward on a canvas.

As they walked, hand-in-hand, she wanted to take a needle and thread to the moment and somehow stitch it inside her forever. Gabriel led her inside the small café that she frequented often and pulled her chair out for her.

"Such a gentleman." She laughed.

"Tell me what you want and I'll grab it."

"Mmm, I will have a cheese Danish and a coffee, please . . . milk only." Gabriel nodded and set off to get their orders. Returning with their fare, he sat.

"Tell me about yourself," he said.

"What exactly would you like to know?"

"Everything."

Celeste laughed at his quick and precise answer. He was so . . . cocky, and assured. It set her on edge a bit, but also piqued her interest in him. Surely he wasn't like this all the time?

Smiling and working hard to swallow her laughter, "Hmm," she hummed as she tapped a finger against her temple.

"Okay, okay. How about, where are you from? What was your childhood like?" he asked.

Celeste frowned at his questions. As a young girl she was always sick, or at least, that's what she could recall. From the age of five until she turned ten, she was in and out of hospitals. Test, after test, after test. Nothing was ever confirmed to be wrong. Everything within her appeared to be in proper, working order. Still, the headaches, stomachaches, and bouts of nausea persisted. Her parents had held her hand through it all. Her mother's warm hugs had eased her fears and comforted her. Her father's happy, crinkled-at-the-edges eyes had assured her that everything would be all right. And it mostly was. Homeschooled through the fifth grade, Celeste had been nervous her first day of middle school.

"My childhood was . . . boring, actually. I was sick a lot, so I didn't get the traditional childhood. There weren't many skinned knees or outdoor games. I was homeschooled until sixth grade."

"Really?"

"Really," she answered.

"Sick how?" He questioned.

Celeste sighed. It wasn't often she opened up and told people about her health. They always seemed to look at her differently somehow afterward and she wasn't sure she wanted to go there with Gabriel.

"Cyclic vomiting syndrome. Or CVS," she told him. "The cause of CVS is unknown."

It was a rare disorder that offered recurrent episodes of severe nausea and vomiting that could last for a few hours to several days. That was how her childhood was spent. The kicker was those episodes were followed by a period of time free of any symptoms, giving the illusion that she was better. She never was. And the nausea and vomiting were severe enough to be incapacitating when they hit. She was pale, lacked energy, had abdominal pain and headaches much of her childhood. As she grew older, she outgrew the frequent episodes, but every so often one crept up on her and struck again.

"Are you cured?" he asked, head cocked sideways.

"No," she stifled a snort and tried to relax a

little. "As an adult, the episodes occur less frequently, but sometimes last longer. It's not contagious or anything, so you don't have to worry." Her joke fell flat. Gabriel's face fell.

"Celeste . . ." He reached across the table for her hand. He brushed his thumb across her knuckles gently. "I'm sorry. I didn't realize what a loaded question I was asking when I brought up your childhood."

She shook her head. "It's all right. It's just not the most cheery subject."

"How'd you end up in France? You're American, aren't you?" he asked as he released her hand and leaned back in his chair.

"Yes. My father was starting up FogPharm and there was interest in their work by French officials. Basically, as I understand it, they made him an offer he couldn't refuse to open up shop here instead of in the U.S." Celeste tilted her head and smiled. "What about you, Gabriel?"

"Ahh, tu connais la musique," *You know the routine,* he said. "I grew up here in France, in a little town north of here. My parents broke their backs working to get me into college. I'm smart. I made the most of it and turns out, I'm pretty gifted in biochemistry to boot. Now I'm just part of métro, boulot, dodo." *The rat race.* Celeste scoffed at his term. *Hardly.* The man across from her was sought after. Pursued for his potential. He was being overly modest about his life.

Celeste laughed at his description and took another sip of her coffee.

"Somehow, I doubt you'll ever be part of the *rat race*." She smiled. "Siblings?"

"I had a brother. He died when I was five."

"I'm so sorry. That's terrible." She felt guilty for bringing it up. Celeste was terrible at first dates. She always felt awkward and unsure of herself.

"It's alright. I was small and it was so long ago." Gabriel sighed and rested his forearms on the table. She reached out and patted his hand in comfort. They finished their pastries in a comfortable silence.

"On y va ?" *Shall we go?* She gave him a blithe smile.

Gabriel stood and reached for her hand. With the coffee fueling her and Gabriel's touch warming her, she felt she could conquer anything.

She smiled up at him. "Oui." She squeezed his hand. With a tug and a quick step forward, they exited the café.

"C'est parti." *Here we go.*

She loved listening to him speak French. It was hot. If she were bolder, she'd tell him as much . . . but she wasn't. Not yet, anyway.

"Yes, here we go," she echoed as she fell in step with him.

"Celeste," he said, "loosen up, this isn't a job interview." His smile was broad and content. She inhaled a deep breath and slowly let it out. How was it that he could read her so well?

"I'm not really that great at this," she admitted.

"At what? Walking?" he asked, smirking. She felt her eyebrows knit together in confusion for a moment before realization hit her; he was making a joke.

Laughter bubbled up and left her mouth in a great burst of noise. "I'm terrible at walking."

"Maybe I should carry you, you know, so it's less awkward for you." He chuckled.

Her eyes grew wide at his response and she shook her head. His laugh was deep and masculine. It did funny things to her belly.

In a quick motion, he bent, scooped her up— one hand under her knees and one wrapped around her back. She squealed at the suddenness of it, causing him to laugh harder. She wrapped her arms around his neck. Their faces were inches apart. His breath hit her collarbone, sending shivers through her as their laughter faded away and silence swept in.

To say that he was handsome was skirting close to an understatement. Their breathing fell in sync, the way the incoming tide kisses the shoreline, the waves lifting and falling until they become a familiar rhythm.

"Celeste." Her name sounded like a wish each and every time it left his lips. She wanted to capture the moment in a jar and keep it locked away, so fifty years from now, she could take it out and turn it over in her hands, re-live the lust-struck heat that currently steeped her body.

Lips: barely touching.

Fingers: tracing soft skin.

Eyes: flickering with hot desire.

She couldn't pull away if she tried. She was captivated.

His breath, hot along her collarbone, made her feel as though she was slowly melting into a pool of sweet caramel. He leaned in just slightly. She inhaled. Their lips met. Moved together. She floated away into the pink hued sky. His tongue burned like the sun colliding with the earth as he pushed deeper. Her fingers gripped his neck tightly, desperate to hold on to the moment. He withdrew slowly and placed a tender kiss at her collarbone before setting her feet to the ground. She felt incoherent.

What was that? How could a man claim her with just three kisses? She felt owned. Wrapped up and presented to him as a gift. It was reckless, unlike her in so many ways. Yet, she couldn't—and if she were being honest with herself—didn't *want* to fight it.

They resumed their walk. "I love that you blush," he said eyes rooted on her face. Celeste felt her cheeks heat more at his words. "What were you thinking about just now?"

She thought for a moment, wanting to tell him anything *but* the truth, only before she could form a respectable answer words tumbled from her mouth. "I want to have a completely adventurous, passionate, wild life."

Gabriel stood stock still and took her in. Every second that passed as he stood there not saying a word made Celeste want to crawl inside a deep dark hole to hide from embarrassment. She'd only ever discussed her longings with Matteo and Mara.

"I think we can arrange that. Don't you?" he finally said. She angled her head up to see his face. "You're really something, you know that?"

"I am?" she questioned.

Gabriel gazed down at her. "You are," he stated. "I want to get inside your head, figure everything out, know every little bit that makes you tick. You're so intriguing, yet you don't see it, so beautiful, yet you choose not to acknowledge it. Why is that?"

Celeste's jaw dropped. She recovered quickly, but she was sure her shock was evident on her face. Her normally cool composure shot to hell.

She shrugged. She had no words to give him as she thought about his statement. She didn't feel intriguing. She also didn't feel that her beauty was something to acknowledge or not. It had never occurred to her that perhaps she came off as meek. Gabriel's words resonated with her. She found herself *wanting* him to forever feel the need to dissect her, to keep his interest.

Parc des Buttes Chaumont has been referred to as the most romantic public park in all of Paris. A calm mood settled over Celeste as they explored the romantic touches of the park. Waterfalls, a grotto, a lake, and a folly—the Temple of Sybil—on top of a cliff with views of Montmartre in the distance. They talked. *Really* talked. She learned of his schooling, his job prospects, and hobbies. It turned out he was an excellent whistler. The tune he carried amazed her. She'd never heard anyone whistle with such precision, clarity and musicality. The conversation flowed. It was open and honest and fun. And she found that he listened . . . *really* listened, when she spoke. She knew she probably bored him when she went on and on about her passion for plants and flowers, yet he smiled, asked questions and always at least feigned interest. They stopped at a street cart and ordered food after more than two hours exploring the park.

She watched as he sunk to his knees in the grass and unwrapped their food. She was starving, the breakfast they ate long ago digested with all their walking. She sat down next to him and folded her legs underneath her.

"What's that one?" he asked, pointing to a flowering plant ahead of them.

Celeste smiled. He was, at the very least, trying and it made her chest tighten with happiness. She drew in a breath and tucked a stray hair behind her ear. "That's a bleeding heart. It's a perennial. Named as such because the blooms hang like a drop from the red petals and its shape suggests the bleeding heart image. Gardeners often tell stories and legends about its meaning, actually."

"Legends? About a plant?" he asked wearing a skeptical expression.

"Yes! Flowers, well a lot of them anyway, have different symbolic meanings."

"Go on," he urged before sinking his teeth into his sandwich.

"Well that one" — she nodded toward the bleeding heart flower " — is sometimes called a *Spurned Suitor*. Gardeners will hold up a bloom and tell a story as they peel away parts of the flower." Raising a finger, she signaled him to wait and then jumped up, jogged to the flower and pulled off a blossom before bringing it back and sitting next to him again. "The removal of the red petals shows the presentation of pink bunnies to a princess by a prince who is courting her."

"Very scientific," he said and grinned.

"Ah, but she is unimpressed, the princess, so he removes two white petals as flashy jewelry." Gabriel's eyes pinned her to her spot. He nodded, waiting for her to continue. "She is still unimpressed." Celeste removed more of the petals. "So the prince reveals a heart-shaped center with a line. The line is the dagger with which he stabs himself in his despair and the princess declares that her heart shall bleed forever."

Gabriel watched her as she set the destroyed flower down. Celeste picked up her sandwich and took a bite. It made her salivate. She hadn't realized exactly how hungry she was. Of course, it was delectable.

"That is seriously the most depressing thing I've ever heard." The deep timbre to his voice sent an eruption of shivers down her spine.

Cutting her eyes to him, she noted his serious demeanor. Covering her mouth, she laughed. "Yes, I guess it is. But just because something has a hidden meaning, doesn't guarantee it will be a good one."

"You're awfully smart, Ms. Fogarty. There are no guarantees in life, that's for sure." He nodded. "What about those there? The tulips." He pointed to a grouping of red tulips.

"Red tulips are mostly associated with true love, and purple symbolizes royalty," she answered. Celeste could get lost in gardens and flowers and plants. She loved the calmness that came with digging in the dirt, planting, and watching seeds grow and transform into something beautiful.

Gabriel's head swiveled around taking in all the enchanting scenery around them. "Hmm, I never thought so much about flowers before." He smiled. And damn it was beautiful.

Celeste giggled as they continued to eat their lunch. "I think flowers are redeeming."

"How so?" he questioned.

"Every flower grows through dirt first. Beauty comes from filth. It makes you think."

"You make me think." He cocked his head.

He licked his lips as he thought. She stole her eyes away, not wanting to be caught staring at his mouth. "About what?"

"Everything. Your passion, especially within your element, is astounding. Your eyes crinkle in this sexy little way when you smirk. Your lips turn up just slightly when you're nervous. I could listen to you talk all day, Celeste." He brushed a flyaway strand of hair from her face. "I could watch your reactions for a lifetime."

Celeste felt the heat warm her chest and cheeks. "That's quite the compliment. Thank you, Gabriel." She looked at the blades of grass swaying gently with the breeze.

"Don't ever thank me," he stated.

"But . . ."

"I don't deserve thanks for telling the truth. Just hear it. Listen to my words and be honest with me in return."

Celeste thought about this before nodding. "Okay." She liked Gabriel more and more as the day wore on. He, too, was passionate, quick-witted and fun to be around. More than that, her body reacted to him physically. She hoped that after today he'd call again.

When they'd finished eating, Gabriel laid back on the grass, staring at the bright sky above. She followed suit. He pulled Celeste into the crook of his arm. Their sides touched from shoulder to ankle. After a moment, she relaxed into him. He rolled slightly toward her and cupped her jaw.

"You're beautiful, you know that?" The pad of his thumb grazed her cheek. "Inside and out."

He kissed her then. His lips warm on hers. Her hand spread across his cheek. She wanted to freeze the moment in time — the feeling of him pressed against her. The scent of him. He made her weak in the knees, he made it hard to breathe, and he made her heart strike at a furious rate.

His large hand cupped her jaw softly. The blue sky was clear and bright. His tongue, delectable like a mouthwatering piece of chocolate, claimed her mouth and neck. The late spring breeze and the scent of the flowers washed over them. Caught up in her overloaded senses the thought that there was never a moment more perfect than this one flitted through her mind.

Chapter 5

Annabelle

"My pride, my light, my energy. My sight to see my way."
~ L'ame Immortelle — Betrayal

Annabelle watched Jezebel closely in silence. She'd stopped speaking moments ago but was lost in her mind somewhere. She coughed to get her attention.

"Oh!" Jezebel squeaked placing a hand over her heart.

"Hi." Annabelle laughed.

Jezebel cleared her throat. "Where was I?"

"Their fourth kiss. You know, Celeste is a little slutty. Four kisses in like two days with an almost stranger?" she jabbed playfully.

Jezebel laughed hard at her remark. "Maybe you're right sport, or maybe she was just a love-struck fool. Love at first sight and all."

Annabelle huffed. "I don't believe in that."

"Well tell me then, what drew you to your boyfriend?" Her question startled her. She'd never really given much thought to why she and Damon were together.

She shrugged. "He was there. Available and

nice to me."

"That my dear is the saddest answer I've ever heard. *EVER.*" Jezebel stated emphatically.

Annabelle twisted in her chair. *Who cared? They weren't getting married.* "We aren't serious really. I mean, I like him and all but I'm eighteen, we're not going to get married."

"How do you know?" Jezebel pressed, wide-eyed.

"Because . . ."

"Because," Jezebel cut in, "you wouldn't say yes if he asked. And why wouldn't you? Because you don't love him."

"No." she stated firmly. "I do love him. He's a good guy."

Jezebel looked skeptical, searching Annabelle's eyes, her expression, for anything she could grab onto. "I don't believe that."

"Why are you picking a fight with me? I was just starting to like you," Annabelle huffed.

Jezebel raised her eyebrows and waited. It made Annabelle anxious, the way this woman seemed to pull information from her. Impatience flickered on her face.

"I don't know okay! I don't know if I love him. I don't know what love is." she blurted sounding more hysterical than she intended. Jezebel's face twitched and Annabelle sensed the woman found her temper amusing.

But Jezebel frowned at her. "Love is easy. You will know it when you have it."

"Why do people say that? It's a lame excuse for: no one's really sure what love is supposed to be or feel like." Annabelle looked away and wrinkled her nose. Love was an elusive bastard. If family love couldn't sustain over time how were two strangers supposed to?

"I didn't realize you needed someone to spell it out for you. Let me." Jezebel let her head sag against the back of the chair for a moment deep in thought. Annabelle watched and waited. She started humming a cheery tune; she was interested in what Jezebel would say but she didn't want a boilerplate definition of love.

Jezebel set her mouth in a grim line at her humming. She speared Annabelle with a murderous look. "When it's right, you will be able to talk about the tough stuff, easy stuff and everything else easily. You won't be able to get enough of each other. You'll *have* to spend all your time together doing absolutely nothing important." As she spoke her eyes danced with delight. "When you touch, your skin will ignite. It will feel like static electricity. His kisses will make you lightheaded. In his eyes you won't have flaws. You *will* sweet beet, but he will love you for them. He will listen to you, treat you with respect and trust." The softness and fondness of Jezebel's voice proved that she was indeed speaking from the heart. From experience. "He will support you emphatically in whatever you choose to pursue. You will *want* to please him. You will do things you normally detest doing simply because it makes him smile and *you* love seeing his smile." She drew in a breath and continued on. "When you're running late for work, you'll find your coffee mug full and your car running with the heat on already. It will feel like a worn-in cashmere blanket has wrapped your heart up. It will feel like you've won the lottery, and really- you will have. Love is powerful. It can heal, it can lift—it can also drag you down into the depths of hell and burn you until you're no longer recognizable—so you must be careful with your heart," she concluded.

Annabelle sat slack-jawed at Jezebel's rant. It was romantic. It was honest. It was . . . she didn't have the right words to sum up what she felt but she knew that the woman sitting across from her was one in a million. She was the kind of mother she wanted, full of solid advice and honest truths. She read into Annabelle's brief words and dug deep forming a bridge between a bad teenage attitude and an actual conversation. The woman was like a magician. Maybe it was simply because she *wasn't* Annabelle's parent or any relative or maybe Jezebel was really just that good. Either way, Annabelle felt a brief moment of luck for sharing any kind of moment with her.

"I . . . No, Damon and I don't have that. It's more of a waste-our-time-together kind of relationship. You know, better than being alone. We have fun. God, this isn't coming out right at all." Annabelle twisted in her seat, trying to appear comfortable and perfectly at ease. She wasn't.

"I understand. It's easy. *Comfortable.* I'm sure he's nice enough and you are too. You're biding your time." She nodded at Jezebel, confirming what she'd said. That *was* it. "Yes."

"But, why? Why waste your time?" she pressed. "You could be missing out on meeting the one who *isn't* a waste of your time."

Annabelle hadn't thought of her time in that way before. Her choices were instant usually. She just felt something then did it. Planning ahead seemed like something for after college. She shrugged, unable to think of a valid answer.

"You shouldn't be scared to dream a little bigger, tiger. There's a great big world waiting for you to actually join it."

~***~

Annabelle schlepped her way home. She hated the bus. Today though, the ride went quickly, Jezebel's words heavy in her mind. She'd avoided emotions, choices that required emotions, for so long now that each time Jezebel spoke, the words assaulted her. She *felt* them all. It was a strange sensation for her. Feeling was something that didn't exist in her home. For eight years her family survived by *not* feeling.

Dinner was on the table waiting by the time she walked through the door. The bus had been late. She dropped her purse in the entryway and toed off her sneakers before padding into the dining room.

"You're late," her mother scolded as Annabelle sat in her chair.

"I'm sorry. The bus was behind."

"Do you have homework?" her father questioned.

"Yes. Not a lot though."

He grunted a response and the room was enveloped in the sound of utensils clanking against plates and food being consumed. Why did they have nothing to talk about? When had they really stopped trying? Annabelle thought hard but couldn't come up with a timeline. It was as if each passing year as a family they interacted less and less. She felt the sting of absence.

"Hey Mom," she blurted, "how was your day? What'd you do?"

Her mother's eyes cut to hers in shock. Her fork, midway to her mouth, was set down to her plate. Her lips pressed tightly together, giving her that pinched look that Annabelle hated. Maybe this was a mistake. Being a functional family was too much work.

"My day?" her mother asked quietly. She stared at her plate as if it held a secret answer.

"Yeah," Annabelle confirmed and held her gaze.

"It was . . . long. Today was long," her mother answered. Annabelle noticed her mother's eyes were on her father now. He stared at his plate, not noticing his wife's sad stare. "Thank you for asking Belle," she said politely.

"Dad?" Annabelle said. "How was your day?"

His brows knit together at her question. "It was busy. Made a few new sales. John was happy with that."

"That's great news," her mother offered, suddenly perking up.

"Yeah," he answered and resumed staring at his plate as he forked bites into his mouth. Annabelle wanted to scream at him. She wanted to fill the room with noise. She wanted him to look at her, at her mother, his wife. To see the wounded expression her mother wore at his neglect. Annabelle didn't though. She simply sat and stewed quietly.

As she ate the last bite on her plate she looked up to her mom. When was the last time she'd seen her mom smile, laugh or relax?

"May I be excused?" she asked.

"Yes." Her mother answered.

Annabelle collected her plate and utensils and stood. The chair made a scraping sound on the hardwood floor. It echoed. "When was the last time we were happy?" she asked the quiet room. It was rhetorical. She didn't expect her parents to give her an answer.

Her father's gaze snapped to hers, a warning look. It was better than no look, but maybe that was just her grasping at straws for attention. She flashed an angelic smile at him. Her mother covered her mouth with her hand to quiet her gasp. Annabelle shook her head frustrated at her parents. This house sucked the soul out of everyone who stayed in it. She stomped to the kitchen to rid herself of her dirty dishes. Dishes. Dirty. She felt dirty. Diseased. Disease clung to this family. Living in this house ensured a miserable existence. She couldn't exactly pass judgment. The reality was that there was no one to fault for any of it. All the hurt, all the hostility, all the misery; it was just there. They were all just victims of life's cruel game.

Once in her room, behind its closed door, she felt her breath seize up in her chest and the weight of panic bearing down on her. It squeezed her until she thought she might crack like an old fragile tea cup. Annabelle set her laptop on her bed and booted it up. She needed a distraction. She opened Facebook and saw she had a message waiting. She half-smiled when she saw Damon's name. At least maybe he could distract her for a bit.

Damon: Sneak out tonight. I need to see you.

Annabelle: *I can't.*

Damon: Come on gorgeous. We can't do anything fun at school.

Annabelle: *Sorry.*

Damon: Sorry? Belle, come on. If you won't sneak out I'll sneak in.

Annabelle: *Damon- DO NOT. If I get caught I'm screwed. I'll see you tomorrow.*

Damon: Yeah, maybe. Whatever. Bye.

Annabelle: *Don't be like that.*

Damon: Belle, this sucks. Six months is a long time.

Annabelle sighed. Six months *was* a long time. A lifetime. She closed his chat message and opened Madison's.

Annabelle: *Damon's a punk.*

Madison: What's new?

Annabelle: *Nothing. Just bored I guess. Parents are being . . .*

Madison: normal? Ha. How was your crazy old lady today?

Annabelle: *She's not old. She was entertaining.*

Madison: Awesome. Gotta run. Mr. Clark killed us with homework tonight.

Annabelle: *See you tomorrow.*

Madison: Later lovah.

She closed the laptop lid and stared at the picture on her nightstand. Four happy faces stared back at her. She was the mistake, she knew that. Brant was the golden child. Coveted by her parents. Her father's *son*. His pride and joy. Daughters apparently didn't count for much. She flipped the photo face down. It hurt to look at it. It hurt to think about it. She missed his smile. His laugh. His noogies. She missed damn near everything about him. She didn't know how to say goodbye, none of them did it seemed. She missed the way he glued their family together. She missed *him*.

~***~

Annabelle tucked a strand of chocolate colored hair behind her ear as she walked down the corridor to suite 208. Over the week she'd found herself looking forward to today. She wasn't sure if it was the story or Jezebel herself but she knew that her lips tipped up into a smile just thinking about her visit.

"Jez? You in here?" she called as she walked through the threshold.

"A moment, dear!" Jezebel answered from the bathroom door.

Annabelle sat in her usual spot and crossed her legs at the knee. Fiddling with her sweater sleeves she waited for Jezebel to join her.

"Ciao!" Jezebel chirped.

"Hi," she answered, jaw tight, posture rigid.

"Why so glum?" Jezebel asked, creases forming on her forehead as she looked over her.

"Does it show?" Her shoulders slumped and she heaved a hopeless sigh.

"Darling, all that make-up you wear—it doesn't cover up your emotions. You wear them plain as the sun shines through that window." Jezebel nodded to the sunlight coming through the window.

"Har, har," she replied dryly. "I tried. It didn't work," she admitted.

"Tried what?"

"Talking. I asked them about their days. Three nights in a row. I gave up after that."

"Did they not answer you?" Jezebel asked indignantly.

"No, no. They did, but that was it. They just answered vaguely and that was that."

Jezebel scrutinized her. It made her uncomfortable. "What happened to your family?"

"Tragedy." Annabelle knew her answer was childish and dramatic but it accurately summed up the truth.

"Expand on that kiddo," Jezebel said with a pointed look.

Annabelle sighed. She really didn't want to

get in to it. "I had a brother. He's dead." She pursed her lips in irritation.

"Ahh, sorry to hear that. And since his death things at home have been . . ."

"Miserable!" she threw her hands in the air and slammed them down on her thighs. "It's like cancer in that house. Everything that tries to live there is devoured from the inside out," she blurted, sounding far more hysterical than she would have liked.

"Maybe you need to try harder." Jezebel's voice was firm, but gentle.

"Me?" she squawked. "I'm the child. They are the adults." She crossed her arms over her chest.

"You're an adult now. Don't leave all the responsibility on their shoulders. If *you* want the family back, *you* should fight for it," Jezebel answered.

Annabelle's shoulders sagged. She could feel the weight of that suggestion without needing to think on it.

"It's impossible. They don't speak to each other, let alone me. We don't talk about him ever. It's eerie silence in my house."

"Be the noise then," Jezebel said. "Be the light. Be the laughter. It's contagious you know, joy. A smile is the best make-up you can wear. Show them how it's done. You are only home for a little more than five months- then you'll be off to college. Take this time and *do* something with it." Jezebel arched a challenging brow at her.

"How? I can't just walk around laughing at nothing, smiling at the walls. They'll think I'm nuts," she crowed, frustrated.

"What do you remember from before your brother died?"

"He didn't *die*. He was killed." Her words were venomous as they left her mouth.

Jezebel's eyes open wide. "That's terrible." Annabelle nodded her agreement.

"I was only ten. I remember my mom's perfume, my dad's big hand holding mine. I remember making cookies together, licking the batter from the mixing spoon. My parents used to come into my room to tuck me in, except when my dad was gone for business." Annabelle chewed her lip to keep from saying any more. She couldn't just air her family's dirty secrets to any stranger. They had a reputation to keep up.

"Does he travel often?" Jezebel questioned.

"Yeah. He's gone almost two weeks every month."

Jezebel nodded. "Well, make cookies with your mom then. Turn music on. Dance around. Hold your dad's hand. Hug them. That's a good start."

"I think they'd die of shock," she stated dryly. Her hands bunched into fists.

"So let them!" Annabelle startled and stared at her wide-eyed. "What are you going to lose by trying?"

Annabelle shrugged. "Nothing I guess."

"Then do it."

She mustered some grit and jutted her chin out. "Can we talk about something else?" Annabelle needed to change the topic. There was only so much family talk her heart could bear. Her pain and grief over the matter made a solid fist in her belly. A tangled knot of emotion forever on the edge of bubbling over the edge.

"If you promise to try, yes."

"Fine, Jez. I promise." She gave in.

"Good, good. Now, our story, are you liking it?"

"It's a little dull. But sure. You tell it well and I trust you when you say there's a twist," she admitted.

Jezebel clapped her hands together. "Well now that you know how they've met and how she was feeling for him- let's skip ahead a bit yeah?"

"Sure."

"Alright, let's see . . . Paris, 1985."

"So much for skipping ahead a bit," she laughed.

"A lot can happen in a year's time. Now, *shh!* I'm trying to talk here," Jezebel teased.

Chapter 6

Celeste

Paris 1985

"Celeste, hurry up!" Mara cried from their room. "He's been waiting ten minutes already."

"For crap's sake woman, I'm almost ready," she answered. Checking herself in the mirror one last time, she decided the reflection staring back at her was as good as it was going to get. She pushed through the door and glanced at Mara.

"Damn. You are smokin,'" Mara said.

"Very funny," she responded dryly.

"No really, Cece. You look rad. Gabriel is going to cream himself when he sees you." Celeste giggled at her friend's choice of words. Mara was all piss and vinegar, which was exactly what Celeste needed. She tended to be too much of an introvert, too polite and too pleasing. She hated to see others irritated at her. She loved bringing smiles to others faces. Mara and Matteo, each in their own way, had helped her come into her own.

Celeste and Mara had spent the last two days shopping for her trip to Italy with Gabriel . He was whisking her away for the weekend. Even her parents were thrilled they were getting away.

In a year, he had managed to charm her parents and *her*. Even Mara and Matteo liked him. Well, Matteo a little less than Mara. She'd understood why Gabriel was so possessive when it came to Matteo.

They'd had their first big fight after he walked into her dorm room and Matteo was in her bed. Sleeping, of course. They'd had a fantastic night out doing a pub crawl and crashed, drunk, when they got home. It wasn't anything new and there was nothing sexual about it, but Gabriel had all but punched Matteo in the face when he'd seen them lying in bed together. She was so mad that she hadn't talked to Gabriel for a week. The things he'd screamed at her were terrible.

Matteo and Mara were her best friends and she couldn't imagine life without them. Gabriel was so mad he'd asked her to choose, and although she had fallen head over heels in love with him, she would not abandon Matteo because a jealous man asked her to.

Obviously it had all worked out over the course of the last year.

Mostly.

Matteo and Gabriel weren't each other's biggest fans, but they put on a front in order to make her happy. Shaking the thoughts from her head she picked up her travel bag and kissed Mara on the cheek. She really needed this break. Gabriel's work at her parent's company kept him busy; too busy. Her school this year was stressful and kept her busy; too busy. They desperately needed this time together to unwind and just be.

Smiling, Celeste all but skipped down the hallway, stairs and out the front door of the dormitory. Her stomach was riddled with knots. The anticipation of the weekend to come set her heart to a frantic beat.

Gabriel scooped her up as she pushed through the door. She squealed with delight and clung to him as he spun her around. He stole her breath away.

"Good morning, mon amour." *My love.* She loved it when he called her that. She peppered his face with kisses as he set her to her feet.

"Morning!"

"Are you ready for our vacation?"

"So ready. I don't think I can stand waiting another minute."

"Could have fooled me. Making me wait out here for ten minutes," he said and gave her a sly smile.

She playfully smacked his arm. "You deserve nothing less than a beautiful woman on your arm. I wanted to look pretty for you."

"Celeste, you always look beautiful, mon amour, you know that." She blushed. He was always telling her that. She still hadn't become immune to hearing it. She pushed up on her toes and kissed him. He groaned into her mouth and wrapped an arm around her as they walked toward his car. He set her bag in the trunk alongside his and opened her door for her. He was always doing sweet things for her. Always thoughtful and respectful. His linen shirt was unbuttoned at the top. It made her mouth water. His hard, defined chest barely peeking out at her. Suddenly she wanted to skip the vacation and rush to his apartment.

Shaking the thoughts from her head she laughed.

"What's so funny?" he asked sliding into the driver's seat.

"Nothing," she laughed again.

"Something!"

"I was thinking I want to skip Italy and spend the weekend in your bed. You look delicious."

Gabriel groaned. "The things you do to me Celeste. If you only knew."

"Oh, I think I have an idea," she responded.

The flight from Paris to Rome was a short two hours. Gabriel spoiled her with champagne on the flight and first class tickets. She knew he was doing well for himself but this seemed like too much to spend on a weekend getaway. From there they rented a car and drove another hour to the Garden of Ninfa. Described as a place that had inspired artists, she was longing to see the secluded, picturesque garden set in fairy tale like surroundings and Gabriel knew it.

Instead of locking themselves away together in a fancy hotel for two nights he was taking her to a garden and she couldn't have loved him more for it. Breath hissed out of her when they entered the stunning microclimate that allowed plants of all varieties to thrive in the location's natural greenhouse environment. The roses, maple trees and lavenders lining paths, a spectacular bamboo pavilion and even tropical plants such as banana trees. Add the ruins with creeping vegetation, the hypnotizing crystal clear river. It was almost too much beauty to take in.

"My god Gabriel, it's heaven," she breathed.

"It's better than I'd thought, and the look on your face is priceless, mon amour." She grinned and grabbed his hand anxious to wander further.

Greeted by a tour guide, they waited with a group of about thirty others before starting the tour. Celeste felt as though she was in a catatonic trance. She barely heard anything the guide mentioned as they went. The place was simply magical.

"Alright," Gabriel started, "start telling me what the plants really mean." She smiled at him before looking around.

"That," she said, then pointed, "is lupine. It represents imagination. And there!" She again pointed excitedly. "Gloxinia; love at first sight." She gazed up into Gabriel's eyes. His smile reached ear to ear. It seemed he got endless pleasure from making her happy. He cupped her chin and kissed her briefly.

"And those?" he asked, pointing to a patch of irises.

"Irises. Faith, hope, wisdom, courage, and admiration. The purple iris is considered the emblem of France," she informed him. He laughed and scooped her up in his arms.

"My little flower brainiac, I do love you."

"I love you too Gabriel. So much. This is fantastic." She kissed his jaw before nuzzling her face into his neck while he held her. She loved the smell of him. She loved everything about the man.

"One last one. What're those?" Gabriel asked pointing to a blue flower.

"Ahh, those are Himalayan blue poppies. They are supposed to represent sleep, peace, and death: sleep because of the opium extracted from them, and death because of the common blood-red color."

"Sounds dangerous, like those bleeding hearts you first told me about."

"They are. Harmless to view, but don't go picking them," she said and winked.

They toured the garden for a little over an hour. Celeste was in her element. Excitement swept through her at every turn, at every new marvel. The garden was enchanting. When they'd viewed all they could, they left for dinner.

Gabriel picked a small restaurant in Prato di Coppola. Our table overlooked Lago di Fogliano. The spectacular orange sunset was shared with sexy man, delectable wine and witty banter. By the time they arrived at their hotel for the evening it took all of Celeste's energy to even think of removing her shoes. It had been whirlwind day.

As she plummeted to the bed Gabriel laughed.

"Tired?"

"Exhausted," she blew out, feeling the day's activities catch up to her.

"Not *too* tired I hope." He smirked while looming over her.

She knew that tone. She knew that innuendo. Suddenly her body came alive. "I suppose if you can help me remove my shoes I might get my energy back." She smiled coyly at him.

"I'm certain that can be arranged."

He knelt at the end of the bed where her feet dangled and softly pulled each shoe off of her. His hands worked methodical circles into her arches, kneading the stress of walking the day away little by little. Bit by bit she relaxed into his touch. If he kept it up, she'd pass out, and she didn't want to miss the fun.

As if reading her mind, Gabriel's hands moved north. His fingers ascended, their progress achingly slow, over her calves and thighs. A gasp flew from her mouth at the teasing pleasure. He continued to trail his fingertips in a straight line up the insides of her thighs. Grabbing at his wrists with both hands, she tried to stop him . . . or urge him on. She didn't know. What she did know was when he touched her, the sky and the ground switched places.

He pushed her dress up slowly, exposing her belly, before hooking his thumbs into her panties and sliding them down over her legs.

"I need to taste you Celeste." She felt her cheeks heat. He was a professional at making her blush.

"Yes," she urged. "Please."

"Please what, Celeste?"

He loved to hear her use her voice. In the bedroom, she still didn't have a confident voice of her own.

"Please, Gabriel, taste me."

He spread her legs, and kissed the inside of her thighs. Each kiss moved closer and closer to her core. When his mouth worked its magic she moaned deeply. She was lust-drunk and weak. He took his time as he discovered every place on her body. He turned her inside out with his reverence. Her insides ached with need as he worked the sensitive bundle of nerves. Gabriel wasn't rushing and she wasn't sure how much she could sustain. He definitely raised the bar for any other man to be compared to. With a bewitching flick of his tongue, the graze of his teeth in just the right spot she was lost. His touch ignited her skin.

Gabriel's head and hands came up. His hot breath on her skin set her soul on fire. He worshipped every inch of her skin before raising himself above her. She wove her fingers through his hair and pulled his mouth to hers.

"I love you."

"Ditto, mon amour."

"I . . ." His lips captured her words as he sank into her. Her breathing labored as she neared the precipice and stars began to dance behind her closed eyes. Every muscle in her body tightened and was set on the brink of imploding when she buried her face against his wide chest. It built slowly, flickering in low but powerful waves of fire through her entire body until she ignited underneath him. Splintering into a wildfire that blazed to life. She was lost in her pleasure, lost to the sensations holding her body captive. She clung to the edge, never wanting the moment to end until she no longer could. They came together, came apart, free fell through space and became one. Sounds escaped them but were incoherent. Each wave moved from her breast to her core.

As they laid in a tangled, sweaty mess, nose-to-nose, toes brushing and hands tucked between their bodies, they talked. They talked about music and food and movies. They traded dreams and history until their voices were scratchy and their eyelids dropped shut.

~***~

Celeste woke to Gabriel nuzzling her neck, his leg between hers as he slid his cheek across her back. His arm draped over her hip, fingers splaying on her stomach possessively. She smiled as shivers trickled across her skin when his warm, soft tongue licked the sensitive skin below her ear.

"Good morning," she breathed, the blood in her veins burned and every inch of her flushed hot, her skin stinging at his touch.

"Morning, mon amour."

"Sleep well?" she hedged.

"Always do when it's with you." He kissed the shell of her ear. She sighed.

Her smile grew. She wanted to finish college before she agreed to move in with him. He'd recently asked and she'd found it ridiculously hard to deny him, but she had. She had three semesters left. It wasn't that long to wait. His little comments didn't go unnoticed. He took every chance he could to slip something in about spending long nights together, especially when their schedules didn't jive, which was often lately. She settled into the feeling of his arms around her, of his breath at her ear, and reveled in it.

Hours later, they finally unraveled from each other. Celeste couldn't stand a moment longer without coffee. She had thrown on a shift dress to run to the lobby and secure two cups of the liquid gold. Returning to the room she heard the shower running so she set Gabriel's coffee on the table and curled up in the chair at the window. They had a spectacular view overlooking the lake. The coffee slid down her throat and started to instantly work its magic. In no time at all she would be ready for the day.

The downside of coffee, she found, was that it ran right through her. After fifteen minutes of blissful peace, a breathtaking view and delicious coffee, she required the bathroom. Knocking on the door first, she waited for Gabriel's grunt of approval before opening it. Steam and the smell of men's aftershave filled the thick air. Gabriel stood in front of the mirror, towel wrapped around his waist, chest bare. Water dripped down his skin, giving it a glistening effect.

"I . . . need to use the room," she stuttered out.

"Go ahead." He stepped aside.

"Gabriel!"

"What? Is it, you know?" A slight tug of a smile on his lips.

Her hand came up to her mouth and her cheeks felt inflamed. She was definitely nowhere near the peeing with him in the room phase, nor the other thing he was suggesting.

"Aww, mon amour, you're so sweet. So innocent." He walked to her and cupped her chin, lifting her gaze to meet his. "I know girls use the bathroom." Again her cheeks heated. She pursed her lips.

"Yeah, and I know you do too, but I don't want to see it." She deadpanned.

Gabriel's face broke into a cat-ate-the-canary grin, laughter rumbled from his mouth, his chest shook and his shoulders rounded. Celeste shuffled left, slowly maneuvering him, as he laughed, toward the door. When he was just far enough through, she smiled at him. He looked at where he stood and a mischievous gleam shone in his eye.

"Oh no. I really have to go!" she squealed, thinking he was going to come back in. She started to close the door on him. He fisted the fabric of the towel at his waist and yanked. She stopped moving. He stood naked and proud as her jaw dropped to the floor. Reaching forward, with a sated smile, he put his hand on the door and pulled it closed, leaving Celeste gawking at the painted door. She snapped out of her daze and hurried to accomplish what she had set out to, so she could hurry to the dashing male prowess that waited for her.

The flight home was quick on Sunday. The drive from the airport even shorter. As he pulled up to her dormitory she frowned not wanting the weekend to be over yet. Saturday had been picture perfect in her opinion. After *finally* leaving the hotel room around noon, they'd rented bikes and peddled for miles exploring. By the time they returned from their exploration, they were both tired and ate together in their room instead of going out.

~***~

Waking in Gabriel's arms this morning, again, had set her belly aflutter. She felt as though she had won the lottery with each look he gave her, each lingering touch, each quiet moment spent together. Now they were home.

"Why the frown?" he asked.

She turned her head to him, reached out and cupped his cheek. "I'm sad the weekend's over. I had so much fun."

"It doesn't have to be, mon amour. Come home with me. We can have all the mornings and all the nights."

She smiled as she rubbed the pad of her thumb over his five o'clock shadow. "I'd never get any studying done. You distract me. *Always.*"

"Celeste," he started.

"No, Gabriel. It's only three semesters. Three semesters and I'm yours."

"I don't like waiting," he complained.

"Don't I know it." She threw her head back and laughed at his little boy pout. He was sexy even when throwing a tantrum.

Turning the car off, he exited and ran around the hood to get her door for her. She took his hand and stepped out. They lingered a moment, chest to chest, before he stepped backward. She watched as he closed her door and then retrieved her bag for her.

"Want me to carry it up?" he asked.

"Sly, Gabriel, real sly," she teased.

"A man can try, can't he?"

"I hope you never stop."

He walked her up the steps to the door and

set her bag down before lifting her into his arms and peppering her face with light kisses.

"I love you. I'll miss you tonight," he whispered in her ear.

She placed her mouth next to his ear. "I'll sleep with you in my heart tonight."

One passionate kiss and lingering hug later he was gone. Celeste pushed through her bedroom door, plodded to her bed and set her bag down.

"You're back!" Mara squealed from the doorway. Matteo stood behind her but quickly pushed past beating Mara to her and wrapping his arms around her in a firm embrace.

"We missed you this weekend," he said.

"I missed you guys too," she said before laughing, "okay, I was a little too . . . preoccupied to miss anyone," she admitted. Mara mock gasped before a laugh tumbled out while Matteo watched her a moment too long before joining in. Briefly she wondered what his issue was before pushing the thought aside.

"You're such a brat." Matteo gave her an exaggerated smile.

"Yes, but that's why you love me," she teased.

"Yeah, that's why I love you all right."

Matteo plopped down on her bed causing her overnight bag to bounce and fall. He lunged to catch it in time but the bag hit the floor upside down with a thud.

"Well thank god it was zipped." Mara quirked.

"Sorry, mio fiore," Matteo muttered bending at the waist to retrieve her bag for her. As he did a long black velvet box fell from the front pocket to the floor.

"What's that?" Mara asked bounding from her perch on her bed. Celeste watched as Mara scooped it up from the floor before she could.

"I don't know, give it here." She held her hand out expectantly. Mara opened the box just a smidge before snapping it shut. A huge grin spread across her face.

"I knew you guys were getting serious," Mara said with assurance.

"What?"

"He's buying you jewelry! What says *serious* more than jewelry?" Mara asked.

"I assure you there was no jewelry given this weekend."

Mara forked over the rectangular box to Celeste. She took a minute to look it over. *Where had it come from?* She peeked inside and saw a note. Opening the box fully she pulled the note from atop a stunning gold locket.

It read; Je suis à vous. *I am yours.*

She picked up the locket and turned it over in

her hand. The cool gold chain snaked between her fingers as she inspected it. The locket was tasteful, heart-shaped with a keyhole emblem on the face of it. She opened it. Vous êtes la clé. *You're the key,* was engraved inside. Her heart felt swollen. She couldn't contain the smile that blossomed across her face. Celeste had never received anything of value from a man before. Her insides grew warm and she was sure her cheeks flushed. *How'd he manage to slip that into her bag without her noticing? And furthermore, what if she hadn't found it straight away? Would he have said something?* Celeste turned it over again and stroked the precious metal between her index finger and thumb.

"What's it say?" Matteo asked peering over her shoulder. Celeste held the locket out for him and Mara to read.

"Damn," Mara breathed. "He is like the king of romance. You are one lucky bitch Celeste Fogarty." Celeste didn't know what to feel. She didn't know what to say. She was lucky and she knew it but Gabriel was different from anyone she'd encountered before. He was vines of honeysuckle and clematis growing up along a trellis, extra-sweet, ripening the surrounding air. He was a house that smelled of potpourri and homemade candles and fresh baked cookies. He was so much more than anything she could imagine. She bit her lip in thought.

"What are you the key to?" Matteo chimed in.

Mara and Celeste shoulder bumped him at the same time while emphatically saying, "His heart!"

"That's cheesy." Matteo chuckled. "And so are you two."

Mara made a face at him but Celeste didn't bother to respond. Matteo was romantic at heart. They'd shared many conversations over the last three years about love and life and she knew that he would gladly give his heart away when the time came, cheesy or not. Instead she held out the locket to him and asked, "Would you?"

Without hesitation he took the necklace from her. Celeste turned her back to him and lifted her hair from her neck. The locket dropped in front of her until it rested in her décolletage. Matteo's warm fingers worked deftly at the nape of her neck securing the clasp. Her skin tingled at the contact and goose bumps broke out down her arms.

"There. Let's see." He asked turning her to face him and Mara. He trailed his hands down her arms, hiding the goose bumps until they were gone.

"It really is beautiful," Mara said. "Simple but stunning."

"It suits you perfectly," Matteo agreed.

"I think maybe I need to make a thank you phone call," she trilled with a flutter in her belly.

Chapter 7

Annabelle

"You left me empty on the floor. Without even looking back."
~ L'ame Immortelle — Betrayal

"Listen, I have to run. My parents get all bent out of shape if I'm late and the bus never seems to be on time," Annabelle complained. She pulled her hair into a ponytail as she stood.

"Yes, yes. We don't want you getting in any *more* trouble." Jezebel gave her a wry smile. Annabelle could not help but think it held a secret. There was something endlessly intriguing about Jezebel.

"Yeah, alright," she responded.

"Annabelle," Jezebel called as she stepped through the doorway into the hall, "there is a part of you that clings to your brother; to a different time. We all cling to that time when we've lost someone, but it doesn't mean we're going to get it back. Things change. As do we. And many things changed the day your brother died and that's okay."

Annabelle thought about her words and nodded to her before turning to leave.

The air was heavy with the earthy scent of

impending rain as she waited at the bus stop. It made her think of her brother. Of how he would have had the window open in his bedroom so he could listen to the storm as it rolled in, bringing in the sodden, earthy smell of rain. She would have been scared when the thunder boomed. The best part of having him around was sneaking into his room when she was scared. Together, they would count the seconds between the strike and the clap of thunder exploding across the night sky. When the storm was far enough away she'd curl up in his bed with him and fall asleep.

The sound of squeaking brakes broke her memory. The bus came to a stop and Annabelle boarded. There were few seats left this evening — people didn't want to chance getting caught in the rain. She pushed through the narrow aisle, found a seat and stared out the window. As the bus moved on to its next stop she watched kids speeding down the sidewalks on bikes, their smiles wide and playful. It made her think about how she and her brother used to get in trouble for riding their bikes on the crowded sidewalk downtown. They'd lean their bikes against the wall of a building, never bothering to lock them, and go inside the stores to buy supplies for whatever Saturday adventure they'd planned for that week.

The bus brakes squeaked before lurching to a stop, jarring her thoughts. Annabelle wiped away the tear rolling down her cheek. She gathered her emotions and blotted her eyes, reminding herself that the world doesn't stop so you can grieve. The death of a loved one doesn't make you special.

The heavy oak door looked oppressive as she climbed her front porch. Once inside, she kicked off her shoes and hurried to the bathroom. Annabelle held on to the edge of the sink. In the mirror, her reflection stared back with flushed cheeks. She took a moment to regroup, turned on the faucet, and splashed cold water on her face. She took a calming breath and headed for the dining room.

Her father drained his glass. The ice clinked. At dinner she had asked them each what the high and low were from their days — a game her mother used to play with them *before*. It was painful, but they'd both answered. After dinner she'd helped her mom with the dirty dishes. She'd switched on the stereo, tuning into the oldies station. Her mother had raised an eyebrow at her but Annabelle caught her humming along after a minute or two. Her dad's office, with its rich, dark molding and wainscoting, made her nervous. It was serious, so formal. He gave her a gentle smile as he stepped behind her and shut the door. She heard the lock click shut. Outside his bay window, rain fell in the shafts of yellow light from the street lamp.

He sat behind his desk and shuffled papers around. "What did you need to ask me?"

"How come we never talk about him?"

Her father huffed and pinched the bridge of his nose. "Belle."

"What?" she replied in a snit.

"Why are you dredging this up?"

"Why are you burying it?" she pushed. It was a tired argument, and she was tired of having it.

"Because," he boomed. She startled. His tone softened. "Because, Belle, it does no one any good to think about it. To feel it." He left the statement hanging in the thick air between them.

"It makes me happy to remember him." She lifted her chin defiantly.

"Then remember him," he said dismissively, "It doesn't mean you need to do it *out loud*." He shut her down, quickly and efficiently.

"This entire family is screwed up. We all stopped talking about him. We all stay silent. The silence in this fucking house is deafening! We used to be a family," she yelled.

Her father stood. "Yes, we did." He looked pained as he let out a long breath. *Good,* she thought. At least it meant he was feeling *something*.

"Dad?" she hedged. He looked to her, "I miss things . . ."

"We all do."

"But, we're still here. *I'm* still here. Why don't *I* get to have a family?"

To this there was no response. She was met with familiar silence. The kind that broke hearts, shattered dreams and slowly ate away at your soul like an insidious parasite. For tonight, she could not, would not try any more. She stormed from his office to her room barely giving her mother a passing look as she inquired what was wrong.

Outside the window, the rain sheeted across the sky and struck hard on the flat roof, pinging as it funneled through the gutters and downspouts. She felt the fatigue in her limbs as she sunk into her bed. Her door creaked open with a soft knock.

"Belle?" Her mother's voice was faint.

"Come in."

Her mother glided across the carpet gracefully and came to a seat on the edge of Annabelle's bed. Her face wasn't pinched like normal. She appeared soft and thoughtful. Annabelle didn't bother moving from her spot. She closed her eyes when she felt her mother's hand run through her long hair. She inched her own hand toward her mother. When Annabelle's hand found her mother's free hand, she laced their fingers together and squeezed gently. Her mother squeezed back.

Annabelle fell asleep thinking how small holding hands seems but how large it *feels*. And about her brother's easy smile.

~***~

A towel turban entwined her hair. She thought about Jezebel. Parents and denial be damned. Annabelle turned on her MP3 player and connected it to the docking speaker. She flicked through playlists until she found one to suit her mood. She sang along to words and danced as she got ready for school. She applied mascara and eye shadow, added a touch of perfume to her wrists and neck, and headed downstairs to the smell of bacon.

"Wow!" Annabelle said entering the kitchen. Her dad stood at the stove flipping eggs. He turned and grinned at her. For a moment she was lost in déjà vu. Her father, when home, always made fabulous breakfasts for her and her brother.

"Coffee?" he asked and nodded at the pot on the counter.

"Yeah, I have a big test today." She shuffled to the counter.

Annabelle poured herself a mug and then asked her father how he took his before fixing one for him as well. He piled her plate with bacon, a side of eggs and a slice of toast. *Just the way she liked it.* She sat at the breakfast bar and dug in as he did the *New York Times* crossword puzzle, which meant the coffee had kicked in.

"What's it in?" he asked after sipping his coffee.

"Calculus," she groaned.

~***~

Her father's surprise breakfast had set the mood for the rest of Annabelle's week. She felt lighter, happier and more secure. He'd left for a business trip the next morning and wouldn't be back for two weeks but the breakfast had made everything, for the moment, better. It was as if he was *trying* or apologizing—she couldn't be sure which, but either option made her heart feel lighter. Maybe he had heard her after all. She had floated into school in a slightly upbeat mood.

"Damon. No."

It had taken Madison until Thursday to tell her about last weekend. Annabelle felt like a fool. For three days she'd been none the wiser. How dumb Damon must think she was.

"Belle, come on." He sounded like a five-year-old. It irritated her. The more he pushed her to disobey her parents' grounding, the more annoyed she became. She propped a hip out and rested her hand on it.

"I can't. What part of that don't you understand?"

"You don't have to be a bitch about it," he snapped.

She snapped her eyes to his and glared. "A bitch? Really Damon? Madison let me know you were at Matt's party Saturday night."

"And? I'm not grounded Belle," he shot back.

"And you had Sierra sitting on your lap," she spit the words at him in quick succession.

Damon reddened slightly and then, "Anything else you'd like to inform me about my life?"

That was the last straw. Annabelle dropped her bag to the hall floor and slapped him across his cheek. Hard. "Yes. You're now single."

She lifted her bag and stomped away from her *ex*-boyfriend. Tears threatened to spill from her eyes, but she pushed them back and willed herself to ignore the sorrow she was feeling. It wasn't real. It was the simple fact that rejection had occurred. It overwhelmed her but it would pass. This pain was nothing to her everyday norm.

Damon was a distraction, and a crappy one at that. She knew it wasn't love but still, hearing about him and Sierra had put a dent in her self-esteem. Madison had tried to make her feel better when she told her about the party Saturday, saying Sierra was sloshed, but it did nothing to ease the hurt she felt. *Fake it 'til you make it.* If you don't feel good, pretend you do because eventually you will. She repeated that mantra the entire bus ride home from school.

As she trudged through the entryway twenty minutes later the sound of *Born in the U.S.A* blared through the house. Annabelle hoofed it to the kitchen and the source of the music. Her parents had often played Bruce Springsteen's CDs growing up. Her mother had claimed it was the secret to baking the perfect cookie. *Ha.* As if Bruce made a cookie good—but it was her mother's tradition and right now, it brought a smile to her face. Traditions proved soothing when you felt less than stellar.

"Hey, Mom."

"Belle! You're just in time," her mother greeted. Her cheer was refreshing, but it also caused confusion to stir in her gut.

"For what?" she asked and offered up a smirk.

"Cookie batter," she stated as she held up a spoon.

Annabelle crossed the kitchen and snatched the spoon from her mother's hand. Depositing it into her mouth she groaned. There really was nothing better than eating cookie dough. The sound of unfamiliar laughter rang out. Opening her eyes she realized it was her mother's.

"Mom?"

"What?" her mother answered cleaning up some of the mess she had made.

"Did you and Dad ever cheat on each other or maybe think the other one was?" Her mother's face clouded over. Her features became pinched and tight. Annabelle instantly wished she could take her words back. She wanted the carefree look back.

"Why would you ask that?" her mother asked carefully.

"Damon," she answered.

"That boy isn't worth a moment of your time. If you suspect or know he cheated, then it's time to cut your losses. He's nothing but trouble, always was." Her mother carried dishes to the sink.

Annabelle fidgeted in her spot. "Mom?" she called.

"Yes?" Her mother looked over her shoulder to her.

"I love you."

"I love you too, hon." Her mother smiled. It didn't quite reach her eyes though and that made Annabelle's heart ache.

They worked silently together placing spoonful's of cookie dough onto greased baking sheets and listening to the E Street Band. It was more than Annabelle could have hoped for on a bad day. She was greedy and would take what she could get.

~***~

One month. This particular Tuesday marked the fourth visit to Glenview. Only five months or twenty more visits until freedom belonged to her again. Strangely, this made Annabelle slightly anxious. She couldn't quite understand why though. A month ago, she'd arrived at the assisted living facility wishing the weeks away. Now, however, she was disturbed at the thought that they would end. Not today, but, they would end. Perhaps it was simply because she had grown to enjoy Jezebel's company or maybe it was just that she liked the woman's story. Either way, she realized that her last visit with the woman would be bittersweet.

"Hi, Jezzie," she greeted as she entered Jezebel's room.

"Well hello to you."

"How was your week?"

"Did you just ask me how *my* week was?" Jezebel balked.

Annabelle shrugged. "Yeah."

"My God, I think you may actually be a human being after all."

"Hey!"

"Don't squawk at me kitten, you're the self-absorbed teen."

"I resent that," she huffed.

Annabelle sat in her chair, kicked off her shoes and tucked her legs up under her, making herself comfortable. She fiddled with the cuffs of her shirt.

"My week was . . . bland. Yes, bland. What a word. Sounds exactly as it means don't you think?"

Annabelle nodded her head. "Yup."

"How was your week?" Jezebel asked.

"Honestly, shitty and awesome."

"Expand on that please."

"I found out my shitty boyfriend cheated on me, or was at the very least about to. I didn't press for details. But, my dad made breakfast for me before his work trip; I can't even remember the last time he did that. *And* my mom made cookies. *Cookies!*"

Jezebel grinned. "Why do you think all that happened out of the blue?"

"Yeah yeah—I get it. I asked them about their days at dinners and I played music in the kitchen, and I asked my dad why we're not allowed to talk about him—my brother. I think it all happened because I made them feel guilty."

"Guilt is a strong motivator, but do you really think it was *just* guilt?"

"Well, I'd like to think no—but yeah, it

probably was just guilt."

"You don't think that, perhaps, they miss the same memories that you do? That maybe you guilted them into action—but that they too enjoyed the result?"

"Were you like a philosophy professor before or something?"

"Hardly," Jezebel scoffed.

"What *were* you?"

"Does it matter?"

"No. But we talk about Celeste—I feel like I know her kinda. But you—we never talk about. I don't really *know* anything about you."

"And, you want to know me?" Jezebel asked.

"Yes," she replied simply and waited. It hadn't really crossed her mind before, but now she wanted to know who exactly Jezebel was.

Jezebel stared out the window for a long moment as if contemplating where to start. Annabelle let her gather her thoughts in silence, curious as to what Jezebel would eventually say.

"Eighteen years ago I was blessed enough to marry my best friend. He's handsome and charming, patient and gentle and smokes like a chimney."

"That's who brought the plant for you?"

"Yes."

"Is it hard to be here . . . away from him?"

"Very. It's hard to be away from someone who saved you. Someone who supported you in ways you never thought another person could."

Annabelle frowned. "I'm sorry. Does he come to visit?"

"Once a week like you. He still works full time, of course, but he spends one entire day with me each week."

"Well that's nice."

"Yes it is."

"How'd he save you?" she asked.

"Oh. I lost someone very close to me many, many years ago. Unexpected death is a terrible thing, as you know." Jezebel sighed. "He held me together when I could not do it myself. He let me fall apart safely. He let me heal properly. I would not be me without him."

"Sorry you lost someone too," she mumbled.

"It was another lifetime. I'm well past it now, dear."

"Was it your idea to come here or his?"

"He travels often for work and I am just so forgetful now. I kept misplacing items. I got lost a couple of times going to a grocery store that I'd been to a thousand times. When I started forgetting the names of simple objects he said it would be safer for me to be well cared for and here, I am well cared for."

Jezebel looked solemn and resigned to the

fact that her life was what it was now. Annabelle felt a pang of sadness deep in her chest for the woman. She didn't seem forgetful in the least and she'd noticed no signs of a deteriorating mind during her visits. Perhaps she had good days and bad days.

"So, do you have kids?"

"Nope."

"Why not?"

"Nosey aren't you?" Jezebel replied.

"Curious," she retorted. Jezebel chuckled at her answer.

"I worked too much to have kids."

"What did you do?"

"I was a veterinary assistant."

"Really? That sounds cool. I love animals." she answered.

"Do you have pets?"

Annabelle frowned. "No. My parents would never allow us—I mean me—to have any."

"Annabelle," Jezebel started, "here, in this room, be you. Remember your brother—your family the way you want—all you want."

Annabelle smiled and nodded at the woman. She understood—this was a safe place for her. She could vent all she wanted. She could *feel* all she wanted. She could just *be*. It was a powerful sensation. Hope burrowed a hole into her heart.

She coddled it, let it snuggle in.

"Are you ready for some more of our story?"

"Yeah. But honestly, I'm waiting for the shoe to drop."

"The shoe to drop?"

"Yeah you know, all this buildup, Celeste being in love with Gabriel—I'm waiting for it to fall apart."

"Why?"

"I don't know—just a gut feeling. Like one of them has a brain tumor and dies or something like that."

"My God kid, that's morbid as hell."

"Is it? I mean is this entire story just going to end at them having a magnificent wedding and lived happily ever after?"

Jezebel snorted, which made her laugh. "No sugar, not at all. The wedding, you could say, was just the beginning of their story really."

"Alright, I guess. You might as well get on with it."

"Well if that's how you feel . . ." Jezebel turned her head and stared out the window.

"Jezzie come on. I mean it. I want to know what happens. Just pick up from 1985. Please?"

Chapter 8

Celeste

Paris 1985

The fall semester ended without fanfare and Celeste was relieved to have the summer at her disposal, as was Gabriel. He would, of course, still be burdened by full-time work, but her evenings were now free allowing them to spend more time together during the week on a consistent basis.

The bar that Matteo, Mara and she were currently sitting in was filled with students letting off steam at the completion of the semester. Mara was waving over a tall, dark, sexy man as Matteo headed toward their table carrying three drinks.

"Who is that?" Celeste asked.

"That, fine stud muffin is Charles. My date for the evening." Mara winked and Celeste doubled over with laughter. Another unsuspecting soul was about to be claimed by her best friend. Mara had the love life of dirty pair of underpants. She was always changing men.

"Charles, this is Cece," Mara introduced. Celeste stuck her hand out. He took it and firmly shook.

"Nice to meet you. I've heard a lot about you."

"I wish I could say the same," she replied. Mara kicked her under the table which made her giggle. Matteo slid in next to her and pushed everyone's glasses to their appropriate owners.

"Matteo," he said to Charles, a cigarette dangling effortlessly between his lips.

"Charles," Mara's date for the night replied.

Their booth was small. Matteo was close enough that whenever he moved, his shoulder brushed hers. His warmth radiated from him. Charles and Matteo struck up an easy conversation allowing Celeste to really look at him and Mara for the first time in months.

He was bigger now somehow, filled out, more manly looking. His expression was droll as he listened to whatever Charles was saying. Sitting smushed between him and the wall Celeste was relaxed; Matteo was as comfortable as her favorite pair of jeans. It was a strange thing to think about. She pushed the thought aside and watched the women moving about the bar. Jealous, catty glances were shot her way. If they only knew Matteo wasn't *with* her. No doubt they would be all over him. How did he not notice?

She turned her attention to Mara who was

gawking at Charles. She looked happy and content, an expressions she didn't often have in the company of her date-of-the-week. She watched as Mara sighed and took a sip of her drink before resting her hand casually over Charles' bicep. A claiming move. A move unlike her dear friend. Mara played the aloof game often and men ate it up, loving the chase of the seemingly unattainable, but not now. Now Mara appeared love-struck. Celeste realized with a hint of anxiety that she hadn't exactly had much time to sit and gossip with Mara lately about life. Could she really be falling for this man? She filed that away for later when they were home alone and could talk and laugh well into the night. She needed to find out what was up with Charles.

After the group's third round, their fourth appeared at the table. Celeste felt the tell-tale signs of being one foot in the land of the buzzed and the other foot firmly planted in drunk land. She leaned her head on Matteo's shoulder, and in return he placed his lips on her hair and kissed her. Not with romantic intentions—no, with friendly affection, as if to say: I know you're here. It made Celeste giggle. Matteo would be so damn perfect for some woman. She wished he'd find that person already. She giggled more as she ticked off women she knew who she might introduce to him. As she ran through the mental list she found something wrong with each, or something that *he* would find wrong with them. It was totally inappropriate laughter bubbling out of her yet she couldn't stop it.

"You alright?" Matteo asked, drawing Mara and Charles' attention to her as well.

"I'm fabulous. Finals are over and there are only two, count 'em one," she held up a finger, "two," she raised another, "semesters left until we graduate!" She was pretty certain that the word graduate came out more like *graayouate.* She was in need of water at this point. Mara and Charles chuckled and Matteo excused himself to procure a tall glass of water for her.

"I need to tinkle." She giggled. Mara outright laughed at her declaration and nodded for her to go ahead.

Celeste wobbled for a moment when she stood. Gathering her wits she, rather ungracefully, made her way to the restroom in the back of the pub. The line, thank God, was short. She was in and out in less than ten minutes. She fumbled her way back toward the table but before she got there a strong arm wrapped around her and tugged.

"Épouse-moi," *marry me,* he said. Celeste felt her brows lift and her eyes grow wide. Gabriel's grin widened. She couldn't help but be swept up in his dimpled smile. His carefree expression was mesmerizing. Hell, everything about him was mesmerizing.

"Gabriel," she squealed while she threw her arms around him.

"I'll ask you every day until I wear you down and the only logical answer becomes yes."

"I've heard that line before," she answered, snorting.

"I know what I want, Celeste." Celeste thought about his words, his *game,* and decided to play along.

"What about next month? Next year? Twenty years from now?" she asked just as she had more than a year ago.

"Je vous veux," *I'll want you,* he answered. The conviction in his voice still made her heart slam against her ribs. She loved this man.

"How are you here?" she asked.

"I came to find you. You said you'd be here with the gang after finals."

"I'm glad you're here. I think Mara might actually be *in love.*" She laughed at the thought. "You have to meet him!"

As Celeste tried to right herself and pull away from Gabriel she lost her grip on him, or he lost his grip on her, and she slammed ass-down on the floor. When she burst out laughing Gabriel stood and grabbed her hands.

He helped her to her feet, and then kept his hand at her elbow as they walked to the table.

She thought how lucky she was that Gabriel was so gentlemanly and chivalrous. Her stomach almost erupted with butterflies from the gesture because it was intimate and familiar and sexy. She was so lucky.

"Maybe we should just head home," Gabriel offered. She shook her head no and he sighed at her before grumbling about something she didn't catch.

"Matteo! Mara! Look who I found."

"Gabriel, glad you could join us," Mara greeted. "This is Charles." The men shook hands and lifted their chins at each other. Celeste took the opportunity to chug the entire glass of water Matteo had placed on the table.

"I was just saying I should take Celeste home. She's . . . drunk."

"Oh come on," she whined.

"I think it's probably for the best," Matteo weighed in.

Celeste suddenly found herself the subject of scrutiny as three faces all watched her for signs that it was indeed time for her to leave. She felt like a scolded child. She wasn't drunk. She wasn't exactly sober either but she didn't need to go home.

"Fine. Let's go." She tugged Gabriel's arm to get him moving. Mara called out for her not to be such a bad sport but Celeste was past that point. She was definitely a poor sport at the moment, it was evident in the way she stomped to the door. "Your place or mine?" she asked agitated.

"Ours."

"Gabriel, I'm not in the mood for your shameless plug for a joint home," she pouted.

"If you'd stop being an idiot for a moment and pay attention . . ."

"An *idiot?*" she screeched. Her arms flailed wildly as she let off a string of curses at her boyfriend. When she was done and silence surrounded them, she found Gabriel smiling. *Smiling.*

"What's your deal?" she asked still angry at everyone's babying treatment of her.

"My *deal*, Celeste," she loved the way her name dripped from his lips, "is that you are ruining a perfectly magical night."

She scoffed. "I am not. What is so magical about tonight?"

"This," he said.

Taking her arm he led her. She followed in silence completely confused. He walked her two blocks to the garden where they'd first met. The more fresh air she took in the less buzzed she felt. Standing under the arbor at the entrance he asked, "Tell me what you see."

She took a moment to look around. "I see

lights, in the garden. But . . . but it's closed now."

He led her into the garden park towards the lights until they were in the exact spot they'd first met. The only things missing were the dance floor, bar and tables. And guests of course. She smiled up at him. *This man.* He was almost too good to be true.

"Celeste, mon amour, I've been trying to figure this out for some time now. Nothing I dream up is quite right though. I admit, as a last resort I called in some favors."

"Favors from whom?" She asked.

Matteo, Mara and Charles stepped from behind a tree across the open space. Celeste gasped. Lights twinkled overhead and a waltz started abruptly. Naturally her head turned to find the source of the music. Matteo held a boom box on his shoulder. He looked ridiculous but adorable.

Turning back to Gabriel she smiled. "Just one dance?"

"No Celeste, je veux que tous d'entre eux." *I want all of them.* He kneeled before her and pulled a small velvet box from his pocket. "Épouse-moi." *Marry me,* he asked.

Temporarily ignoring the ring, Celeste sank to her knees in front of him. The moment felt like a scene out of *Sixteen Candles*. Excited tears dripped down her cheeks. She was flabbergasted. They'd discussed moving in together but not marriage. Shock and joy coursed through her.

"Oui, cent fois oui," *yes, a hundred times yes,* she cried.

Matteo, Mara and Charles clapped and whooped in delight as Celeste and Gabriel shared a passionate kiss that seemed to seal their fate. Gabriel's hands tangled in her hair, his lips on hers. She was cherished, he gave her his heart and they would build their own world, their own happiness. He ended their kiss reverently placing soft kisses at the corners of her lips.

"Show us the ring!" Mara whooped. Celeste laughed. Gabriel stood with her and tucked her into his side. She plucked the large solitaire from the lush padding and held it up to inspect it. The inside of the band glinted in the light. She squinted and inspected it more: à une vie de découverte, *to a life of discovery.* She glanced up to Gabriel, not understanding.

"You are the key to a life of discovery." He touched her necklace. She swooned.

This man, the one who held doors, made love to her, who was playful, demanding and thoughtful, was going to be her husband. "It's perfect," she breathed. Gabriel slid the ring onto her finger. A perfect fit.

Celeste extended her hand to her friends.

Mara made a sound in the back of her throat that sounded odd as she examined the ring. It wasn't easy to surprise or impress her. Gabriel had done an excellent job choosing. Matteo clapped Gabriel on the back before pulling Celeste into a tight hug and whispering, "I'm happy for you fiore mio." She squeezed him back hard. Now he just needed to find the perfect woman.

"Congratulations," Charles offered.

All four heads turned to the stranger of the group and they promptly burst out laughing. Having Mara's new date sharing in the very private moment was completely absurd and totally welcome. The tape in the boom box stopped and with it the music.

"Excuse me, everyone, while I whisk my fiancé away to properly celebrate her acceptance," Gabriel stated.

Charles laughed and Mara elbowed him in the side. He looked to her with a look that screamed *What'd I do wrong?* Matteo laughed at the two of them before she and Gabriel quietly snuck away.

~***~

Where are we going?" she questioned as they passed her dorm, then Gabriel's apartment.

"Shhh, mon amour, don't make me blindfold you," he threatened playfully.

"I could still talk with a blindfold," she deadpanned. He chuckled, filling the car with the deep sound.

"Touché. Maybe a gag would suit you better."

"I'm hurt!" she feigned offence.

"We're almost there. I promise," he said. He took her hand and brought it to rest on his thigh. She loved that he did that. Always in contact somehow, always wanting to be connected. It was endearing.

Almost there in Celeste's opinion and almost there in Gabriel's turned out to be two very different things. They drove to the opposite side of Paris and into an adorable small neighborhood made up of beautiful houses that had plots of land with them. A place like this would be the best place to have a garden of her own and still be fairly central to all the happenings in the city. In biking distance from Pantheon and Luxembourg Gardens, she would be able to cruise the Seine for an intimate look at the city, people-watch at a sidewalk café with a pain au chocolat on the beautiful Left Bank or simply wander through the streets when it the mood struck.

Gabriel pulled into a small driveway that accommodated his car but not much more. *What was he up to?* He motioned for her to stay put so she did. She watched as he jogged around to her door and opened it for her. He looked like he could grace the cover of a magazine even in his faded jeans with a hole in one knee and his black V-neck sweater. He led her to the bottom step of the tall, narrow house.

"Gabriel?" she questioned.

He folded in half and scooped her up bridal style. Taking the stairs slowly she clung to his warm, firm body. At the door, he dug one hand in his pocket while holding her and unlocked the front door. Celeste had no words. She wasn't sure if this was a rental for the night or if Gabriel had done something much, much more permanent before knowing if she'd have said yes.

"I kind of always wanted to do that," he admitted as they stepped into the foyer.

She met his eyes. "What?"

"Carry you over our threshold," he whispered.

"Our?" she asked.

"Ours," he stated firmly.

"Like, to rent?" she pushed.

"Like we own," he clarified. Shell-shocked, Celeste turned her head a fraction to the left, then right, before her lips tipped upwards into an enormous grin.

"Oh, oh oh oh," she panted. Celeste was at a loss for words as he spun them around slowly giving her a glimpse of the house. This was theirs. Theirs. Hers. His. She could hardly catch a breath.

"I hope *oh* is a good thing."

"The best," she answered peppering his face with small kisses.

"No, the best is waiting," he said. He set her down and with a smile that showcased his dimple he her tugged hurriedly down a hallway to a set of French Doors. Pushing through, she followed him outside. She watched as he searched around for a moment, one hand fumbling against the outside of the house. His brow was furrowed and he huffed as he tried to find it. He looked adorable.

Suddenly lights flicked on and filled the space with a soft ambiance. Celeste gasped at the perfection that was their back yard. She stepped from the small deck down two steps to the grass in a trance-like state trying to take it all in. Trees lined the property giving them ample privacy. The rest of the space was vast and untouched. She could create the most beautiful getaway here. One lone potted plant sat in the grass near her feet. Gloxinia.

"I hear it means love at first sight or something like that." Gabriel's voice rang out in the quiet night. It surrounded her, enveloped her entire body and made her feel warm and fuzzy.

"Gabriel Fontaine, I think it's time for you to make love to me." She crooked a finger at him beckoning him to her.

"Here?" he asked pointing to where she stood. Celeste felt bold and lust-drunk. She nodded yes and smiled coyly. He all but bounded down the steps to her. She laughed as he tackled her to the ground gently.

Her teeth clamped down on her bottom lip gently as he rocked his hips against her with slow, but aggressive, abandon. The moon illuminated the inky black sky. The grass was cool against her back and the stars overhead shone brilliantly. He moved over her fluidly. Touching all the right spots. A firm but gentle lover. His rhythmic thrusts hurdled her into oblivion until she was no longer thinking, just reacting, primal in nature, to the motion of his body and the touch of his hands.

In the moment she fell apart beneath him, she knew her life consisted of what sayings were coined from, because this was *as good as it got.* She clung to him, letting the waves of pleasure crash over her, not wanting the feeling, or him, to leave her. She wanted to live in this moment forever, or at the very least, capture it and stow it away deep inside her heart. Something in her soul told her she'd be full of these moments in the years to come. That Gabriel would fill her up to the brim with happiness, love and joy. She clung to that thought as he kissed her again.

Chapter 9

Annabelle

"And then you walked through the door. And my life turned black."

~ L'ame Immortelle—Betrayal

"So he proposed when she was drunk?" Annabelle's words reeked of disdain as they cut through the air.

"Well, hate to break it to you kid, but not all proposals are picture perfect. But, I will say this, she'd only had four drinks before Gabriel swooped in to steal her away, and there was plenty of time walking to the garden for her to sober up a bit."

"I still think it's lame. He should have waited."

"Well, what's done is done—can't go back and change history, now can we?" Jezebel answered.

Annabelle shrugged. "Nope."

"What are your plans for this week?" Jezebel asked.

"I don't know. It seems I'm single, grounded and pathetic."

"Buck up child. Your life is not over. You

should be happy that you ditched the loser before it got serious. I'd say you dodged a bullet."

Annabelle smiled. Maybe the woman was right. "Yeah, probably," she admitted.

"Not probably—absolutely. Now, indulge me, what do you do while you aren't visiting me?"

"School and homework. I need a hobby or something to keep me busy at home."

"Music! Listen to music. Dance around and be silly."

"I have music."

"Learn to cook! You are allowed to use the kitchen, aren't you?" Jezebel asked.

"I am. Yeah. And my mom's cooking blows, so that's not a terrible idea." She admitted.

"Brava darling. Now, go home and whip up dinner for your parents. Maybe you'll even get them to smile before the night is out."

Annabelle slid her sneakers on and stretched. Jezebel stuffed her feet into slippers and pulled a blanket across her lap. Stopping in the threshold Annabelle turned.

"See you next Tuesday Jez." Jezebel lifted a hand, her long slender fingers waved Annabelle off.

~***~

Annabelle sang along to the lyrics of the music that played in the kitchen. The floorboards creaked slightly under her feet as she walked from the stove to the refrigerator and back. The lace curtains danced in the breeze at the open window by the opposite counter. A swirl of Spring air gently worked its way around the kitchen. It would just be her mom and her tonight. Her father wasn't due home for another week.

Annabelle whipped together a heavy cream sauce per the recipe. Her mother's book club had ended and she was going to walk through the door any moment. Annabelle wanted everything to be close to finished before then. The table was set, just the way her mom liked it: candles lit, plates, utensils and napkins at their settings and the overhead light set to dim. She lifted the cover off the pot. Steam billowed up, snaking white tendrils that danced in the air. She put the pasta in the boiling water and set the timer for ten minutes. Everything else was done. The Carbonara only needed the pasta to be ready. It even smelled perfect. Pride brimmed in her heart. Cooking was kind of fun.

Heels clacked on the hardwood floor signaling her mother's arrival. A pang of anxiety shot through her. *Would she be impressed or would she be irritated?*

"Wow," her mother stated as she entered the

kitchen. "What's all this?"

"I was bored, so I tried my hand at cooking?" Annabelle wasn't sure if her question was a statement or vice versa. Her mother chuckled.

"Well, let's hope you got your father's cooking skills and not mine." Annabelle's eyes widened in disbelief.

"Why the face? You couldn't honestly believe that I wasn't aware of how awful my cooking is."

"You know?" Annabelle crowed.

Her mother's laugh, light and breezy filled the air. "Oh yes. I know."

"Why do you make us all suffer then?"

Her mother shrugged. "I'm bored. Cooking, or trying to gives me something to do."

The honesty in her mother's words hit Annabelle in the chest. All this time, how did she not notice how broken each of them was? Was she really so focused on only herself?

"But," she started, "you never got better." Now it was her mother's turn to look shocked. They stared at each other a moment before both doubled over laughing. Warmth crept in, filling Annabelle's soul with a light and airy feeling. The timer dinged and Annabelle turned the burner off before carrying the pot to the sink and draining the water from the pasta.

"You know what I *am* good at?" Her mother

asked.

"What?" she answered.

"Getting the serving bowl out."

Annabelle smiled as she watched her mother retrieve a serving dish before filling it with the sauce she'd made. Annabelle added the pasta and her mother stirred it all together before bumping her hip to Annabelle's and carrying their dinner to the table.

Annabelle smiled as she chewed. "Could we read tonight? I know it's silly . . . but—"

"What did you want to read?" her mother asked, grinning. She resumed eating while waiting for Annabelle to answer. She thought on it and remembered how when she was younger, before life was altered, her mother used to read her chapters from an old book. Annabelle swallowed her last bite.

"Would you do a chapter aloud from *Little Women?*" she asked feeling hopeful.

Her mother nodded and smiled as she walked to the bookshelf in the den. Annabelle hurried after her, following her lead and leaving the dirty dinner plates on the table.

"I love you Belle." The words created a cavernous ache deep in her chest but she didn't quite understand why. Maybe it was simply because it had been too long since she'd heard them said. Maybe it was something else entirely.

Fighting the emotional overload, she replied, "I love you too."

Her mother pulled her into her warm embrace and held her as she melted into her mother's side. Without hesitation, she laid her head on her mother's shoulder and listened to her narrate one of Annabelle's favorite stories. Her mother kissed the top of her head and Annabelle's breath caught in her chest. As she settled in, the rain became a soft hiss behind her mother's words.

The grandfather clock sat in the corner near the door, tall and stately, marking the unwavering constant of time as it ticked past, second by second. It chimed nine times marking the time and woke Annabelle from her nap. She was tucked into her mother's side still. The book lay open but flat on her mother's chest, which rose and fell steadily as she slept.

Annabelle grinned and laid her head back down. She pulled a throw from the back of the couch and pulled it over them both before settling back to sleep.

~***~

She woke in the best mood she could remember in a long time even though she was alone on the couch. Stretching her neck and arms she pushed up and off the couch to head upstairs. She counted each gleaming mahogany step as she went. As she entered her bedroom she thought of Jezebel. There seemed to be an unconscious pull to the woman, a call that she desperately wanted to answer. Part of her attributed her family's slow but steady progress of fixing their broken bonds to Jezebel. Another part genuinely liked the woman. She looked forward to her Tuesdays now. She liked listening to Jezebel's story and liked the conversations they always seemed to find themselves in.

A warm breeze blew through her brown hair. Today after school she would ask her mom if she would take her to Skillins Nursery to buy Jezebel a plant for her windowsill. She wanted to do something nice for her. She wanted to make the woman smile and possibly feel less alone during the week.

The day ticked by in minutes instead of hours, dragging excessively. By the time school let out Annabelle felt worn out from the effort it took to will the day by. She gathered what she needed from her locker and slammed the door shut.

"Hey!" Madison called. Annabelle spun around to face her friend.

"Hi."

"How're things? I feel like we never talk anymore." Madison frowned.

Annabelle knew the feeling. Being cut off from her best friend hurt. She worried that by the time she was allowed to do *anything* Madison would be gone. Gone to school or just moved on—gone. "Yeah. It sucks. But, I'm alright. I mean, bored a lot but the volunteer gig isn't so bad. Jezebel and I spend my time in her room. I just listen to her talk."

They moved together down the hall. Madison's sneakers squeaked on the linoleum flooring. "Is she really old?"

"No. She's actually like, my parents' age and she's kinda cool. I like her."

"What does she talk about?" Madison asked.

"Life. I guess. Mostly she tells a story about some lady from Paris in the Eighties."

Madison's brow furrowed. "Sounds . . ."

"Lame," Annabelle giggled. Because it did. But it wasn't. Not at all. "I guess you have to be there to get it. I swear though, she's pretty interesting."

"Hey!" Madison chirped. "You can't go out and I can't go to your house, but . . . can I come to a volunteer day with you? Maybe we could hang that way."

Annabelle liked the idea but wasn't sure if it would fly. Sure anyone could volunteer at Glenview but her gut grew anxious at the thought of sharing Jezebel. The woman seemed like magic somehow and she, quite frankly, wanted to keep her all to herself.

"Yeah," she answered instead of saying no. "Tuesday, after school. Room two-oh-eight. I have to take the bus but meet me there."

"This'll be fun! I mean, I'm not going to do it every week, but I miss you, Belle. And it'll be nice just to hang out for an afternoon."

Annabelle smiled at her friend. It would be nice, and maybe Jezebel would like the extra company too. She hurried to the bus and waved bye to Madison who was parked in the student lot. Another reminder of her punishment, she was reduced to riding the bus again. She sighed and climbed up and onto the bus that perpetually reeked of garlic.

~***~

It had been raining for five days straight. Her boots created puddles on the floor as she stepped across the foyer. Her mother would be pissed at the mess. The overcast sky mimicked her mood. She'd been naïve in thinking that her home life was looking up. Friday, she'd heard her mother on the phone, presumably with her father, and it had left a sour feeling in the pit of her belly. She kicked off her boots and trudged upstairs. Her mother had gone from lighthearted to glum after she hung up. There had been no more music in the kitchen, no more shared moments after dinner and no more cheer in the air. There had only been silence. Again.

Annabelle had tried everything Jezebel had

encouraged her too. She'd listened to music, she'd smiled non-stop and she'd tried to strike up easy conversation with her mom but it was all met with a pinched expression and not much else.

She didn't understand it. She scooped up her laundry basket and carried it down the hall. She opened the washer door and haphazardly threw things into the machine. She poured liquid detergent in and started the water.

"What're you doing?" Her mother stared at her, eyes chilly.

Annabelle shrugged. "Laundry?"

"How very . . . adult of you," her mother said. Confused by her iciness, by her mother's words, she shut the washer door before starting the appropriate wash cycle.

"Rude much?" she muttered.

Her mother sighed long and hard. Her heels clicked on the hardwood floor. "I have . . . I'm sorry," she said turning to Annabelle. "I have time, now, to bring you to Skillins if you want." Annabelle considered her mother's apology and decided it was the best she was going to get. She nodded at her mother and shuffled in her wake down the hall.

~***~

Feeling rebellious, Annabelle let Madison drive her to Glenview Tuesday after school; no one would know. It lifted her spirit giggling in the car with her best friend while belting out lyrics to their favorite songs on the drive over.

"Listen Madison, I know it's weird, sitting with a stranger and listening to them talk but, be polite okay?" She wasn't asking. It was an instruction. And surprisingly, Madison nodded. Annabelle carried the potted flower down the corridor with Madison dragging her feet behind her.

"Hi, Jez!" Annabelle greeted, entering the room.

"Hi," Madison said and smiled uncomfortably.

"Well! What do we have here?" Jezebel asked, pointing to the flower.

Annabelle shrugged. "This is for you." She walked to Jezebel and handed her the gift.

"Ah, an orchid. Do you know what it means?"

"Um, captivating, I think," she answered.

"Yes and strength," Jezebel added. "It's beautiful. Why did you choose it?"

"When the lady told me what it meant it just seemed fitting for you. I dunno, it's how I see you I guess."

"That's quite the compliment. Thank you." A bright smile graced Jezebel's face. "Annabelle, who is this?" Jezebel gestured to Madison.

"My best friend Madison. I thought it was okay for her to come today."

"Oh why not!" Jezebel answered. "So Madison, what's your deal?"

Annabelle snickered at Jezebel's question as she pulled a small chair from the opposite corner of the room for Madison to sit in.

"I don't know. I just wanted to spend some time with Belle. I miss her."

"Interesting, so you chose to come here with her?"

"She's grounded. No friends over and no leaving her house, this was the only way," Madison answered matter-of-factly.

Annabelle sat and toed off her shoes before tucking her legs underneath her. She motioned for Madison to get comfortable.

"So, my dear, how was your week? Still pining over the boyfriend?" Jezebel asked.

Madison snorted. "No. Actually I didn't really think about him at all," Annabelle answered.

"Well at least you didn't waste brain cells."

Annabelle noticed Madison absentmindedly navigating her phone. It struck her as rude, but she knew that if hers hadn't been confiscated by her parents, she'd be doing exactly the same thing. Still, it bothered her. "I made dinner for my mom." she blurted.

Jezebel raised an eyebrow at her and grinned. Madison's thumb stopped moving on the screen. "I made pasta carbonara. And you know what? It was really freakin' good. Actually, my mom even admitted to being a terrible cook that night—which was hilarious. And we read. Well, she read to me after we ate and fell asleep together on the couch." Her words were rushed and enthusiastic. She felt pride about her small accomplishment and wanted to share it.

"Are you for real?" Madison asked without bothering to look up from her phone.

"Girl, put that away," Jezebel snapped at Madison. "You don't need it, those damn phones are automating our humanity. Talking in person, touching in person, seeing a smile in person, those are the things in life that will carry you through your hardships. And trust me, you *will* have hardships. Do you really think five years from now you will remember a sweet text your boyfriend sent? No, don't be silly, if you remember anything about him *at all* it will be something that was tangible, the feeling of his lips on yours, the softness of his hair or perhaps the way he held your hand."

Madison stared slack-jawed at Jezebel, thumb hovering above the phone screen. Annabelle snickered. She couldn't help it. Madison looked to her and she shrugged because quite frankly, she agreed with Jezebel. She watched as

Madison powered off the screen and tucked the phone in her purse.

"Uh, sorry," Madison stammered.

Jezebel cocked her head to the left and scrutinized Madison for a moment. "Now, Annabelle, I think it's wonderful news that you had a good week."

"No. Just a good twenty-four hours. My dad called the next day and somehow killed mom's mood. The rest of the week was back to miserable silence," she answered, deflated.

"You cooked? And hung out with your *mom?*" Madison asked shocked.

Annabelle nodded.

"Child, do you really think that eight *years* of behavior would be changed overnight?" Jezebel asked.

"No. I mean, I was hopeful though." She frowned. She *had* thought that maybe everything was truly going to be better. How foolish.

"Hope is a nasty little bitch isn't she?" Jezebel laughed.

"That's a depressing sentiment," Madison balked.

"Not at all kiddo, it's just a realistic one," Jezebel retorted.

Annabelle found herself agreeing with both of them. What kind of a life could a person have without hope? But, hope alone couldn't make a person happy. There had to be a middle ground, one where expectations, hope and reality coexisted. The large diamond on Jezebel's wedding ring sparkled in the light, catching Annabelle's eye.

"How was your week? Did your husband visit?" she asked hoping to change the subject.

"You're married?" Madison asked.

"Why is that shocking?" Jezebel retorted, not missing a beat.

"I don't know, I guess I just assume that people in these places aren't."

"These places?" Jezebel prompted. Her tone dripping with disdain.

"Yeah, nursing homes, or assisted living places. Like—if you had a husband at home, you wouldn't be here because he'd take care of you. These are the places you go when there's no one left to take care of you." Madison answered, brow furrowed.

"Do a husband and wife love each other?"

"Of course." Madison replied.

"And, if you had a husband, and you were still relatively *young*, would you want him to be saddled with taking care of you alone, worrying about you all the time, while he still works all day? Would you feel terrible knowing that *he* feels terrible about having to go to work while you struggle at home alone?"

"Well sure. I mean, that sounds like a lot of pressure," Madison conceded.

"It is. And it also wasn't fair to either of us, or feasible, as my episodes worsened. So here I am, fifty years young and in one of *these places*."

"Yeah," Madison replied sheepishly.

"To answer your question Annabelle, yes he visited. We had a splendid dinner together and spent the rest of our time snuggling in my bed and reading."

Annabelle noticed that Madison's expression mirrored her own. Their noses both wrinkled up in revolt at the thought of anyone their parent's ages snuggling in bed together. It made her laugh. Madison giggled beside her.

"We're middle-aged dears, not dead," Jezebel chuckled. "Shall we start?"

Madison and Annabelle nodded in unison.

"Hm, okay, Paris . . ."

"Nineteen eighty-five," Annabelle finished for her. Jezebel smiled and began.

Chapter 10

Celeste

Paris 1985

Gabriel whistled a song while he unpacked. The tune carried throughout the house. Celeste stopped what she was doing and listened, a smile creeping over her face. This would be her every day. This would be her norm now and it made her heart lift and stomach flutter. She put her stocking-clad feet up on the coffee table while she listened to his whistle, sipped her coffee and tried to find motivation to tackle unpacking. She had convinced Gabriel to wait until they had told everyone of their engagement before moving into the house he'd purchased for them. It bought her time to pack and figure out how she would get through her last year of college with him around to distract her.

Matteo, the genius that he was, had suggested he and Mara and her meet three nights a week at the library, strictly to do homework and study. It was a solid plan. It put her out of the house and with people who she knew she could get the work done with. Gabriel supported her one hundred percent in her studies, but whenever he was physically near she found herself watching him, daydreaming about what they *could* be doing instead of homework. She needed to focus.

The hours passed by slowly, the time filled with unpacking boxes and organizing. By late afternoon, Celeste felt completely burnt out in the moving department. She rummaged through Gabriel's bedside drawers trying to find extra space for the small items in the open box at her feet. A deck of cards, a few concert tickets and the watch she gave him last Christmas sat in it. She picked up the tickets and grinned. He had kept all the tickets from the shows they had seen together. She liked that he was sentimental that way.

Hours later when their eyes were so heavy they couldn't keep them open any longer, they lay down in bed together. *Their* bed. She entwined herself in his limbs and fought visions of endless boxes stacked all around her, until she finally fell into a dark and fitful sleep.

The sun streamed through the curtain-less windows. It was too early to be up yet. Gabriel lightly snored next to her. Snuggling back under the blankets Celeste savored the last few moments of peace before facing the day ahead. There was still a lot of work to be done. They had unpacked most of the boxes, but the house was still in need of some serious cleaning and arranging. She'd need to enlist Mara's help today if she was going to accomplish it all.

Celeste ticked off a mental list as she slid out of bed hours later. She softly padded down the hall, descended the stairs and promptly started a pot of coffee. As she waited for the glorious liquid gold to brew she picked up the phone and dialed Mara's number.

Chapter 11

Annabelle

"And I didn't see the future coming. Because I've been too blind"

~ L'ame Immortelle, Betrayal

"Does this story have a point? I mean she's met the handsome guy and they've fallen in love. What could possibly happen now?" Madison interrupted.

"You can't rush perfection. I promise you this story will make your head spin. It's worth hearing."

Madison slumped back into her chair and huffed.

"Please, continue," Annabelle spoke up as irritation at her friend festered.

"You could always go make yourself useful somewhere else," Jezebel snapped at Madison.

Jezebel was the only reason Annabelle wasn't yanking her hair out of her head or dying from boredom. She'd grown fond of the woman and her story and she was pissed at Madison's crappy attitude.

"I'm sorry Jez," Annabelle offered.

"Oh hush. It's fine, I remember being

eighteen once. Old people sucked."

Annabelle laughed loudly at the woman's remark.

"I promise, you don't suck Jez. I'd tell you." She glared at Madison.

"Well thank God for small miracles. Now, are we done for today or are you ready for more?"

"More please," she answered. Jezebel looked to Madison and waited.

"Yeah. Sorry. Keep going," Madison answered with an expression of embarrassment plastered on her face.

Jezebel quieted for a moment. She looked lost in thought. Annabelle wondered if she'd lost her train of thought, or perhaps had forgotten where she was in the story. Normally she didn't care for busybodies but Jezebel had a way of spinning tales and rumors like they were harmless bits of nonsense. She was about to remind her but she'd learned Jezebel had her own pace when telling the story and Annabelle didn't want to disrupt it.

Chapter 12

Celeste

Paris 1986

Celeste stared at the bottom of her white satin shoe—at the handwritten note from Gabriel on the sole.

Chaque pas que vous faites aujourd'hui vous rapproche de mon cœur.

Every step you take today brings you closer to my heart.

She could practically hear him speaking the words he wrote. A delightful mix of melody and syllables that could charm a snake. When Celeste thought about her future it was lavender and wrapped in satin. Gabriel was the epitome of her wildest fantasies. Handsome, glamorous, smart and down to earth. Everything he did seemed so effortless. The way he held her, kissed her, cared for her was nothing short of a romance novel. While her friends were enduring heart-wrenching breakups, lost in questions like, "How could I have loved that boy?" and, "What did I see in him?," she was up in the clouds floating in brilliant hues of oranges, reds and blues.

"My God, does the man have *any* flaws?" Mara asked staring at the handwritten words on the bottom of the shoe.

Celeste shrugged. "Not really," she answered and smiled.

"Charles would never think to do something that sweet. I swear Celeste, how you managed to snag a man like Gabriel, I will never know." It wasn't an affront. She knew exactly what her friend meant and agreed with her. She was still in shock that Charles had lasted a year with Mara. He'd tamed her a bit, wormed his way into her best friend's heart and managed to keep Mara wanting him. And she liked Charles; he was a good man.

"I know." The words left her mouth in a breathy puff of air.

Today was *the* day. Last night Mara and a few other girls from school had gone out on the town celebrating her bachelorette party. They had ended their girls evening at BC Black Calvados, the *branché* black and chrome nightclub. It had been so much fun, almost too much. She had been adamant about being back to the hotel by ten to get a good night's rest but they had ended up out until one a.m.

Mara and her mother helped Celeste into her dress. The pearl buttons skillfully done up the length of her back. The photographer took pictures as they each slid on her shoes for her and fixed her hair and makeup just right.

Now, ready to walk down the aisle, the romantic lace *Catherine Walker* dress combined with the stunning Paris cathedral backdrop made Celeste feel like the quintessential bride, delicate and elegant like a ballerina atop an antique music box. She rolled her neck, the tiny hairs on her back prickling as she waited for Mara to descend the aisle. The cathedral doors, open behind her, let the summer wind whip her hair, whip her dress around her legs, but she didn't care. Her father, at her elbow, gave a gentle squeeze. Matteo, at her other elbow, beamed at her. She couldn't imagine a more fitting scenario. But now, all she could focus on was the man waiting for her at the end of the aisle. With one glance, even in the crowded room, he made her feel vulnerable and exposed, as if he could see a side of her that no one else bothered to notice.

He watched reverently as she neared him. She felt her father and Matteo release her. A bittersweet wave engulfed her as she took Gabriel's hands. Her father kissed her cheek and Matteo followed suit. In the moment when Gabriel closed his hands around hers she felt her heart nearly explode with joy. He clutched her hands tightly as the minister said his piece. They promised they would love each other for all their years. His happy tears fell, his smile full of promise of their future. She couldn't wait to pull him close, wanting to be lost in the smell and sight and feel of him. The press of his lips to hers calmed the chaos of the day away.

They had taken a year to plan the wedding. She and Gabriel had gone with the soft, romantic colors of white, peach, and pink, with dusty miller accents. To add to the ambiance they also chose amber up-lighting around the perimeter and tall candelabras for the center tables to fill the space and draw the guests' eyes up towards the gorgeous ceiling. The food— from the chicken confit appetizer to the espresso crème brûlée cups, and the home-made foie gras to the truffle "lollipops" served with a refreshing black cocktail—made their way around the open space where their guests mingled. Music was cafe-inspired, including many Django Reinhardt jazz pieces. And finally, to add to the formal, romantic mood, they chose black tuxedos for the men, and she chose lacy dresses and pearl accessories for the women. Looking around, she couldn't have been happier with how the event turned out and now they could finally enjoy all of the romance they had worked so hard to create.

The entire celebration left Celeste feeling warm and grateful. The reception had been a

K. LARSEN

whirlwind of smiles, hugs and warm wishes. Gabriel looked nothing short of dashing in his tux. She relished the dances they shared, the private moments spent in each other's arms moving to the cadence of the quartet. It was magical and breathtaking.

The music was cranked up full-blast and a swirl of summer air gently worked its way through the crowd. The scent of his aftershave filled her nostrils as he held her close. It was familiar and calming.

"So, how does it feel to be my husband?" she joked as he swept her around the dance floor.

"I'm a scientist. Not enough empirical data yet." He feigned seriousness.

"Well, we'll have to change that." She tilted back her head and met his lips, kissing him. "Take me home and make love to me, Gabriel," she whispered.

He grinned and danced her right off the floor toward the exit causing her to laugh at his little show. "I'm sorry, all!" he yelled out to their guests, "But husbandly duties call!"

He carried her through the very same door to their house he had before, and to their room where he laid her down and began to give her his love, and she gave hers to him. His hand lowered to the hem of her dress and began to lift. She tilted her hips to arch her back allowing the dress to be pushed up higher. His fingers slid over her thighs, so near, yet not touching where her body wanted. His movements were beautifully slow, deliberate.

He moved steadily deeper into her and paused just to watch her. His lips brushed her neck. His touch warm and electric. Nuzzling her exposed neck and shoulder, her hips tilted forward, stalling the thoughts in her head. His hand slid down her stomach. The path he'd traveled tingled from the warmth of his touch, igniting her skin. She reached for his shoulders as one then two fingers slid inside her and let out a gasp. Heat burned through her as his fingers worked magic, building, building, building, until she exploded in ecstasy. Gabriel withdrew his fingers and moved over her, hovering chest to chest before slipping inside.

Pounding into her, he found his release as he let out a roar that echoed through their room. Her eyes went wide and her mouth fell open as he made the final push. She was so full of him. He watched as lust mired her features. When the final ripple of crazed pleasure subsided, Gabriel kissed her forehead and rubbed his cheek against hers. Uninhibited and delicate. The two of them tangled up and sweaty. "You're incredible, mon amour." He continued to brush her arms in a ghostly caress until she fell asleep sated and still in her wedding dress.

~***~

Their honeymoon began the morning after the wedding. Their bags were packed days in advance which made their morning stress-free and easy. Gabriel sat at the breakfast table, a mug of coffee and *The New York Times* crossword puzzle in hand. As he thought, he whistled. It was endearing. After warming and buttering a scone she sat next to him and sighed.

"What's wrong?"

"Nothing. I'm perfectly happy." She tucked a strand of hair behind her ear and smiled.

"You'd better be," he chuckled.

"Anyone who could find reason to be unhappy after yesterday's fairytale-come-true and an impending trip to Capri would be insane."

"Oh, so happy has nothing to do with me?" He laughed. She crumpled her napkin and threw it at him as they both laughed.

~***~

Capri. Her breath might as well have just disappeared altogether. She had never been to Capri and it was stunning. Exiting the ferry from Naples Celeste was speechless. Her mouth hung agape as she took in her surroundings. She licked the briny air from her lips while the breeze rustled the hair away from her face. She thought she knew what beauty was, she had an idea in her mind, but what she saw when they arrived in Capri was a beauty she didn't know existed. Her heart, wide open, oozed uncontrollable joy.

After exploring a bit of one side of the island, they got on the tram and started the climb up to the hotel Punta Tragara. Littered along the way were extravagant shops, beautiful flower lined pathways and inviting rich patios. It was almost too beautiful to bear. The sound of Gabriel's camera shutter snapped her from her thoughts.

Celeste fiddled with the chain of her locket. "This place is like a dream."

"I knew you'd like it." He let the camera rest against his chest and kissed the crown of her head. Her first love, her husband. She was too high, floating in the clouds to ever step foot on land again. She pushed up and pressed her lips to his. Gabriel groaned in response.

"*Mon amour,* your lips were made for mine."

When they finally arrived at their hotel near the top of the island she was floored by the extraordinary charm of the hotel. The room and the service were perfection, and the view of legendary Faraglioni cliffs was incredible. After dropping their bags and fooling around for a while like giddy teenagers they checked out the heated pool. On the coast the summer breeze made the heated pool the perfect temperature for a night swim.

She found that looking up at the stars into

space makes one reconnect with what is important. Gabriel's strong arms wrapped around her, his wet hair flopping into his face, and the champagne may have helped that revelation come about. They floated together, her back to his chest, his hands wandering. Celeste smiled up at the stars as she covered his hand with hers and guided it down her stomach and beneath the elastic waist of her bikini.

~***~

The sun beat down through the thin material of her sleeves. Moving through the water, over swells and farther into the ocean, they rowed out in a tiny boat after their lunch to see the grotto. It didn't seem all that amazing until they reached the water *inside* the grotto. When it was finally their turn, they were instructed to lay down on their backs in the boat, and the guide pulled the boat through an impossibly small cavern entrance. When Celeste's eyes adjusted and she resumed her upright position, she gasped. She was dazzled by the luminescent waters beneath them. It glowed a stunning electric blue.

"It's breathtaking," Gabriel said grinning. He ran his fingers through his hair and pulled Celeste closer.

"Breathtaking doesn't even seem to do it justice," she answered, wishing she knew a word—any word—that could encompass the stunning natural phenomenon they were seeing.

"I'm happy you're enjoying this." Gabriel bared his dimple at her. Forgetting the guide was with them, she reached out to touch it. He cupped her chin and pulled her face to his before pushing his warm lips against her own.

At dinner they tried to steer lighter in the food department with mixed bruschetta, prosciutto, and buffalo mozzarella sliced cheese, all so flavorful under the sun. A salty warm breeze captured their memorable honeymoon like a dream in every way possible.

That evening, when they finally decided to call it a night and return to their room, he took her hands and pulled her around to face him. Then he grabbed her by the hips and lifted her up onto the window ledge where he fed her grapes and wine. His eyes lingered everywhere as if memorizing each curve and angle of her. It was sweet.

"Those taste so much better than the grapes at home," she groaned in appreciation.

"Well it's because they're magical," Gabriel whispered. Celeste laughed and swatted at his chest.

Capturing her hands he brought the wine glass up to her lips. "Drink up."

"Are you trying to get me drunk? Take advantage of me?" She took in the moment with him like a refreshing drink, savoring each and every moment they were collecting together.

"It seemed like a solid plan," he retorted and grinned. He lifted the cup a little more. Celeste parted her lips and he groaned as she took her sip and savored it.

"You don't need a plan," she whispered leaning into him. "I'm Mrs. Fontaine now. You can have me, whenever, wherever, and *how*ever you like." She giggled and hopped down from the window ledge to head out to the balcony. The night stars glittered overhead and the sea breeze whipped her hair around.

Oh really? Then I say we skinny-dip, Mrs. Fontaine. You up for it?" he asked. his eyes sparkling with mischief. The corner of her mouth turned up at his suggestion. She nodded and willed her heart to slow down. "I never say no to an adventure."

Celeste ran past him, grabbing towels from the bed and hurrying toward the pool. She'd never skinny dipped before and didn't want to lose her courage. She'd meant what she'd told him about having her. She could hear Gabriel laughing behind her as he tried to keep up. She pushed through the double doors to the pool terrace and stopped at the first lounge chair, dropping their towels. Gabriel came to a stop a mere inch from her.

Lifting her sundress slowly she stripped for

him. She wanted him to kiss her. She imagined the way his full lips would feel, firm, yet soft. She imagined the way his hands would feel on her back, pulling her closer, closer, closer. His sharp intake of breath broke her thoughts as her dress hit the pool deck. She reached out, sliding his shirt up and over his defined torso until it, too, lay in a puddle at their feet. His eyes danced with delight as he reached behind her and unclasped her bra. Sweat formed in tiny drops at her forehead and the base of her neck. She pulled her thick hair back into a messy ponytail, instantly feeling relief as the breeze slides along the back of her neck. Her panties went next and his shorts and boxers followed.

He scooped her up into his arms. "One."

"Gabriel—no."

"Two." He took a step closer to the edge.

"Really, I'll get in on my own!"

"Three!" He boomed and leapt into the pool, plunging them both into the chilled, dark water.

She fought to swim up, breaking the surface of the water and spluttering. Gabriel's head popped up a moment later. One look at her and he burst out laughing.

"You little shit!" she squealed in good humor.

"Come here," he demanded. She watched the muscles in his back as she swam to the edge of the pool before following his lead. He propped his arms up on the pool edge to hold himself in place. She wrapped her legs around his waist and her arms around his neck.

"Tell me what you want Celeste."

"What do you mean?" she questioned, her brow furrowed.

"What do you need me to give you to make you look like this forever?"

This man. She thought about his words, about the weight of them. Rain started to drip from the sky.

"You," she answered simply. He grinned and kissed her just as the rain came heavy and fast. They scrambled from the pool and laughed and ran all the way back to their room.

His biceps stretched the fabric of his shirt, which was wet and sticking to his chest. Wave after wave of appreciation moved through her fluidly as they gazed at the each other. Celeste moved to the window overlooking the sea. Gabriel came up behind her and swept her hair aside with the lightest touch of his finger. She turned, facing him, and jumped up wrapping her legs around his waist. He wasted no time walking her to the bed where they ended up laying tangled together for days, smiling and sighing and wishing they could somehow stop time.

She awoke to a stream of sunlight shining

into the room. Little particles of dust danced in and out, through the rays, and she lay there a moment, thinking about the past few days' events. She felt like she was soaring and never wanted to come down.

Chapter 13

Annabelle

"Why did you do the things you've done? Destroyed my life with so much fun"
~ L'âme Immortelle, Betrayal

"Can you say honeymoon baby?" Madison snorted. Annabelle's thoughts halted to a stop. "Their honeymoon sounds like my parents.' My mom gets this crazy look in her eye when she talks about it and she gets all breathy and weird, smiling at my dad like he's a prime piece of meat." Madison shuddered and wrapped her arms around herself.

Annabelle was envious of Madison, of her parents who openly still touched, talked and *tried*. Madison had no idea how good she had it. "I think that's nice," she stated.

"It's gross. Trust me. No one wants to imagine their parents doing it." Cue another shudder.

"Your parents obviously love each other. You don't see that? Like that? Jesus, Mad, look at my parents! Would you rather have them?" She raised her voice. Some people just didn't know how good they had it.

Madison looked to the floor and slid one shoe

back and forth. "No. I mean, it would suck if no one talked or gave a shit. But, no one in my family died either, I have no idea how that would change them."

Annabelle was shocked that Madison brought that up. She knew of course, but it was something that they never really discussed as Annabelle's entire motto for years had been avoidance. "Yeah," she retorted coldly.

"Belle, I wasn't trying to be a jerk," Madison whined.

"I know. I just . . . you're right."

"Annabelle," Jezebel cut in slapping her thigh. "This girl," she pointed one of those long delicate looking fingers at Madison, "is your *best* friend and she doesn't know your deepest, darkest thoughts? She doesn't know how your home life affects you? She doesn't know how your brother's death affects you?"

Annabelle wished Jezebel would shut her mouth. Some things she just didn't discuss with anyone—well, anyone before Jezebel. Madison furrowed her brow and watched her friend for confirmation of the woman's words.

"Belle doesn't talk about it. Her brother I mean." Madison interjected and ran a hand through her long hair. "She complains about her parents and yeah, going over there is about as fun as visiting a mausoleum. But no, we never really talk about it."

Annabelle huffed, feeling as if she were now part of some ridiculous intervention. One she did *not* need. "There's no point. Why would we talk about him? He died before I even knew you."

"Bullcrap!" Jezebel shouted. Madison startled and she jumped a good inch in her seat.

"Jez. Stop," Annabelle glared.

"I will not. Your only alternative is hoofing it to the kitchen or common room to finish out your *sentence*. I'm quite confident you'll endure my two cents before volunteering for the kitchen. Hair nets darling. *Hair nets.*"

Madison shivered and looked horrified. Annabelle fumed but remained silent. Jezebel had her there; she'd take anything—even Jezebel's meddling—before hair nets and latex gloves again.

"Let's get something out, yes?" Jezebel started. "Your brother died. A horrible event." Jezebel looked to her and Madison. They both nodded. Jezebel pulled a bobby pin from the back of her head letting her long peppered hair cascade down around her shoulders. "Your parents are a different problem that I'm not going to address. I am going to address your grief Annabelle, for that's the only one you have any control over." Starting to feel parched, Annabelle got up and helped herself to a glass of water. She noticed her hands were shaking.

Her grief. Her grief. Her grief.

No one had referred to it that way. Ever. It was *the family's* grief. It was her parents' grief — for losing a child. It was never hers — never hers alone. As she sat back down in her chair Jezebel dove in.

"How did he die?"

Annabelle closed her eyes and drew in a breath. "It was a hit and run."

"Did they catch the person?" Madison asked.

"No," she shook her head. "He didn't come home that night. My parents got worried and called the police but they wouldn't do anything until he'd been missing for twenty-four hours. My parents rallied some other neighborhood parents and searched for hours." The words fell from her mouth in a hateful tone. She noticed a calm expression fall over Jezebel's face and it made her angry.

"What happened next?" Jezebel asked.

"I found him. The next morning I was walking to school he was right there, on a dead-end side street near ours. We used to take it as a shortcut to get home. No one had thought to look near the path. Most kids didn't walk through the woods." Visions pummeled her, of her brother, bloody and prone on the sidewalk, his gangly twelve year old body set at an awkward angle , of her younger self trying to wake him up, .the way her backpack had spilled its contents on the ground because she was always forgetting to zip it up. Of the walk back to her house. Of her parents' faces. Of the way from that moment on she became a shadow, simply left in the background as her parents struggled to get through that year—and every year since. She squeezed her eyes shut against the memory. "I was ten. He was twelve."

"Oh my God," Madison breathed. Annabelle watched as Madison hopped up from her chair and rushed at her. Her arms wrapped around her tightly and held on as sobs wracked her friend's body. The room echoed with her heartache. It could be heard in the sobs, heard in the sniffles, heard in the gasps for air as she struggled to breathe.

Reluctantly, Madison released her. Annabelle watched as she pulled her chair closer, tucked right in next to hers and reached out for her hand. She took it and wiped her eyes with her opposite sleeve.

"That my, dear girl, is why you need friends who know your secrets," Jezebel offered quietly while brushing a clump of hair back over her shoulder. "Comfort. Friends are the family we get to choose. They will lift you up during your lows and cheer you on during your highs. If they don't, they aren't truly your friends."

~***~

The bell rang. It was loud and jarring and irritated Annabelle. She stuffed her notes into her backpack and trudged out the classroom door into the hallway packed with students hurrying to leave the building.

"Yo," Madison greeted and bumped her shoulder. She smiled and bumped her back.

"What's up?"

"I have a date tonight." Madison bit her lip.

"Do tell."

"Andy Kessler, and we're going to dinner and then paintballing. I have no idea what the hell to wear for that! Could you score your laptop before dinner maybe? We could Skype and I could show you my outfits," Madison rambled. She was nervous. It was adorable. Madison rarely got nervous. She was full of light and confidence normally. Annabelle smiled at her friend.

"Yeah," she said. "I'll make it happen."

"Score!" Madison chirped.

~***~

Annabelle rushed off the bus and down her street. Blowing through the foyer she heard her parents arguing in her dad's office.

"Christ, Gavin, can't you just let it go?" Her mother's voice was hot and angry.

"This could be it though, don't you

understand? How can you *not* support me on this? It's what we've been working on for years."

Her mother barked out a laugh. "No, honey, it's what *you've* been working on for years. I've just been along for the ride. You had your chance at greatness and you let it slip through your hands." Her words were bitter and angry.

A stinging crack resounded from the other side of the door. Annabelle gasped. The door was yanked viscously open and her mother stormed out red cheeked. Without acknowledging her, her mother stomped passed and up the gleaming mahogany staircase to her room. Her parents' bedroom door slammed shut with enough force to shake the pictures hanging on the surrounding walls. Surely her father hadn't actually hit her mom.

She poked her head into her father's office slowly. "Dad?"

"What?" he grumbled without meeting her eyes.

"Uh, I have a load of homework, could you get me my laptop?"

"Now's not a good time. Do it after dinner." He waved her off without looking up from the papers spread out across his desk. Anger bubbled in her chest.

"Dad," she said firmly. He looked up. "It

can't wait."

"Fine," he boomed. Pushing away from his desk he pounded his way to the kitchen to unlock her laptop. Annabelle, curious, made her way into his office to his desk. Sheets of paper littered his desk, notes scribbled in his familiar handwriting all over them. She didn't know what she was looking at. She couldn't understand why they were so important to him. Medical jargon and chemistry-like equations were sketched on each one. Formulas, probably, for whatever new drug he was peddling these days to the doctors. But why? He was simply a sales rep. The company he worked for had teams of scientists. She backed away just in time.

Her father waltzed back into the office, laptop in hand. He thrust it at her. "Here."

She took it and scrambled up to her room, confused. She didn't understand why her father had slapped her mother. It didn't make sense. Her mother's days of working were long over. Her mom stayed home, she wouldn't know anything about her father's work. She certainly wouldn't *be* any part of it, other than in marital support . Her mother kept the home running while her father went to work every day to provide for them. But, she thought, the house was as spotless as ever. Everything in its place as he liked it. How could he be such an asshole? Disgust burrowed a tunnel in her chest. How could her mother let that happen? Why did she not stand up for herself?

She fired up her laptop and opened Skype. She would *never* let anyone hit her. Her mother's soft cries could be heard even from behind the closed door of her room.

~***~

Annabelle's weekend had sucked. No Internet, crappy TV and being stuck at home had made the time pass uber slowly. Her parents hadn't helped either. They had avoided each other the entire weekend. Poisonous silence blanketed the Fortin household once again. She had reverted to her head-in-the-sand avoidance tactics. She found that thinking about that slap was more than she could deal with. She had never been so grateful for Monday morning and school. As she pushed through the crowded hallway she spotted Madison.

"Hey Ho!" she called out snagging Madison's attention. She watched a brilliant smile light up her friend's face. She jogged, closing the gap between them. "How was the date?"

Madison groaned and lifted the hem of her shirt showing a purple bruise atop her hip. "It was awesome, and painful," she laughed.

"Who knew paintball could be so dangerous."

"He made up for it. He felt so bad. It was

adorable. He asked if I wanted him to kiss it better."

Annabelle snorted and adjusted her bag on her shoulder. "So—did you let him?"

"No!" Madison laughed and winked. "I'm no hussy. But seriously Belle, it was such a fun night. Like . . . the *best*." Madison sighed with a dreamy look in her eye. Happiness bloomed in her heart for her friend. She was genuinely happy to see Madison so happy.

"Aww, yay. I'm glad for you."

"How was your weekend?" Madison asked. "It was torture not having any way to get in touch with you after I got home Friday night." She pouted at Annabelle.

Annabelle frowned. "My weekend was long. You know, big house, full of silence." She shrugged. "I was bored senseless."

"Ugh. I'm sorry. I really freakin' wish there was something I could do."

"Yeah, well . . . me too, but I'm the idiot who drank and then drove home."

"I meant about your family, but you are an idiot for that stunt," Madison said and slanted her eyes to Annabelle. "Speaking of idiots—did you hear about Damon?"

Annabelle turned to face Madison. "No."

"He was busted Saturday night. Got pulled over for speeding or something, I guess. Had a big bag of coke on him and an open six-pack. They nailed him. It probably didn't help he had a car full of people who were so high they didn't know their asses from their heads," Madison snickered.

"Can you please tell me what I saw in him?" she groaned. Madison switched her bag to her other shoulder and shrugged.

"Escape and a seriously ripped bod."

The girls laughed together. Damon *was* gorgeous and he had offered her an escape of sorts. He wasn't deep. He didn't question anything and he had been available.

"He's eighteen—how's this going to play out for him?" Annabelle asked.

"I dunno. My dad said he's looking at probation, with lots of counseling and rehab, and maybe even some community service." Madison's father was a hot shot attorney who never lost a trial. Annabelle knew—he'd been hers. Thank God for that. If not for him, her sentence would have surely been a lot worse.

"Is he repping Damon?" she asked.

"Not a chance. His words—not mine," Madison answered. "Hey, tomorrow . . . want me to come along again?"

Annabelle thought about her offer for a second. "Naw. No offense. I just think two visits in a row might be pushing my luck. Don't want to get caught."

"Cool. That lady is freakin' pushy and weirdly wise. She made my head spin," Madison admitted.

Annabelle grinned and nodded. "I think that's why I like her so much."

~***~

Annabelle practically skipped to Jezebel's room. She was excited to see her. The week since her last visit had been long and stressful and today would be a nice reprieve. Today she came armed with something she hoped Jezebel would find fun.

"Jezzie," she sang as she pushed into the woman's room. Instantly she was concerned. Jezebel was lying on her side in bed staring out the window. Annabelle noticed a faint but thick scar that crept out from her tank top near her shoulder blade. Annabelle wondered what could have left such a mark. "Jez? Everything alright?"

"Hello darling. Fine, fine, just a bit under the weather I'm afraid."

"Should I . . . do something else today and let you rest?" Annabelle stuttered out. She didn't want to do anything else and she hoped Jezebel would still let her sit with her.

"God no! Please, I'll die of boredom if you leave. Drag that chair over so you're closer. It's just my stomach." Annabelle scooted her usual chair close to the bed. Jezebel looked flushed and she wondered if she was more sick than she let on.

"Okay. Well." Annabelle pulled her nail kit from her bag. "I thought maybe we could paint each other's nails today while we talk?"

Jezebel's face lit up with excitement and it made Annabelle happy, a warm heat spreading throughout her chest. "I'd love that! Do you have Harlot Red?" Jezebel asked.

Annabelle burst out laughing. Only Jezebel would ask something like that. Rummaging through her container of polishes, she pulled out a vibrant red color. "This work?" she asked as she held it up. Jezebel grinned and nodded.

"Let's dive in," Jezebel said as Annabelle pulled out a file and nail scissors. Jezebel gently placed one hand in hers and Annabelle happily started working on the woman's nails. "Paris, nineteen eighty-six."

Chapter 14

Celeste

Paris 1986

Their clothes were spilled across the bedroom carpet, along with the decorative pillows from the bed. Celeste lay beneath the sheet catching her breath. They'd kicked off the covers and the down comforter. She ran her fingers over Gabriel's chest. He kissed her sweetly and rolled onto his side to get out of the bed, but she reached for his shoulder and pulled him back down. "Tell Monique I'm sorry you were late," she winked, rolling on top of him and feeling him harden beneath her.

After their morning quickie, she lay on the bed watching him dress. The scent of his masculine cologne filled the room. Gabriel adjusted his tie and padded over to her. "Good luck today," he said and bent over placing a gentle kiss to her temple.

"Thanks love." She sighed.

"I'm sure you'll get the job. The man would have to be an idiot not to see how perfect you are." He grinned, bearing the dimple she loved so much.

"Well he's hiring me for the gardens — not

because I'm perfect," she laughed.

"Regardless of why — he's hiring you. Or . . . he'd better."

She laughed and shooed him off. "You're already late. Get going Mr. Fontaine."

"True. Monique will have my hide Mrs. Fontaine." He laughed and headed downstairs.

Celeste tried not to let it bother her, but she wasn't a fan of her husband's assistant. Monique was a tall, beautiful model-esque woman who also happened to be an intelligent blood specialist. They spent more time together than she and Gabriel got to and it made her flutter with insecurity. She saw the way Monique looked at him when she thought no one was watching and she saw the jealous glint in Monique's eyes whenever Celeste showed up to see her husband. It made her uneasy to say the least. She trusted Gabriel with her soul, but she didn't trust Monique, not one iota.

Celeste applied mascara, a little eye shadow, added a touch of perfume to her wrists and neck, and headed downstairs to the smell of bacon and coffee. *Gabriel.* She sighed and smiled. He'd taken the time to leave her a pile of bacon — her favorite — and a half pot of hot coffee. He was always doing things like that. Grocery shopping, he'd carry in six bags to her three. In the winter she'd go outside to a cleaned-off car, warm and running, just waiting for her.

Even cleaning the house he helped out more than she had expected, and she'd noticed that even her hairbrush was always hair free. At first she'd thought it was odd that he'd do *that* for her but over time she figured he just liked his bathroom clean and hair free and she *did* shed a lot. When he shaved he always cleaned up the mess immediately, so it made sense.

Flowers die, Celeste had told Gabriel that when they first started dating. Not because they weren't welcome or beautiful but because they weren't everlasting. They contradicted everything her soul felt about love and her husband. So he began sending her plants. Within eight months, their garden was reminiscent of the Butchart Gardens in Canada. Every single time she looked out a window facing the backyard she smiled. The flowers and plants had bloomed and grew and spread over time, much like their love and relationship had. She smiled at the back yard and set her empty coffee mug in the sink—she needed to leave.

At the heart of Villiers sur Marne, in a private location enclosed by a stone wall, a charming Napoleon III property rose up from the hillside. The main house looked to be at least 400 square meters, with two Baltard pavilions renovated to the highest standards she'd ever seen. Matteo was Dr. Basle's veterinarian. He'd been hired just over a year ago after graduating, and he'd taken a real shining to Dr. Basle. When the doctor had mentioned his groundskeeper leaving, Matteo had set Celeste up to meet with him in hopes she could replace the man leaving. She had been over the moon at the prospect.

Driving through the gate she passed by a sparkling pool accompanied by a cottage style pool house. The grounds were covered in trees and a French garden. She passed a gatehouse and various outbuildings, a tennis court and small stables, kitchen garden and greenhouses. A prestigious property on a human scale, full of historical charm. Matteo had been humble in his description of the place. She was thrilled that if everything worked out, she'd not only see Matteo regularly again but also have the job she'd always wished for.

Celeste climbed from the car, insects dancing and buzzing about her, and she started down a stone path in a rich-green lawn that looked and smelled like it had been freshly mowed. An older man stepped out from an alcove. A monk's ring of hair and a full brow that seemed perpetually furrowed greeted her. "Ciao. You must be Celeste." He looked rail thin. Thick lenses magnified his eyes and made them appear watery. She stepped closer.

"Yes. Dr. Basle?" she extended her hand now that she was close enough. Peering through his thick lenses, the doctor gasped. He laid one hand over his heart and stared at her. "It can't be! The resemblance is amazing."

"Is everything alright sir?" Celeste asked.

He shook his head and blinked. "I'm sorry." He smiled but it looked forced. "Yes, yes. I'm Dr. Basle, but please, call me Leo." He jutted his hand outward towards her. She took it. His shake was firm and brief. "Come, let's sit in the kitchen." He motioned to the door. Celeste followed.

Celeste noticed a tremor in his hands when he unzipped his jacket and hung it on a hook inside the door. She followed as they entered a den that flowed into a kitchen with a table and chairs, granite counters, bar stools, and ornate lights that hung from the house's intricate box-beam ceiling.

Leo filled a kettle at the faucet before setting it on a burner. "Can I help with something?" Celeste offered. He waved her off, pulled two mugs from a cabinet and dropping in tea bags and lumps of sugar.

Steam whistled from the spout of the kettle, and Leo shuffled about to fill both mugs. Celeste declined milk. Leo set the mugs on the table and sat across from her dunking his tea bag. The mug shook when he raised it to take a sip.

"So, Matteo tells me you're a fantastic gardener."

Celeste blushed. Her green thumb was worth bragging about but she didn't. It was her passion and she didn't really care if she was good at it or not—she did it because it made her heart smile. "I'm flattered he would say that. I suppose my talents in the garden are nothing to sneeze at."

Leo chuckled. "Well my dear, Matteo vouches for you and the grounds are too big for me to keep up with. I have an immediate need. The garden around back is where I need someone. The grounds are mowed by a crew every week, and Matteo takes care of the stables, not just the horses but the surrounding area as well. He's a dear man. I've told him it's not his job but he won't hear it."

"I've known Matteo for years, he's definitely a good man." Celeste grinned. She liked that Leo was fond of Matteo.

"The garden spans about an acre. There are all kinds of plants and landscaping to maintain but you'd also have free reign to add more as you see fit. Also, I'd like to do more around the pool eventually." Celeste nodded. A dog padded over and stuck his head in her lap, a sign of affection. "You need some attention?" she asked, and gently caressed the dog's head.

"Careful. He's a master manipulator. What Max wants is some table food." Leo said. She scratched Max behind the ears. Leo snapped his fingers and pointed, and the dog dutifully went into the next room and lay on the rug.

"Honestly Dr. Basle, the job sounds wonderful and I'd love to be a part of the crew here."

"It's Leo, please. I'd like to do a trial run. See how we both fit together and go from there, yeah?" Celeste beamed at him and nodded her agreement. "Fantastic. Come tomorrow, eight a.m. sharp, and I'll give you the official tour of the grounds and introduce you to the others."

"Thank you so much for the opportunity, Leo. I promise I won't disappoint," she rushed.

"I've no doubt. I'll see you out to the stables. Matteo is here today and he'd think poorly of me if I sent you away without visiting him first."

Celeste laughed and finished her tea. It had been a few weeks since she last saw Matteo and she couldn't wait to hug him and thank him for thinking of her for the job.

Matteo sauntered lazily from the barn as she and Leo approached. He looked handsome in his blazer, jeans and muck boots. When he caught sight of them he picked up his pace. Celeste beamed at him and jogged to meet him. He wrapped his arms around her and twirled her once. "It's good to see you fiore mio."

"You too," she replied.

"I've decided to let her stay." Leo said in

greeting when he finally caught up to them.

"Bravo, Dr. B," Matteo chuckled. "You won't regret it. You just watch, you'll have the most stunning garden in all of France in a year's time."

Celeste blushed and shook her head. "Thank you Matteo for thinking of me."

"I always think of you. Who else has a green charmed thumb of your caliber?" he laughed. She ruefully shook her head at him.

"Has he always been such a charmer?" Leo asked. Celeste liked Matteo's nickname for him. Dr. B seemed fitting for the man. She turned to him and nodded vigorously.

"He's hopeless really."

"Well the animals love him—they'll have to keep him company until he can find a good woman."

"Agreed," she answered. Matteo *did* need a good woman. He was always dating and none of the women seemed to stick. It made her heart pang. She didn't want him to be alone.

"When will people learn that I'm perfectly happy as I am?" Matteo cut in. Dr. B chuckled and threw his hands up in mock surrender.

"Fine, fine. I'm going to the study, Matteo. If you need me stop in. Celeste, it was a pleasure, I will see you tomorrow morning."

Celeste reached out and shook Dr. B's

weathered hand and said goodbye. Matteo pulled her into his side as they watched him slowly shuffle back to the house. When he was out of sight Celeste turned in Matteo's arm and squealed her excitement.

"This is amazing!"

"I'm glad to see you so happy," Matteo returned.

"Happy? I'm ecstatic! Matteo," she enthused and twirled around, "look at this place. It's reminiscent of something from a fairytale."

Matteo laughed, it was loud and genuine. "Ah, Celeste, your outlook is refreshing as always."

She pushed his shoulder playfully. "Will you be here tomorrow?" She watched Matteo light a cigarette, the length of it hanging from his lips. She wasn't fond of the habit but somehow Matteo managed to make it look good.

"No, I'm here about three times a week usually. Good luck tomorrow, not that you need it. You'll be loved by everyone."

"Thank you. Alright, I'd better get going. I think tonight calls for a celebratory dinner out! There are reservations to be made, a new outfit to buy and a husband to tell."

"Then allow me to walk you to your car so you can get going." Matteo ran a hand through his midnight hair and smiled widely at her.

Hooking his arm at her elbow, they walked side by side to the front of the house and Celeste felt the strangest sense of peace.

Chapter 15

Annabelle

"I think of your betrayal. Which still echoes with your voice."
~ L'ame Immortelle — Betrayal

Annabelle reviewed her work. Red suited Jezebel. It made her long delicate looking fingers look even more refined. She blew on them lightly as Jezebel inspected her free hand.

"You did quite well. They look perfect. Thank you."

"Jez," she started looking up, "why didn't Celeste and Matteo ever hook up?"

Jezebel drew in a long, slow breath. "They were best friends. It's complicated to explain I suppose. In a way, it worked out for the best. They really did value their friendship too much to risk ruining it by making it romantic. Are you not a fan of Gabriel?"

"No, no," Annabelle shook her head. "It's not that. He sounds perfect. Almost too perfect. I mean, no one can really be that wonderful right?"

"Oh, of course there were things that irked them about one another but darling, when you're in love you tend to let those things go.

For the greater good and what not. Not everyone is so lucky to experience a love like Celeste and Gabriel's."

Annabelle studied Jezebel's mouth as she spoke. Everything about her was graceful, from the way she carried herself to the way her mouth moved while she told a story. Annabelle found herself wishing that she could be more like Jezebel.

Annabelle pulled out an electric blue nail polish from her kit as she pondered what Jezebel told her. "We have a little more time, would you do mine?" She held the bottle of polish out to Jezebel.

"I'm not sure how good I'll be but let's try. You can always wash it off if I butcher it."

Annabelle laughed as Jezebel took the polish from her. "Deal."

Jezebel grabbed her hand and squeezed. Annabelle could feel Jezebel's contentment and joy flowing through her. She let go and the feeling lingered with her for a time.

On the bus ride home Annabelle wondered if her parents had ever been like Celeste and Gabriel. If they had, something inside them had been extinguished. Her chest tightened at the thought. Her parents still had decades left to live, to be happy, to enjoy each other. There had to be a way for them to get what they had back. What was the point otherwise?

Walking from the bus stop to her house she wondered if she suggested something as simple as painting her nails with her mother it would go over with the same ease as it had with Jezebel. She resolved to make the effort. For some reason, her parents felt the need to hide how broken they were, as if they were ashamed by their lack of progress in the grieving department.

When inside the house, she tossed her keys and purse onto the kitchen counter. She went to the fridge and stuffed two bottled waters into her arms and sought out her mom. She poked her head into the den. Her father sat on the couch alone.

"Hi Dad," she called out softly.

"Hi Belle."

Instead of leaving it at that, like she normally would, Annabelle took a chance. She walked into the den and planted her rear on the couch right next to her dad. She looked up at him wishing that he'd sling an arm around her, pull her close and kiss her temple. Or maybe he'd simply ask how her day was or what was on her mind.

He stared down at her. His eyes dissected her. Took in each detail of her face. She was utterly speechless because her father's expression was so knowing. Like he looked inside her head and saw the thoughts that whizzed around.

His arm wrapped around her, tucked her into his side and he asked, "You know I love you right?" Unable to form words she nodded her response. He kissed the top of her head. "Dinner's in twenty." With that, he pushed off the couch and headed toward the kitchen, leaving Annabelle stupefied.

Dinner was yummy. Her father had cooked and it was delicious. In typical fashion there had been only curt conversation. Afterward, Annabelle put on music as she helped her mom wash dinner dishes.

"Mom, do you have half an hour? I thought maybe we could give each other pedicures."

"Now? It's getting late Belle," her mom said with a hint of annoyance in her voice.

"Are you busy doing something else?" she pushed and set the last clean dish in the drying rack. She picked at the skin around her nail beds, fidgeting, waiting.

Her mother chewed her lip. "Well, no."

"Come on. Please. It will be fun," she urged. Her mother gave a soft smile and nodded. Annabelle threw her arms around her and squeezed.

They headed up the stairs, her mother following close behind her. She could hear the box fan on full blast humming from her bedroom. The air conditioner in her room had broken last summer and she'd never bothered to tell her parents because they never seemed to listen to her anyway.

Annabelle and her mom sat on her bed as she laid out all the necessary items for their mock-spa fun. She picked out a dark plum color for her toes and her mother laughed, citing that it was a very morbid look. Her mom chose a pale rose color that she said would complement almost anything.

"How very practical of you Mom," Annabelle said with a roll of her eyes and gave her mother a sardonic smile.

Her mother shrugged. "Hey. They're *my* toes."

"Yup. Okay, let me fill up the tubs so we can soak first. Do you have any of those smelly salts?"

"Oh! That's a great idea. You fill, I'll grab the bath salts."

Her mom scooted from the bed and hurried to the master suite. When she shuffled back into the bedroom, Annabelle had two comfy chairs pulled next to each other from her reading nook with soaking tubs at the foot of each and the bottles of water from earlier next to them. She watched her mother mix in the bath salts before plunking down into the chair next to her.

"Ready?" she asked holding her feet just above the water.

"Go!" her mother exclaimed. They sunk their feet into the plastic tubs simultaneously. She groaned at the feeling of the hot water seeping into her feet. Her mother rested her head on the back of the chair and sighed.

"This was a good idea Belle."

"Thanks."

"Your nails look nice, did you do those today?" her mother asked as her fingers trailed over Annabelle's fingers.

"Jezebel painted them for me. I did hers too."

"Jezebel?"

"The lady at Glenview." She answered.

"That was nice of you to do for her. You like her very much don't you?"

"Yeah. She's pretty awesome."

"Good. You deserve that."

Annabelle didn't quite understand her mother's meaning. It was an odd thing to say, she thought. She wanted to scrutinize and analyze everything her mother said but it would only ruin the moment so she bit her lip and stayed silent.

By eight thirty their toes were painted to perfection. She wiggled her toes at her mother and smiled. "Nice work."

Her mother snorted. "I'm surprised I didn't mess up. It's been ages since I've done this." Watching her mother push up from her spot, she felt hopeful and content. It had been fun spending the evening together. Her mother looked child-like as she moved through Annabelle's room trailing a finger over things. Actually *looking* at her room. Her mom picked up the picture on her nightstand, her fingers tracing the outline of her brother's carefree face. A pang of grief hit her. Annabelle studied her mother as she clutched the picture in her hands. Her knuckles growing white as she gripped it. The color slowly drained from her mom's face and she set the picture back in its spot softly. Drawing in a deep breath she turned, faced Annabelle and walked past her. Annabelle followed her mom into the hallway, confused.

"I miss him you know," her mother blurted out. Annabelle stood, unmoving, trying desperately to think of something to say, something that would ease her mother's pain just for a brief moment. A million things passed through her mind but nothing came out. She watched as her mom walked distractedly down the stairs, leaving Annabelle standing in the hall, listening to her mother's footsteps fading, and finally the sound of nothing. She suddenly felt lonely. The poisoned silence left in her mother's wake felt like acid slowly burning her from the inside out.

The sky faded fast into dark shades of purple and navy. There were no clouds, leaving the stars free to sparkle as they do. There were so many of them, so much sky occupied by them, she didn't know how anyone could ever feel alone looking at them. But she did.

~***~

Waking up to sunshine did not seem right after a long night of melancholy dreams. The sky should be gray and the rain heavy and angry. Annabelle stretched and yawned wishing it were the weekend and she could go back to sleep. But it wasn't and she couldn't. She dreamed of Brant and it was torturous. The dream, plagued by images of his stiff, unmoving body lying on the sidewalk made her feel useless and frightened. Sometimes, in her dreams, she rewound to the day before. To just after school.

And in her dream she didn't have piano lessons that afternoon. She walked home from school with her brother instead of being picked up and shuffled off by her mother. They arrived home from school together. Alive. And the four of them would sit together at the table and eat dinner. They'd talk, joke, clown around and maybe even bicker a little, but they were together, and happy.

She flung the covers away from her and shuffled to the bathroom feeling sullen. At least it was Tuesday. A smile played on her lips as she thought about her upcoming afternoon with Jezebel.

"Hey," Madison greeted falling in step next to her.

"Hi."

"So, I know it's kinda far off and all, but do you think your parents will give you a reprieve for graduation?" Madison mused.

"I don't know. I can ask I guess. I mean obviously I will attend graduation but I doubt I will get to do anything afterward."

"Don't they notice?"

She arched a brow at her friend. "Notice what?"

Madison sighed, completely exasperated. "How much you've changed." Annabelle's nose flared.

"Is that a joke?" she frowned and adjusted her backpack on her shoulder.

Lines creased Madison's forehead. "No Belle, I'm serious. You're different somehow. Not bad, just different."

"Am I?"

Madison nodded proudly. "Yeah, I mean it's not like world changing or anything, but I noticed. You seem . . . less uptight."

Annabelle groaned and wanted to smack her palm to her forehead but refrained. "I was uptight?"

"Kinda. Well, high-strung I guess. Some people are! I'm not complaining, I just . . . *frack,* this isn't coming out right at all." Madison pouted.

Annabelle shook her head, unconcerned. "No, it's okay. I mean, I feel less angry lately. Maybe that's it." She gave a shrug as they continued walking.

"I think it's that looney lady you spend time with. I think she's making you deal with crap you didn't want to—but in a really good way." Madison rushed. "She's one of those 'tough love' people as my mom would say. But really, I think maybe it's what you needed."

"Gee thanks?" she said tartly.

Madison didn't bow down, instead, she speared Annabelle with a pointed look. "I'm sorry, but I wanted to tell you."

"And you did." Annabelle confirmed and crossed her arms over her chest with a scowl.

"Right—so moving on . . ." Madison bit her lip in thought as they shifted through the crowded hall.

"Mad," Annabelle started. If she was honest with herself she *felt* what Madison noticed.

Madison looked to her expectantly. "Yeah?"

"I *might* agree with you but . . . why did you ever want to be my friend in the first place if I was so miserable to be around?"

Madison's lips tilt into a slow, lazy smile. "You remember the first day of ninth grade?"

"Of course," she said, thinking back to that day.

"When you sat down next to me in class and I said 'hi,' and you just shrugged at me all aloof and shit, but your eyes were so tired and sad. We were just kids. I didn't understand why, but I wanted to find out. I wanted to help. It was stupid, maybe, but then we ended up being friends—and at my house you were lighter, different and I liked *that* Belle, so I stuck around." Annabelle had never realized how deep Madison was, or how perceptive. She was a crappy friend for not noticing these things before. She resolved to change that—to be a better friend to Madison.

"I'm glad you did," she admitted.

"Yeah me too. You're alright," Madison snickered.

"Why thank you." Annabelle gave Madison an over-dramatic curtsy and a sweet, sarcastic smile for good measure.

"You're welcome?" Madison laughed her rebuttal before disappearing into her first period class.

~***~

Annabelle hopped off the bus and headed directly across the street into Rite-Aid. She weaved in and out of the aisles until she found what she was looking for. She grabbed the first one that sparked her interest and carried it to the front to pay before she headed into Glenview. She stopped at the front desk, checked in with her supervisor and made her way down the corridor.

Jezebel's eyes crinkled with amusement as she took the bag. She pulled out the box of hair dye and stared at it. "What do you do plan to do with this?" A look of dumb innocence crossed her face.

"Put it in my hair." Annabelle answered as she rolled her sapphire blue eyes.

"Your witty banter is charming," Jezebel said dryly and shot her a sardonic smile.

"Oh, quit your fretting. I have nothing but the best intentions," she said with a grin.

Stifling a snort, Jezebel visibly relaxed a little. "Well, I guess you expect me to do this for you." Jezebel's lips flinched as she held back a smile. A sure sign she was up to no good. Annabelle nodded slowly. Jezebel worried her lip while she examined the box of color in her hand. "Ok. One condition." She held up a solitary finger.

Annabelle smirked. "Shoot."

"You can't see until I say so." Annabelle peeled her eyes away from the woman and her wrinkled nose as she thought. "You look like you bit a lemon with that sour expression." Jezebel commented.

Annabelle stood up a little straighter, determined not to let Jezebel ruffle her feathers . "Fine. I won't look until you're done," she conceded.

"Brava, darling. A little mystery will do you good."

"You aren't going to ruin my hair right?" she asked grimacing.

Jezebel simply shrugged as she opened the top of the box and pulled the paper instructions free. "Be a good girl and grab me those reading glasses over there," she murmured wiggling two fingers in the direction of her night stand. Annabelle did as she was told.

Annabelle sat patiently as Jezebel pulled on the latex gloves and mixed the solutions just as the directions said to. She clutched the towel over her shoulders at her throat as Jezebel massaged the dye into her hair. It felt heavenly. Her favorite part of haircuts was always the way they washed your hair before the cut. A small groan escaped her lips and Jezebel chuckled. The massaging stopped. "Says here we have to let it sit for twenty minutes."

"Okay, then we let it sit." Annabelle

shrugged.

"Let's skip ahead in our story a bit while we wait." Jezebel suggested.

"Sounds good to me."

Jezebel winked. "Paris, nineteen eighty-eight."

Chapter 16

Celeste

Paris 1988

Gabriel's fingers swept into her hair and weaved through the strands. She tensed. So, so close to the edge, nearly pushed over right then and there. He drove in again and she toppled over the peak panting and shuddering with each sensation that passed through her. Their mornings were often spent like this, tangled in each other's limbs.

"Celeste," he drew her name out on an exhale. "Let's make a baby." He kissed her. "We'd have a Spring baby. Perfect for taking long walks outdoors," he murmured. Celeste's stomach dropped out as her brain went into overdrive. She froze beneath him. How could it have never have come up before? How utterly preposterous was it that they had never discussed children before. *How rich was that?* she thought angrily. Of course he knew she loved children and vice versa, yet the subject of having their own had never been broached.

"Mon amour, what is it?" Gabriel asked as he inspected her sour expression.

She pushed him aside and sat up, pulling the

sheet with her. She couldn't breathe. Sweat started to bead along her hairline and at the nape of her neck. "Celeste," he snapped and shook her by the shoulders before he cupped her face, and his eyes softened while his thumbs stroked back and forth over her cheeks.

"Gabriel." Her wide eyes caught his. "I can't have children." The beating of her heart echoed in her ears. It resonated deeply as the scent of her own failings. She saw pain flicker in his eyes and her heart broke for him. For his unexpected loss. For her having caused it.

"Nonsense. Is that what has you so worked up?" he asked shaking his head left to right slowly. She hurt for him, he wasn't understanding the situation.

She nodded solemnly. "But it's not nonsense. All those tests . . ." her chin quivered a little, her courage faltering. She could feel the muscles in her jaw working hard as she fought back tears. "When I was little . . . the CVS. There were experimental drugs. I'm . . . I'm sterile." Two tears spilled over and trailed down her cheek.

His eyes followed her tear drops. "Are you sure? I thought CVS was the only side-" he stopped himself short, brows furrowed in confusion. Swiping at her tears, she grunted a yes. Gabriel sighed, clearly exasperated with the situation. He pulled her into a tight embrace. "We'll figure this out." Her breath caught in her chest.

"There is always adoption." But her voice lacked enthusiasm.

"No," his voice was firm, harsh even. She bristled at his tone. "No Celeste. I only want my *own* kids." She could hear the defeat in his voice, the longing. She silently berated herself. They should have talked about this much earlier in their relationship. She should have thought to bring it up. With both of them working full time, and Gabriel's long hours at the lab, children had never crossed her mind. Or maybe that was simply because she already knew and therefore never considered his feelings.

"I'm an awful wife," she sobbed into his chest. He kissed her hair and pushed her back from his chest.

"You're not. You're twenty-four, still young enough that we didn't really need to think about kids before this. I can't believe it never came up but it doesn't make you a bad wife. I could easily make the argument that it makes me a bad husband, for never having asked you about it."

"Right." She rolled her eyes at him and huffed. "Nothing about you is 'bad husband' material."

"Oh come on, you can think of something I'm sure." He raised an eyebrow at her.

She smiled and wracked her brain for any small thing. "You stay late at work too much leaving me home alone," she pouted. He grinned and pressed a light kiss to her lips. He brushed his thumb over her bottom lip and stood.

~***~

Celeste headed off to the estate. She treasured her job. She got to be outside daily, mumble to herself a lot, plant things, saw Matteo routinely and had a dog named Max to follow her around everywhere. It was pure bliss. She'd come to think of Dr. B as family. He was ornery and witty and kind. In the winter months she spent four days a week there just helping out around the house and keeping him company. Their relationship was warm and comforting and she couldn't help but care for him as if he were her own grandfather.

Shafts of morning light filtered through the trees surrounding the stables. She descended the rock staircase into the garden. Water swept like tears down the stone face of the fountain near the entrance. It was peaceful and serene. Over the last two years she had transformed his beautiful garden into an enchanted secluded getaway. The garden was truly magical now. Moss created a pathway to follow through the weeping branches of trees, flowering plants and greenery. Matteo appeared near the trickling fountain at the center. She grinned at him and waved.

"Dr. B sent me to find you." Matteo smelled like a fresh shower and soap, like clothes that were hung to dry in the sunshine. She loved the smell of him. It was uniquely his.

"Is everything alright?" she questioned with a small smile.

"I'm sure it is. He didn't seem upset about anything."

"Alright then," she answered.

"And you, Celeste? What is on your mind?" he asked as he ran a hand over a day's growth of stubble on his chin.

"Nothing. What makes you ask?" His piercing gaze much too perceptive for her liking today.

He raised both hands in mock surrender. "We've got two minds that think as one, fiore mio. Our hearts march to the same beat. Always have."

"I hate that you can read me so well. This morning was disastrous." She threw her hands into the air dramatically then sat down in the grass with a thud. "Gabriel found out I'm sterile this morning." She looked up to him, wishing he could offer her more than just sympathy but knowing he couldn't. The anxious twisting in her stomach told her so.

"I'd hug you but you're all . . ." Matteo gestured to her clothes and graced her with a playful smile. She glanced down to inspect herself. She was covered elbow to toes in mud. "I didn't realize he wasn't aware already."

"That's just it. He seemed so . . . so crushed. I want to kick myself for never having brought it up before now. It was the worst timing too—if you catch my drift."

Matteo nodded and offered her a weak smile. They had long ago talked about this very issue. "He loves you and he will get over this. He's only had hours to adjust to something you've known your entire life," he reminded her.

"You're irritatingly wise." She scowled but laughed. He held his hand out to her and she took the offered pull to her feet.

"You've commented on that before." He winked. "Now get your ass inside. Dr. B is waiting." Celeste leaned forward popping a quick, muddy kiss to his cheek and made her way to the main house leaving Matteo blustering about mud behind her. She pushed the side door open. Dr. B stood just inside the kitchen waiting.

"Sorry I'm all muddy. I've been weeding in the garden. They grow so thick in the summer."

"Well, at least you know what you're doing," Dr. B said, attempting to compliment her. "I don't have a green thumb at all." Dr. B waved her farther into the house after she removed her mud-caked shoes.

"It takes practice. Lots of practice. When I first started gardening, I killed everything . . . twice!" Celeste laughed heartily.

"I doubt that dear," he answered wearing a sincere smile. She entered Dr. B's study close on his heels. She'd been in this room only a handful of times. She took in picture-clad walls and mahogany furniture. There were several spots where pictures that had once hung but were now missing, the sun-faded wallpaper making their absence obvious. Dr. B looked off, grimacing, an indication that something more than his hip was bothering him. After years working for him, she knew Dr. B's tells. She sat next to him on the couch careful not to get it too dirty. He handed her a cup of coffee before speaking. She took a sip.

"I don't get around so well anymore, as you know," he started. Celeste nodded. "I've been torn over how much to tell you dear, but it seems that now I must at the very least share something before asking you to run an errand for me."

Celeste felt herself squint at him as if that would help her decipher what he was getting at. "Okay," she responded slowly. He set his coffee down and placed his hand over her knee. This was far more serious than she expected.

"You know I consider you family yes?" he said warmly.

"Yes, of course and likewise." She smiled.

"In another lifetime, I was an important doctor. I frequently consult on projects for different governments still. Occasionally, that means visiting the Embassy to deliver my reports."

"Do you understand?" he questioned seriously. But his words had fallen on deaf ears. Celeste's mind was running a thousand miles a second, conjuring up ideas on secret missions the doctor might be part of. Her imagination had never been lacking. His wealth wasn't simply from making house calls or doing rounds in a Hospital. Come to think of it, she didn't even know what kind of doctor he had been before he retired. "Celeste?"

She snapped out of her thoughts and met his eyes. "Yes, yes. I understand."

"I have a report that needs to be delivered today. Frankly, I'm just not feeling up to the trek. Can I count on you to drop it off for me?"

"Of course, I'd be happy to," she returned. It was endearing that Dr. B trusted her with something he obviously felt was so important.

"That's a great weight off my shoulders. I appreciate it my dear." He stood and shuffled to his desk. Pushing various papers aside he found the ones he was looking for, gathered them together, tapped them on his desk, aligning them, and tucked them into a plain manila envelope. She watched as he scrawled a name across the front and made his way back to her.

She took the envelope from him and mentally repeated the directions he gave her before heading out.

The opulent, two-story brick building had been carved into office space long ago.

As she climbed the interior staircase, she looked down on the intricate mosaic floor that depicted an American eagle with an olive branch in its right foot. She looked at the directory board on the wall and found the name she was looking for. The trudged to the office on the second floor and stepped into a tiny reception area with a vacant desk. A sign told her to ring the bell. She slapped it with the palm of her hand, resulting in an obnoxious clang and giggled. She wasn't sure what drove her to do it but it had felt good. A man came around the corner in khakis, leather boat shoes, and a blue-and-white-striped button-down shirt. She shrunk a little at his presence, feeling juvenile for the bell ringing.

"What can I do you for?"

Celeste held up the envelope. "I'm here to drop this off for Dr. Basle," she said. The man's eyebrows rose and he took a step closer to her.

"He sent you." It was a statement, rather than a question.

"Yes. He wasn't feeling up to making the trip. I work for him." Her explanation felt less than satisfactory.

He stared at her a bit, hands shoved in his pockets. "And you are?"

"Celeste Fontaine," she stated.

"Well Celeste, this is rather unusual. If you don't mind I'd like to ring him to double check. You understand of course."

Celeste shrugged. "Sure."

Celeste watched as the man, who didn't introduce himself, wandered back around the corner and shut his office door. She sighed and shifted her weight. When he returned, he was smiling.

"I'm Dan. Looks like we're all set here." He commented, reaching his hand out. Celeste handed the envelope to him.

"Well, Dan, thanks."

"No, no Celeste, thank you. I'm sure we'll see each other again."

She smiled at Dan, offered him a curt wave and turned on her heel to leave. She was done for the day and instead of heading home, she was going to pop by Gabriel's office for a quick hello.

Chapter 17

Annabelle

"There's nothing I wouldn't do to hear your voice again."
~ Hurt, Christina Aguilera

Jezebel had been silent for the last five minutes. It made her apprehensive.

"Jez?" Annabelle touched her friend's arm. Jezebel snapped her eyes to Annabelle's, her expression slightly confused before she smiled.

"It's time to rinse!" she exclaimed looking at Annabelle's head. Annabelle grinned and followed Jezebel's lead into the bathroom.

"Lean your back on the edge of the tub there," she pointed, "and I'll rinse for you."

Annabelle did as she instructed. It was an awkward and uncomfortable position but she didn't have much of a choice. Jezebel leaned over her and started the water. After a few moments, she ran her hand under the stream from the faucet, checking the temperature. Holding a cup under the flow of water she filled it up.

"Close your eyes kiddo." Annabelle did as she was told. Warm water followed by the soft stroke of Jezebels hand. Annabelle couldn't remember the last time someone had washed her hair this way, outside of a salon of course. Jezebel repeated the process over and over again. Warm water, the soft stroke of her hand over Annabelle's head. Small trickles of water that ran into her ears or eyes were wiped away gently and quickly. It was motherly, tender even. Annabelle relaxed, savoring the moment.

When the water shut off she opened her eyes just as Jezebel covered her head in a towel and placed a palm on the back of her neck, pulling her to an upright position. With two hands, Jezebel ruffled the towel around on Annabelle's head, like a mother would a small child. She chuckled.

"We need to blow dry it now." Jezebel tossed the now damp towel into a nearby hamper.

"I can do that," Annabelle answered.

"Absolutely not. There is no looking until it's done." Jezebel winked.

Annabelle planted her rear on the toilet, straddling it facing the tank. Jezebel ran a brush through her long hair, working out the knots one by one. When was the last time her own mother had done this? She couldn't remember. Her throat tightened and she bit her lip and closed her eyes to ward off the tears she felt coming. Once the tangles were worked through, Jezebel blow dried her hair, every so often pulling out the collar of Annabelle's shirt, sending the hot air rushing down her back. When she squealed and laughed, Jezebel did too.

"Can I see yet?" she said as she studied her cuticles and chewed her nails—effectively ruining the manicure she'd received last week.

Jezebel's hands snaked through her hair a few more times before she sighed and leaned back against the opposite wall. "There. You can look now." Jezebel replied, sounding very pleased with herself. A thought hit her hard and fast, Jezebel was like the North Star, there to guide her, although to where—she wasn't sure. A freeing sort of feeling moved through her, a self-effacing smile bloomed on her face, as she stood slowly and stretched her cramped legs.

Moving to the mirror she drew in a breath and looked. A gasp left her mouth. It was beautiful. Her dark locks weren't all dyed, the way she had imagined. Jezebel had woven the dye throughout her hair in highlights, caramel streaks peaking and popping from all angles. She loved it. It was infinitely better than having done her entire head the one color. Beyond that, Jezebel had blown her hair out to epic proportions and somehow managed to create loose curls at the bottoms of the strands so they all curled the same way.

"It's amazing!" she squeaked. Behind her in the mirror, Jezebel grinned widely.

"Yes, it is."

"You're such a smart-ass sometimes." Annabelle laughed.

Jezebel raised her brows. "I'm allowed," she said dryly.

"Yeah, you are." She snorted and rolled her eyes.

~***~

Neither of her parents had mentioned her hair for two days. She forked a bite of meatloaf into her mouth. It was becoming increasingly difficult to deal with her home life in the absence of any technology to distract her. Everything appeared more pronounced: the silence, the denial, the animosity between her parents.

"It's all a farce isn't it?" her mother said, a distant expression on her face.

"What?" Annabelle's brows knit together at her mother's strange outburst.

"Life," her mother answered.

"Mom, what are you talking about?"

"You think you have it all but really, you have nothing. Things—people, can just be stripped away from you." Her mother's voice held no emotion. It made Annabelle's stomach twist into a knot.

"Jesus, Monica." Her father snapped. Her

mother speared him with a scathing expression and pushed away from the table disappearing into the kitchen. Annabelle shot up to follow her mother.

"Sit down Belle," her father barked. She skidded to a stop and cut her eyes to her father. "Sit and finish your dinner. Let her be."

Annabelle fumed but stopped herself before responding with some flippant, sarcastic remark. It wouldn't help anything. She bunched up her fists in irritation and sat down hard in her seat.

~***~

Six nights.

Four dreams.

All different.

All upsetting.

Annabelle shoved her way through the school hallway and out the front doors. She skipped the bus and decided to walk the four miles to Glenview. It would cut into their time a bit, but she didn't think Jezebel would mind. She hoped the long walk would help clear her head. What it really did was leave her lingering with her thoughts for too long.

She was grumpy and irritable, and she had been since her mother's strange words days ago and her father's seemingly cruel reaction. She blew into Glenview barely registering anyone on her way in forty minutes later than she normally arrived. She didn't care though. She pushed Jezebel's door open with force, dumped her bag to the floor and settled down into her chair near tears.

"Well aren't we a ray of sunshine," Jezebel tittered. She stood at the windowsill watering her plants.

"I'm not in the mood," Annabelle said curtly.

"And what makes you think *I'm* in the mood for *you?*" Jezebel volleyed back as she approached.

Annabelle scowled as Jezebel sat across from her. "What is *with* people?" she slapped her palms on the arms of the chair. "They're hot then cold. Every freakin' step forward sends us all back ten steps. It's been years! Eight years! I'm so lost." A sob tore from her throat. "I'm so lost. We all are." Her voice faltered and broke. Tears streamed down her face and she let them.

Jezebel stood without answering her. She crossed the room and climbed into her bed, stretching out and making herself comfortable. Then, she patted the space next to her. Annabelle gave her a confused expression.

"Don't be daft kiddo, get up here with me." There was only a moment of hesitation before Annabelle did what Jezebel asked. As she crawled into the bed, Jezebel hooked an arm around her shoulders and pulled her into a silent embrace. Relief flooded her. Nothing felt better than being snuggled in Jezebel's arms like this. Two months ago she couldn't have dreamed up this scenario but now . . . now it was exactly perfect. She cried — no — she sobbed openly into Jezebel's shoulder as she clung to the woman she'd grown so fond of. Long quiet moments passed. She finally ran out of tears. Her sniffles and choppy breaths evened out.

"The world is a complex place tiger. If you try to make sense of it you'll end up reflecting your whole life away. Good intentions aren't enough. You've got to act on them."

"Can I tell you a secret?" Annabelle's voice was scratchy and hoarse.

"If you'd like," Jezebel answered.

"It was his birthday."

"Today?"

"No, no. the night I got the DUI. It was his birthday, or would have been. I wanted to forget so badly. He would have been twenty. I lied to my parents, told them I was hanging out at Madison's that night. I went to Damon's instead. We drank. I got emotional and claustrophobic and needed to just be alone so I ran out on him. I was driving home and instead of turning down my street, I went down *that* street. I left the car running and sat on the pavement where I found his body. I was a mess. The cops were just doing a normal patrol that night. I had just gotten back into the driver's seat when they pulled up behind me. The car was still in park. Not that it mattered. It was stupid to begin with and I should have never driven that night anyways. But the rules are . . . if the keys are in the ignition and you blow drunk, you're going down. I never told my parents that. I don't even know if they paid enough attention to the report to notice *where* I was bagged." There was a brief moment where Jezebel's eyes clouded over and she appeared heartsick as Annabelle met her gaze. Was she heartsick for her? She didn't have the time to decipher before Jezebel's expression changed.

"I don't know what losing a child or sibling is like honey, but I imagine it changes a person."

"It's not unique though. It happens. Every. Single. Day. People get over it. They move forward. Why are we so broken? So stuck?" she asked.

"I don't have the answer to that one," Jezebel said and tucked a lock of highlighted hair behind her ear. "Just think though, you only have four more months and then you're free. You can go off to college and be whoever you want, move forward however you want and feel however you want."

Jezebel was right. She had four months left before she could leave this town and choose her own path for moving on. It lightened her mood a smidge. "Well in the meantime—you got any sage advice for me? Four months can seem like a lifetime in my house."

Jezebel snorted and grinned at her. "Sorry kiddo, I got nothing. Your house sounds miserable and without knowing your parents, I can't really offer anything up as far as insight. I can only show you the door, you're the one who will have to walk through it."

"Maybe I should make them come and visit you too. You're better than a grief counselor." She chuckled at the thought of her parents sitting in this room and taking Jezebel's crap. What a freaking show that would be.

Jezebel startled and made a choking sound. "That's a terrible idea."

"Jeez, I was kidding. Relax," she assured her. Jezebel blinked a few times. "Tell me more about Celeste."

"You sure?"

"Yeah, I'm ready."

"Hmm," Jezebel scrutinized her for a moment. "Alright then, Paris, nineteen eighty-nine."

Chapter 18

Celeste

Paris 1989

Celeste loved watching Gabriel work. It was as though nothing else in the world existed except that very moment. His white lab coat suited his frame and his pocket protector was adorable and made her giggle. She watched his mouth pucker as his brow furrowed, a sure sign he was stumped.

Monique, his assistant, said something she couldn't hear. He laughed, brushed a swath of dark blond hair out of his eyes and tied his hair back in a low ponytail. Celeste loved his laugh—it was throaty and deep and sent her pulse racing. She watched Monique and realized their expressions mimicked each other's. Her pulse raced for her husband but her blood boiled over his assistant as she looked at him from under her veil of black eyelashes.

She knocked on the glass barrier between them securing his attention. A wide, dimpled grin appeared on his face that made her feel warm inside. She noted Monique's expression fall but paid it no attention.

"Quand on parle du loup," *speak of the devil,*

Gabriel said opening the door and stepping into the corridor. She chewed her lip to keep from saying something she might regret involving Monique.

Monique stepped out of the lab behind him, her mouth settled into a grim line. "You're not due here for another four hours," she stated. "Gabriel," she nearly purred his name, "we have a lot to tie up."

Celeste's nostrils flared. She peeled her eyes from Monique and set them on her husband and held up a full white paper sack. "I come bearing lunch. My husband has to eat right?"

"We ate." Monique commented before Gabriel had a chance to speak.

Incredulous, Celeste drew a deep breath in and chose instead to focus on her husband.

"It was a snack," Gabriel scoffed, "I'd love to have lunch with you. I'm the luckiest lab rat here you know—stunning wife bringing me lunch." Monique made a garbled sound and speared Celeste with a murderous look before stomping away.

"Gabriel, can't you do something about her?" she pouted.

"Celeste," he drew her name out in that sexy way only Gabriel could, "she's harmless. It's a pathetic crush that I don't respond too. You are the only woman for me." He rubbed his palm on his forehead as though he had a headache.

"Are you feeling okay?" she asked.

"Yes, just tired and stumped today, *Il y a quelque chose qui cloche* and I can't figure it out." *Something's amiss.* "What did you bring for lunch?" Celeste smiled at him and ran off the list of things she'd picked up as his hand landed on the small of her back and guided them toward his office.

When they had finished the bulk of the food she had brought, he propped her up on his desk and placed a fresh cherry into her mouth. His eyes grew dark as she bit into the flesh surrounding the pit. Cherry juice trickled down her chin as he removed the pit from her mouth for her. His thumb caught it and wiped it up. He leaned forward and whispered in her ear how much he wanted to slip his finger between her legs and feel how wet she was. Her breath hitched, and she swore her body combusted. She wrapped her legs around his waist and a hand around his neck—drew him to her and kissed him hard. As he worked the buttons on her jeans, she swore she saw someone standing outside his office through the blinds, and she had an inkling she knew who it was. She said nothing. *Good,* she thought. Let her watch.

~***~

Saturday, Celeste cooked supper for them. Gabriel's favorite—pot roast, potatoes and carrots in a red wine sauce. She hated that he had to spend his Saturday in the lab but he'd promised to be home by dinner and kept that promise. More than that he'd walked through their door whistling a light, upbeat tune, a sure sign he was in a good mood.

"Friday, I'd like to leave by nine," she said after swallowing a bite.

Gabriel moaned as he chewed. "Fine by me. I still can't believe she's getting married."

"I think Charles is perfect for her. No one else could have tamed Mara," Celeste laughed.

"Well I certainly couldn't have done it," he chuckled.

"I can't wait to see you all dressed up," she mused.

"I can't wait to strip you out of your bridesmaid dress. I peeked the other day when you tried it on—you looked edible."

Celeste blushed and shook her head at him. "You're devious."

"No," he stood and took her plate. "I'm lucky." She grabbed his elbow as he passed. He stopped, leaned down and kissed her forehead. Gabriel was uncompromising about doing the cleanup himself. After some bickering about it, he shooed her into the living room, insisting that she relax while he finished cleaning up. The cushions and throw pillows surrounded her as she sank into them.

Gabriel joined her and they watched *Quantum Leap* before retiring to the bedroom and reading together for hours snuggled under their duvet.

~***~

Breakfast was a long and lazy affair. It was Sunday and they had nowhere to be. They ate on the bed like children, Indian-style with trays on the wrinkled bedspread. Their home was cozy and homey, replete with overstuffed furniture and bursting bookcases and she loved it. In the afternoon they walked to the farmer's market and snatched up enough fresh produce for the week. They sampled various mouth-watering cheeses and stopped for a Parisian hot chocolate, Celeste's favorite treat.

As they curled up in the living room together that evening Celeste felt full and complete. She put her stocking clad feet up on the coffee table as he ran his hand down her side, finding her hand and intertwining their fingers. Bringing them to his lips, he kissed each one. She felt content knowing she had managed to create a life that not only appeared wonderful on the outside but one that felt perfect on the inside. She looked down at the twinkling of her wedding rings and smiled.

Chapter 19

Annabelle

*"Some days I feel broke inside but I won't admit.
Sometimes I just wanna hide 'cause it's you I miss.
And it's so hard to say goodbye."*
~ Hurt, Christina Aguilera

"Jez, this story is nice. I mean, I like it and all—but it's not exactly a thriller or mind-blowing." Annabelle gave her a pointed look. Jezebel furrowed her brow and shook her head.

"Patience is a virtue that you clearly do not have."

"You said my brain would explode." Annabelle tugged on a strand of hair, exasperated.

"And it will. Don't rush it, Sport. It will lose its luster if you do," Jezebel tsked.

"You keep saying that but I swear, nothing life-altering has happened yet. Can't we skip to the exciting part?" she returned dryly.

"It would be a tragedy to end this too early. The timing must be perfect." Jezebel fingered the chain of the necklace she wore. Annabelle slapped her palm to her forehead and groaned. "Nothing was ever solved by being dramatic, kiddo." Jezebel chuckled.

"Says you." She rolled her eyes and slumped her shoulders.

"Yes, says me. Drama belongs in the theatre."

Annabelle huffed out a sigh and checked the clock that hung across from the bed. "I have to get going. This week is going to blow," she grumbled.

"Annabelle, you need someone who will be there for you when you fall apart. Guiding your direction when you're too blind to see the way."

"That's why I have you, Jez," she returned.

Jezebel sat up and rolled her shoulders. She looked tense. "It can't be me. Sometimes writing can do that. Do you keep a journal?"

"Not since I was little." Annabelle wrinkled her nose at the thought.

"Write then. Write your week away."

"Maybe." Annabelle shrugged, stood and stretched. "Til next week, Jezzie."

"Adios, cherie."

~***~

Annabelle was bored and restless. Her mother was at the country club and her father was hiding in the house somewhere. She'd finished her homework, messaged Madison for a while before her laptop time was up and rearranged her closet — twice.

Taking a note from Jezebel she dug out her

old diary and started to write.

> *Dear Diary,*
> *Hey, it's Belle, back from sixth grade.*
> *I know the last time I wrote I was crushing hard on Danny and wondering when I'd get my period and boobs but hey, I'm back. And by the way, thanks for filling me on how NOT awesome periods are.*

She felt lame trying to write in a diary again so she tried a different approach. She wrote a letter to her brother.

> *Brant,*
> *I'm not irritable today. I feel something else. Like change is in the air. Somewhere just out of my grasp, but still near enough that I can sense it. I think Jezebel gives me that feeling. You'd like her.*
> *They say everything happens for a reason. Slamming doors are the only sound now, Brant. You didn't die for a reason because the only reason I can see, all these miserable years later, is to break us. To break the ones you left behind. And you wouldn't do that.*
> *I want you here to fix this mess. To*

fix the never-ending rain that douses us, cold and raw. Am I wrong for saying that I'd choose another way if I could? This road you've abandoned us on is worn down to just cracks and chunks of the asphalt that used to make a perfectly smooth street. Am I wrong for trying to reach the things that I can't see? They used to exist. They must still be there somewhere.

You were cool and sweet like ice cream. You made us all orbit around you. You and your stupid spirit and big heart. But now what Brant . . . NOW WHAT?

I dreamed last night. I laid your ashes to rest but when I looked down, I had blood on my sleeve. I hate when I dream of you. You pick and pick and pick at my scabs, keeping the wounds forever open. The damage was done though; you're gone and I'm here, stuck with them.

How could they be one way, simply because you were here, and so different now that you're gone? I have never left. I am still here. Sitting at the table with them, eating Mom's terrible food. I am still right in front of them, except without you none of us exist. I hate you for it. I hate you so much *sometimes. I hate that I feel guilty for hating you because really, I love you so much it hurts.*

Jezebel told me you can't have love without hate. She's cryptically smart.

"You need someone who will be there for you when you fall apart. Guiding your direction when you're too blind to see the way."—*Jezebel*

Peace out bro,

Belle

She felt a bit lighter after writing. She didn't go back and read her words. She didn't edit. She simply ended her letter, slammed the journal shut and sat cross-legged on her bed breathing deeply until her emotions felt stable.

~***~

Brant,

I don't want to be filled with sorrow and grief anymore. I want to be free. I'm going to be free. I'm going to tell you I miss you—right now—and move forward. I'm going to learn who I am.

Who I am without you.

Who I am without Mom and Dad.

Just who I would have grown up to be if things were different.

Later, Belle.

Annabelle breezed through the entrance at Glenview and damn near tripped over her own two feet when she saw *him*. Standing just inside the reception area was quite possibly the most gorgeous guy she had ever seen. Dark hair flipped up at his collar and around his ears. His eyes were two piercing blue sapphires. Her heart stuttered and skipped and a knot formed in her throat. She swallowed past it, dropped her eyes to the ground and willed her feet to move: left, right, left.

"Hola," Jezebel chirped.

Annabelle cut her eyes to Jezebel's and cocked an eyebrow up. "What's with the Spanish lately?" Jezebel shrugged but said nothing. "Um, so . . . are there any, ah, new employees here?" she hedged.

"Oh, you saw Mark." Jezebel chuckled. "Dark hair, the prettiest blue eyes, tall." Annabelle swallowed the lump in her throat and nodded.

"He'll be by in a bit."

"What?" she squawked.

"He is just a person you know, he holds no super powers." Jezebel chuckled.

"Whatever. He . . . oh, never mind."

"Do not never-mind me." Jezebel wagged a hand through the air. "Spit it out."

"I got all . . . weird when I saw him," she admitted.

"Did your pulse pick up?" Annabelle nodded. "Did you instantly feel hot?" She nodded again. "How about breathing—were you able to?" Annabelle shook her head no. "Oh boy. Hormones, honey—you've got a bad case of them."

"Gee thanks for that helpful insight," she delivered with a hefty dose of snark.

"You're very welcome," Jezebel deadpanned. Annabelle snorted and sank into her usual spot. She dropped her bag between the two of them and curled her legs under her.

"Jezebel! My best girl, how's it going today?"

Annabelle jumped at least six inches in her seat and spun her head around toward the deep baritone voice behind her.

"Mark," Jezebel batted her lashes, "you're too sweet," Jezebel complimented as Mark strode up to her and planted a kiss on her cheek.

Turning to her, Mark said, "Hey, who's this?"

"Annabelle. She visits me every week, on Tuesdays," Jezebel informed. A wicked glint shone in her eyes and Annabelle wanted to slap her upside the head to knock the look right off her face.

Mark smiled.

"Nice to meet you." His large hand shot out toward her. She took the proffered hand robotically and stared at where their bodies joined as a slight buzz travelled up her arm. He squeezed gently and moved their hands up and down while she watched.

"Yup."

Yup? YUP!? Annabelle wanted to crawl into a hole, curl up and never come out. Ever.

Mark chuckled. "Well, alright ladies, if you need anything just holler."

"Absolutely stud," Jezebel shouted after him. Annabelle mewled and pulled the neck of her shirt up over her eyes, mortified.

Jezebel snorted. "Wow, you weren't kidding about getting weird." Annabelle scowled at Jezebel and felt her face tint red.

"Can we just, I don't know . . . dive into the story?"

"After that fiasco! No way. Fess up kiddo. You're smitten."

"Obviously." Sarcasm laced her voice.

"It helps if you form words, and look someone in the eye, if you want them to notice you."

"Doesn't matter," she said and ground her teeth.

"Of course it matters!" Jezebel boomed.

"No, it doesn't when you're grounded and have no way to communicate outside of one day a week." she elaborated, adjusting herself in the chair.

Jezebel frowned and nodded. "I see your point. But there's nothing wrong with building up slowly to something. You never know how things can turn out."

Annabelle rolled her shoulders and tilted her head side to side. "I won't rule anything out. *Now* can we have story time?"

"Fine, brat. Paris, nineteen eighty-nine."

Chapter 20

Celeste

Paris 1989

Celeste looked only at Gabriel's face, but still she felt exposed by his penetrating gaze, torn open. The chapel was crowded as her husband undressed her with his eyes. She knew her chest and cheeks were tinged red at his lingering stare but she couldn't do anything about it. She resolved that having a husband who could still make you blush was a good thing. She focused her attention back to the gorgeous woman in white next to her.

Mara was stunning. She radiated a calm contentment that Celeste didn't think her friend would ever find just five years ago. Charles stood facing Mara wearing a shit-eating grin. Celeste was happy that they'd found each other. He was a good man and Mara was her best friend. Happiness bloomed in her heart for them.

Vows were exchanged. Rings were placed on fingers and the groom swept the bride up into his arms and claimed her with a kiss. White hydrangea littered the reception hall. Mixed with the lights, music and people it was the perfect backdrop for Mara's big day. Matteo crossed the room in a tux, looking extra handsome. A beautiful redhead hung on his arm.

"Fiore mio," he greeted using his nickname for her. Celeste beamed and kissed his cheek. "Where's the husband?"

"Grabbing drinks. Are you going to introduce me?" she prodded.

"Celeste, this is Aria. Aria, Celeste."

She took the redhead's hand and gave her a warm smile. She was excited to meet anyone Matteo deemed worthy of bringing as a date. "I've heard a lot about you," Aria said curtly.

"All decent I hope," Celeste laughed.

Gabriel appeared at Celeste's side then, champagne in hand. "Love, this is Aria, Matteo's date. Aria, my husband Gabriel," she introduced.

Gabriel clapped Matteo on the back, as men did, murmuring something about how nice it was to see him, and then took Aria's hand in his and kissed the back of it. "Lovely to meet you Aria."

Celeste chuckled at her husband's chivalry. It was in earnest but she also found it adorably amusing. Matteo saw the star-struck look on Aria's face and grumbled at Gabriel. "How do you get used to it?"

"I've found that flattery is a cheap distraction from truth," Gabriel answered. They all shared a good laugh as Mara finally found the time to stop by and chat with them.

"I'm so happy for you!" Celeste squealed pulling her friend into a tight hug. Matteo wrapped his arms around them both, sealing the three of them in an embrace. "Me too, Mara. You look stunning."

Mara sniffled and wiped happy tears from her eyes. "Psst. Can I borrow you two for a minute in private?" she asked. She and Matteo both nodded as Mara grabbed each of their hands and tugged to get them following her.

Just outside the chaos of the reception Mara stopped and turned to face them.

"I'm pregnant!" Mara squealed.

Matteo's brows shot up to the top of his forehead and Celeste gasped in shock.

"And before you two jerks say anything," Mara said, eyeing them, "no. That's not why we got married. I just found out last night and—don't hate me Celeste, but I wanted to wait and tell you together!"

Matteo shook his head and laughed his congratulations to her. Celeste tugged Mara into an epic hug and told her how happy she was for her. And, despite the small pang of jealousy that bumped against her heart, she *was* happy for her friend.

"Hey! Three musketeers, the groom is looking for his bride," Gabriel shouted toward them.

"No one else knows besides Charles, so mum's the word, okay?" Mara whispered, then pretended to zip her lips and toss away the key. They both nodded.

The reception was the most fun Celeste had had in years. They danced, they drank, they danced some more, they re-lived old stories and ate too much while doing it. As they headed upstairs at the end of the evening Gabriel swept her up into his arms and planted tender kisses where her shoulder and neck met. She laughed as goosebumps broke out across her skin.

Inside their hotel room, Gabriel stripped her as bare as his eyes had made her feel earlier in the day and cherished each and every centimeter of her skin. As they lay together tangled in a knot, she thought about Mara's news.

"Mara's pregnant," she blurted into the silence surrounding their breathing.

"Is that . . ."

"No, she only found out last night," Celeste explained, knowing his question.

Gabriel twisted her in his arms to face him. "We could try, you know. Look into options . . . there has to be one."

Snippets of a hundred 'what ifs' ran through her mind. She shot them all down. She expelled a heavy breath that felt like it carried the weight of the universe. "Gabriel," she fought, trying to find the right words, "there is no treatment that will magically allow me to carry a baby."

He huffed and stared at her hard. Disappointment etched in the lines of his face. She started to speak but he stopped her. "Drop it, Celeste." His words were cold and raw. She blinked back tears and nuzzled her face into his neck while she whispered that she was sorry. She would have to be patient with him and he would have to, ultimately, be strong. As she lay there wishing her truth was different she tried to keep in mind that no marriage was perfect. No person was perfect. They would conquer this hurdle together. They had to.

Chapter 21

Annabelle

"Oh, it's dangerous, It's so out of line, To try and turn back time."
~ Hurt, Christina Aguilera

At six, Annabelle noticed the time. She had completely zoned out to the story today. She jumped up from the chair and scurried to the bathroom to relieve herself before heading home.

Emerging from the bathroom she apologized to Jezebel. "Sorry to run, Jez, but . . ."

"You're going to be late." Jezebel nodded in understanding and Annabelle scooped up her bag and made a beeline for the front doors. She had ten minutes to get to the bus stop and catch her bus home.

"Hey! Wait!" Annabelle stopped her feet and skidded to a halt. She turned and found herself chest to chest with a breathless Mark. "Uh, Jezebel said you forgot this." He held out her wallet.

Baffled, she unzipped the outermost pocket of her backpack to check. Her wallet *was* missing. But she hadn't touched her bag the entire visit.

Brows furrowed, she looked up to Mark.

"Weird. Thanks," she mumbled, taking the wallet from him.

"So, Jez says you visit her every week. That's real sweet. Is she family?"

"No," she answered. Confusion swept over his face and she knew what he'd ask next. Embarrassed about the circumstances for her being at Glenview, Annabelle preferred to avoid that particular conversation with Mark.

"So, why do you come here then?" he asked, just as she figured he would. She waved her hand to stop him. "Can we just talk about something else?" He mulled that over, his eyes never leaving hers.

It was obvious he did not want to drop it, but he gave her an acknowledging shrug anyway. "What would you like to talk about instead?" There was a playful edge to his voice. Annabelle suddenly felt apprehensive. "I don't know . . . actually . . ."

He cut in, "Alright, I'll pick." He seemed like the kind of guy who didn't have a care in the world.

"Um," she cut him off, "I really have to go. I can't miss the bus. Sorry." She gave a small wave as she turned to go.

His hand caught her arm, slid gently up to her neck and stroked her bottom lip with his thumb. Her breathing halted. Her muscles froze.

His expression was tight, like he was fighting for restraint. "Are you sure you have to go? I'm off in ten." The gravelly sound of his voice almost convinced her to stay. *Almost.*

She pressed her lips tightly together and took a step back from him. "I'm sure. Uh, see you around." She turned on her heel, bolted out the doors and ran the entire way to the bus stop. Another two seconds and she would have missed the bus. As it was, she could barely catch her breath from the impromptu sprint—or maybe it was because of Mark. She couldn't be sure.

On the bus ride she took time to gather her thoughts. She had definitely *not* left that pocket on her bag unzipped and she had *not* taken her wallet out for anything while visiting. Jezebel set her up. It had to be when she used the bathroom before she left. *That sneaky brat.* Annabelle smiled to herself and watched the town blur by the window.

~***~

Mark.

Mark.

Mark.

Mark.

His name seemed to play on an endless loop in her head. It was foolish and embarrassing but she couldn't put him out of her mind. The feeling of his thumb grazing her cheek. The way his eyes sparkled. The way the fine hairs on the back of her neck stood at attention from his touch.

Mark. When she dreamed.

Mark. When her teacher's voice droned on and on.

Mark. When she was restless at home.

Mark. When she talked with Madison.

He filled up space inside her soul alongside the ever-present grief and sorrow, somehow making it, briefly and ever so subtly, more tolerable.

Brant,

I met a guy. His name is Mark. I know absolutely nothing about him. I think you'd tell me how ridiculous it is that I'm obsessed with him. I think you'd tell me that if he wants a shot at your baby sister he has to get by you, but I think you'd approve. I have no facts to base this off of, but I want you to approve.

I guess maybe you wouldn't, simply because there's nothing to approve of. Not yet anyways. Maybe I'll see him again Tuesday.

Your psycho sister,

Belle

She tucked the journal into her desk drawer and lay on her bed, staring at the patterns the moonlight cast on her ceiling thinking about . . . of course, Mark.

~***~

Annabelle startled awake. She threw the covers off and sat up in bed, panting. *Just another stupid dream.* She chastised herself quietly as she slipped from bed and walked to the kitchen. She flipped on the overhead light and squinted against its glare. Her eyes adjusted swiftly as she scanned the bleak kitchen for some kind of purpose. She let out a yawn before the fridge caught her interest. That was, until she opened it and realized there was barely anything in it. Without much thought, her hand closed around a can of whipped cream. She checked the expiration date, saw that it was still good and nudged the fridge door closed with her foot.

She hopped up on the counter and stared at the can. Why had she grabbed it? *Brant.* She didn't think sugar would exactly help her sleep but at the moment she didn't really care. Annabelle removed the cover and angled the can over her open mouth before she depressed the lever. Creamy, delicious, sugary-sweet goodness piled on her tongue. She wiped at a bit that had spluttered on her cheek with a paper towel, then crumpled it into a ball and tossed it in the trashcan and whispered, "Score!" when it swooshed in.

A low chuckle startled her. She let out a yelp as her father entered the kitchen. "What are you doing up?"

She relaxed and shrugged. "Can't sleep."

A glimmer of a smile played on her father's lips. Grimly, she realized how very little anyone in the house ever smiled. She lifted the can and squirted another clump of whipped cream into her mouth.

"You should try it," she mumbled, mouth full.

"Brant used to do that."

Annabelle tensed and looked away. When he said his son's name, his voice was pained.

"Yeah," she said after a pause. Her father cleared his throat. She pictured a big, raw knot of emotion blocking his throat. He reached into the fridge and pulled out a bottle of water. "Finish up your whipped binge and get back to bed."

"Okay," she answered.

He turned in the doorway. "Night, Belle."

"Night." He had almost reached the stairs when she called after him. Glancing at her from over his shoulder, he said, "Yes?"

"Why are you up?" His eyes held her for an instant and then his shoulders drooped. "I couldn't sleep either." With that, he retreated, leaving her alone in the kitchen again.

~***~

When Tuesday arrived Annabelle was a tightly-wound bundle of nerves. The anticipation of seeing Mark had her stomach bubbling with excitement and fear. Fear that she'd become a bumbling idiot again in his presence.

She showered, dressed and headed to school thinking how there was no dignity in grief. She was bored and disgusted with her family's sorrow. It had to end. She was here. Brant was not. That should have provided some comfort *eight* years later for her parents yet her presence seemed to only serve as a morbid reminder of all they had lost. She slapped a smile on her face as she pushed through the double doors of the high school. She only had a month until graduation.

Her day whizzed by. Nothing exciting marked its presence. She stared blankly from the window of the bus the entire trip to Glenview, her mind strangely quiet.

Jezebel grinned as Annabelle entered her suite. "Tell me how your week was."

"Eh. Fine I guess." Annabelle couldn't stop her eyes from skirting back and forth from the door and Jezebel. She hadn't seen Mark when she came in today and she was disappointed.

"Fine?" Jezebel pushed.

"Status quo? Ugh. Okay it blew. I had a hard time sleeping but I did have a weird two a.m. run-in with my dad."

"Oh?"

"I don't know. He was up, getting water and I was shooting whipped cream down my throat."

Jezebel gasped. "My God girl, take your sexcapades outside the house! In the kitchen?"

Annabelle stared, confounded, as her friend's brows knit together.

"Huh?" Then realization hit. "Gross Jez!" she squealed. "I was eating whipped cream, as in, the dessert topping?"

Jezebel's face smoothed out from its disgusted expression and she smiled. Annabelle scoffed. "You have a dirty, dirty mind."

"I suppose I do, don't I?" Jezebel laughed. "So what did you talk about?"

"Nothing. That was the point. There we were, alone, in the dead of the night, with nothing at all to talk about."

Jezebel nodded her head solemnly. "Pity he doesn't see what's right in front of him. You'd think he'd want to hold onto you for dear life."

Jezebel's words hit hard. Didn't everyone need someone to hold their hands, give them a reason to get up in the morning? Didn't everyone deserve that in life? Why had her parents abandoned the very idea of her?

"Jez, I'd like to hear more about Celeste." Annabelle had been enjoying her lack of thoughts this afternoon and didn't feel up to digging into her pathetic home life at the moment.

Jezebel seemed to take her cue. "If that's what you'd like."

Annabelle nodded.

"Celeste, Paris, nineteen ninety."

Chapter 22

Celeste

Paris 1990

On her way to the Embassy, Celeste couldn't help but notice each and every baby that passed by. And so many did. They passed by, unaware of the aching need rooted deep in her belly. Gabriel desperately wanted children. A fact that was cemented further after Mara had given birth six months ago.

They had fought about it after visiting Mara and Charles in the hospital. It had been a fight that no one could win. Her hormones were revved up and she finally felt that ticking time bomb people referred to as baby fever. She had it bad. At twenty-six her body knew it was ripe and ready to make babies but her brain hadn't sent the message to her hormones that she wasn't physically capable. It was torture.

She passed the envelope to Dan as was customary and tried to make a hasty exit. She wasn't up for chit-chat today. She wanted to be back at the estate with Dr. B and Matteo. She wanted the comfort of distraction.

"Whoa, what's up?" Dan asked catching her arm and stopping her escape.

"I . . ." she didn't know what to say. She wasn't about to delve into her marriage issues with Dan.

"You seem off today," he said.

"I guess I am."

"You didn't look inside the envelope did you? I'd hate to have to kill you."

Celeste bit her lip and shook her head. "I'd hate for our visits to end that way."

"Cheer up. Nothing in life is permanent," he offered. She reached out and placed her hand on his forearm. "Some things are."

~***~

She drove on autopilot, radio off, mind numb, all the way back to the estate. Once there, she dug into her duties, relishing the relief it provided from her endless thoughts.

It was late by the time Celeste arrived home that day. Gabriel wasn't home. He'd been spending more and more time at work. The light on the answering machine blinked a steady meter. She pushed play and Mara's frantic voice filled the silence surrounding her. She smiled at the sound of her friend's voice. She leaned a hip on the counter as she listened.

"Cece! I think I'm losing my mind. DO NOT LAUGH. I'm serious. I tried to watch a show with Charles last night on the couch but I fell asleep at ten. At midnight Matthew woke up hysterical. I've been

up with him ever since. I tried medicine, bourbon on his gums, letting him cry it out, putting him in the guest room bed with me, walking around the house, giving him a hot bath, then finally driving around the block for an hour. Just now, I put him down in his bed and he's wide awake and fussing. No temperature. Ugh. I think it's his teeth. Worst night of my life. Well, besides the night during our sophomore year when I went home with that guy who farted non-stop. Do you remember that? I think I'm delusional. Don't think that dropping him off at a fire station or church didn't cross my mind at four a.m. He's in bed now, babbling to invisible friends. I want to sleep for a week straight. Sorry for the early call. I need to see you soon. Oh hey . . ."

The message cut off. The next one began.

"What the hell? I didn't talk for that long. Or did I? So, last night, I didn't wake Charles up because he has a very long day today and won't be home until after nine tonight, and you know what he says when he woke up and found me crying in bed with Matthew? 'You shouldn't have driven around with him. We don't want him to get used to it.' I looked straight in his eyes and said, 'WALK AWAY NOW OR I WILL LITERALLY CUT YOU.' That's the mindset I was in. What the hell, Cece? Who says that? How does one even 'cut' someone? I'm losing my mind. I just know it."

Celeste didn't call Mara back. Fighting emotional overload, she deleted both messages and pushed her way out the French doors to the back patio—she needed air. She didn't mean to be a bad friend. She loved Mara. But Mara's life currently represented all hers didn't have in it. She walked past the spot where Gabriel made love to her for the first time at their new house. She continued down the path through her garden as she had hundreds of times before. The world was immersed in moonlight, the trees stretched up and whispering in the wind. She sat. Or dropped to the ground like an anchor.

She thought about Gabriel, about his hands in her hair, his lips on her own. She felt his hand on her cheek, remembering how he cherished her and gave her his heart, and how they had built their own world, built their own contentment.

She never believed his love would die, but each day that passed drove the baby wedge further, deeper. It felt like they were repelling magnets. Time passed through her fingers slick and easy as water. As every second and minute passed, she felt like she disappeared piece by piece because she couldn't give him what he wanted most.

That morning when he left for work there had been a stiffness in the way he kissed her and in the way he held her. It was as if he was doing something automated, devoid of any sentiment or affection. And now, her heart felt frozen, her hands numb.

She missed him. She tried to recall one of her favorite nights in the kitchen with Gabriel, a few weeks ago, a few decades ago. When was the last time she'd thought of him with lust. When the thought of seeing him for dinner made her smile all day? When the scent of his cologne was the first thing she wanted to smell in the morning and the last thing she wanted to smell at night? When they used to sleep intertwined like vines, legs and arms coiling, her head planted securely on his chest. Things had slowly changed. His work hours increased, her free ones were spent alone. She made a note to get back to how they were, to put in the effort—for him, for them.

~***~

In the sun-drenched yard, Celeste covered her eyes with dark glasses and got to work. She pulled weed after weed. The yanking, purging, of the little devils was cathartic.

It hit hard and fast—abdominal pain, vomiting, a rush of heat and vertigo that brought Celeste to her knees. The excessive vomiting was causing her body to lose water too quickly, and her esophagus became so irritated it began to bleed. The vomit tinged red. Panic overtook her. She could barely catch a breath between retching. She felt like she was drowning.

Celeste crawled in the direction of the stables

as she heaved and retched. It hadn't happened in so long. She had been episode-free for years now. Her vision grew hazy and she opened her mouth to call for help but only vomit came out. She felt weak and lethargic. Max nuzzled her side as she continued to vomit. *Please*, she thought, *please Max, get help.*

"Cece," Matteo's voice was close. She opened her eyes slowly, taking in her surroundings. "You had an episode. How're you feeling?" Celeste wanted to answer but couldn't. Her throat felt like the cracked, heat-scorched earth of the desert. Matteo squeezed her hand gently. She squeezed his hand. "You gave me a scare fiore mio. I found you about fifty yards from the barn, unconscious."

Celeste frowned. She could only imagine what a sight she was laying on the ground in her own vomit. Her eyes scanned the room. *Where was Gabriel,* she wondered. As if able to read her mind Matteo cleared his throat, drawing her attention back to him. "Gabriel is just outside, talking with the doctors." She nodded her head in understanding. She was happy she hadn't woken up alone. She was happy she'd woken up at all.

Later that afternoon her doctor made his rounds. He stepped into her room and stood at the end of her bed. "Research designates that half of people with cyclic vomiting syndrome also have depression or anxiety. Mrs. Fontaine, your medical history shows no signs of depression or anxiety issues. If vomiting episodes are triggered by stress or excitement, we need to find ways to reduce stress and keep you calm. Continued episodes could cause severe dehydration that can be life threatening. We're confident the tests will give us a better picture of what's really going on." Celeste nodded and thanked the doctor before he continued on with his rounds.

Gabriel looked tired, with his long hair unruly, like when he first woke in the morning. Celeste wished he wouldn't worry so much. This was nothing new. It had followed her around her entire life.

Celeste's parents stopped and visited for a few hours. Her mother's worried face upset Celeste. She didn't want everyone fretting over her. Her father and Gabriel had gone through her medical chart at the end of her bed together, their minds trying to piece together why, after all this time, she'd had such a severe attack.

After a bland cafeteria dinner Gabriel sat near Celeste's bed as they watched TV. Celeste looked at her husband and smiled. "Hop in," she said and patted the spot on the mattress beside her. He laughed but she wasn't joking. "Please," she urged softly. Gabriel carefully crawled into her hospital bed and slid under the wires and tubes. He stretched out next to her. She wrapped an IV-ed arm over him and lay against his chest and closed her eyes. He cupped her chin and lifted her eyes toward his. Grasping her firmly, his large hands ignited her skin as his masculine command flowed through his touch. He kissed her then. Her sigh caught between his lips. She relished the tender moment. She fell asleep nested in his embrace.

Over the course of three days in the hospital, Celeste endured an endoscopy, a CT scan to check for blockages in her digestive system, motility tests to monitor the movement of food through her digestive system, and finally, an MRI to check for a brain tumor or other central nervous system disorders. She was exhausted and stressed with all the chaos of the last few days. Gabriel had personally run lab tests to check for thyroid problems or other metabolic conditions.

She understood. All results pointed to something else—that CVS was likely not causing her current issues. The results all concluded that one reality. She had found Gabriel's overwhelming concern for her sweet. He had insisted with her doctor that he take the blood samples and personally run her blood panels himself, at his lab.

When she was finally discharged they were no closer to answers, but Celeste assured Gabriel that she was used to this, that for years at a time she was fine and whatever caused her episodes would be figured out eventually. After all, she had been dealing with this her entire life. Reluctantly, Gabriel agreed with her, vowing to find out on his own, if he had to, what was causing her strange illness.

Chapter 23

Annabelle

"You gave me strength gave me hope for a lifetime. I never was satisfied"
~ Save Me, Nicki Minaj

Annabelle shifted in her seat. Her left butt cheek was numb and tingling painfully.

"Do you think the ache of not being able to have your own child is the same as losing a child?"

Jezebel stiffened in her seat. Her shoulders pulled up and back and she crossed her arms over her chest protectively.

"I, obviously, couldn't say." Jezebel's words were devoid of emotion, which was odd for her. Annabelle let it go.

"Is it weird that I like hanging out with you?" she asked.

Jezebel cocked her head, tucked her hair behind an ear and thought on Annabelle's question. "You and me, we're searching for the same light, desperate for a remedy for this ailment."

"What ailment?"

"Grief," she answered plainly, as if it were the

most apparent thing ever.

"So what? That makes us kindred spirits or something?"

"Something like that," Jezebel answered, a half-smile emerging.

Annabelle slouched in her seat going over everything in her mind that she knew of Celeste and Gabriel. "I feel bad for Celeste. The whole baby thing and weird throwing-up thing. She doesn't deserve it," she concluded.

"What makes anyone deserve anything dear?"

Annabelle shrugged. "I guess nothing."

Jezebel caught her gaze and held it firmly. "Who's to say that we don't get what we deserve?"

"No one. It just seems like . . . like Celeste should have more luck. She's this super nice person who never did anything wrong."

Jezebel turned her head and stared out the window wearing a lost expression. "What if the greater plan for her life was just because she hadn't done anything wrong . . . yet?"

Annabelle fidgeted in her seat. "What? Like fate is a determined based on what it knows what will happen in the future? So she's being punished in the now for sins she will commit later on?" Annabelle gaffed. "No, I don't believe in that."

Jezebel shrugged and ran her fingers through her hair. "How would one ever know though? Can you prove that's *not* how things work?"

"Of course not. But, it's so farfetched. Think about it, there are a million choices you're hit with in a lifetime. If fate punished you for future happenings, that implies that no matter what choice you made, it would always lead to the same outcome. There'd be no free will."

Jezebel clapped her hands together. The sound echoed in the room. "Brava, darling. I love it when you get riled up. You're so feisty when you put that brain to work. I love a gal with spunk." Her eyes sparkled.

Annabelle smirked. "Are you always playing devil's advocate?"

"Do you really care?" Jezebel asked.

Annabelle thought about it for a moment. She laughed. She didn't care. Jezebel challenged her, made the dull flicker in her spark to life. "No," she answered.

Nodding, Jezebel changed the subject. "Mark was asking about you."

"What?" Annabelle squeaked as a warm swarm of butterflies came to life in her belly.

"Mark was asking about you."

Annabelle rolled her eyes and leaned forward in her chair. "I heard you," she clarified. "What did he ask?"

"Oh, this and that," Jezebel answered flippantly.

"Jez! Come on."

"He asked what you were like, how old you were and other drab questions." Jezebel waved her hand in the air as if swatting away a pesky fly.

Annabelle, on the edge of her seat, could not tolerate Jezebel's lax attitude. This was a big deal. "Are you going to give me details or just leave me hanging like it doesn't matter?"

Jezebel laughed loudly. "You like him."

"I thought we established that when I all but drooled and stuttered around him. Don't think I didn't know it was you who stole my wallet." She speared Jezebel with a pointed look.

"I thought it was a rather brilliant move," Jezebel smirked. Annabelle widened her eyes and said nothing. She waited Jezebel out. Silence sat heavy between them.

"Alright, alright! I told him you were a lovely young woman nearing graduation and that he'd better be nothing short of a gentleman to you."

Annabelle smiled, shaking her head at her friend. "How you manage to answer everything without giving up any real information is a mystery." She rose, taking her bag with her and slinging it over her shoulder. "I'll see you next week."

Annabelle ambled slowly down the corridor toward the entrance hoping to see Mark. As she checked out with reception she heard her name called. Spinning around toward the sound she smiled as Mark skidded to a stop a few feet from her.

"Hey," he said. He wore a half-smile that made him look dopey, but adorable.

"Hi." She adjusted her bag strap on her shoulder.

"I know you take the bus, but, I'm done in like, five, and I thought I'd offer you a ride home," he rushed his words. "It's probably quicker than the bus."

Annabelle wanted to accept. "I'm not really supposed to," she said instead.

"Supposed to what?" he asked.

"Supposed to . . ." her words faded. Was getting a ride home against her parents' rule? It was a gray area, they'd never really discussed it. Mark's eyes burned bright with hope and it melted her. She wanted to get to know him. "You know what, sure. I'd love a ride." Impossibly, his grin grew.

"'Kay, give me five." He turned, his sneakers squeaking on the floor, and disappeared into the employee room.

Annabelle plopped down into one of the reception area chairs while she waited, an insistent flutter residing in her belly. She jammed her hand into the largest outside pocket and fished out her tinted lip balm. It was all she had on her and it would have to do.

Mark emerged from the employee break room quickly. She stood and smiled shyly. "So, you ready?" he asked.

"Yup." What was it with her and that response? She wanted to plant her palm firmly to her forehead, but refrained. Mark led them to a jacked-up truck in the parking lot.

"This is . . . large," she commented. Mark laughed. It was boisterous and confident.

"Yeah. It is." Planting a foot on the chrome foot rail he tugged her door open for her.

"Need help getting in?"

"I think I got it," she said, stepping onto the running board. She hoisted herself into the passenger seat and blushed. That wasn't the most graceful maneuver. Mark closed her door and jogged around the front of the truck to his side.

"So, first, where am I going and second, tell me about yourself," he said.

Annabelle gave him her address. He nodded and started the truck.

"Why are you doing that?" he asked as he put the truck in reverse.

She strapped on her seat belt, confused.

"Doing what?"

His eyebrows shot up. "Sitting against the door as far away from me as possible. I don't bite." He grinned as she blushed. She looked to her right. Annabelle grimaced, unnerved. Yep, she had wedged herself against the door. Immediately, she slid over a few inches, forcing herself to relax. Annabelle pulled the elastic band from her ponytail and shook her hair free. It fell past her shoulders in wavy strands. She ran her fingers through it and twisted in her seat, trying to appear comfortable and at ease. Mostly, she tried to keep her eyes off of Mark and on anything else. She concentrated on the scenery out the window. At the speed he was going, the sky and the trees melted into each other.

"I'm not sure what you want to know," she finally said.

"Anything is a good start."

"How old are you?" she asked.

Mark cocked his head to the side. "I'm twenty, but I feel like that says nothing about you," he joked. Annabelle blushed, again. Yes she was keeping count. How was it that he made her feel screwed up tight with nerves without doing anything at all?

"I'm eighteen. A senior at Walsh. I don't know what to tell you that Jezebel hasn't."

Mark smiled. "You're cute. How 'bout this, I'll ask questions and you answer."

Annabelle nodded. "Sounds easy enough."

"What's your favorite color?"

"Gray," she answered without hesitation.

"No one likes gray," he chuckled and shot her a look from the corner of his eye.

"Someone does."

Mark tried to hide his amused expression but Annabelle caught it. "Okay, what's your favorite restaurant?" he asked.

"Walters. Best eggplant parm in three towns," she gushed. She hadn't been in ages but years ago her family had gone once a week for family dinner night out. She'd always loved it there.

"Eggplant parm, huh? You vegetarian?" he asked, eyes cutting to hers.

"No," she shook her head. "If you'd had it, you'd understand my sentiment."

"How about I try it with you, Friday," he stated boldly. She thought she noticed the barest hint of nervousness in his voice though.

Annabelle sighed. "I can't."

Mark snapped his eyes to hers. "Please don't be one of those chicks who says 'I don't date.'"

"Har, har, no . . . I'd love to, but I'm grounded until I leave for college in August. I literally *can't* date." She tilted her head to the side and her unruly dark hair fell over her forehead, veiling her eyes.

"Oh," he said, brows knit together. "I wasn't expecting that."

Annabelle laughed. "Yeah."

"You're eighteen and grounded," he stated.

"That's accurate."

"So what'd you do?" he asked. His candor surprised her.

Annabelle looked out the window. "I'd rather not get into that."

"Well, how am I supposed to wait until August to take you out?" He flashed a friendly smile, his dimples popping.

Annabelle flushed and bit her lip to keep from blurting out something ridiculous. His question caught her off guard. After a moment she finally spoke. "Why would you wait?"

"I hear you and Jezebel talking. I see you, all smiles and stuff when you're with her. Jezebel's a good shit. Spunky and funny and, don't take this the wrong way, but you're hot. I'd want to ask you out for that alone." He cringed at his own words. "But knowing that you also have substance makes me curious."

"Substance?" She turned to meet his gaze.

"You spend every Tuesday at Glenview, you sit with someone who's not related to you for *hours*. It shows you're a good person—that you've got a lot going on in there." He pointed to her head. For a moment she felt guilty, like she was lying to him. What he said was true *now* — but that's not how her time with Jezebel started out.

"I think maybe you have the wrong perception of me. I go because I don't have a choice. Meeting Jezebel was just lucky. Really lucky. If it wasn't for her I'd be doomed to wear a hairnet and work in the kitchen."

Mark considered her for a moment as they pulled onto her street. "Well, I suppose you'd still look hot in a hairnet."

Annabelle chuckled. "You're funny."

"You're a puzzle," he responded with a warmhearted smile. "One I'd like to put together." Annabelle blushed — again.

"Pull over here," she said, not wanting him to stop at her house.

If her mother was home, and saw, it could mean the end of rides with Mark. "Okay. Listen, I'm just going to shoot straight," Annabelle started as he pulled to the side and put the truck in park. "I got in a bit of trouble. I'm serving six months of community service, which have turned out to be six months spent with Jezebel, so it isn't so bad really. My parents also piled on their own punishment to my court-ordered one. No going out. No friends over. No phone and very limited laptop use. I'm rambling . . ." she stated flustered. "I guess what I'm trying to say is . . . I have no life right now. I'm happy you're interested but, outside of possibly Facebooking you for an hour a night or seeing you Tuesdays at Glenview, I'm inaccessible," she finished, and frowned.

"Whoa. Ramble doesn't seem like the right term . . . rant maybe," he said. Annabelle leaned back in her seat and bit her lip. "I'm cool with that. I can give you a ride home Tuesdays—if you want, that is," he finished.

He reached out and took her hand in his. Annabelle noticed the warmth of his fingers on hers. His smell floating in the cab of the truck. The way his eyes held hers right then. She wasn't sure how to deal with the scandalous thoughts her mind was throwing at her. Mark's hair looked towel-dried and annoyingly attractive all messy, his face clean shaven, and the red T-shirt he wore not only accentuated his tanned arms but highlighted his muscular physique. She was suddenly and uncomfortably aware of the long, bare curve of his neck, his broad shoulders. She turned and smiled at him as her stomach dropped a few feet and landed somewhere in the vicinity of the floor. She pulled herself together as much as possible. Raising a perfectly plucked brow, she smiled and said, "I want."

~***~

Brant,

Today I smiled at every single person I passed. I'm happy. I don't even think my feet touch the ground when I walk. It's just a dream and if I started to sing and dance, I wouldn't be surprised if all the strangers I've smiled at join in as some sort of flash mob or something. I really like Mark. It's not exactly rational since I barely know him. I'm sure you don't want to hear this boy talk but I can't help it. Mom has become one of those not-good-enough moms. She's an imperfect, crap mother. And even that doesn't bother me today. Intense 'like' has burrowed a deep hole into my heart.

I want to coddle it, let it snuggle in. Do you think it's weird that lately I think about other people's lives and all the love they don't have, the friends they don't really connect with, the boring routines that make up their sad existences, the weight of the pressures that crush their spirits? That in those moments I realize how much I have and how precious it is? I'm going to stay happy. I'm going to. For you. For me. For everyone else.

-Belle

Annabelle and Jezebel were stretched out side by side on the bed together listening to old mix tapes Jezebel had requested her husband bring in. Annabelle lay there, eyes closed, music playing loudly, thinking about her Facebook messages with Mark throughout the last week. *Duran Duran, the Cars, Phil Collins* and *Billy Joel* were the strange soundtrack to her thoughts as they laid still and just listened. Annabelle knew many of the songs but there were also many that she wasn't familiar with.

A smile crept over her face as they lay shoulder to shoulder. Jezebel's warm hand found hers, clutched it, and squeezed. Everything in that moment felt just right. She was exactly where she was supposed to be, with who she was supposed to be with. It was a liberating feeling.

Her week had been bland. Madison missed three days of school because she was sick, her classes didn't hold her interest and her parents, well . . . they were the same. Everything was horrifically quiet at the house as always. She'd cranked up her music. She'd smiled non-stop, she'd asked questions to prompt conversations with her parents who responded in the moment briefly before they slipped into their normal routines of discontent. Messaging Mark was the only real highlight of her days.

"Do you like *10,000 Maniacs?*" Jezebel said,

cutting into her thoughts.

"Sure," she shrugged.

Jezebel hopped off the bed and switched sides of the tape that was playing. When the familiar opening of a classic began, she smiled widely and spun around in a circle. Her hair lifted from her neck and blew in the breeze she created. Her lips were upturned and her eyes closed. Annabelle felt jealous. Jealous that she could just let go, feel a moment and enjoy it. She wanted that so badly. Annabelle yanked her elastic from her hair and resolved that she could have that and she would.

Right now.

"Dance party!" Annabelle cheered.

She joined Jezebel, spinning and shaking and laughing as the song played. They swung their hair, shook their hips and danced. Jezebel took her hands and spun her out, then back in, she swayed them together and dipped Annabelle dramatically. She couldn't catch her breath she was laughing so hard. It had been ages since she'd done anything so silly. When the song wound down Jezebel dimmed the volume and snuggled into her chair. Annabelle followed her lead.

Breathless she tucked her legs under her and waited for Jezebel to take the lead. Moments passed in silence and Annabelle wondered if something was wrong. Jezebel stared at the flowers on her windowsill solemnly.

"Jez?"

"Yes?" Jezebel croaked and swiveled her head to meet her gaze.

"Where were you?"

Jezebel grinned but it didn't quite reach her eyes. "In the past."

"Tell me about it?" Annabelle hedged.

"Not a chance kiddo. My past is a whole other story." Jezebel winked and pulled her hair over one shoulder. "For now, we should stick to Celeste. Did you know that the song *Jezebel* is written from the perspective of a woman who has realized that she is no longer in love with her husband and wants to dissolve their marriage?"

Annabelle stared at Jezebel a second and blinked before sucking in a deep breath. "Nope."

Jezebel sighed and nodded. "It was."

"Okay," Annabelle said unsure where Jezebel was going with the conversation.

"Oh never mind." Jezebel waved her hand through the air. "Shall we get to it then?"

"You mean Celeste's story?" she asked. Jezebel nodded. "Yeah. Let's."

"Paris, nineteen ninety-two," Jezebel began, and Annabelle settled into her seat a little more.

Chapter 24

Celeste

Paris 1992

Hi Cece,

How is my favorite lady? Things are going well here. The weather is just beautiful and there's so much to do! We went apple picking, raspberry picking, picked pumpkins at the pumpkin farm, went on hayrides, you name it we did it. Love all the color and the kids have had a blast with all the leaf piles. I really miss you but am keeping busy taking care of the house and the family.

Kids are all doing very well in daycare and are actually ahead of where they should be which is a relief! Molly just started talking. Matthew is doing soccer—it's adorable, they all swarm the ball. We are all excited awaiting the first snow which may happen on Saturday. I can't wait to do some skiing. I hope you are doing great and enjoying your beautiful weather in Paris. Everything, including snow, is more magical there.

Hope all is well with Gabriel and

work! Please tell Matteo I send my love. Ok, enough of my rambling, I know you are busy. Take care and hope to hear from you soon.
Your Favorite Lady, Mara

Celeste smiled as she set the letter down on the counter. The last two years had brought many changes. Mara and Charles had moved to the States for Charles' work. She missed her best friend dearly but it was what was best for their family. Matthew, their first born, was three now and Molly was pushing ten months. As their godmother, Celeste took her role seriously, spoiling them with gifts at every occasion she deemed appropriate.

Gabriel and she had pushed through the roughest patches in their marriage and were, for the most part, back on track. For Gabriel, desire and logic had been two very separate things when coming to terms with not being able to have a child of his own. Of course, there were still bouts of disappointment and longing when it came to friends and co-workers having babies but they knew now how to get through it— together.

Gabriel descended the stairs with heavy footsteps. He fiddled with his tie as he entered the kitchen. Ambling up to him she swatted his hand away from his tie. She handed him a mug of coffee and fixed his tie for him while he took that first glorious sip.

"What would I do without you?" he asked. His eyes crinkled as he smiled appreciatively at her.

"Indeed," she answered with a smile. Gabriel leaned down and kissed her temple. She rested her head on his chest and sighed.

"Will you be home tonight for dinner?"

"Chances are slim, mon amour, we're very close to working out the side effects finally."

"Congratulations love, it must feel good to be close to the finish line," she offered, tamping down her disappointment.

He nodded. "Six years in the making."

"Almost there now, keep your chin up," she encouraged.

Gabriel cupped her chin and looked tenderly into her eyes. She wondered if when he finally worked out all the kinks of the drug he was working on, he'd have normal hours or if a new project would magically appear to soak up his time. She brushed the thought away as he kissed her and nodded. He set the mug on the counter and headed to the lab. She gripped her mug, still warm from the steaming liquid inside. She picked up his mug and stared inside. He'd drained it to the dregs.

~***~

Dr. B sat in the kitchen, his hands wrapped

around a cup of steaming tea. His warm eyes crinkled at the edges when he smiled at her.

"Afternoon dear," he greeted.

"Hi."

"Tea?"

"That would be nice, thanks." She watched him shuffle around the kitchen to fix her some tea and she laughed. He grumbled the entire time about nothing and everything. He always appeared grumpy — unless you knew him.

"Something amusing?" he asked.

"You," she said and batted her eyelashes at him in mock innocence.

"I've been called many things dear, but never *amusing*," he grumbled good-naturedly. He walked past a bare spot on the wall where a picture had hung.

She couldn't help her curiosity and asked, "Dr. B?" as he set her teacup in front of her. "Why is it that there are pictures missing on the walls?" She noticed he startled slightly before he studied Celeste's face.

"Some things are better left as memories and some memories are too painful to view. I don't need the pictures. My memories are all up here," he said and tapped his head.

"I'm sorry," she offered. She didn't want to pry but longed to know Dr. B's story.

"Don't be. You had no way of knowing. I lost

a great deal in my lifetime Celeste, but I've also gained a great deal. You and Matteo for instance." He gave her a warm, easy smile.

Celeste blushed at his affection. She often wondered about Dr. B's life. He was a private man, who had amassed quite a bit of wealth in his years, but had no family to speak of. She knew he'd been married at one point but didn't know anything else. Had his wife passed on? Left him? She burned to know the answers but knew it wasn't her place to pry. Over the years he had shared tidbits here and there as he saw fit and that would have to be enough for her.

"We've gained you, not the other way around," she said. Max curled up at her feet. She wiggled her foot gently under him.

"Aww, child, you never know who is really benefitting now do you?" He quirked a bushy eyebrow at her and smirked.

"You're much too kind for your own good," she teased.

"Maybe so, but I'm old and a good judge of character." Celeste laughed; that certainly couldn't be denied. "How's everything at home?" he asked.

"We're good." Dr. B and Matteo had been a great source of comfort to Celeste in the last two years. She was able to talk with them about wanting children and Gabriel's moods and get not only good advice for her well-being, but insight into how the male mind worked. "Gabriel spends most of his time at the lab working on God knows what drug. Six years and he's finally making progress, from what he says."

"Interesting. You must be proud of his work," Dr. B commented.

"I support him of course, but honestly I know very little about what he works on. It's all very hush-hush. New compounds, new side effects, old drugs tweaked to perform differently or to enhance their ability. I sort of zone out when he tries to explain what he can to me," she said and laughed.

"My wife did the same. She was smart as a whip but really had no understanding when I started jabbering on about work. The look on her face . . ." he started, his voice fading as he shook his head at the memory, a quiet smirk on his face.

Celeste conjured up the last time Gabriel had droned on about the intricate chemical compounds that made up his work. She let her face relax. "Like this?" she said. Dr. B laughed heartily at her expression.

"Yes dear, you look just like her." He reached across the table and patted her hand.

Celeste warmed at Dr. B's gaze. Sometimes she noticed him watching her with a fondness in his eyes. She wasn't sure why but she was happy that she gave him something to smile about. She relished their time together and was happy that he seemed to share the sentiment. She loved her parents dearly but their relationship was more formal. What she had at work with Dr. B and Matteo was what she imagined most families to have. And she loved it.

"Cece, fiore mio," Matteo greeted her, and kissing Celeste's cheek. He looked sharp in a navy-blue suit, white shirt, and solid blue tie. He definitely wasn't working the stables today.

"Teo! I wasn't expecting you today," Dr. B said. He gave Matteo a wolfish grin.

"Celeste is here . . . of course I'd be here," Matteo answered.

Celeste threw a crumpled napkin at him. "As if," she covered a laugh with a cough.

"Celeste is here *every* day," Dr. B pointed out.

"I really enjoy your tea?" Matteo tried again.

"You are hopeless." Matteo glanced up at the ceiling as if it would give him a hint to his next comeback.

"Dare I admit that I enjoy your company old man?" he said, narrowing his eyes playfully at Dr. B.

"Oh, hogwash," Dr. B deadpanned as his eyes flashed with amusement.

Matteo sat then, joining them at the table

where the three of them laughed and chatted about nothing in particular for hours.

~***~

The rain cast a dreary feel over everything as it sped by her windows. She only needed to drop off something for Dr. B at the embassy before heading home for the day. The weather made her sleepy and quiet. She found a parking spot with ease, close enough that she wouldn't get soaked jogging from her car to the entrance, and snatched the envelope from the passenger seat after putting the car in park.

She made her way through the now familiar halls until she reached Dan's office. She didn't bother knocking anymore as Dr. B generally called to let Dan know she was on her way. She pushed through the door, bypassed the empty reception desk and walked into his office.

Dan sat reclined in his chair, feet propped up on his desk, a book in his hands. "Working hard I see," Celeste said with snark. Dan set the book down and smiled at her. Over the years they had developed an easy rapport with each other.

"Nice to see you too Celeste." Dan gave her a smug smile. He dropped his feet to the floor and stood to greet her. She glanced at the clock on the wall and saw that it was just a little after five in the evening. Celeste wrapped her hand around his and shook his offered palm.

"I didn't expect the good doctor to turn this around so fast," he said, pointing to the envelope in her left hand.

"Are you disappointed to see me?" She laughed.

"Never, Celeste," he laughed heartily.

"How're the wife and kids doing?" she asked sincerely. She propped her hip against the wall and watched Dan run his fingers through his hair.

"Grace hates it here. She's about ready to graduate and says she's moving back to the States." Dan chuckled and shook his head.

"You'd think after the last four years she'd have grown fond of Paris in some way." suggested Celeste.

"Not a chance. That girl was pissed when I was transferred here and she's pissed we've stayed so long. Sheila is beside herself," he huffed and rolled his eyes.

Celeste gave him a heartfelt grin. "I imagine a mother would want to keep her baby near no matter how old."

"Absolutely. They're both stubborn and buttheads non-stop. I'm about to lose my damn mind trying to keep the peace," Dan chuckled.

"I'm sure you're exaggerating. Sheila and Grace are both lovely." She gave him a rueful smirk.

He raised an eyebrow at her that said 'if you only knew' and added, "Thank God I have Jim. Without that kid, I'd be outnumbered and out-witted."

Celeste smiled and thought of what Dan's household must be like. A teenage daughter, a middle school-aged son and a feisty wife who lit up any room she entered. It made her heart warm to think that Dan was in good hands, that he had something meaningful to go home to at night. He was a good man.

"You're tough, you'll make it," she joked. Celeste handed the manila envelope to him and said, "It's after five Dan, go home to your family." Dan nodded and took the envelope from her.

"It's after five Celeste, go home to your husband," he threw back at her with a wide grin. Celeste only chuckled before turning and heading back out to her car.

The rain soaked her thoroughly as she rummaged through her pocket trying to pull her keys out. She shivered as she finally plunked into her seat and yanked the door shut. When she pulled into her drive she turned the car off and stared at the dark house. Sitting in the shadow of her car she imagined what Gabriel would be doing if he were home. He would most likely be reading, legs crossed, note pad on his leg, documents resting on the arm of that tattered but comfortable armchair they used to play-fight over. She smiled briefly at the thought and then frowned. He wasn't home and he likely wouldn't be before she retired for the night. With a heavy sigh, she opened her door and readied herself for the rain-laden sprint to the front door, feeling his absence more vividly than his presence.

Chapter 25

Annabelle

"I was taught to love, But I learned to hate. Bisect me. I will regenerate"
~ Earthworm, Grief

Mark waited for Annabelle at his truck looking delectable. For the first time in her life, she was completely breathless in the presence of a guy, and she didn't want the feeling to end.

"Sorry I'm late!" she called as she quickly made her way across the parking lot. He reached out and snagged her bag from her shoulder, setting it in the truck for her.

"No worries," he said reaching for her hand. Annabelle gave it to him. "Hi," he said in a hoarse voice. He tugged her to him and hugged her. A feeling of euphoria rushed through her. She burst out laughing. It was so ridiculous to be so affected by such a simple gesture, yet she was. It was a warm, sincere, affectionate hug. "Is this amusing?" Mark asked releasing her.

"Not at all," she giggled, willing herself to stop. "Sometimes, I laugh at inappropriate situations."

"That was inappropriate?" Mark scratched his neck, a bewildered expression on his face.

"Not at all, that's why it was inappropriate to laugh." Mark shook his head at her still not understanding. "You hugged me. I liked it. It was nice. I'll stop laughing now if you do it again."

He gave her a wry look before tugging her to his chest and squeezing her. This time, she squeezed back and found the sound of his heart beat calming and reassuring. Mark helped her into his behemoth of a truck and bowed to her before closing her door and climbing into the driver's seat.

"Will we get to chat tonight?" he asked.

"I'll have a little time," she smiled.

Mark had embedded himself into her life over the last week. He made it a point to message her daily and she found by the end of the day the anticipation of reading his thoughts and having a few minutes to message back and forth with him left her breathless and excited.

"Only seventy-seven days you know."

"Until what?" Annabelle's forehead wrinkled in confusion.

"Until I can take you on a date, inmate." Annabelle smiled and swatted his thigh. He caught her hand, pinning it to his leg and said, "I'm really happy we met."

Annabelle let her hand relax as she blushed. He removed his hand from hers but she left her hand where it was. Mark looked down quickly before focusing on the road ahead and grinned. And Annabelle wished the trip home were longer.

~***~

With one hand and one eye on the steering wheel, Annabelle's mother started digging through her bottomless purse. The Coach bag was busting at the seams full of *'essential'* items, as her mother liked to call them. Annabelle cringed to think of how much she would pack on an actual trip somewhere. Her mother had the car swerving all over the road when she finally pulled her hand out of the bag, looking victorious and producing a perfume bottle. Annabelle scrunched her nose. Her mother popped the cap off and spritzed herself and then took aim at Annabelle.

"Mom! No," she protested, leaning right until she was pressed firmly into her door. Her mother smirked and spritzed anyway. Annabelle groaned and tried to waft the air around her away. She wasn't a big perfume fan. Pulling out a tube of lipstick next, her mother smoothed a generous amount on her lips, using the rearview mirror as her guide. *At least there wasn't any traffic on the road right now,* Annabelle thought. Still, she tightened the strap of her seat belt more. Her mother smacked and rubbed her now coral-colored lips together, then reached over to Annabelle. "Here."

"I'm okay, coral isn't really my color," she stated dryly, and pushed her mother's extended hand away.

"Oh, come on," her mother said with a pout.

"Fine," Annabelle groaned and carefully dabbed on the tiniest bit using the mirror in her visor to guide her. She pressed her lips together and dropped the lipstick back into her mother's bag.

"So what's this surprise?" she asked.

Her mother grinned at her and shook her head. "Not telling, you'll find out soon enough."

Annabelle stared out the window; it was a sunny Saturday and although she was happy to have something do outside of the house, her mother's surprises usually weren't her idea of fun. On that thought, Annabelle's head bumped her window as her mother veered right into a parking lot. She pulled upright and rubbed the spot gently. Looking around she spotted the surprise—apparently it was spa day. Annabelle half-smiled. Maybe a little pampering would do her good.

~***~

She sat beside her mother as estheticians poked and prodded at her, willing to take whatever moments with her mother she could get. All the while she kept trying to think of something to discuss, a light topic that would keep their conversation upbeat and flowing. Despite her best efforts, nothing came to mind. She never used to have such a hard time talking to her mother, but that was long before.

"Did you know your father and I met at work?" Her mother smoothed her shirt.

"No, you've told me about your first date but not where you actually met," Annabelle answered. She wanted to know, but mostly she just wanted to keep her mother talking. It was a rare and pleasant surprise.

"Oh Annabelle, he was so determined and driven and handsome," her mother gushed, a soft smile playing on her lips. "There was never anyone who caught my eye like he did. I was a goner from day one." Watching her mother lean back into the pedicure massage chair Annabelle thought about how when she was a child and sad, that woman held her. Her mother who sacrificed so much for her *before*. There she was sitting right there, the same but so different. She listened to her mom chatter on about her father and wondered how a person was able to change so vastly in the span of a lifetime, how, the highs and lows of life could change the fiber of your soul, creating a different person altogether.

Five hours later, Annabelle was relaxed and ready for a nap. They'd each had a pedicure, manicure, massage and facial. It was a decadent treat that should have left Annabelle on a high. Five hours alone with her mother was unheard of. Instead of the high she craved, her stomach twisted into knots on their drive home. She had noticed the sorrow-filled gazes her mother had cast her way at the spa. They talked about superficial things to pass the time they were seated next to each other. There was a longing in her mother's voice that she couldn't place. When her mother had stroked her hair and murmured, "Always be a good girl," Annabelle hadn't responded. She had been too in shock. Her mother's words hit her as a goodbye rather than a simple reminder.

The sun was sitting on the edge of the earth as they drove home. They spilled through the door together and the weight of the silence in the house visibly hit them both. Annabelle noticed her mother's face fall as she looked around. Her mother sighed, dropped her bag on the table in the foyer, kicked off her shoes and moved quietly into the depths of the house without a word. Annabelle closed her eyes and shook her head, warding off all the negative energy floating around her.

Brant,

What's up? How's life in the afterworld? Here's not so great. Well, just here, as in, the house. School is fine. I'm pretty excited to graduate and be out of here. And Glenview is great. Mark. He makes me smile and forget that there are shitty circumstances in life. Jezebel, dude, you'd adore her. I know—I've written that before but she's like Mom from before. She's firm, but gentle and caring. It's hard to explain I guess. Do you remember when we used to go with Dad and get fresh honey? How it melted on your tongue as soon as it hit? It was so sweet. It went down so easily and we always begged for more. Jezebel's like that feeling. Mark is a warm summer breeze that makes you think of windy days and salt and sand and Jezebel is like honey.

Does that make any sense?

-Annabelle

~***~

The sun woke Annabelle as it rose over the horizon and the muted glow began to light her bedroom. A tranquil breeze blew the curtains. She yawned and stretched wishing she never needed to get out of her bed as she basked in the soft down against her skin. For the first time in years she woke feeling content and grateful; she had Mark, Jezebel and Madison in her life. The silence of her home didn't seem so profoundly deafening any more. With a content heart she hopped out of bed to prepare for her big day.

With big bright eyes and rosy cheeks Annabelle headed downstairs. Graduation Day. She could barely contain her excitement as she gathered her things and headed for the bus stop. A car horn honked as she rounded the corner of her street. She lifted her head.

"Get in! No bus for you today!" Madison called from her open driver's side window. Annabelle grinned, loving her best friend, and jogged to the car.

"Can you believe it?" Madison said excitedly.

"Hardly. I don't think it will seem real until we're at the ceremony," she said.

"In two hours we will be officially free," Madison sighed with delight.

"Thank God."

~***~

"Annabelle Fortin." Her name rang out in the auditorium and echoed. Annabelle stood, mumbling 'excuse me's' to her peers as she shuffled to the end of her row. She walked up onto the stage and approached the faculty. Her principal extended her diploma with his left hand and shook her hand with his right. She scanned the crowd quickly and smiled as flash bulbs went off. Mark stood near the back of the auditorium and waved. She grinned and lifted her hand low next to her hip back at him. She scanned the crowd again. Her parents were nowhere to be found. Disappointment flooded her. Surely they hadn't forgotten.

~***~

Brant,

I'm on the bus. I graduated today. It's a feeling I can't quite describe. It's also one you will never know. There's so much you won't know. So much you missed out on. It's bittersweet. I know you would have been there today. Standing next to Mark. You would have hollered the loudest when I took my diploma in my hand. You would have made Mom and Dad be there. The whole family would have been there.

I'm off to see Jez today. I should have invited her. She would have, if I'd thought to make the arrangements.

-Belle

Annabelle entered suite 208 and startled as Mark, Jezebel and Madison boomed "Congratulations!" in unison. She clutched her chest, squeaked and then laughed.

Madison lunged forward, embraced Annabelle then stuffed a small gift in her hands.

"I can't stay, you know—party at my house. But I wanted to be here for the surprise."

"Who planned this?" she asked.

"Jez and Mark."

"How'd they get you in on it?"

"Jez told Mark to let me know, he messaged me on Facebook a week ago. I'm on your friends list you know, it's not like I'm hard to find." Madison winked. "Speaking of, message me later okay." Annabelle stifled a laugh as her best friend darted around the room collecting her belongings. "I'd stay if I could you know. I mean, I wanted you to know that I wanted to celebrate with you," Madison said and shot out the door to head home.

Mark kissed the top of her head as he wrapped one arm around her and squeezed. "I'll be right back," he said. Annabelle nodded, then approached Jezebel.

"Thanks for this," she said sincerely. Jezebel opened her arms and pulled her into a bear hug. Annabelle let a single tear leak from her eye. That was all she would allow herself to shed over her parents gaff. Pulling away she moved to her spot and sat.

"What is it?" Jezebel asked.

"My parents didn't come," she answered. Her voice shook as she tried to compose herself.

"Fuck them!" Jezebel crowed.

Annabelle snapped her gaze to Jezebel, mouth agape. She snorted followed by a shy smile before she lost it. She laughed so hard that she clutched at her stomach and fought to catch her breath, the sound of it maniacal in the quiet space between them.

"What'd I miss?" Mark asked as he sauntered back in looking between them.

"Nothing," Jezebel said with a mischievous look to Annabelle. Gratitude washed through her at having someone who really understood her. Who saw her, every side of her. Someone who could even reveal her own self to her. Jezebel's words weaved with her words into a blanket that held them both. And she was safe. Even in turmoil, she felt safe. The connection was so deep, she almost couldn't see the sliver of space that existed between them. She shook her head and looked to Mark and plastered a smile on her face. "Yup. Nothing."

"I come bearing champagne!" he replied holding up the bottle. Jezebel clapped her hands together and snatched the bottle from him.

"Did you forget my second request?" Jezebel asked.

"Nope." From behind his back he produced a plate with a single cupcake on it, an unlit candle in its center. Jezebel uncorked the champagne bottle with a grin. The cork shot out and bounced off a wall. She caught the overflowing liquid in her mouth. Annabelle giggled at the sight.

Jezebel lit the candle and set the cupcake and a champagne glass on a tray and set it on Annabelle's lap. Jezebel looked at her. "Make a wish, kid, and make it count." The candle's small flame flickered and danced. Annabelle closed her eyes and blew the candle out. Her wish would never come true but she sent it off into the universe just the same. Jezebel raised her glass up for a toast and Annabelle and Mark clasped theirs and followed suit.

"To new beginnings."

"To new beginnings," she and Mark repeated with grins.

After slicing the cupcake into thirds and downing the entire bottle of champagne between the three of them, Mark left to do work. Jezebel twisted her hair up and secured it while Annabelle tucked her legs under her and got comfortable. As Jezebel picked up with Celeste's story her fingers toyed with the gold chain of her necklace.

Chapter 26

Celeste

Paris 1993

Celeste missed her play-fights with Gabriel in the kitchen and the bargains they struck to make up. He would take the trash out for a week if she would wear the lingerie he'd gotten her for her birthday. Or perhaps she'd flick flour at him and he'd ravish her right there on the kitchen floor as punishment. She missed their weekend mornings spent in bed. The simplicity of being home together with nothing to do. The way he'd brush his hand at her waist whenever he passed by.

She was excited for a real date night, finally. There were days when she felt she was losing him. First he'd stopped making their coffee in the mornings. Another few months passed and he stopped reading with her in the evenings, coming home long after bedtime. Gabriel didn't leave all at once. No. Just moment by moment it seemed. Those thoughts, when voiced, were always brushed aside as irrational. And on some level she knew he was right. Gabriel's hours at work resulted in her being alone often and that resulted in her feeling like he was disappearing when in reality he wasn't. Was he?

Still, she took great care in getting ready for their evening out together. Painstakingly, she curled her hair into a perfect mass of curls — just the way he liked it. Expertly she applied her make-up and dabbed on perfume that he could smell but wouldn't know where it had been applied until they got back to their bed. She put on her dress, careful not to ruffle her hair or touch her make-up, and wandered downstairs to find her shoes. She wanted to take his breath away. She wanted the validation of seeing his eyes alight with passion when he saw her.

~***~

Celeste and Gabriel sat two feet from each other, a candle on the table casting a romantic glow between them. It might as well have been two miles. It felt like a vast abyss separated them. It was as if shims had been placed between them over time, carefully moving them further apart until all those shims amassed an enormous wedge. She couldn't fault Gabriel. It wasn't him persé. It was them both and she knew that. She smiled lovingly at her handsome husband and reached for his hand. It was at least a small step to bridge the distance she felt. Gabriel covered her small hand with his much larger one. She took a shallow breath. The warmth of his hand heated her own.

He smiled at her warmly, one dimple gracing

his face. "Everything alright?"

"Yes," she sighed.

"Did I mention you look edible tonight?" he said, desire lacing his words.

"No," Celeste smirked at him and shook her head.

"You do, mon amour." Gabriel gave her hand a small squeeze. Celeste sighed as he ran his thumb rhythmically over her skin. The contact made her heart speed up. "So very delicious."

"Tell me, how is work going?"

That dimple appeared on his handsome face again. His eyes lit up and his smile reached ear to ear. "Fantastic," he gushed. "Very close to it all coming together now."

Their waiter arrived and set their plates in front of them. Gabriel released her hand to make room. Reluctantly, she slid her hand back across the table.

"Bon appétit," he said, his native tongue melting her heart.

Dinner was delicious and the movie they caught afterward had them laughing and quoting one-liners on the way home. It had been ages since they'd had such fun, shared such laughs. Gabriel's hand rested on her thigh the entire drive and she took joy in tracing the length and lines of his fingers. As they pushed through their front door laughing at each other's terrible celebrity impressions Celeste found herself happier than she had been in a long time. Perhaps they just needed to make time for more date nights together. Her full and warm heart boosted her mind-set and gave her a sense of peace.

Gabriel peeled back the blanket and crawled into bed next to her. She stared at the ceiling watching the moonlight shift the shadows around from the window. "What are you working on exactly?" She asked resolving that she wanted to be more invested in her husbands 'other' love.

Gabriel rolled to his side and ran a finger from her temple to her jaw. "Celeste you know I'm not allowed to talk about it."

"Oh come on, who would I tell, Gabriel?" she exasperated.

"Your father would have my head." His voice was firm.

She sighed and rolled her eyes at her husband. "I'm not going to tell my *dad* anything. I just feel like I don't understand what you're doing all day-why it's so important. Are you curing cancer?" she asked a playful hint in her voice.

Gabriel scoffed. "Hardly. It's much more devious than that. In 1960 the French government commissioned a team of biochemists to develop a biowarfare drug that would incapacitate, say, an opposing army or base of some sort."

Celeste gasped at his words. "Not to kill them Celeste, just keep them down long enough to infiltrate or acquire information. Basically something that worked to paralyze their bodies yet keep their minds and speech functioning.

"In 1967 they had run animal trials successfully for years so the government sanctioned a human trial. It was a blind study. They contaminated the water at a small restaurant in some remote location in Spain. It failed. Horribly, actually. Everyone who was at the restaurant died. Well, almost; there was one survivor. But after that, the program was shut down. Obviously."

Celeste worked to wrap her mind around his words. "Jesus Gabriel. They killed people?" she said shocked. "I don't understand . . . how does this tie in to what you're working on?"

"Celeste, I'm really not sanctioned to tell you more. I've said too much already."

Celeste pouted. "I just want to understand better. It's not really the details I want, it's just . . . I want to understand what you spend all your time on. Why it matters." She gave him a pleading look. Their night was going so well. Her spirits boosted, soul light. She didn't want top-secret information. She hoped her expression conveyed to him that she was just . . .

trying. Trying to be more invested. Trying to understand his passion. Trying. Gabriel held her eyes. She could see his mind turning over whether or not to give in. "We've been testing the survivor's DNA for years now trying to determine what the key was. We're so close. I can taste it, mon amour. If we can alter the original drug so that it performs the way it was meant—my God Celeste, we'd be rich." He kissed her jaw and nibbled her earlobe. His dedication to his work was obvious in his passionate rambling.

"We are rather wealthy already," she pointed out wrapping her arms around him. Celeste didn't care about money or material things. She felt like she'd already won just having Gabriel in her life. She just had to be strong until his work was completed. They'd have more time together then.

"The kind of wealth I'm talking about is different. Governments would kill for this drug. It would change the way wars are fought. My name would be legendary. It would be a major breakthrough." Gabriel rolled on top of her and stared down at her, eyes hungry.

"It sounds dangerous," she breathed. He dipped his head and stole her breath with a kiss.

"It is. Then again, any work with any government has the ability to be dangerous."

"Are you working with French government?"

she asked wriggling out of her pajama pants.

"No, no mon amour," he answered between kisses he trailed down her chest.

"Are you testing on people Gabriel?" The thought was blurted before she could stop it.

His head popped up, above her navel and he stared at her. She couldn't quite decipher his expression. "Please, there is no need to worry about my work. We're not doing anything we aren't supposed to. Everything is by the book," he answered.

"Well I'd hope so. How many died?" she asked. He stared blankly at her. "At the restaurant?" she said.

"Oh. I don't know . . . thirty-two maybe," he answered. Celeste pushed up on her elbows, eyes wide. "My God, Gabriel, how did that never make the news? History? How were all those deaths explained? Those poor families," she said her voice full of sorrow for the people affected.

"Celeste, my beautiful wife," he kissed her forehead. "I suspect that governments can and will cover up anything they want. It was a long time ago. It's not for us to worry about." His head dipped to the spot where her shoulder and neck met and he bit lightly. A great sigh escaped her and she sunk back into the bed as Gabriel continued his plight down her torso. "Let me give you something *better* to worry about." He smirked up at her and spread her legs wider. She pushed aside her thoughts of deaths, drugs and governments, swatted at his head, laughed, and let her husband do as he pleased.

Chapter 27

Annabelle

"after the bliss has long ended-this caution this fault, give me a breeze that's long winded."
~ Exhausted, Foo Fighters

Mark drove, one hand on the wheel, the other holding her hand. Annabelle smiled. She thought about her parents. Would they be at home to greet her, to wish her congratulations, to offer a hug? She was nervous.

"Congrats again babe," Mark said throwing the truck in park. She still hadn't told him it wasn't her house. She always waved him off and waited until he pulled away to walk a few doors down to hers. She didn't know why exactly. At first she didn't want her parents seeing her get dropped off, but today, it felt like something more.

"Thanks," she answered. Mark leaned across the cab to her, his face hovering just inches from hers.

"Annabelle," he said.

"Yes."

"I'm going to kiss you now." One hand slid around the back of her neck and tugged, closing the distance between their lips. When they met, she stilled at the sensation. She wasn't inexperienced but Mark's kiss felt unlike all the previous ones she'd received. It was warm, gentle and flawless. Unspoiled by a bad attitude or grief or sorrow. She let herself go and gave into the moment, feeling the high of it. When he finally pulled away she was breathless, dazed, content and full.

"We should do that again," she said. Mark's laugh filled the cab of the truck as he hugged her. He kissed the top of her head.

"We will," he answered. "Talk to you later on?"

"Definitely." She hopped out of the truck and waved Mark off as he pulled away.

When his taillights disappeared she walked three houses down to hers and climbed the front steps. The answer to all of her earlier questions about her parents was: no. The house was dark and silent when she arrived and she was glad she wasn't dumb enough to get her hopes up. After reading the note taped to the fridge door, saying her mother was at the country club at some meeting, she headed straight for her room. She noticed her father in his office as she walked by. She didn't bother to stop. What was the point?

~***~

Annabelle tossed and turned. It was well after

midnight and despite all the tricks she could think of to try, she couldn't trick herself into falling asleep. The disappointment of her parents missing her graduate coursed through her. She kicked the blankets off and stared at the ceiling. In the silence, a sudden sound rang out. *Tink. Tink. Tink.* Annabelle swung her legs over the edge of the bed, irritated, and walked to the window. *Tink. Tink. Tink.* She brushed the curtain aside. Squinting, she peered out the window.

Mark.

Standing under a tree, Mark smiled. His teeth almost glowed in the moonlight. He bowed in her direction before holding up a wrapped box toward her. Annabelle stifled a giggle. What was he doing here? She held up a finger to indicate she needed a minute. He nodded and sat at the base of the tree.

She tugged on yoga pants under her nightshirt and carefully opened the window. It squeaked when it got to a certain point. She threw one leg out and found her footing on the trellis before swinging her other leg out too.

"What are you doing?" Mark whisper yelled.

"Coming out."

"Are you too cool for the door?" he asked.

"Shhh."

Annabelle jumped down the last two feet and

landed with a soft thud in the dewy grass.

"What are *you* doing here?" she asked.

Mark ran a hand through his hair and smiled at her before looking at the ground. "I couldn't sleep. I kept thinking about how disappointed you looked and I wanted to do something about it."

"How'd you even know where I live?"

"I know you wait for me to drive off before walking here. I can still see you in my rearview." Annabelle squeezed her eyes shut, embarrassed. "Figuring out which window was yours was the tough part."

"How many rocks did you have to throw?"

Mark laughed and shook his head. "Come here," he said pulling on the front of her shirt. The look in his eyes had Annabelle's heart stumbling in her chest. She moved toward him, but only a little. He pulled her closer still. She reached out and traced a finger from jaw to neck to shoulder and down his stomach. He was so much harder than she expected. Like all his muscles were right on the surface. He sucked a breath in through his teeth at the contact as her fingers hooked the waistline of his jeans and hung there.

"I got you something."

Annabelle looked up at him. When she didn't take the present, he took her hand and pressed the box into it. The present was wrapped in sparkling paper, Annabelle's favorite kind, celestial stars glittered in gold against a black background. She took the package from him and lead him away from the house. She didn't want to risk getting caught.

She led Mark through the backyard until they reached the treehouse that had long been abandoned, but that she thought should still be able to hold them. She watched as he looked up into the tree.

"Ahh," he gave her a sideways glance. "You sure this will hold us?"

Annabelle shrugged. "Let's find out." She tucked the box into the waistband of her yoga pants and started climbing the ladder. Mark followed behind.

Brushing aside some stray leaves and dust she sat on the floor Indian-style. Mark did the same. She tore the paper from the box and opened the lid. A gold nautical compass pendant sat nestled in velvet.

"It's queer," he said. Annabelle shook her head. "It's perfect. It's beautiful," she said. "Thank you."

"Will you wear it?" he asked. Annabelle nodded.

"Will you help?"

Mark grinned and nodded. He took the

necklace out of the box and carefully fastened it around her neck. Maybe that's why he bought it, so they'd have this moment, with his hands warm on the back of her neck, under her hair. He ran his fingertips along the chain and settled the pendant on her throat. She shivered.

"I can't really picture you as a treehouse kind of kid."

"I wasn't," she sighed. She laid down on her back. Mark scooted next to her and followed suit. His warm hand enveloped hers as they stared silently up at the endless, star-littered sky. She didn't feel disappointed anymore.

~***~

Annabelle's mother breezed in through the front door wearing a fitted white skirt and a tailored black blouse. Her hair was swept up in a loose knot and she wore a little superficial smirk at the corner of her full lips.

"Monica!" her father roared from his office. Annabelle startled from the den where she was curled on the couch watching TV. The sound of her mother's heels clacked on the hardwood as she waltzed through the den to her father's office. She muted the TV and watched her parents instead.

Both her mother's and her father's mouths were tight and firmly shut, as if they were using all their willpower to contain their anger from exploding out, able only to stay composed for the moment. Her father's nostrils flared, his chest heaved. Her mother crossed her arms over her chest and leaned against the door jam.

"What happened?" her father asked. Annabelle shifted her position on the couch to get a better view. She needed to know what was going on.

"What?" her mother spit out curtly.

"I waited at the restaurant for an hour. I texted. I called. Where the hell have you been?" her father boomed.

"My phone's on silent. I was at the club," her mother stated. Her posture changed then. Slumped slightly, her mother let out an audible sigh. She pushed from the doorframe and took a step into the office. A step toward her father.

"Don't." Her father raised his hand. Her mother froze where she was. Her father ran his hands through his hair and looked straight up, something he always did when thinking deeply.

"Gavin, I'm sorry," her mother offered quietly, her head hung as she stared at the floor.

"Sorry? It's our *anniversary*," her father said, the hurt evident in his voice.

Her mother snorted. "Yes, what a joyous thing," she offered dryly. Her father's eyes grew dark and narrowed. He stood from his desk and marched up to her mother, fuming.

Annabelle silently pushed off the couch and tiptoed out of the den toward her room. She could already hear their yelling as she moved through the hallway. Her parents were crumbling under the weight of their bitterness. A knot formed in her gut and she wanted nothing more than to bury her head under her pillow and forget about this week.

~***~

Jezebel waited in her usual spot for Annabelle. She had her nose in a book and a fan in the window blowing in the warm early summer air.

"Whatcha reading?" Annabelle greeted. She dropped her bag to the floor near the door and kicked off her flip-flops before sitting. She felt lighter in Jezebel's presence. No bitterness or grief assaulted her here. Two glasses of water waited on the table. She picked one up and took a sip.

Jezebel looked over the top of her book at Annabelle. "The Other Typist."

"Any good?"

"It's a total mind-fuck—so yes, it's brilliant."

"Maybe I'll borrow it when you're done."

Jezebel dog-eared her page and shut the book, setting it on a side table. Annabelle picked at a hangnail on her middle finger and bit her lip.

"Kid?" Jezebel said.

"Jez, did you ever forget your wedding anniversary?" Annabelle asked while still studying her cuticles.

"Never! It's a sacred day between married people. It doesn't mean you have to celebrate it grandly, but it should most certainly be noticed and revered," Jezebel answered.

Annabelle nodded her head in agreement. In years past her parents always did something together. Her mother had once told her, when she was little and wanted to celebrate with them, that it was a private day for the mom and the dad to remind each other of their commitment and renew their love. She'd cried, feeling left out when their parents spent an overnight at a hotel that year.

"Yeah," she said blandly.

"You're dismal today," Jezebel said. Annabelle snapped her eyes up.

"Yeah. Just a long week I guess, but not all bad," she answered.

"Tell me the good then." Jezebel settled deeper into her chair, making herself comfortable.

"Mark kissed me," she breathed, recalling the memory of his lips on hers, how he'd kissed her goodnight and cupped her butt as she started back up the trellis to her room.

"Finally," Jezebel said with barely concealed amusement. "When I told him to be a gentleman I didn't mean be a prude!" Annabelle laughed loudly, a grin taking over her features. "Well . . . don't just sit there looking starry-eyed — details!" Jezebel exclaimed.

"Well, we were in his truck. Mark leaned across the cab. 'Annabelle' he said. I said 'Yes,' and then he was all . . . 'I'm going to kiss you now.'" Annabelle sighed, happy. "It was tender and flawless. When he pulled away I was breathless." Jezebel pushed her sleeves up her forearms and leaned her elbows on her knees.

Jezebel waited. "And . . ." Annabelle didn't want to finish her story, but she knew she didn't really have much say on the matter around Jezebel.

"And then like a fool I blurted out 'We should do that again.'" Annabelle flushed and buried her face in her hands.

"Brava! Did you?" Jezebel asked.

"He said, 'We will,' and then I got out of the truck. Why am I such an idiot around him?"

"You're not! He probably thinks you're just about the most adorable thing to ever land in his lap. Trust me." Jezebel stated. Annabelle shook her head in protest but smiled at the thought.

"Trust . . . you," Annabelle deadpanned.

"Well, I do see him more often than you,"

Jezebel countered with a sly expression. Annabelle chuckled. Jezebel was always one step ahead of her. But she didn't know about the treehouse and for an unknown reason, she didn't want Jezebel to know. She kept that moment to herself.

"You're so infuriating sometimes," Annabelle commented playfully. "I can never beat you."

"You can't beat someone at their own game, dear."

Annabelle stifled a laugh and surrendered. "Let's just move along, yeah?"

"To Celeste?"

"Yes . . . to Celeste," she answered.

Chapter 28

Celeste

Paris 1994

"Cece?" Matteo's deep voice came through the receiver. Celeste smiled.

"Matteo, hi," she greeted. She propped her hip against the kitchen counter and twirled the cord through her fingers.

"Have you spoken with Dr. B?"

"Not since I left yesterday. Why?" she questioned.

"Can you stop over at my office this morning on your way to work?"

"Matteo, you're scaring me. What's wrong?" Celeste's fingers stilled, the cord dropping from them. Gabriel strode into the kitchen and fixed himself a mug of coffee. He stopped and gave Celeste an 'everything-ok?'look. She shrugged in response.

"He left me the strangest message last night on my work answering machine."

She breathed a sigh of relief. "So?" Looking to Gabriel she nodded that things seemed fine. He leaned in, kissed her temple and scooped up his briefcase as he breezed out of the kitchen and headed to work.

"Cece, just come here. Listen. Please," Matteo pleaded. Celeste would never say no to Matteo when he sounded so bewildered and nervous.

"Of course, give me forty minutes. I need to throw clothes on," she answered.

Matteo exhaled a relief-filled sigh. "Thank you."

Celeste tossed clothes out of her way, shirts and pants flying out the closet door behind her. She grabbed the pair of jeans she was looking for and tugged them on one leg and a time, doing a little hopping dance to get them up over her hips. She and Gabriel really needed to do laundry this week. Their closet was a sad affair at the moment. Grabbing a white button-up shirt she stepped out of the closet and addressed each button as she walked down the hall and descended the stairs. Slipping her feet into clogs she snatched her purse from the console table by the front door and left for Matteo's.

Carly Simon and James Taylor songs kept her company as she made the twenty minute drive. They also helped her mind not to wander. Matteo was never riled up. Matteo was solid, calm and rational. The waver in his voice had her stomach twisted up with worry. She was anxious. She doubled parked behind his car and bolted from the car into his office where she found Matteo pacing.

"Cece, thank God," he said. Three powerful strides brought him just short of her. His arms engulfed her in a hug. A tight, scared hug.

"You're kind of freaking me out Matteo, what's going on?" she asked looking up at him as he dropped his arms.

"Come on." She followed him to his office and motioned for her to sit. She did. He pushed play on the answering machine and Dr. B's voice filled the cozy room.

"Teo, Teo, Teo, I've stumbled across something." Papers shuffled in the background. "It's rather urgent that you get to Celeste. Please." Dr. B's voice shook as he spoke and Celeste winced. He sounded rushed and scared. "There are things . . . many things I should have told her . . . told you. I suspected for years . . . but the impossibility . . . such an impossibility . . ."

The message cut off, the room silent again. Celeste sat confused and staring at the machine. What was Dr. B going on about? His message made no sense.

She looked to Matteo. "I don't understand." And she didn't.

"Neither do I. I was hoping he called you, too. That maybe you knew what was going on. In nine years Cece, I've never heard that man's voice quake once. Something is wrong."

"Let's go then."

"I have a parrot arriving any moment for its annual exam." Matteo frowned. He was clearly conflicted. Despite the mood, Celeste smiled.

"Damn parrots." She grinned. "Alright, I'll go and I'll call you with news if you haven't arrived by the time I figure all this out." She stood as Matteo rounded his desk before embracing her.

"Okay," he answered. "Okay."

"Relax Matteo, I'm sure everything is fine." Matteo ran his fingers through his hair then tugged an earlobe. It was his go-to habit when he was stressed out. He kissed her cheek and sent her off without another word.

Celeste threw her bag and herself inside her car and started the engine. The thirty minute drive was thirty minutes too long. Her mind wandered and her heart raced. Matteo was right, she'd never heard that particular panic in Dr. B's voice before and it worried her. It worried her deeply. Her stomach swarmed with anxiety.

When she arrived at the estate she slammed the brakes so hard the car skidded to a halt. Celeste killed the engine and jogged to the front door. She mentally berated herself for the frenzy she was creating. Surely she'd be laughed at by Dr. B as soon as she waltzed through the door.

On a deep breath she pushed through the kitchen entrance. The house was quiet. The tea kettle whistled on the burner. Her panic grew. She switched the burner off and began frantically calling out Dr. B's name.

Chapter 29

Annabelle

"And I ever want, Is just a little love."
~ Toes, Glass Animal

Annabelle groaned. "You can't stop there."

"Sorry kiddo, the clock says otherwise," Jezebel stated before stretching her legs. A quick glance at the clock confirmed Jezebel was right. *Damn.* "You wouldn't want to miss your moment with Mark would you?" Jezebel added.

"Har har," she returned dryly as she stood and stretched. Annabelle collected her things before stepping into the hall. She paused and looked over her shoulder at Jezebel.

"Thank you," she said.

Jezebel stiffened slightly, something flashing in her eyes. Disbelief maybe? Or was it mirth? "For what?"

"For . . ." Annabelle wracked her brain for the right word, "everything." She didn't wait for Jezebel's response as she headed to the parking lot and a waiting Mark.

Mark scanned her head to toe as she approached him. She breathed in and inhaled his scent as a thrill shot straight into her stomach. She wrapped her arms around his waist and hugged him tight. Pulling back slightly to look at her he reached out and caressed her lips with his fingertips. She stared at his mouth, thinking how amazing it would feel to have his lips move with hers again.

"Kiss me," she whispered hoarsely.

"Yes, ma'am," Mark said with barely concealed amusement.

Annabelle closed her eyes, imagining what she might do if Mark were to suddenly kiss her neck or *other* places. Her knees felt weak at the thought. Butterflies took flight in her belly. He intertwined their fingers and it seemed like such a natural fit; and imagining what his fingers would feel like caressing her skin almost caused her pants to incinerate in a cloud of ash. His lips were warm and moist as they pressed to hers. The kiss felt as natural as their hands felt twined together. She leaned into him and let herself get lost in an utterly perfect moment of bliss.

~***~

The sound of a whistling tea kettle drove Annabelle toward the kitchen. Obviously her mother was already up and about this morning. She lifted the kettle from the stove and turned off the burner. Her mind was spinning at how similar this particular situation was to Dr. B's in Jezebel's story. Helping herself to a cup, she added a sprinkling of sugar and a touch of honey. She leaned up against the counter and slowly sipped at her tea and wondered, if she put the kettle back on the stove, how many minutes of whistling it would take before her mother heard it. Before she went through with the ludicrous idea, a blur of movement outside the kitchen window arrested her attention.

Her mother moved across the yard, a lost look plaguing her face. The back door squeaked. Her mother had been after her father for months to fix it. Clearly he hadn't. Annabelle turned to find her mother entering the kitchen. Things were unbearably tense between her parents lately. It was obvious they hadn't spoken since their fight last week. In fact, she didn't think they had spoken a single word to each other since it happened. The habit of burying things instead of resolving them was going to have severe consequences on their family soon. She could feel it in the air, wrought with tension.

"Want me to fix you a cup?" Annabelle asked. She watched her mother stride to the bar and perch on one of the stools.

"Alright." For a long time her mother stared around the room, seemingly without seeing anything.

Annabelle shifted from one foot to the other. Her mother's stiff posture and her refusal to make eye contact with her did not signify anything good. She smiled anyway as she fixed her mother a cup. Setting it down her mother gave her a weak smile that didn't reach her eyes. Annabelle shuddered involuntarily as her thoughts drifted to dark musings—her family living under the same roof but existing in two different worlds.

~***~

Summer was in full force. At least the heat was anyway. Annabelle swiped at the back of her knees before she plopped into the chair opposite Jezebel.

"My mom's freaking me out," Annabelle blurted.

Jezebel raised an eyebrow.

"Care to elaborate? Hi, how are ya?"

Annabelle huffed as she sank down into her seat and explained the strange behavior her mother exhibited over the last week. The distance. The lost look on her face. The casual indifference that rolled off her. "They've been married for like twenty friggin' years . . . Why now is everything falling apart? I don't understand!" she finished, anger rolling off her in great waves. She twisted her back to the side and let out a small grunt of pain-pleasure as it loudly popped.

"The difference between men and women in marriage is this: a woman marries a man thinking he'll change, but he doesn't. He won't.

A *man* marries a woman thinking she won't ever change, but she *does*. Sometimes, those things can't be reconciled after so many years. You're family has also suffered a great loss Annabelle. That changes people and it takes time to have enough courage to accept that."

"I don't think either of them have accepted that. They've barely been parents, let alone partners, for years." She seethed.

"What exactly do you want from your mother?" Jezebel asked as she floated across the room and turned the fan in the window up a notch. Annabelle welcomed the steady breeze.

"A mom is supposed to know everything about her kids. Dentist appointments, crushes, best friends, favorite foods, secret fears and hopes and dreams. Right? My mom knows none of that. But you Jez, you *do.* You're more motherly to me than she's even tried to be in the last eight years."

Jezebel's eyes popped open wide and studied Annabelle as she returned to her chair. "That is quite the compliment, sweet beet."

Annabelle shrugged before she slumped into her seat. "It's true though. Somehow in like four months you've done more to . . ."

She wasn't sure what exactly. "Heal me? Guide me? I don't know, but it's leaps and bounds more than my own parents have accomplished in the last eight years."

"I like you kid, it's too bad our time is running out. It'll be difficult for me when you're gone," Jezebel said. She turned her face away, admiring the flowers on the windowsill.

"Me too," Annabelle answered, fidgeting; she didn't know what else to do with herself in the moment. She hadn't even considered Jezebel's point before. This would all end and she'd have what, *who?* Struggling to grasp the thought, she shoved them down to the pit of her belly and changed the subject. "Tell me about Dr. B."

Jezebel regarded her for a moment before she nodded her head. Wisps of her hair bobbed in the breeze as she did so. "Paris, nineteen ninety-four," Jezebel started.

Chapter 30

Celeste

Paris 1994

Celeste entered Dr. B's study and let out a sonic boom of a scream. Her arms fell like dead weight to her sides and her knees buckled. Dr. B was slumped at an awkward position in his chair behind his desk. His hands rested on the arms of the chair, but his head hung listlessly to the right. The phone receiver hovered just above the floor. The obnoxious tell-tale *beep-beep-beep* gave away its off-the-hook status. His skin, pale gray. Eyes open. An unopened envelope stuck beneath the wheel of his desk chair. When she was finally able to, she stood up, walked on shell-shocked feet toward the phone and depressed the release button before picking up the receiver. The dial tone reminded her of her goal. She dialed the police.

The house was eerily quiet. The weekday staff always had Saturdays off at Dr. B's insistence. He made it clear he could fend for himself one day of the week. That never stopped Tilda, the head chef, from making sure there were ample re-heatable meals stocked in the fridge in her absence.

Within the hour the house was swarming with paramedics, police officers, and crime scene technicians. The eerie quiet replaced with loud static radio bleeps, tape being ripped and gum snapping. As she watched everyone take statements and collect evidence, she closed her eyes and tears poured down her face. How could this be?

~***~

His light scent wafted around her, igniting her senses. Unlike the heavy masculine cologne her husband wore, Matteo smelled of filterless cigarettes and summer breezes. A gentle hand on her shoulder roused her from her thoughts. It was comforting in the moment, familiar and safe. She inhaled hard and met Matteo's eyes. Grief pummeled her.

"He was fine on Friday," she choked out through her tears. Matteo swept her into a tight embrace, his own tears soaking her blouse at the shoulder. "What's going to happen? The estate? All the employees?" Celeste asked, her voice muted in Matteo's chest.

"I don't know fiore mio. We should call Bourassa." Celeste nodded into his chest. Of course they would have to let Dr. B's attorney know. She pulled away from Matteo and looked into his red-rimmed eyes. What a pair they must look like right now.

"We should do that sooner than later,"

Matteo stated. His voice quivered, breaking at the last word just slightly.

"Do you think he was in pain? Panicked? Oh, God, Teo—his phone call to you, do you think he knew he was dying?" she cried out, unsure if she truly wanted to know the answer.

Matteo smoothed her hair, tucking it behind her ear. She leaned into his palm as fresh tears presented themselves. He nodded and shrugged. Of course he knew no more than she did. His thumb swept back and forth over the apple of her cheek. Celeste swiped the falling tears away and looked around. She needed a purpose. Right now. She ticked off a mental check list call the house staff, Dr. B's lawyer Taylor Bourassa, and Gabriel, and start putting together an obituary and funeral arrangements. With a heavy heart she took a deep breath determined to do something. First up, find the doctor's address book. Weak and lightheaded, she stumbled. Matteo steadied her.

"Sit. I'll grab his contact book and we can do this together," he offered. Celeste planted her rear in the chair nearest the phone, thankful for Matteo.

~***~

Celeste watched as Gabriel's stomach rose and fell, the occasional snore sounding through the silence. She couldn't sleep. His skin had such a beautiful glow to it. It almost shimmered in the moonlight. She looked away, to the window, and wondered what Monday would bring.

Gabriel had left work immediately and driven all the way out to the estate to be with Celeste, knowing how much her employer's death would affect her. He and Matteo had taken over the difficult tasks of phoning people to deliver the bad news. She had tried but failed miserably to do so herself, her sobs and hiccups and sniffles preventing her from forming coherent words.

She looked to Gabriel again, envious that he could sleep so soundly right now. She wanted nothing more than respite from her aching heart and sorrow-filled thoughts. The world had lost an amazing man today and the loss cut her deeply. Dr. B's message on Matteo's answering machine replayed on an endless loop in her thoughts. His death didn't sit right with her. Something seemed wrong with the whole thing. She couldn't find anything alarming of course. He *was* old. But his message held such an air of importance to it. She needed to figure it out. She needed closure.

Chapter 31

Annabelle

"Hanging so high for your return, But the stillness is a burn"
~ Infinity, The XX

She couldn't sleep. Annabelle curled her legs to her chest and reached for the framed photograph that sat on the corner of her nightstand. She stared at it longingly in the moonlight. Finally she sat up in bed; in the darkness with nothing but the moon casting silver beams on her wall, stood and stretched her body, and started pacing her room. Something was wrong. She could feel it. Her gut clenched as heat—so hot it felt cold—spread throughout her chest. She treaded silently into her bathroom and rummaged around the medicine cabinet until she found what she was looking for. Popping the little white pill that had provided her with relief from panic in the past, she ground it between her teeth before she headed back to her bed.

To say that Annabelle was dog-tired was an understatement. She and sleep were at odds. She walked into the kitchen, still in her pajamas, and glanced around. Two envelopes rested on the countertop. Her brow furrowed and she fought a wave of nausea. Her mother's graceful cursive was plain as day on each envelope. *Gavin* was scrawled on one; the other read *Annabelle*. She picked hers up and noted that for something so small it seemed to weigh so much.

Belle,

You're much too young, even still, to understand the delicate workings of life and intimate relationships.

There are things you don't know. Things you will never know about your father and me. Things a child shouldn't know about their parents.

I'm sorry. I am so sorry. You will never grasp how much I love you and your brother.

I've tried and tried for years.

I'm tired Belle, so tired. And I'm so sorry for leaving you. But I have to.

I can't cope. I can't grieve here. I can't move forward and I need to. I need to so badly.

I was naive to think we could walk away and have it all.

I should have known better. I should have realized. I didn't though and now—now, I have to do what's best for me.

Sometimes we're too far gone to fix

what's broken.
I love you,
Mom

What. The. Hell.

Annabelle read the letter again and still had the same reaction. Her mother was lost. The more her mind churned over the contents, the more her stomach twisted with confusion and doubt. Gone. Abandoning her and her father. It felt as though someone had punched her in the gut. She struggled to catch a breath. Unshed tears burned her eyes. Why now? What would this solve? Annabelle's questions wouldn't likely ever be answered and that made her stomach ache even more.

She stomped from the kitchen, anger and hurt boiling within, to her father's office. Flinging the letter at him she crossed her arms in front of her chest and leaned against the door jam. Her father ran his hands through his hair and looked straight up, his usual position of deep reflection. Something he did when deep in thought. She was beginning to hate that habit.

"Belle," he started. Annabelle looked at him, exhaled slowly, and sent him a pleading look, but she didn't speak; she was afraid to shatter the silence. "Your mother . . .." His voice faltered, and Annabelle suddenly realized that her father was just as hurt as she was. "She just needs time," he said firmly with a succinct nod of his head.

"You didn't even open your letter!" She didn't care if she shouted. She didn't care if he couldn't face it just yet.

"I don't need to." He cast his eyes downward.

Annabelle didn't agree, but if her father needed to hold out hope, who was she to tell him differently? Irritated and angry and confused Annabelle bolted. She took nothing but what was already on her and just ran—out of her house and down her street. Neighbors shot funny looks at her as she ran, tears streaming down her face, in no particular direction. By the time she stopped to catch her breath and take in her surroundings, she was a good three miles from home and only two streets over from Mark's apartment. She'd not been able to see it yet, but he'd showed her pictures and knew the address. Grounding and punishment be damned-she strode purposefully to his building and rang his bell.

~***~

Mark expertly sliced through the skin of a ripe avocado. "You're sure everything's alright?" he asked, popping a chunk of avocado into his mouth. Cutting an avocado seemed so trivial. She'd shown up in pajamas, tear stained and refused to really dive into what was wrong. She was doing to Mark what her parents did to each other, and it made her skin crawl.

"No. No, it's not," she answered finally. Mark was to her in three decisive strides. He pulled her to his chest and rested his chin on top of her head. "Tell me," he said.

Annabelle didn't hesitate. She explained her fairytale childhood right up until her brother died. Then she explained a Grimm's Brothers-sounding tale about the years since then. She realized he didn't judge or comment or criticize as she spun her story. He simply listened. It was truly the only thing she needed right in the moment and she felt a warm feeling bloom in her chest.

"Annabelle, I'm so sorry. Things sound pretty messed up."

"Yeah," she answered solemnly. She pushed the heels of her hands into her eyes attempting to relieve the building pressure.

"Should I bring you home? Your dad is probably worried sick by now."

"No, Mark. Not tonight." She rested her palm against his face gently. "Tonight I'm staying here. Tomorrow I'll go home."

She needed him. Annabelle needed whatever he could offer her until she left for school. He distracted her from life—which was more than she could ask for. Mark left her for less than a minute while he ran back to his room. He returned holding up a clean pair of his boxer shorts and one of his t-shirts. Annabelle grinned.

~***~

Annabelle entered Jezebel's suite with a heavy heart. Her father was still in some state of blissful denial but she knew better; her mother wouldn't be coming home—ever. She sunk into her chair and kicked off her shoes. Tucking her feet up into the chair with her, she took slow, purposeful breaths to calm herself. She didn't want to lose it, again, now.

"How goes it?" Jezebel asked as she made her way to her chair.

"It sucks," she answered.

"Doesn't it always?" Jezebel quipped.

"This time it *really* sucks," she grumbled.

"Care to share?"

"My mom . . . left." Her voice broke on the last word.

"Left where?"

Anger, red-hot, rushed through her. "Jez— I'm not in the mood. She left, left me, left my dad . . . left the family. She's gone."

Jezebel stilled. Then, "Oh, dear, that *does* suck."

Annabelle bristled. "That's all you have to say?"

"What would you like me to say? I'm so

sorry? Would that be comforting? Was it such a shock really? She seemed so miserable."

"She was, but . . ."

"But what, kiddo?"

"But she just gave up. I'm . . . I'm angry. She took the coward's way out."

"Ahh, there we have it."

"Have what?" Annabelle fumed.

"The root of the issue. You're angry." Jezebel nodded. "You're disappointed in her, but the act itself isn't surprising to you. You felt it coming."

"Yeah. I guess. She was a shadow that sulked around mostly. If she just talked, if any of us had just talked . . ."

"You can't live your life with maybes . . . maybe if you talked things would be different, maybe they wouldn't. You will never know the answer to those questions so it's best to just take it for what it is and move on," Jezebel said while giving her a pointed look.

"I hate you sometimes, you must know that, right?"

Jezebel laughed at her statement. "I suspect love and hate are so similar that it's hard to tell the difference sometimes, yes."

"That's not exactly what I was saying."

"Oh, but my dear, it was. You hate me because I make you face the ugly truths in your world, yet you love me for the very same reason. Even the darkness of night brings the promise of daybreak. You're a good girl. You'll find your way."

"I stayed at Mark's the other night. My dad was furious when I came home the next day but you know what? I didn't really care. They've forced these rules and punishments on me and for what? I told him I'm done with my grounding. I respect what their goal was so I still won't go out, but I will have people over and I get my phone and laptop back."

"Taking a stand! I like it." Jezebel cheered.

"Yeah, well, my dad didn't."

"Par for the course, don't you think?"

Annabelle shrugged. It probably was, but what was he going to do about it? "I need to know what Dr. B's lawyer had to say."

"Right on." Jezebel grinned accepting her obvious topic change. "Paris, nineteen ninety-four."

Chapter 32

Celeste

Paris 1994

Taylor Bourassa was a short and squat man. He was balding at the top of his head and he attempted to hide that fact with a hideous comb-over. "The last person to see Dr. Basle alive was one Monique Watson," Taylor said.

Celeste stilled. She most certainly did *not* hear him right.

"That's impossible," she breathed. "How would they even know each other? That's . . . I would have known." Celeste looked to Matteo who looked equally lost. Matteo stood and snatched the police report from Taylor's hand. His eyes scanned the report, widened and slid up to hers.

"It's true. Tilda said that before she left Friday night she let Monique Watson in to visit with Leo." He handed the report to Celeste. She carefully read the words stated on the page but none of it made any sense to her. Surely Dr. B would have told her if he was friends with her husband's assistant. He would know. He would have told her. Celeste's stomach burned.

"Why would she visit him?" she murmured

more to herself than anyone else.

"Perhaps we can address that after we go through Leo's will. I'm glad both of you could make it today as he spoke very highly of you two and left you both a great deal."

Matteo and Celeste's heads snapped up in unison. "What?" Celeste asked.

"Of course he left certain things to different staff members with whom I will schedule meetings over the next week, but you two were the primary benefactors. As you may be aware, Leo Basle Germain had no living relatives." Celeste's brow scrunched up. *Germain?* She looked again to Matteo but he appeared as confused as she did — again. "Basle wasn't his last name?" Matteo asked, stupefied.

"No. Dr. Germain changed his last name, legally, to his middle name, Basle, in 1967. I've represented him since 1965. I assure you there are probably a great many things you do not know about our late friend, but in an effort to quickly and succinctly execute his estate, I'd appreciate it if you held all questions until the end." Taylor paused before pressing on, leaving no room for argument.

Matteo's hand reached out and clasped hers. She squeezed back and refocused her attention to Taylor.

"What I am at liberty to tell you isn't much," Taylor said. "But he came to France for a consulting job with a team of other scientists and doctors. He was married and had a grown daughter, also married. He also had a granddaughter that he raved about." Taylor's face lit up as he recalled the memory. "That little girl just adored him and vice versa. In 1967, his wife, daughter, son-in-law and granddaughter were found dead after a nasty virus from something they ate, or so they speculated."

Celeste broke into a round of fresh tears. *Poor Dr. B.*

"He was devastated, of course, and due to the nature of his work and his personal family tragedy, he opted to change his name and remove himself from the public eye. Which he did with flare." Taylor drew a deep breath. "Celeste, Leo's wishes state very clearly that you are to inherit half of the estate." Taylor looked to Matteo. "And you Matteo, the other half."

"I will of course send you a list of possessions that he has willed to other employee's who he was close with. Those will be theirs to take. The value of the house, land and stables is to be split between the two of you. You may choose to sell but it is not a stipulation in the will."

Celeste blinked hard, squeezing her eyes closed tightly before snapping them back open. The entire estate? That was worth more than her family was. An unfathomable amount, even at only half. She didn't want it. She didn't want

~ 361 ~

any of it without Dr. B around to enjoy it with. "It's too much," she said quietly. Her breath caught in her chest. Matteo nodded in agreement. She squeezed his hand hoping it would quell the tears streaming down her face. He squeezed hers back. It didn't stop the floodgates.

"It is indeed a lot, but it is also his final wish," Taylor stated.

After working through a hefty pile of paperwork, Celeste and Matteo left in daze. They parted ways with a hug and a promise to meet at Dr. B's the following day; they needed to pull some boxes down from the attic for some of the other employees. Celeste was overcome by the irrevocable loss of such a wonderful man. She longed for the warmth of her bed, the smell of the flowers outside her window, the feeling of beauty that used to ooze from her every pore. Everything felt dark and cold now. She couldn't wrap her mind around Dr. B's parting gift; granted he had no one else to leave his fortune to but a charity would have benefitted greatly from his wealth. Even dividing his assets among his employees would have greatly enhanced many lives.

Her heart felt heavy as she schlepped her way to her car. She wanted the comfort of her husband's arms around her. She wanted the comfort of his soft voice in her ear, consoling her. She popped in at home to call her mother and father. She would need a good lawyer to handle the wealth she was about to come into and her parents employed only the best. Her mother's calm voice aided in settling Celeste down and making her feel more composed. By the time she hung up with them she almost mustered a smile. Knowing that Gabriel would likely be working late she decided to drop in at the lab and see him. She craved the solace his embrace evoked. With a clear mind, she changed her clothes, ran a brush through her hair and touched up her make-up. Then she climbed into her car, headed for her husband.

Chapter 33

Annabelle

"Wish the best for you. Wish the best for me. Wished for infinity."
~ Infinity, The XX

"Gabriel is going to lose his shit," Annabelle laughed. "All that money, he's going to flip."

Jezebel gave her a curious look. "Do you think so?" Jezebel asked.

She took a sip of water from the glass set out for her before answering. "Yeah, I mean he wants globs of it and the notoriety that comes with it and here Celeste is about to go and give it to him and he doesn't even have to put in the work. She's about to make him the happiest man alive," she explained.

Jezebel studied her cuticles for a moment before bringing her gaze back to Annabelle's. Shrugging she said, "Sometimes, it isn't the money people dream of but being recognized for something that *brings* money with it."

"So he's going to be mad?" Annabelle asked.

"Not at all. I'm sure he wouldn't have been," Jezebel answered.

"What does that mean? He either was or

wasn't," she said, pushing Jezebel for an answer. Jezebel stroked the chain of her necklace softly. She looked at Annabelle but she didn't think she actually saw her. Her eyes were fixated on something far away.

"I think our time is up for today," Jezebel said.

Annabelle made a face and looked at the clock. "We have thirty minutes before I have to leave," she volleyed back.

"I have an appointment dear, have to cut our visit short," Jezebel said.

Annabelle watched her stand up and rummage through a drawer mumbling to herself. Irritated at Jezebel's clear dismissal she stood and scooped up her purse while jamming her feet into her shoes.

"Whatever, I'll see you next week," she said through gritted teeth.

"Yes, yes kiddo, next week," Jezebel called over her shoulder without looking at her. Annabelle rolled her eyes and stomped out of the suite and down the hall.

"Whoa!" Mark said and caught her by the arm as she attempted to stomp past him. "What's the issue?" he asked.

"Jezebel," she grumbled.

Mark laughed loudly, "What did she do this time?"

Annabelle shrugged. Nothing, she'd done nothing, not really. Annabelle was in a rotten mood in general and even her visit with Jezebel hadn't helped relieve that today. "Nothing. She did nothing," she said. Her shoulders slumped. Mark stuck his arms under her limp ones and lifted up and down. She pouted as he flapped her arms like wings.

"What are you doing?" she squawked.

"Making you look like a fool." She scrunched up her nose and stared at him, arms still flapping. Looking left, then right, she noted she *did* look like a fool. In the middle of the hall her arms flapped loosely and Mark stood facing her moving her arms like it was nothing. She tensed her arms and bore down trying to stop the movement but Mark was stronger. She gave up trying to push down as he thrust upward. Her arms jerked up and she squealed as her purse flew off her wrist. Mark raised one eyebrow at her. She wanted to scowl but he looked so adorable and she . . . she looked, so . . . ridiculous.

Annabelle let a huge grin consume her face and laughed. They stood there together flapping their arms and laughing until she couldn't breathe and tears formed in the corners of her eyes. In her peripheral vision she noticed Jezebel's head poking out from her room watching them with a grin.

~***~

Brant,

Hate to be the bearer of bad news but our mom is an asshole. I'm angry. I'm hurt. I'm about a thousand things that I can't even begin to express but I'm all of them. She left. Did you hear me . . . SHE LEFT!

She wrote Dad a note. A NOTE. Me too, actually. It pretty much said nothing. It just said-nothing. I'm sure the death of your child will drive you to do crazy things but seriously-eight freakin' years later? Why not right after you were taken from us? Why not that first year? Why try for so long only to give up and bail. What was the point of the last eight years?

I hate you right now, too. I hate you for leaving me here alone to deal with this. I hate . . .

As the sun finally sank over the horizon Annabelle was bored and restless. She sat cross-legged on her bed with her laptop open on her legs. She closed her computer and lay back on her bed. Emptying her mind, she slowed her breathing and focused only on the beating of her heart. It struck hard, almost audibly. She breathed deep again but the pounding only grew louder. Groaning she raised a hand to forehead and called out, "Go away!"

"Belle, love, it's me, can I come in?" her father said in his most ingratiating voice. Of course it was him, who else would it be? *Her mother?* she scoffed silently. What a joke.

"Why?" she answered. She heard him try to laugh but the sound didn't come out quite right.

"Belle, yes or no? Are you decent?" Annabelle laughed, low and throaty, at his question.

"Yeah Dad, I'm decent," she called out and promptly rolled her eyes.

The door yawned open and her father stepped over the threshold. She tilted her head to the side and her dark hair fell over her forehead, veiling her eyes. Annabelle looked at her father. Disappointment was more and more etched onto his face as time passed and her mother didn't return. He stuffed his hands in his pockets, looking very much like a boy who's just had all his fun spoiled. A cold, hard fist of anguish in the pit of her stomach made her cringe. She rolled over on her side so he could no longer see her face.

"Belle . . ." he started. She felt the mattress shift as he sat on the bed.

"Uh huh?" she offered.

"I thought, maybe, we could do something?" he said softly. Annabelle rolled over to face him.

"Do something?"

"Yes. See a movie? Go to dinner?"

"Why?" she asked. Her father sighed and dragged a hand down his face.

"We should try Annabelle," he said.

"Try *what?*" she answered.

"Try to be a family," he said. One hand absent-mindedly clenched and unclenched at his side and she wondered if he truly wanted to try or was just doing so because it was expected?

Annabelle thought about his offer, his suggestion. Did she even want that anymore? In two months she would be packed and moved into her dorm at college, free to turn a new page and be the kind of person she wanted to be. Happy, free, grounded in the present instead of trapped in the past.

"Maybe tomorrow," she answered.

Her father stared at her a beat before standing and nodding. He heaved a sigh, and left her room, shutting the door quietly behind him. For a brief moment something like guilt hit her but it passed quickly. Madison was due to arrive with pizza any moment. Cracking her neck, Annabelle yawned and pushed herself from the bed to head downstairs.

~***~

"Hey," Annabelle called as she stepped through the threshold into Jezebel's suite. Music was cranked up loud and Jezebel stood at the window watering her plants and swaying her hips in time with the rhythm.

Jezebel whipped around, shook her shoulders and grinned at Annabelle. "Hey is for horses," she said. Jezebel crooked a finger at her and beckoned her over. Annabelle rolled her eyes before casually making her way to the window. "Look at that," Jezebel sighed, pointing to the view from her window.

A lush garden in all its summer splendor bloomed below in the courtyard. Bright reds, oranges and purples, and lush greens filled the space symmetrically.

"It's pretty," she said.

"It's pretty?" Jezebel mocked indignantly.

"Yeah," she said.

"That's it? Look at those colors . . . the symmetry. The way the sky looks impossibly brighter blue against the flowers."

"Alright, it's beautiful. Better?" Annabelle asked giving Jezebel a lazy smile.

"You. Are. Hopeless," Jezebel answered as she walked to the stereo and turned the music to a low din before sitting in her chair and sweeping her hair up into an effortless loose bun. Annabelle rolled her eyes at the woman before following her lead. "How was your week?"

"It was good. Madison came over a couple of times. I cooked dinner for Mark one night. He met my dad, finally," she said.

"Oh? How was that?"

Annabelle tucked herself comfortably into her chair. "Good, I think. I mean Dad asked all the perfunctory questions, Mark answered, and we ate," Annabelle said.

"That sounds promising."

"Oh! And, weird, Dad asked me if I wanted to do dinner and a movie with him. Alone. Together," Annabelle blurted.

"Why do you say that as if it's strange kiddo?" Jezebel gave her a curious look.

"Because it is."

"You won't know that until you actually do it," Jezebel answered.

Annabelle shrugged. "I guess, but we haven't done anything together in years."

"You haven't been happy in years either, do you think it's strange to want *that*?" Jezebel asked.

"No. Point made," she said before lifting her hair from her neck and securing it in a ponytail. "Do you have any random appointments today that will cut our time short?" Annabelle snickered.

"Touché dear. No. I do not."

"Good, then let's get crackin,'" Annabelle replied. She settled back into her chair and waited.

"Very well. Paris, nineteen ninety-four," Jezebel said. Annabelle studied Jezebel as she closed her eyes and took a few deep breaths before diving in.

Chapter 34

Celeste

Paris 1994
April

Celeste headed to Gabriel's favorite café. She wanted to tell him about the meeting with Taylor over delicious food. She parked a block away from the café, the closest spot she could find, and walked briskly to her destination mulling over the absolute craziness of her morning. Who the hell was Dr. Basle? For a man she thought she knew, knew well, she was beginning to think he had a lot of secrets.

Her breath caught in her throat as she entered the cafe. A hollow feeling overcame her.

"We need another sample," Monique said as the two of them waited in line to place their lunch orders. Celeste stayed put just behind the display case that blocked her from her husband's view.

"Shouldn't be an issue. I'll bring one tomorrow," Gabriel answered casually.

Celeste watched. They stood close. *Too* close. Something in Gabriel's smile announced his intentions, and Monique responded in kind with a bright smile, her cheeks rosy as she laughed at something he said. *La vérité va sortir (the truth will come out)*, Celeste thought. Monique's belly was swollen just enough to notice. Gabriel's hand reached out, his fingers spread wide, feeling his very single assistant's pregnant stomach.

Celeste turned on her heel and bolted from the cesspool of activity without being noticed. Her heart splintered as she sprinted to her car. If she had known she was about to enter the gates of hell she would have chosen to remain blissfully unaware. But like the inescapable pull of gravity, there was nothing she could do about it now. Perhaps it wasn't what it looked like. Perhaps, Monique was dating someone and Gabriel was merely excited to somehow be a part of a pregnancy. Any pregnancy. Her heart and throat constricted painfully as she slid into the driver's seat. Slamming the car door shut she cranked the engine and peeled out of her spot needing the comfort of her home.

She had watched the sky change from the yellow cheer of afternoon to the soft oranges of dusk and into a cool navy night. The key made a turning sound that echoed severely in the silent house. It was nearly midnight. She peeled her heavy body from the restraints of her refuge and walked down the stairs. It felt like the longest journey. What would he say when she told him?

Gabriel's eyes never left her, his feet rooted to the floor of the foyer, his face drawn tight, lips flat as he watched her approach.

"Where have you been?" Celeste asked. Her heart thumped, kicking her ribs as her fingers gripped the polished rail secured to the stairs. Gabriel swallowed and took a breath. She took a step forward, thinking if she could touch him, if she could reach him, if only—but Gabriel took a stride backward, keeping the distance between them. Her hand fell and hung limply at her side. There it was. Clear as day. Muddy and cold and rotten—like his deceit.

Gabriel's expression softened. "Work, as always."

She laughed then, loud and punitive. Celeste knew every curve of this man's lips, every expression of his face, and the moment she laid eyes on him tonight, she had known. It was in the tilt of his head, the angle of his shoulders. Before, she had been living with eyes wide open but somehow fast asleep; not anymore. He was lying to her. She wanted to hide, to turn away, to run . . . but something held her there, something kept her from running.

"Gabriel . . ." her voice faltered. "I stopped by the café to pick up lunch for us. You were already there though." The planes of the face she loved so much sharpened as quickly as they'd smoothed, and he spun abruptly and walked into the kitchen without a word. Celeste closed her eyes as her pain stretched out before her in agonizing silence.

Unable to quell her anxiety or face her husband, Celeste walked ten steps forward, yanked the door open and walked through it. She jumped in her car at just past midnight and drove out to her former employer's home. Not a light was on as she approached, and a fresh wave of grief engulfed her. Too many thoughts and emotions competed for her attention but she shoved each one away, unwilling to face any of them. How had her life been turned so upside down? How would she get through this? Would he go to Monique now seeking solace-a shoulder to cry on? Would he worry about her and stay put?

The thought of Gabriel's infidelity made it hard to breathe. She couldn't get air. He'd refused to admit verbally to anything but she didn't need him to. She could see it written all over his face, pronounced in his posture. Her heart was alone, shrouded in darkness as she pushed through the kitchen door of Dr. B's house and let the tears come. Silently walking to the study she let her thoughts wander dangerously. She entered and stood stiffly, taking in the mess that needed to be cleaned up before the funeral and subsequent gathering here.

"My God, what has happened to my life?" she sobbed and collapsed into one of the stately wingback chairs adorning the room. She looked up to the ceiling and said a silent prayer that the baby wasn't Gabriel's. She could overlook his betrayal, his infidelity-but she couldn't overlook a child. Gabriel was her sun. Her gravity. She'd thought she was his as well. The pain cut deep, a dull knife dragged through the very core of her.

Alone in a safe place she let the tears come. She hung her head and cried for her marriage. For Dr. B. For the dreams and hopes that somehow slipped through her fingers.

"Cece, *fiore mio,* I'm right here, you're not alone." Matteo's deep soothing voice cut through the silence. Celeste turned her head marginally. "What's got you so upset?" he asked, kneeling beside her. She stared into Matteo's handsome face and felt a tug in her chest. Her Matteo. Always there. Always true.

"Gabriel, he . . . today . . ."

Her voice faded. She couldn't bring herself to say the words aloud. She didn't want to make them true. She didn't want any of this. "What are you doing here?" she asked instead of saying those dreadful words poised too closely at the tip of her tongue.

Matteo sighed and rubbed the top of his head. "I'm having trouble sleeping. I thought I'd get a head start on making this place presentable." She wanted Matteo to wrap his arms around her. She craved comfort.

"Well that makes two of us," she said

despondently and looked away. She couldn't bring herself to ask for what she needed.

"Let's just focus on the study tonight," Matteo suggested.

Celeste nodded her head and Matteo offered her a hand up from her seat. "I'll grab some trash bags," he said. When he was out of sight, she spun around taking in all the items they needed to clean up. She busied her mind. An envelope stuck beneath Dr. Basle's chair caught her attention, for a second time. That had been there when she found him. Partially tucked under the area rug and partially stuck beneath the foot of his chair it seemed odd. She walked on numb feet to the last place she had seen the doctor and bent to retrieve it.

She turned it over in her palm. A familiar FogPharm logo adorned the top left corner. What business did Dr. B have with her parents' company? Matteo appeared at her side. She looked to him, hoping, on a whim, that he would have an explanation.

"What's that?" he asked. His breath tickled her neck and a shiver ran through her.

"It was stuck under his chair. I noticed it when I found him but in all the hubbub forgot about it," she answered. She ran her fingers over the penned *Dr. Basle* in the recipient location.

"FogPharm?" he asked hesitantly.

Celeste nodded. "I know. Strange."

"Monique visited. Maybe that's why," he said. At the mention of her name, Celeste cringed and fought tears back. If she never heard that name again it would be too soon. It would make sense that Monique had been here if it had to do with her family's company. "Open it," Matteo urged.

Celeste tore open the envelope judiciously and withdrew the contents. Unfolding the paper, she stared at a printed table full of numbers. The column headers read: Child, Maternal Grandfather. The bottom of the page showed a percentage rate followed by 99.9996% probability.

"Matteo?" Celeste called out bewildered.

"Celeste," he breathed, taking the paper from her. He pointed to the *Child* column, under it a date: Celeste's birthday. "That is Dr. B's birthdate. And yours."

"I don't understand," she mumbled. She stared harder at the print on the paper as if it would suddenly speak and tell her the secrets of the world. What would prompt Dr. B to think such a thing? How did he get a DNA sample to even test with? Endless thoughts barraged her mind. Too many conflicting emotions; betrayal and hurt, grief and sorrow. Bittersweet agony coursed through her unabashed. Her mind raced and spun until she felt lightheaded.

"Cece, this DNA report says you're without a doubt his granddaughter," Matteo stated. He rested a palm on her lower back to steady her as she swayed slightly and blinked. What the hell was going on?

Chapter 35

Annabelle

"Let me find out what you hide. Way down there deep inside."
~ Let Me, Phoebe Killdeer & The Short Straws

Annabelle sat with bated breath waiting for Jezebel's next line. It never came. Jezebel appeared frozen in time. Her hand clutched her shirt at her chest. Her eyes were blank, staring ahead yet taking nothing in, her expression flat.

"Jez?" Annabelle said.

Jezebel snapped to from whatever state she was stuck in. She shook her head and blinked as if trying to clear away cobwebs. "Yes, dear?"

Annabelle gave her a wide-eyed look, "You kinda zoned out on me there."

"My mind, it gets . . . what's the word?" Jezebel wrinkled her face in concentration. "Lost. I get lost."

Jezebel's behavior scared Annabelle. Most of the time, Annabelle thought she didn't really belong in Glenview, but right now she couldn't deny that Jezebel seemed off. She frowned at her thoughts. She didn't want Jezebel to deteriorate. She was so full of life, so challenging—it would be heartbreaking to watch her slide into a state of bland lifeless nothing. "It's okay," she said and smiled.

"Where were we?" Jezebel asked and gave her a bright, but bemused smile.

Looking to the clock Annabelle observed it was nearing time to leave. "It's about time for me to meet Mark for my ride home," she said. Jezebel glanced at the clock before nodding. Annabelle stood and stretched her limbs, feeling the delicious pop in her back as she leaned side to side. She approached Jezebel, bent at the waist and embraced her in a hug.

"Can't wait till next week," she whispered in her ear.

Jezebel rubbed a hand between her shoulder blades. "Me either, sweet beet."

~***~

Annabelle sat on the counter humming and swinging her feet as if she were a kid again. Her father chopped peaches for her favorite dessert. With every slice of the knife blade, a portion of the peach fell away revealing orange flesh under the fuzzy skin.

"Belle," her father called over the music filtering through the speaker. "Take over." He motioned for her to take the knife from him. She hopped off the counter too quickly, wincing at a hard landing into the reality that she was not a small child anymore, and took the knife from her father's hand.

Slicing peaches, Annabelle watched from the corner of her eye as her dad flipped a hotcake onto a plate, the action instantaneously followed by the sizzle of a fresh dab of butter in the skillet and a generous amount of batter. Peering over her father's shoulder, she saw the perfect discs of batter cook. Butter snapped underneath them and looked a little browner than normal. Annabelle silently wondered if her favorite addition, bacon grease, had been added.

She watched as he slipped the spatula under the little rounds and, with a flick of his wrist, revealed golden undersides smelling of butter and ever so slightly of bacon. *Definitely bacon grease.* She smiled to herself and returned to chopping peaches.

"Who taught you how to cook?" she asked as she popped the peach cobbler into the oven.

"My mother."

"What was she like?" Annabelle asked.

Her father sighed and planted his butt on the seat of a stiff wooden stool at the kitchen bar. "She was like summer," he started. "Always baking treats, and yelling at me to wash up for something." *Like summer,* Annabelle thought. What a perfect way to describe someone. Summer felt like warmth and bright skies and cool evening breezes.

"Do you miss her?"

"Sure, sometimes," her father answered. "Why?"

"Because I . . . I don't really notice Mom's absence now." It was a rotten thing to say but it was also the truth. Her father stared at her a long moment before rounding the island and pulling her into his chest. Annabelle stiffened and held her breath. When was the last time he had hugged her? When was the last time they had any sort of tender moment like this? She wasn't sure what to do, how to react, so she stood woodenly in his arms.

"You'll burn the hotcakes," she mumbled into his chest. He pulled back and gazed down at her for a moment before nodding and tending to the frying pan. Annabelle slumped with relief.

"Plates out, breakfast for dinner is ready," he called out. Annabelle grinned and set two plates at the bar top. Breakfast for dinner was the best.

~***~

Annabelle's cellphone bleated. It startled her. She found it strange that six months ago she couldn't go thirty minutes without using or checking her phone for something. But now, finally having technology at her disposal again, she found she didn't really enjoy it. She'd coveted her phone, her laptop ever since she'd had them, but now scrolling through her newsfeeds on Facebook, Instagram, Twitter and all the other pointless apps she'd used daily made her feel disconnected and despondent. She'd spent the better part of the last four months technology free and had built a different set of values in that short time.

She found she preferred her face-to-face interactions over the anonymity that the Internet offered. She felt connected and alive *in person* now. She stared at the blinking light on her phone and sighed. She really didn't want to be tethered to it ever again. It served as nothing more than a time-suck these days, and she found it a boring one at that.

Foregoing the notification she switched her phone to silent and tucked it in the outermost pocket of her purse. Whatever it was could wait. She had a living, breathing person to see.

"What's shaking sport?" Jezebel greeted, an easy smile on her face.

Annabelle shook her head and chuckled. "What's with all the nicknames?"

Jezebel half-shrugged. "They add flare."

Annabelle rolled her eyes and set her things down. "Can't argue that," she said.

"Did you have decent week?" Jezebel asked.

Annabelle took her seat and smiled. "You know what?" she started, "I did. Great even."

Jezebel smiled widely and clapped her hands

together. "Fabulous, kid."

"Not to be greedy, Jez, but I'm dying to know what happens next," Annabelle said, excitement lacing her voice.

"Ah, and we've arrived," Jezebel said.

"At what?"

"At the *good* part," Jezebel answered.

Annabelle laughed. Indeed they had. She was more invested in the story now than ever. "Please don't keep me waiting. Please."

"Greedy little thing aren't you?"

Annabelle speared Jezebel with a look.

"Is there any Mark news?"

"Stop stalling woman!" she laughed.

"Hmm. I suppose your cheery disposition leaves me no choice but to indulge you. Paris, nineteen ninety-four."

Annabelle grinned and relaxed in her spot.

Chapter 36

Celeste

Paris 1994
April

Celeste's emotions were raw, the line between composure and tears thin. Thoughts rolled around her head endlessly. Her world had fallen apart in matter of days. The impossible seemed possible and that terrified her. She moved on auto-pilot across the study and sat heavily in a chair.

"Cece," Matteo called. She waved a hand at him to stop. She needed everything to stop-the noise, the motion, everything. It was spiraling around her like a tornado. She felt dizzy. It was as though she was outside herself, watching. A man she regarded as family was dead. A man who was, so it seemed, actually family. Her husband was clearly having an affair, possibly bringing a child into the world with someone other than her. And now, she was going to have to confront her parents and ask them the most ludicrous question she'd ever conjured: was she adopted? She wanted to laugh at the absurdity of it all. She imagined it-a maniacal laugh, one of a woman gone mad.

A large, firm hand clamped around her jaw and drew her head back, her eyes forced upward. Matteo had a cigarette dangling from his lips, a habit he routinely denied still having these days. He must be very frazzled to be smoking in front of her now, indoors no less. "Cece, please, *fiore mio*, what is going on in that head of yours?" he asked. "I know something is wrong. I gave you space but you look . . . *non lo so-alla deriva.*" *I don't know-adrift,* he said.

Celeste felt foolish trying to spare her closest friend from her woes. Of course he would notice.

"Gabriel is sleeping with Monique—I'm *almost* positive. It appears I may be adopted and a close friend just passed away," she stated robotically. Matteo dropped her chin and sat on the floor beside her chair, head in his hands.

"I'm so sorry Cece. So sorry," he said softly. The words struck her as odd, almost insulting. She was no weakling who broke under the weight of stress. She straightened in her chair. Bristled.

"I'm not. I'm not sorry at all. It's not the end of the world. I can talk to Gabriel about it. We will work it out." Celeste's mind shut down, denial and avoidance taking root in her head.

"Cece . . ." Matteo tried, but let his thought drop off.

"I can handle this," she resolved, waving a

hand through the air. "All of this." She inhaled deeply, sucking the air in before pushing it out forcefully. Standing, she strode to the door and picked up a trash bag. "Get up," she commanded. "There's a lot to do."

Matteo gave her a pitiful look. Angst and denial and grief—for her. Wordlessly he stood, snatching the bag from her. "You start there," he said and pointed to the corner near a closet.

Unable to execute her decision on her own, Matteo's direction was appreciated and followed. She wandered to the corner, picking up scattered papers along the way. She shuffled through them, deciding what to keep and what should be trashed. She opened the closet door and flicked the light on. Stacked along the left wall were boxes. She tried lifting one and gasped at the weight. *What the hell could weigh so much?*

"Need help?" Matteo asked.

"Looks like it."

Matteo took the box from her arms just before she dropped it. He set it on the floor and pulled the top open. "Framed pictures. All pictures," he said. He lifted one from the box and dusted the glass off. "Cece look, it's his wife."

Celeste leaned over him and took the photo from him while he dug another and another from the box. Dr. B's wife was stunning. Her long black hair shined in the photo and she had a perfect smattering of freckles over the bridge of her nose. Her smile was warm and bright and her eyes shone with love as she laughed at her husband. Matteo coughed and tried to stick a frame back in the box.

"What is it?" she asked.

"A family photo," he said slowly. He sounded unsure. Obviously he would know whether or not it was a family photo.

"Matteo, give it here, I want to see," she complained and reached over him. His hand came down on hers, roughly stopping her motion.

"I don't think right now's the time for this," he said firmly.

Ignoring him she pulled the frame out and gasped. Standing arm in arm, Dr. B, his wife, and a younger woman who was the spitting image of Celeste stared back at her. She ran her fingertip over the younger woman's face. Dr. B had said she reminded him of someone years ago. Now she understood. Staring back at her through the pane of glass was Dr. B's daughter. There was no doubt in Celeste's mind that this woman was her mother. It would be uncanny if it wasn't. The resemblance was too strong. She knelt on the floor and rummaged through the box further almost rabid in her need to see more.

Picture after picture after picture of Dr. B's daughter, of his granddaughter- Celeste-as an infant, as a toddler. It was her. She was his. The world fainted left then right in her head. She fought to get air. Dimly in the recesses of her mind she could hear Matteo's voice. She couldn't understand his words while she stared at undeniable proof that she was not who she thought she was. She was not Celeste Fontaine. No. She wasn't even Celeste Fogarty.

She squeezed the frame tightly in her hand. The pane of glass cracked under the intense pressure of her fingers. Blood smeared the glass as it slowly trickled from the cut on Celeste's finger. She felt like she'd taken a punch to the head and was still clearing cobwebs. She squinted. Opened her eyes. Squinted again.

"Cece . . . *please*," Matteo begged somewhere far away. A switch snapped in her mind.

"What?" She turned to look at him. Worry etched lines in his face and it concerned her.

"You're bleeding, *fiore mio*, let me clean you up." His voice was smooth, gentle and comforting. She looked down. She was. When had that happened? She nodded absently and took his outstretched hand. She couldn't be getting blood on everything.

Laugh or cry? She wasn't sure what was about to erupt from her.

Chapter 37

Annabelle

"Why don't you tell me what's on your mind. I feel there's something's been left behind. Don't be scared now and don't delay, I assure you'll be ok."

~ Let Me, Phoebe Killdeer & The Short Straws

Annabelle studied Jezebel. Each fine wrinkle seemed to tell a story. Stories of happiness, sorrow and joy. Jezebel presented herself with so much poise and confidence Annabelle envied her. She wanted to emulate Jezebel's demeanor.

"Intense," Annabelle breathed after a long moment of silence.

Jezebel's face snapped to hers. "Yes," she stated. "It was, wasn't it?"

Annabelle nodded her head. "I better get going."

"Alright kid."

Annabelle stood and collected her things before wandering down the corridor toward the parking lot. She thought of Celeste and Matteo and Dr. B and Gabriel and wondered briefly if Jezebel was simply an exceptional storyteller or if the story was in fact true. She resolved to Google Celeste Fontaine after dinner. She smiled then, happy that her father and she had started a new tradition. For the past three weeks they had started cooking dinner together. They cooked together, ate together and cleaned up afterward together. It was easy and comfortable and the closest Annabelle had felt to her father in years.

Mark sat on the tailgate of his truck waiting. Upon spotting her, a grin took over his face and Annabelle's heart took flight. She took him in as she approached. His well-defined jaw, his clear skin and sparkling eyes. The hair that fell in his eyes every so often. The way his forearms flexed as he pushed it out of his face. Never had she felt so continuously elated to see someone. Week after week it never waned.

"Hello there beautiful," he greeted as his arms wrapped around her. She inhaled his scent as she squeezed him to her in return.

"Hi," she said. He leaned down and touched his lips to hers in a gentle, tender kiss.

"I missed you."

"Oh?"

"Don't play coy with me, you missed me too," he said. Annabelle smirked and kissed him again.

"I did."

"What's tomorrow like for you? I'm off tomorrow and thought we could do something."

"For you? I'm wide open," she said.

"Wide open huh?" She swatted his shoulder

playfully and nodded. "Good. Pick you up 'round ten then," he said and waggled his eyebrows.

Annabelle laughed. "Get in the truck, Romeo."

~***~

Annabelle realized she had no documentation of Jezebel's and her time together beyond her own memories, and that wouldn't do. She'd scoured the Internet looking for any truth in Celeste Fontaine's life. Celeste did exist. She found a marriage certificate to Gabriel Fontaine online. Her parents had owned a pharmaceutical company named FogPharm that was long since dissolved. Beyond that, there wasn't much for information. Anything before nineteen ninety-four was available but there seemed to be no information or proof of their lives after that point.

As she waltzed into Jezebel's room she made a note to ask the woman about her findings. But first, she wanted to have a little fun.

"Hey there tiger," Jezebel said.

"Hi."

"You look . . . dare I say it, happy today," Jezebel said dryly. Annabelle laughed at her delivery.

"I am," she answered kicking off her shoes as she rummaged through her purse. Finding her phone she held it up victoriously and smirked.

"What the hell is *that* face for?" Jezebel asked, a weary look on her face.

"We are going to have some fun," she started. "I want some pictures of you and me together."

"Oh, no no no," Jezebel clucked, looking horrified.

"OH, yes yes yes," Annabelle answered. She walked to Jezebel and perched on the arm of her chair, leaning her head in near Jezebel's. "We're taking a series of selfies together."

"What the hell is a selfie?" Jezebel balked.

"Okay, it's like this, we make faces at the camera. There's duck face, where you make your pursed lips sexy and your eyes sultry." Annabelle demonstrated the expression while Jezebel laughed at it heartily.

"You look ridiculous!" Jezebel squawked.

"Then there's sparrow face-open your eyes as wide as possible, and then you make your mouth like a chirping sparrow," she continued, unfazed by Jezebel's ribbing. "Frog face is where you stick your tongue out sideways and squint, and fish lips is the duck face move that requires you to suck in a little bit of your cheek. Well, expects you to *completely* suck it in, like you would like to swallow your face until it disappears." Annabelle laughed trying to demonstrate.

Jezebel struggled to catch her breath as she doubled over laughing loudly. Annabelle snapped a picture, it was perfect. Jezebel's hair cascaded over one shoulder, her eyes crinkled at the edges and her smile filled her entire face.

"Please," Annabelle pleaded and gave Jezebel her best puppy dog face.

"You'll have to explain them again, but why the hell not!" Annabelle squealed and flipped the camera on her phone to front facing before she explained, again, the different faces to make.

By the time they'd run through them all they were both hysterical with laughter. The reel of pictures she'd captured were priceless and it warmed Annabelle's heart to know that she would always have a piece of Jezebel with her wherever she went.

"My God, child, you should delete those. I don't want anyone seeing me with any of those faces — ever," Jezebel said while fixing her hair. She swept it up and off her neck and secured it in a neat bun at the nape of her neck. Effortlessly as always.

Annabelle went wide-eyed. "Never. I'm printing them all and plastering my locker with them when I get to school," she proclaimed.

Jezebel chuckled and shook her head at Annabelle. "You're a silly girl, a very silly girl. It's much better than the bad attitude shithead that first showed up here."

Annabelle's jaw dropped before she could think better of her reaction. "You are still a mean old woman," she retorted.

The two stared at each other a moment before dissolving into giggles again.

"We've wasted enough precious time today and there is much to tell you still. Are you ready for Celeste?" Jezebel asked.

Annabelle chugged her water before setting the empty glass on the side table. "Yes. Oh! I have questions — remind me before I go," Annabelle said.

Jezebel nodded her head and thought in silence a moment.

"Paris, nineteen ninety-four."

Chapter 38

Celeste

Paris 1994
April

She squeezed her eyes shut and crossed her arms against the chilled breeze blowing. The night sky had clouded over, blotting out the stars and calming the wind. A chime hung motionless from the roof eaves as she pulled into the driveway of her childhood home.

A fireplace piled high with logs cast light and warmth into the dismal gray foyer of her parents' home as she entered.

"Celeste, honey, what a surprise. Is everything alright?" her mother said rounding the corner.

She thought about the question and exhaled harshly, shaking her head. "No. No Mom, it's not."

Her mother closed the remaining distance between them quickly, worry evident on her face, and enveloped Celeste in a fierce hug. "Tell me," she breathed into Celeste's ear.

Two insignificant words. Two words that seemed so utterly ridiculous yet rocked her to the core. *Tell her?* Her mind circled around ways to spit out the question that needed to be said but none seemed right.

"Mom, I think Dad needs to be here for this too," she said, backing out of her mother's embrace.

"What's going on? Celeste, just spit it out." Her mother stood wide-eyed expecting the worst. It was written all over her face, lines creased across her forehead, her eyes slits. Celeste didn't want to drag this out. No one was dead, but she felt it best to have both her parents sitting with her for this particular conversation.

Celeste sighed and ran a hand through her hair. "Just . . . please, Mom."

Her mother looked over her shoulder and bellowed into the cavernous house for her husband before ushering Celeste into the living room. Her father's lazy stride made Celeste happy as he entered the room. He sat, settling into his favorite chair, before giving her that look—that skeptical, eyebrow-half-cocked look that never boded well for anybody on the receiving end.

"I was in the middle of my show," he grumbled. Her mother made a choking sound next to her. Celeste inhaled sharply. They'd all been so good together in this house. She'd been so happy growing up. They were a family. Would all that be ruined now?

"I need to ask you a question," Celeste began.

"What kind of question is so important that it necessitates a late night visit?" her father grumped.

"Stop that!" her mother scolded. "Celeste, please . . . get on with it."

"Am I adopted?"

Her words hung in the air. Two sets of eyes snapped at her. Two quiet gasps filled the large room. Two faces paled. Two incredulous looks faced her. Celeste didn't need their answer, it was given without words. She slumped into the couch and rested her head in her hands and started to cry. It was her father's hand that came down on her back and rubbed slow circles, which surprised her. His voice was raspy as he attempted to comfort her. "Celeste, you're our daughter. We love you."

"How could you never tell me?" she asked. Her heart beat frantically against her ribs.

"We made a decision around the time you were ten that we didn't want to tell you," her mother answered pushing loose strands of Celeste's hair behind her ear.

"That seems unfair."

"Not to us. We love you. You belong to us. We're a family. We didn't want to change any of that," her father offered.

Anger crept up Celeste's esophagus. Her words bubbled out laced with resentment.

"Who the hell am I though?"

"You're Celeste Fontaine. You're our daughter. Celeste, please, this doesn't change anything," her mother said.

"It changes everything," Celeste scoffed, sitting up straighter. "It changes everything because I found out whose family I really am."

"What?" her mother gasped. "That's impossible! We don't even know who your birth family is."

"Dr. B." she said.

"What about him?" her father asked still kneeling in front of her.

"He was my grandfather. There is a DNA report from FogPharm to prove it. My God, there are pictures of me in his house!" she shrieked.

Her mother shook her head repeatedly. As if it would stop the moment from happening. Her father knelt, blinking, clearly shocked.

"Matteo and I were going through his things, as his will stated, and there are . . . boxes and boxes of family photos. I look just like his daughter. There are pictures of me at two and three. The DNA report, I don't know why he requested it or how he managed to get a sample, but he clearly had enough suspicion to do so."

"Unbelievable," her father breathed before rocking back on to his rear. He stared at his thighs as if they might provide some great insight. Her mother clutched her shirt at the chest, her knuckles white.

"My God, all this time . . . you've been working for him," her mother said.

She believed her parents. There astonishment was too evident to be anything but the truth. "Tell me everything," Celeste urged.

Her parents took their time telling her their story: her mother desperate to have children but unable. Wandering through the adoption center looking at babies to bring home. The way Celeste smiled at them, timid but genuine when they passed by her. The liaison informing them that she was anonymously dropped at the center months before and that they couldn't turn a three-year-old away but didn't expect to place her any time soon; people wanted infants. The way she knew her name, but not much else that was useful. Her illness, they thought, had impacted her memory, or perhaps some form of trauma had occurred. Celeste took it all in silently, letting her parents tell their tale. She needed to understand.

By the end of their conversation, Celeste was exhausted. She didn't dare drive home, but she knew she needed to deal with Gabriel. Her father phoned him for her, knowing only that they needed to talk, assuming perhaps it was about Celeste's adoption. Her parents turned down her old bed for her and Gabriel before each kissing her on the forehead and retiring for the night. Her mother's tears trailing down her cheeks as she told Celeste how much she loved her nearly broke her heart.

~***~

Celeste rested her chin on her hand and stared into the fireplace, deep in deliberation as she waited for Gabriel to arrive. The heat from the fireplace seeped through her clothes, through her chilled skin and into the core of her. She wanted to sleep for days, for years even. She'd suffered the distresses of a thousand lifetimes in just days and it was taking a toll on her. She tried to will herself to be calm. It would be fine. Everything would be fine. They just needed to talk about their marriage. Everything else could wait for now.

Celeste felt his eyes on her and found herself suddenly shy. She looked up from the flames that licked the logs to Gabriel. He towered in the entrance to the living room, lips pressed in a firm line, dark circles under his eyes, his hair sticking out every which way as if he'd run his hands through it repeatedly. He looked skyward. He looked like she felt. How would this go, she wondered. She felt her courage, her fight, was all used up already and yet her marriage needed her to make it a priority. To fight.

"Hi," she whispered. Gabriel closed his eyes and leaned on the door frame. Shadows from the fire danced around him.

"*Tiens.*" *Hi,* he said.

An abyss between them stretched on infinitely. "I don't know how to do this," she started.

"Celeste, I need you in my life." He spoke the words slowly, deliberately, as if imparting a threat instead of simple declaration of love.

Celeste shook her head left to right and back. "Need and want aren't the same, Gabriel," she said. Her heart felt cracked, a crack so deep that surely at any moment it would drop into two even halves inside her chest and she'd cease breathing.

"Need trumps want, mon amour."

She shook her head violently at his words. "No. No it doesn't. I need to know the truth even though I don't *want* to. Are you and Monique sleeping together?" Her heart hung in the balance as she awaited his answer. She was angry. Tired and angry. She felt small. Inconsequential. It hurt.

"Non."

She huffed irritated at his brevity. "Were you?" she restructured her question.

"Oui."

Celeste's heart jumped into her throat. She

tried to swallow but couldn't. Her hands shook with such force that the after-effect left her arms shaking too. Her entire marriage flashed in her head: so many happy times, the love, the devotion, the rough patches, working through them. Did she want to forgive him? Could she? Her anxiety spiked as she swallowed huge gulps of air. She finally managed to ask. "Is the baby yours?"

"Non," he answered simply. Did she believe him? Could she? He didn't lie about sleeping with his assistant, so why lie about the baby? Celeste knew in her heart he would spare her the hurt of having a baby, maybe above anything else. He would lie, she thought.

"Gabriel," she started. Her voice cracked. She didn't know what she needed or wanted to ask. Words sat poised on her tongue ready to lash out but for reasons unknown she couldn't make them come out. Anguish and rage, hot and swift, rushed through her as she tried to wrangle her thoughts into something constructive.

"*Je suis à vous,* Celeste." *I am yours,* he cut her off. Moving toward her with purposeful strides, he collapsed to the floor next to her. "You are my world." The deep timbre to his voice sent an eruption of shivers down through her spine.

He rubbed his palm against his forehead as if he had a headache. He looked tortured. His green eyes bored into hers in that deep, intense way only he could manage. His words were her undoing.

Tears poured unapologetically down her face. Her heart stuttered and in that moment she didn't care about anything as long as she and Gabriel were together. Tears slid from his eyes, rolled down his cheeks, as he took her face in his hands. "*Je suis tellement désolé*. Tell me how to fix this, I will do anything, *mon amour*." I'm so sorry, he said, his voice hoarse. Celeste didn't have answers. She didn't know if she ever would. What would the first step be?

"I don't know," she said just before he kissed her. She melted into his lips, the warmth of them, the passion they produced, the comfort and familiarity of them. Gabriel scooped her into his arms and stood slowly. Celeste wrapped her arms around his neck and nuzzled her face into that perfect spot where his neck met his shoulder as he carried her to the bedroom. She was exhausted. Her husband was there, with her. Sleep would be the most logical choice for now. They'd have the start of a new day to dig in deep and begin repairing their marriage tomorrow.

She fell asleep nestled in her husband's embrace. She dreamed of a hospital room, the sounds of a baby crying and her husband's face beaming with pride. She woke up just as the mother of the infant began to appear from the hospital room. Her eyes shot open and she sat up in bed, panting. Raising a hand to her forehead, she felt her sweat-soaked skin. She ran her fingers through her long, wet hair and snuck out of bed silently. Gabriel lay in the bed still, chest rising and falling evenly. Her heart felt like a fist in her chest as she stood looking at him. She pulled back the drapes and saw a white curtain of rain falling from a low gray sky outside the window. The light of day was faded, the sky hidden beneath a low-lying fog that continued to spew rain and did not appear ready to let up anytime soon. The thermometer mounted outside on a tree indicated the temperature had fallen to thirty degrees and Celeste thought that was just fine; it suited her very mood.

Spring was upon them and she wanted no part of it. Spring brought new beginnings and currently all she felt in her gut were endings. The turmoil of her situation, of her life, hammered down on her. She felt paralyzed.

Chapter 39

Annabelle

"Remember, tick tock, tick tock, tick tock people. Time's tickin' away."
~ Tick Tock, Stevie Ray Vaughan

"Oh, my God, this is getting insane," Annabelle commented.

Jezebel nodded her head excitedly. "It is. Just wait until next week."

"I'll be on pins and needles waiting." She laughed.

"Mark's probably cursing up a storm at me right now."

"He can wait a couple minutes," she assured Jezebel.

"What were these questions you had?" Jezebel asked.

"Oh! Right. Okay, so I looked up FogPharm and Celeste," she rushed. Jezebel's face had a curious look. Nervous, even. "And, well it's all true! But there's nothing to find after nineteen ninety-four. Why is that?"

Jezebel smiled and relaxed into her chair. "I will explain that to you soon. It's all part of the story."

"So, was Celeste really your friend?"

"Yes."

"This is so cool. I mean sad kinda too, since you probably liked her a lot," Annabelle offered as she slipped her feet into her shoes.

"It was very difficult, yes," Jezebel answered.

"Oh, hey, so next week, I want to do something drastic. I gotta run but I'm super excited for the rest of this story," Annabelle said. "I think we need some excitement together." She popped a kiss on Jezebel's cheek and snatched her bag from the floor before sprinting down the hall to go see Mark.

~***~

"So tell me about this lady you visit with," her father asked through a mouthful of food. Annabelle made a disgusted face at him and finished chewing and swallowing her bite before speaking.

"Jezebel. She's . . . I don't know, Dad. She's amazing. She's telling me this story . . . it's a love story, kinda, well it's turning into more of a horror story now but she's got me on the edge of my seat," she happily rambled.

"Wow, edge of your seat, huh?"

Annabelle blushed. "Yeah. Dorky I know, but she tells it really well. Oh! And it's true! A true story. Very cool."

"Seems like it. Anything that gets you smiling

~ 412 ~

and excited like she does is a good thing," her father said.

"Dad?"

Her father grunted in response as he shoveled another forkful of dinner into his mouth.

"What makes you excited like that?" she asked.

He set his fork down and looked to her. "My work used to. And your mother, I guess." He looked out the window behind her. "Coffee in the morning, concerts, that music you refer to as 'bad' eighties music, and well . . . you my love."

Annabelle smiled at her dad and tried to think of ways she could make any of that happen for him. Coffee was easy enough but maybe they could catch a concert down on the mall together before summer ended.

"I love you," she said.

"Love you too," he answered.

~***~

Annabelle all but ran into Jezebel's room. "Piercing or tattoo?" Annabelle asked Jezebel. She had wanted a tattoo for a while now and was excited that her plan for their afternoon seemed flawless.

"What? Neither," Jezebel answered wrinkling her nose up.

"You have to pick one," she said.

"Why? If this is that drastic something-or-other you saddled me with upon leaving last week, I'm out."

"Come on! I have a surprise for you," she said, still standing in the doorway.

"I think not, tiger." Jezebel chuckled.

"Put shoes on. I'm busting you out of this place for a bit."

"Sugar, you don't have the authority, or a license . . . or a car. And I am not hoofing it." Jezebel laughed and stuck her chin out stubbornly.

"Put your shoes on or I will do it for you," she commanded. Jezebel looked at her, arms crossed over her chest, nostrils flaring.

"Make me."

Annabelle smirked. She knew it would be a task to *make* Jezebel do anything but she was prepared.

"Fine," she said. Annabelle marched to the woman and kneeled at her feet. Reaching under her chair she pulled Jezebel's sneakers out and started to shove one onto her foot. Jezebel swatted her hands away.

"Oh good grief! You're serious! Back away before you snap my foot off with that brute force of yours," Jezebel complained and snatched her sneakers up. "This better be damned good," she grumbled as she tied her sneakers and stood.

"I promise. It will be great."

They walked together hand in hand through the common room and out the back door into the gardens. From there, Annabelle led them down a path that rounded the side of the building and came out into the employee parking lot.

"Where exactly are we going?" Jezebel asked, looking around.

"To that truck," she said, pointing at Mark's enormous truck.

"Jesus! Is that beast yours?" she asked wide-eyed.

Annabelle laughed and tugged her along. "Nope, it's Mark's."

"Does Mark know you're stealing his truck?"

"Borrowing and no. Come on Jez, just . . . roll with it," she urged. She pulled open the passenger side door and waited expectantly. "Please?"

"You're stealing your boyfriend's truck, you don't have a license and are serving probation, which includes spending time with me, and you want me to approve of this?" Jezebel asked cocking her head to the side.

"Yup."

"Fine. But I'm driving," Jezebel stated. Annabelle squealed with delight and tossed the keys to her. She climbed up into the passenger seat and watched Jezebel round the hood and open the driver's side door.

Watching Jezebel try to navigate Mark's giant truck was amusing. She fumbled for the directional signals and the wiper blades went into a frenzy. Annabelle laughed and directed her where to go. By the time they pulled into the strip mall parking lot Jezebel was a frazzled mess.

"Okay," Jezebel said as she put the truck in park. "Where to?" she huffed.

Annabelle pointed out the windshield in front of them to *Hallowed Ground.* "There," she said.

"What the hell is *Hallowed Ground?*" Jezebel asked, her face a mask of disdain.

"Come on old fart," Annabelle chuckled as she unclasped her seatbelt and threw her door open. Jezebel followed suit.

"Here's the deal," she started, "I've decided that you're getting a nose piercing today. I'm going to get a tattoo and while they're doing it, you tell me more of the story."

Jezebel stopped dead in her tracks. "I am not getting anything *pierced.*"

"Oh yes, you are." Annabelle tugged on her arm and pulled Jezebel through the entrance to the shop. She watched as Jezebel took in her surroundings, the heavy death metal blaring in the background, the employees covered in tattoos and the smell of antiseptic. "Come on," Annabelle said.

Jezebel made a face and stood motionless as Annabelle talked with Chad, the owner, about what she wanted done: a small nautical compass. A reminder to always let the universe lead her in the right direction. A reminder that even when things weren't perfect, perfection could thrive. A reminder of Mark. In the depths of her heart she knew she would need the reminder of him. Of their time. That it was meaningful and right and pure. The tattoo would be small and tasteful on the inside of her wrist. Once she was set, she instructed Chad to sit Jezebel down and pierce her nose. Annabelle picked out a tiny diamond stud and after inspecting it and asking Chad a zillion questions Jezebel gave in with a great sigh.

Annabelle had been prepped and was anxiously waiting for Chad to start as Jezebel stood before the shop mirror examining her new piercing.

"It's not terrible," Jezebel said resolutely.

"It's sick."

"What?"

"Sick . . . cool . . . it looks good," Annabelle explained. "Now would you please distract me while this guy stabs me a thousand times over?" she asked.

Jezebel grinned and took a seat on a small stool next to her free hand. She picked it up and held on to it as the needle started buzzing.

"I think this entire trip is hogwash, you know. But I'm stuck here now. Paris, nineteen ninety-four," she started.

Chapter 40

Celeste

Paris 1994
May

Celeste brushed her teeth and examined herself in the mirror. She was thirty, and it was evident by the faint lines starting at the corners of her eyes. She thought it unfair that on Gabriel they made him more handsome, yet on her they made it appear she was tired. Spitting and rinsing she set her toothbrush aside and tugged her dress over her head before slipping on her heels.

The sun shone brilliantly, and the warm color of the late Spring day seemed offensively bright and cheerful. It was as if the heavens conspired to show her how the world would go on without him while she thought everything should be as grey and foggy as her emotions. Cold and damp with silent air. But the birds still sang and the flowers still bloomed.

She walked through the churchyard and into the church, arm hooked to Gabriel's elbow, like a silhouette of herself. She wished she really was as insubstantial as shadows so that her insides might not feel so mangled. As she took a pew near the front and long held back tears began to flow. Matteo sat to her left and Gabriel to her right. Matteo clutched her hand and waited in silent grief for the start of the funeral service.

Struggling to hold back sorrow, tears flowed steadily, silently down all the immobile faces surrounding her. At the end of the service Celeste felt bruised inside, numb, empty as she walked behind a mahogany coffin, saying goodbye with everyone else who so dearly loved Dr. B.

"Although he is gone already, the soul, unwilling to acknowledge the finality of death, never to look upon his face again or feel his embrace, see the warmth in his eyes, be surrounded by his love." Words from the Minister were heartfelt.

The speech brought a fresh onslaught of tears from the small crowd. Everyone stood in black as dusky white roses were placed on the casket one by one. Celeste watched it being lowered into the grave through tear-stained eyes.

After the funeral everyone gathered at the estate for food and drinks and quiet stories of Dr. B's benevolence. Celeste wandered through the small groupings of people offering condolences as well as receiving them. Matteo, every so often, would catch her eye and offer her a small smile. She wiped more tears from her eyes than she thought possible. She listened to story after story after story of Dr. B's goodwill and generosity and her heart swelled knowing that she came from such good stock. Matteo let her cling to him when she needed a break and she let him disappear outside to smoke without nagging him on the terrible habit.

Only one person looked as if he'd enjoyed the day's events. Gabriel rocked onto his heels, hands tucked in his pockets, smiling like a man who had just had his fill at a fine restaurant and had savored every last mouthful. It irked Celeste that he could be so jovial while the world seemed to crumble around her. She'd yet to tell him of her parents or of Dr. B's will. She wasn't sure why she held back. It was just too much to fight all at once. Maybe it was simply self-perseverance. She knew the path to a solid marriage was founded on truth. She knew that. But she hadn't lied-yet. She'd just not had the right moment to explain.

She watched Gabriel's smile with a scowl on her face. He had been eating and drinking all day while she had been crying and using up tissues. Matteo stepped to her left and smiled half-heartedly at her before noticing what she was looking at. He kept smiling, but it looked strained as he took in Gabriel's indifferent aura.

"Cece, are you alright?" he asked.

She turned to Matteo and looked him in the eyes. "No. I don't think I am."

Chapter 41

Annabelle

"Everything was clean and pretty and safe for you and me. The worst of enemies became the best of friends."

~ Tick Tock, Stevie Ray Vaughn

"We have to hurry!" Annabelle shrieked as they ran from the shop. "Mark will kill me if he finds out I took the truck." Annabelle and Jezebel looked like quite the pair sprinting to the truck and jumping in. This time Annabelle drove—they didn't have enough time to be cautious.

"Child! You're going to kill us!" Jezebel squawked as Annabelle took the turn into Glenview's parking lot at thirty miles per hour.

"Shhh!" Annabelle scolded. Throwing the truck in park, she hopped out and scooted around the hood to help Jezebel down. She locked the doors and hurried them along the path through the back garden until they made it to the common room. Looking around Annabelle hurried Jezebel back to her suite. The second they were seated she let out a great sigh.

"You're a badass," Jezebel said and licked her lips.

"No way, you're the old fart with a nose piercing!" Annabelle retorted and grinned.

Jezebel touched her nose gingerly and smirked. "Yes. I am."

~***~

Annabelle lay on Mark's bed face up. "God . . ." Mark's lips on her silenced her. He slowly, gently kissed her breathless. Her mouth . . . her neck . . . her collarbone and chest received nearly five full minutes of attention. It was beautiful torture. Mark slid his hand down the center of Annabelle's chest, over her stomach, creeping ever lower. His hands and mouth roamed over every inch of her . . . except for the inches she most needed kissed, most desperately desired touched. Annabelle raised her hips, seeking some sort of pleasure but feeling nothing but renewed pressure in her belly.

"You're going to kill me," she breathed.

"I think you exaggerate," he chuckled into her belly. "You should really get going."

"No," she whined and popped her head up to see him.

"Annabelle, your father will kill me," he said, giving her an authoritative look.

She pushed his hair from his forehead and looked at him. "No, he won't. I told him I was staying here tonight."

"What?" he asked.

"He wasn't exactly pleased, but I'm not a child anymore. He didn't have much choice other than to remind me to stay *safe*." She laughed, recalling the embarrassing talk her father tried to give her before she left. Little did he know, she'd had the talk years before with Madison's mother.

"Hmm," he started, sliding his hands over her inner thighs, massaging them, running his fingers to the very edge of her painfully aroused center before pulling away again. "I suppose I'll keep you then." Mark kissed her rib cage, her stomach, lower and lower, until his mouth was only an inch away from where she so desperately wanted him to kiss. She blocked out the thoughts that their time together was dwindling and threw herself into the physical sensations he was offering up.

~***~

Jezebel handed Annabelle a flat rectangular gift. "What is this?" she asked.

"It's a graduation present—a little late," Jezebel answered.

Annabelle smiled and ripped open the paper to find the book Oh The Places You'll Go. She looked up to Jezebel, "Thank you," she said.

"Don't give me that face—I know your reading level is above Dr. Seuss, but that book is a goldmine of wisdom," Jezebel said.

"Oh really?"

"Yes really—it's speaks to the importance of seizing new opportunities, keeping an open mind, trying new things, taking chances and pushing beyond your comfort zone."

"I'm sure it will be riveting," Annabelle deadpanned.

"Ahh, there's my little shithead," Jezebel smirked. Annabelle laughed and flipped through the pages. She stopped when she saw the inscription from Jezebel.

> *Oh the places you'll go darling, never forget the strength you possess.*
>
> *I have the utmost faith that your life will be anything but bland.*
>
> *Seize the day, my dear Annabelle, and find your happiness—a great life awaits you.—-Jezebel*

"It's great Jezebel, thank you. Really," she said sincerely.

"I'm aware . . . now, there is a lot to fit into this week's story because you hijacked our last visit."

"Don't let me keep you," Annabelle said sarcastically.

"I won't. Paris, nineteen ninety-four," Jezebel said.

Chapter 42

Celeste

Paris 1994
May

Celeste looked around. Small aging chandeliers hung from hooks. The dim bulb overhead cast broken light over the dusty attic. She knew she was being shamefully nosy but she couldn't stop herself from opening some as she sorted through the contents of dozens of boxes. As she sorted she set aside the ones willed to others with a green dot sticker so Matteo could carry them downstairs later.

"Crap," she grumbled at the box she hefted up only to have the bottom drop out of it. Papers scattered across the floor. She knelt to retrieve them all.

FILE: CLASSIFIED
PROJECT: TKDM, CIA
DRUG: Zemtranium besylate

Celeste furrowed her brows. What was she looking at? She picked another paper up from the floor.

Targeting: *Short range*
Transmission and Reception: ███████
███████
Purpose: ███████████████████
Effects: ███████████████ *Defection
against will*
Subprojects: ████████████ *Many*
Pseudonym: *Project Domino*
Functional Basis:
███████████████

*Black budget funded TKDM.

Celeste read further, grabbing the other pages from the floor. Skimming through partially blacked out pages of acronyms and military jargon she gleaned what she could. It wasn't much. Government-sponsored murder, biological warfare, secret weapons, a CIA classified research program from the CIA's scientific intelligence division, French-American relations. The main point seemed to be that a small amount of some substance, placed in a liquid, could render an entire company of soldiers unable to fight, all upon consumption. The papers were dusty, crinkled and weathered.

*Note: Given the CIA's failure to follow informed consent protocols with participants, the uncontrolled nature of the experiments, and the lack of data, the full impact of TKDM experiments, including the

*resulting deaths, will never be known. Director
Richards has instructed all records of these
activities destroyed. Myocardial infarction recorded
for all deceased.*

"Black budget funded TKDM? Everything in
here is coded. I don't know what all these terms
mean." Celeste huffed and tossed the file on the
floor. A photograph slid out, skittered across the
floor and wedged under the foot of a dusty
chair. She walked to it, bent to pick it up and
examined it. Three men in lab coats stood
together, clutching hands. They all wore glasses
that were long outdated. The big frames covered
their faces, but one of the three was definitely
Dr. Basle. Celeste flipped the photo over.
Nineteen sixty-five. She tucked the photo back
into the file and inhaled sharply.

The file seemed such a gross invasion of
privacy it turned her stomach to even have it in
her hands. And yet she couldn't stop, even after
learning of the atrocities that Dr. B had been
involved in. Unease settled deep in her gut. She
had to get to the bottom of this.

~***~

Celeste, file in hand, went to the only person
she knew that could help her with what she was
looking at. As she marched purposefully
through the hallways of the embassy she felt like
goo, her knees barely able to keep her upright.

Pushing through Dan's office door she marched to where he sat and flung the file onto his desk, popped her hip out and waited, arms crossed over her chest. His eyes scanned the blacked out label on the front of the file. Tentatively he opened it. She watched as his eyes scanned some of the pages. He grimaced. He groaned and finally he spoke.

"Aww hell Celeste, I wrote a report to the Commissioner years ago for Dr. Basle, but when he confronted the CIA director, they said the incident never happened." Dan shrugged. "The CIA would do anything to meet its goals and the public has been lied to for so long, they wouldn't be able to recognize the truth if Jesus himself told them. Where the hell did you get this?" he asked, pinning her with a look that meant business.

Celeste arched a challenging brow at him. "Why would Dr. Basle be consulting with them?" she asked, ignoring his question.

"The CIA cooperates with its French counterpart, the DGSE. The countries collect information on one another, especially in the economic and scientific areas. I'm just a middleman really."

"Dan. Layman's terms, please," she urged, frustrated.

"He was a brilliant biochemist, Celeste. I thought you knew that."

She shook her head. Dan sighed. "CIA operatives here in France do good work, but there were times we needed Dr. Basle's expertise to review some reports in return. He got his much wanted privacy. He was under one gag order or another most of his professional life."

Celeste knew her sour expression couldn't be hidden. "Operatives. Here. In France." She pointed to the floor while trying to comprehend.

"Sure, the CIA has contracted scientists all over the world." Dan shrugged.

"Scientists," she repeated absently.

Dan cocked his head to the side. "Celeste, is everything alright?"

She shook her head again. "What was my part in all this?" she asked quietly as she thought about all the times she had run files to the embassy for Dr. B over the years.

Dan looked stricken and fumbled for an answer. "Nothing. You were just a courier."

"No, Dan, I was more than that. Look at that file. Look hard." She pointed and Dan looked.

She waited as Dan skimmed the contents further. He flipped a page, then another and another. His eyes stopped their movement. He squinted and shook his head slowly. "No way," he mumbled. "No *fucking* way," he breathed.

"Dan, it appears I'm Dr. B's granddaughter." Dan's eyes snapped to hers, wide and disbelieving. "Start explaining what you're reading to me because I'm starting to freak the hell out," she ordered.

"I can't say a damn thing, Celeste." Dan inhaled and blew out a heavy breath.

"I don't give a shit! This is my life!"

Dan held her eyes, clearly deliberating if he should share information. He got up, strode past her and shut his office door before returning to his seat. "What you found is a file on a covert project that involved biochemical warfare and human testing. The written reports covering the experiments in 1965 were supposed to be destroyed. Three scientists were secretly employed by the CIA. Spanish citizens were drugged without their knowledge or consent. He wasn't supposed to keep this," Dan said, scrubbing his face with a hand.

"What was studied? And why was it supposed to be destroyed?" Celeste pushed for more information.

"Because in the last experiment, the drug killed every patron at a small restaurant. And even more disturbing is that the extent of experimentation on human subjects is still unknown. They tested on unsuspecting people, *without consent,* Celeste. The drug failed miserably and the project was transferred back to the States where it was abandoned."

"What killed them?" she asked.

"Myocardial infarction-heart attack," he answered. Celeste paled. Everything came flooding back like a tsunami. "What if it wasn't?" she asked.

Dan leaned back in his chair and furrowed his brow. "What if what wasn't?"

"What if the project wasn't abandoned?" she said, stunned, Gabriel's late-night story, detail for detail, running through her mind.

"It was," he stated definitively.

Celeste shook her head as nausea swelled within her. "No, no Dan, I don't think it was . . ."

~***~

When she arrived home from the embassy, she couldn't get Dan's words out of her head. She knew the story already, but couldn't wrap her mind around the truth of it all. Gabriel had told her a similar story years ago. *Too similar.* Celeste studied her husband as he reclined in his chair with a book. She mentally dug deep, to inspect the layers of him. She peeled each one away like gift paper. He glanced up at her.

"Mon amour, I didn't hear you come in," he said, grinning at her. Raising a hand, he crooked his finger to beckon her.

Gabriel was an expert in deception—that much was clear. The small blushes he'd caused so many times toyed with her sensual side, the soft smiles he doled out over the years had appealed to her playful side and the knight in shining armor *act* had guaranteed her trust in him from the very beginning. She'd spent long nights making love to him, a man she had given her soul to, a man she thought had returned that precious gift. Now she had an inkling she'd been in bed with the devil.

Instead of going to him, Celeste wandered up the staircase to their bedroom and packed her things. She heard him call for her, a sound that nearly destroyed her heart right there. But she couldn't stay. As she slipped out the front door, she heard her name called again. This time, tears spilled down her cheeks relentlessly as she forced herself to follow through with her plan. She needed a few days to clear her head, to sort this mess out. Celeste sank into the driver's seat heavily and slammed the door closed.

Celeste drove for hours before ending up at the only logical place she could think of. Matteo's. She wanted to be left alone with her wounds, with the absurd love she still harbored for her husband, and Matteo would allow her that without judgment.

She knocked harshly on the door. It swung open before her. Matteo took one look at her and pulled her through the threshold and into his arms.

"*Fiore mio*, tell me," he said. She pulled back

slightly to see his face. One hand released her waist and came up to her cheek, wiping away her tears.

"Not now, Teo. Please. I need time. I need to be alone. There was nowhere else . . ."

Matteo nodded. He helped her from her shoes and coat before showing her to his spare room.

Alone, she cried as she tried to stand up, but landed solid on her knees. Alone, she cried as she crawled to the guest bed and buried herself beneath unfamiliar blankets. Alone, she curled up into the fetal position and wished a hundred wishes that when she awoke the next day the past two months would be nothing more than a terrible dream-or that she wouldn't wake at all. Alone, the next morning when she slumped into a dining room chair, eyes fixed on her best friend and worst enemy. Celeste snatched a bottle of wine from the sideboard and uncorked it. Alone, she lifted it to her lips and willed it to take away her thoughts. One swig. Then another and she smiled. Celeste swigged again and chuckled. She raised the bottle to her mouth, taking the wine down in great gulps.

Her body was on fire and she began to feel at ease. There would be no more hiding from Gabriel. No more fear. She was doing the right thing. Inside, Celeste felt happy, at peace, but her body was betraying her. The bottle paused at her mouth as her eyes rested on the photo from their wedding day again, propped on Matteo's sideboard. Disgust settled in. A tear forced its way out and slid down her cheek. Celeste's head dropped forward and tears dropped onto her cheeks, then fell onto her legs.

Chapter 43

Annabelle

"Try to wake up. Don't have the power. I'm a daughter in the choir."
~ Curbstomp, Meg Myers

The suspense was more than Annabelle could handle. She raised her hand to her mouth and mindlessly rubbed her bottom lip with the tip of her thumb. Disappointment coursed through her over their time being up but, for the first time in a long time, Annabelle couldn't wait to get home. It was Tuesday-not only Jezebel day, but now father-daughter dinner night, and it was something that over the last month she'd grown to love.

"Jez, this story is cray," Annabelle breathed.

Jezebel looked at her perplexed. "What in God's name is cray?" she laughed.

"Short for crazy," she explained.

"It's not exactly any shorter than crazy. Cray, crazy, is the z really such a nuisance?"

Annabelle burst out laughing at Jezebel's rant.

"No, I guess not," she said when she finally composed herself.

"Take your ridiculous terms home to your father for dinner. What are you two making tonight?" Jezebel asked.

"Crepes, I think." Annabelle slid her feet into her flip flops and hoisted her purse up onto her shoulder.

"Mmm, make sure you have *Nutella* at home — a must for crepes."

She smiled at Jezebel and nodded. "I'll pick some up and surprise Dad."

"Au revoir kid," Jezebel called after her.

~***~

Annabelle's week passed quickly now that summer was in full swing. Her dad even went to Madison's family's cookout with her — and enjoyed himself. She and Mark and Madison had spent days at the lake getting tan and swimming to keep cool. Over the weekend her father had brought her up to the college she'd be leaving for in just a few short weeks, and explored the campus with her. She couldn't remember a time when things had gone this smoothly. A small part of her that she tried to keep hidden was waiting for something to give but she consistently shoved that niggling doubt, that naysayer voice in her head, to the dark recesses of her soul. She was happy. Things were falling into place seamlessly and she wouldn't let her own insecurities or hang-ups ruin that.

"Someone is tan and glowing," Jezebel greeted. Annabelle breezed into the room and plunked down into the seat waiting for her.

"Why thank you," she answered.

"I rather like you looking all," Jezebel waved her hand around in the air, "laid back."

"I had a good week. How 'bout you? How was your visit with your husband? By the way—what's his name?" she rambled.

"Our visit was much needed!" Jezebel clapped her hands together. "He always renews my drive to stay on task."

"Uh," Annabelle breathed.

"You'll understand someday, trust me," Jezebel said.

"Okay. Whatever. You're so strange sometimes."

Jezebel winked at her and grinned. "Nothing wrong with that. Now let's hop to it. We're running out of visits and there's much left to tell you."

"Oh! Wait, I brought snacks for us to have while you talk. I made them myself," Annabelle beamed and dug through the large bag she'd schlepped in with her today. She pulled out a *Tupperware* container and popped the lid off before setting it on the side table between them.

"These look scrumptious," Jezebel said. She

picked up a cookie and took a bite. Letting out a groan she swallowed and started. "Paris, nineteen ninety-four."

Chapter 44

Celeste

Paris 1994
May

When she woke the world still spun, the truth still hung thick in the air and she still hurt deeply. Irrationally she scribbled Gabriel's name on a scrap of paper. She stared at it for what felt like an eternity. She scratched it out, angry black slash marks, but it was still there, underneath, lingering. She hated knowing it was still there. She lit a match and smiled as she watched his name burn. Celeste shoved her hand into the pocket of her purse where she now kept the locket he gave her and rubbed the cool precious metal of the chain between her fingers. She couldn't bear to throw it away so she resolved to carry it with her always-like a charm, like a burden, like a reminder.

Celeste had stumbled through the first three days, barely registering anything around her. She made the effort to seem aware and awake and cognizant of her surroundings. She sat with Matteo in the evenings. She chatted and ate whatever he put in front of her and she busied herself cleaning his house. But her mind ran solely on Gabriel and his unfathomable betrayal.

By day eight, Celeste was sure she would die. Her mind just couldn't wrap around the scandal. The hows and whys circled ferociously in her thoughts. She couldn't make sense of anything and she wasn't sleeping at night. She knew she needed to present the information to someone else. To get logical feedback. She was too hurt, too angry, to find logic on her own. To know what the next steps were for her. Matteo was the only person she trusted. Her parents loved her, but had lied to her over the course of her entire life. Dan was loyal, surely, but to his position and government. Gabriel had used her for research. *Research.* Like a rat. Like a guinea pig. Monique and him probably laughed about it daily through the years and years of her blindness. She had only Matteo.

This game had an hourglass for a timer and she saw the sand running out. Gabriel had said so himself a thousand times and she just hadn't understood. How could she? He was close. His work was drawing to an end. She'd been happy for him. Hopeful that once he accomplished his task, they'd have more time together. She was the task. Had he ever planned to stay with her once he completed his objective? She couldn't know and she didn't want to find out.

~***~

Celeste sat on the couch, listening as Matteo

alternately asked questions and thought out loud. He scoured every last document she had. He had even run out to the estate to grab the rest of the scattered papers in the attic. And now, here he was, without question, without judgment, trying to make sense of what was in front of them. His lit cigarette rested in the ashtray on the table, smoke billowing up and dissolving into nothing. Celeste thought it ironic. She felt like the smoke looked. Fading. Dissolving. Ending.

Celeste pushed out of her chair and wandered to the kitchen to fix herself a cup of tea. Matteo followed Celeste and gave her a sheepish smile. He ran a hand over a day's growth of stubble on his chin. "How are you holding up?"

"Me?"

She felt the fatigue in her limbs and heard it in her voice as she continued. "What do you want me to say, Matteo? Do you want me to go to pieces and break down and cry? What good is that going to do?" He raised both hands in mock surrender, pulled out his chair at the kitchen table, and sat. He gave her a weary look. She could see his worry every time he looked at her. Or when he lingered just a moment longer than he should, to make certain she wasn't about to crumble.

"I told you if you called I would always come

running, Celeste. Did you think I'd leave you at your highest or your lowest? I'm just checking in *fiore mio*. This is heavy shit."

Celeste looked at him as she propped a hip against the countertop. Matteo, who took the trash out for his elderly neighbors. Matteo, faithful and loyal and compassionate. Matteo, who had *always* been there. Matteo, who was not a liar.

"I'm . . . I feel like I've been balled up, thrown in the road and driven over a thousand times, only to be kicked around afterward by some kids with nothing better to do. That's what I am," she grumbled. "All of this hurts, but you know what hurts the most?"

"Tell me,"

"Gabriel's infidelity. How ridiculous is that?"

"*Fiore mio,* when we commit to someone, we promise to do our best to be aware of their needs and desires, to be sensitive to signs of distress and respond accordingly. We don't promise to give the *appearance* of fidelity and sensitivity." His words slammed into her with such force that her foot slid on the kitchen floor jarring her hip and sense of balance. Matteo leapt up from his seat, caught her in his arms and steadied her.

He squeezed her close and kissed her forehead. "Celeste, you and I were always with each other before we knew the other was ever there." Celeste sniffled and nuzzled her face into his chest. He smelled of summer and cigarette smoke and earth. "We belong together, just like a breath needs the air. That's why you're here now. That's why we've spent nearly a lifetime as best friends and that's why I will help you any way I can."

Celeste nodded her head as she took stock in his words. She let them sink into her soul and ease some of her pain. She wasn't alone and with Matteo near, she never would be.

Releasing him, she grabbed her tea and ambled back into the living room. Papers were strewn everywhere. Matteo was worried for her safety and had voiced that concern a dozen times already. He narrowed his eyes as he read stacks of redacted papers and stroked his chin. He urged her to go home, grab her things and come back to his house while he attempted to sort things out.

~***~

Matteo left for work early the next morning, citing something about a llama with a sinus infection. Celeste had laughed at the serious tone in his voice and sent her mouthful of coffee out her nose. Matteo joked that it served her right and let her know he'd call to check in on her later. In her darkest hour he was her light.

Celeste wandered the streets of Paris for hours that day. She stopped at cafés and picked up tasty treats for she and Matteo to snack on over the weekend. She bought some clothes and window-shopped to kill time. Walking back to Matteo's she noticed a car parked on the street. Light rain had started to come down and she noticed that although it appeared no one was in the car the windshield had been cleared. Shaking her head she hurried the last few blocks to Matteo's, the rain starting to collect on the ground and the wind picking up around her.

Celeste pushed through the front door, bags in hand. She dropped her things on the kitchen floor and started the kettle. Glancing at the clock she realized Matteo wouldn't be home for hours still. Sighing she dipped her teabag robotically into the mug of steaming hot water.

Celeste stood for a solid hour in the shower, letting the hot water and the steam soothe her aching body and soul. As she stepped out and wrapped a towel around herself she wiped the fog on the bathroom window and stared out at the street below. She noticed the same car again, parked down the street—not the car so much as its windshield. It had been cleared. Once was odd. Twice was purposeful. Celeste looked to the other end of the street then back to the car. The car was gone. The hairs at the back of her neck tingled. She went to the front door, bolted it, and called Matteo home urgently.

~***~

From what they could ascertain, Celeste was being watched. Matteo grew more paranoid as hours ticked by. Afraid for her life.

"Cece, if he's done this to you . . . if he's been doing this to you . . . for years . . . I will punish him. I cannot stand by and let this happen. We need to talk to a lawyer."

"Matteo . . . stop. Please. We just need to figure this out. What good is a lawyer going to do against the federal government?"

Angry, he shook his head and kicked the chair to his left.

Chapter 45

Annabelle

"When everyone has their disguise. I'll show you my heart is real."
~ After You, Meg Myers

"I am freaking out. Freaking. Out. I can't go home now!" Annabelle cried out. She wanted — no, needed — more.

"I told you there was more to tell but you'll have to wait," Jezebel said and popped another cookie into her mouth. "These are seriously amazing. Bring more."

Annabelle laughed, "You can keep those. I'll bring something else next time. Dad's trying to teach me how to bake this week."

"Good man! I am benefitting greatly from this lesson," Jezebel said setting the *Tupperware* container in her lap.

"Next week Jez . . . can't wait," Annabelle said as she exited the room. A warm feeling blossomed in her gut and a smile broke out on her face. Jezebel was a tough cookie to crack so it pleased her tremendously to know she had impressed the woman.

~***~

"No woman in the history of the world has ever looked so beautiful standing in my doorway in nothing but my shirt." Mark's voice startled Annabelle. She spun around to face him with a hand over her jumping heart. He crossed the short distance between them, stroked her hair and caressed her arms. She kissed his neck and muscular shoulders.

Their trip to the bed was inevitable. Her back pressed his chest while he moved slowly and gently in her. As he thrust into her, he whispered how deeply he loved her, how much he would miss her and what he would do to her when she came home to visit. Annabelle realized she didn't have a care in the world-she was happy.

~***~

Annabelle smiled the entire ride to Glenview. Her father belted out the lyrics to some tune from his youth as they drove. The windows were down and the wind whipped around them. She felt free and content.

"Tell Mark I'll pick you up today too," her father called out the window as she shut the car door.

"Dad."

"Belle, humor me," he said.

"Fine, but I'm spending tomorrow night at his house," she answered.

Her father groaned and dragged a hand down his face. "I do not want to hear about you spending the night at anyone's house besides Madison's."

Annabelle laughed. "Fine Dad, tomorrow I'm spending the night at Madison's—happy now?" He shot her a look that could kill, as she smirked back at him, before he pulled away from the curb. Annabelle turned on her heel and headed into Glenview.

"What's shakin'?" Jezebel said as she rounded the corner.

"Hey! No time for small talk—I need more Celeste," Annabelle said dropping her things. She slid out of her shoes and curled up in the chair.

"What about my snacks?" jezebel asked.

"Oh right." Annabelle chuckled and leaned down. She rummaged through the large bag and pulled out a container then handed it to Jezebel. "Peanut butter chocolate balls."

"Tiger, you shouldn't have," Jezebel grinned and popped the lid off. She took one of the treats balls and popped it into her mouth. Her eyes closed and she looked like she'd gone to heaven. "These. Are. Amazing."

"Why thank you," Annabelle returned.

"You are most welcome, kid, you may have found your talent in life."

Annabelle wrinkled her nose. "I don't really want to cook for a living."

"Bake. Not cook. But I hear you—long hours, hot environment . . . could trigger your inner attitude to reappear," Jezebel said with snark.

"We wouldn't want that," Annabelle said dryly.

Jezebel shook her head furiously before laughing. "Alright, You're in such a damned rush-Paris, nineteen ninety-four," she said.

Chapter 46

Celeste

Paris 1994
June, Saturday

One day she was on the right track; the next she was a train wreck. Each day a new drop or lift on a roller coaster. As she pulled into her driveway she breathed deep trying to calm her nerves. As ridiculous as it was, she still loved her husband. It seemed nearly impossible to erase the good memories of a decade. She'd never for a moment thought their marriage was a ruse and that truth hurt deeply.

She needed to pick up some things. Matteo had encouraged, and finally convinced, her to do it. Here she was. At her house. Feeling like a stranger.

"Celeste."

Gabriel drew her name out in that seductive way only he could as she stood in the foyer.

She took him in. "Gabriel."

"*Mon amour,* where have you been? I've been mad with worry," he said approaching her.

"I can't do this," she answered putting her hands up in front of her to stop him from coming closer. Gabriel grabbed her hands and tugged her to his chest. "Please . . ." she tried.

"Non. Non, you are mine, *mon amour,* we will work this out. All of it. I've fired Monique. Celeste, you are my heart. Please, please just talk to me," he begged in between placing kisses on the crown of her head.

Celeste tilted her head up to look at him. His face, that handsome face, nearly shattered her heart. She wanted his words. She wanted to believe him. She wanted him, just a piece to keep with her always. Backing up a step she pushed past him and took the stairs two at a time to their bedroom. She tugged her suitcase from the closet and began throwing things haphazardly into it. She shoved her tears away and repeated her actions: grab then toss into the suitcase. *Do not cave, do not cave,* her mantra.

Gabriel yanked her from the closet, lifting her off her feet and setting her on the bed with him.

"Stop it," she cried. She didn't want to be reminded of the connection she felt to him. She didn't want the memory of the way his arms felt around her.

"Non. You just need a reminder. We're good together. I love you. I love you more than there are stars in the night sky. I love your smart mouth and your perfect curves. I love you," he pleaded. His hands lifted her knit dress and something snapped inside of her. A switch was flicked. She raised her arms and allowed him to pull her dress off and toss it to the floor. Frantic passion consumed her. Her brain was useless, her body consumed with need.

She pushed Gabriel onto his back and straddled him. He tugged her neck, bringing their lips together. Anger poured out of her and into him as she kissed him back roughly. His hands found her panties and ripped them from her before he flipped her onto her back. She fumbled with his pants until they finally slid down his thighs and she laughed, crazed, when he kicked them to the floor. Thrusting into her she let out a scream. They moved together. They loved together. They hurt together. But, no, that wasn't right. It was all her love, her hurt. Celeste's eyes snapped open as he moved over her, in her. His thumb pressed against her most sensitive spot and circled. Her pleasure built until it erupted in a magnificent burst. So caught up in her own mind and desire she barely noticed when Gabriel finished.

She placed a hand on his cheek. She kissed his lips then rolled him off her and stood. "I'm going, Gabriel." She wriggled into her dress and tucked her curves out of view before turning to survey herself in the mirror. "Please know that I wouldn't have stooped to deception if I didn't hold you in such high regard, but I've known about you since after Dr. B's funeral. I was angry at first, you know-*so* angry," she said.

Eight years. In eight years Dr. B had never breathed a word of his inclination that Celeste was his granddaughter. Now she understood why. She was not merely his granddaughter, she was a commodity. An exception people wanted to use to discover a rule. The truth had exploded inside her like a bomb and she'd splintered under the force of it. She was the key-not to Gabriel's heart, but to his work. Celeste steeled herself.

"You know, after being betrayed, initially, I wanted two things. I wanted to wound you—as deeply and as excruciatingly as I was wounded, and strangely enough, I wanted to be able to rise above the situation and forgive you," she chuckled. "But neither of those tactics work. Every hurt has its own journey, and so does every healing. Love fuses you with another person, makes you capable of feeling their emotions as acutely as you feel your own. For us there is no cure for that Gabriel. I'm leaving you," she said boldly. Celeste felt powerful suddenly.

Gabriel snarled at her, raw and savage, and in the depths of his rage, she saw his true colors. "Celeste." he thundered, chest heaving, nostrils flaring, "You. Cannot. Leave. I need you."

Celeste backed toward the door. "Of course I can," she stated firmly. "You've given me no room to stay."

She watched as he tried to calm himself, to appear rational. It was laughable really. "Celeste, *mon amour*. We're so close. We can work this out. I need you, you're the key," he pleaded.

Celeste knew information was power and she now had all the information she needed. "I am, aren't I?" She cocked her head and looked at him. "I was so foolish all those years ago to think the *key* you were referring to was the key to your heart." She laughed bitterly. Heartbreak, abhorrent and vicious betrayal and a desperate need to understand the motive behind it slammed into her. It ran rampant through her body; her heart had been broken not just by her husband, who she was still in love with, but by someone she thought was a true friend.

"If I can't have you, no one will. Don't you understand?" he thundered. "Celeste, you can't walk away from me or the CIA, not after they've invested years of operatives' lives in you." She froze in her spot. She *was* being watched. Fear rippled through her.

She straightened her shoulders. "Oh, I'm not walking, Gabriel—I'm running." Celeste turned on her heel and strode resolutely downstairs and away from her house, from their house, from *his* house.

As she put the car in reverse Gabriel tumbled out the front door in only his boxers after her. A tremble ran through her at the pure rage that exuded from him. She had no doubt that he spoke the truth. Someone would come for her, be it a government agent or Gabriel himself-she was a walking dead woman. One who at least now was able to prepare.

Later that evening as Celeste told Matteo how the day's events had unfolded an unsettling moment embraced her, fraught with tangled layers of love, hate and power. Matteo and Celeste sat side by side and came up with a plan of action that might possibly remove her from this situation permanently. She would need to play the part. She and Matteo had money. Enough to disappear. Money that Gabriel didn't know about. They talked about Matteo sticking close. About moving money around in the next few days and setting up a safe place where they could go.

Celeste wanted to shatter Gabriel's entire perception of reality and force him into the despair he forced on her. If only wishes were truths.

Chapter 47

Annabelle

"I'm writing letters in my head. I sign my name but never send."

~ After You, Meg Myers

"What?" Annabelle squawked throwing her arms in the air.

"What?" Jezebel answered settling back into her chair. She popped another chocolate peanut butter ball into her mouth.

"What!"

"I feel like we're not communicating," Jezebel said dryly.

"I'm . . . shocked. Stunned. Holy hell, Jez, did Gabriel really do that to her? Was it all a game? He just used her for his work? Oh. My. God. I can't . . . I can't even," Annabelle spluttered. She readjusted her position in her seat and ran her fingers through her hair repeatedly.

"You're awfully worked up," Jezebel commented, then took a sip of water.

"Well yeah! I mean, how can this possibly end well? We only have two more visits, Jez, I just . . . ugh," she sighed. "I hate him." Annabelle took a sip of water to cool down.

"You don't know the whole story yet—you might not hate him at the end," Jezebel clucked as Annabelle slipped her shoes on.

"Yeah right. He's an asshole! He totally used her . . . and for what!? For her DNA? To solve some stupid issue with a drug that armies want to use? It's not like he was curing AIDS or something." She felt hot with anger. Annabelle couldn't even begin to imagine what Celeste had felt.

"True, dear, but who knows how the story really ends."

"Jez, you're killing me here," she grumbled.

"The next two visits will blow your mind, Now get going," Jezebel said.

"My mind has already been blown," Annabelle muttered before taking the empty *Tupperware* container and shoving it in her bag.

"Bring me another treat?" Jezebel asked and batted her lashes.

"I don't know if I like you enough to bake anymore—you're totally holding out on me," Annabelle scowled.

"Oh please, you'll be back; it would drive you mad to not know the ending."

"It's really irritating when I'm irritated and you're right," she said as she paused in the doorframe.

"It is maddening isn't it?" Jezebel laughed.

Annabelle gave her a small wave and stomped all the way to her father's car. Slamming the door shut she heaved out a breath.

"What's your issue? Is it really that bad being seen with me?" her father asked. She turned to him. He looked worried. Annabelle rested her head against the headrest and smiled.

"No Dad, it's not you. I'm not really in a bad mood — it was just . . . theatrics."

"Maybe you should be going to a performing arts college then because that performance was definitely convincing," her father said. Annabelle laughed loud and hard until her father joined in as well.

~***~

Picking out a gift for Jezebel was harder than she thought it would be. She wanted to give her something that was meaningful. Something that would reflect their time together accurately. Thinking back on their time together Annabelle was embarrassed at the way she had behaved six months ago. She'd been so angry and withdrawn. It was hard for her to really believe she had changed, but things had changed-so much in half a year.

"Dad, I want to get Jez a gift, but I'm having a hard time. She's your age, kinda . . . what do you like?" she asked as she pushed her food around on her plate.

"Like my age? That's really useful information," he said sarcastically.

"Okay, she likes music, she likes plants and my baking, but none of those are permanent. I want to give her something she can keep forever," she explained and leaned back in her seat.

Her father stared at her blinking. "That's very thoughtful of you." Annabelle shrugged. "What about a book? Or a framed photo or something like that?"

Annabelle brightened at the ideas. "That's perfect Dad," she said and jumped from her seat. "I need to borrow fifty bucks, is that okay? I know the perfect place to make a really nice photo book."

Her father smiled at her and pointed to her chair. "Yes, you can—after we finish eating. Your pictures aren't going anywhere."

Annabelle chuckled and sank back into her chair. "Yes sir."

~***~

Annabelle was excited as she bounced down the hall to Jezebel's suite. She had put all the ridiculous photos she'd taken into a hardcover photo book she'd created. Each page held a picture of the two of them with a caption, and the last page was the picture she snapped of just

Jezebel when she looked so utterly happy. She scoured stock photo sites to find the perfect picture of Paris for the cover. Never having been, she ended up purchasing one of the Eiffel Tower. It felt right to her. She skipped through the doorway and found Jezebel's room empty.

"Jez?" she called out.

"A moment!" Jezebel answered.

Annabelle kicked off her sneakers and sank into the wingback chair she always sat in and waited. She fidgeted with the wrapped photo book, tightening the bow, smoothing the paper.

Jezebel glided from the bathroom with two glasses of water. She set them down, one for herself and one for Annabelle, then sat.

"That looks awfully flat for treats," Jezebel said with sarcasm.

"Truth," Annabelle chuckled. "But it is for you!" Annabelle handed the gift wrapped book to Jezebel and held her breath as she opened it. She tossed the paper to the floor and smiled as she looked at the cover. Flipping through the pages, she laughed and smiled brightly. Finally Jezebel caught her eyes.

"This is beautiful. You have no idea how perfect this is," she said. Jezebel stood and Annabelle followed suit. She took comfort in Jezebel's arms as she wrapped her own arms around Jezebel's slender waist. Jezebel placed a kiss on top of her head and sighed as she stroked Annabelle's hair. "Are you sure you're ready for today?"

Annabelle pulled back and looked at Jezebel's face. "That is the most ridiculous question ever . . . I *have* to know what happens."

"Alright, alright, sweet beet, I get it," she said, then sat.

"Aww, you'll miss me," Annabelle teased.

"I will."

"If you're good, maybe I'll come back and visit," she said and winked at Jezebel.

"Good lord, don't ever wink at anything—you looked like you were having a seizure." Annabelle laughed at her deflection. She would miss Jezebel, too. So much.

"Alright, let's dig in," Annabelle said.

Jezebel nodded. "Paris, nineteen ninety-four,"

Chapter 48

Celeste

Paris 1994
June, Thursday

The morning of Celeste's death was spectacular. Oranges, pinks and blues set the sky ablaze in splendid glory. She gazed out the window from where she laid in bed, stunned by the raw beauty. Breathing in the spectacular show before her, her mind wandered to uglier things.

She popped out of bed late in the morning before wandering, one last time, to the City of Lights, which lived up to its name. For all its fanfare, the Eiffel Tower rarely disappointed; at night, its thousands of twinkling lights turned on to dazzle onlookers. It would make the perfect backdrop. A dazzling finale for a naive life, she thought bitterly. No more. Her life as she knew it was nothing more than a masterful illusion. She knew she couldn't keep holding out for a miracle. She and Matteo knew too much.

Celeste wandered aimlessly for hours. She admired the stone gargoyles, the fresh smells that wafted from the bakeries and the bustle of the arts district. Finally, armed with a full belly she winked at the black sedan that had been tailing her all week. At the base of the tower, away from the crowds, she sat in wait.

At a quarter past five, she heard a whistle cut through the still chilled air. A jolly intricate tune. Clear, every note carrying beautifully. The whistler was not in sight yet but getting closer. She never could whistle. It had never really bothered her until that moment. The slap of dress shoes on pavement added a beat line to the whistled tune. Her rear was numb from sitting still for so long. Wind rustled leaves faintly. The tune gained volume as the perpetrator neared. She should practice whistling, she thought arbitrarily.

She had known someone would come for her when he found out she knew, because she would never willingly consent to further testing, but . . . she realized that she would rather die in truth than live a life consumed by betrayal. Celeste waited on a bed of nails. She was surprised that Gabriel was the one to arrive. The whistling stopped and she knew her time was nearing its end. Turning her head left, just slightly, he smiled a wicked smile at her. "Celeste." His voice was emotionless and she wondered how. Was he not ever truly in love with her? All these years—an act? It didn't matter anymore; she resolved to look at his betrayal as a gift.

"Gabriel," she greeted. Her eyes scanned her surroundings looking for reassurance. She blinked once when she found it. "Where will you take me?" she asked.

His expression softened. "Nowhere, *mon amour*. Come here." His hands stretched out to embrace her. Celeste found herself wrapping her arms around him, as she'd done so many times in the years past. What they must look like, she thought, to passersby. A loving couple? The lie behind the picture struck deep still. Holding her tight his voice came in a thick breeze at her neck. In everyone's lives there is a crossroads where what is said next will define the future, and this was hers-she could feel it. Her stomach turned. *Don't speak!* she wanted to shout. She understood what was coming and didn't need his reasons.

"You destroyed *everything*. My life's work, my reputation." His snarl was low, menacing. White-hot pain seared the skin of her shoulder blade. She couldn't inhale, her lungs filling with blood. Stepping back, Gabriel wiped a blood-tinged blade on his hankie, as she dropped to the ground, sputtering. He did it. *He really did it*, she thought. The moment stole her breath. She stupidly thought she had the situation under control. She was stripped down to something she didn't understand.

Realization hit her like a freight train-that the

real betrayal would be if Gabriel were able to make her stop loving him, stop believing in what had been *her* truth all these years. She owned that. Clinging to that thought, she looked him in the eye.

"I still love you," she whispered, her voice faint but clear.

His cruel eyes widened in disbelief at her final words. His lips opened and closed, not forming any distinct word or sound. Gabriel stepped backward once, then twice. *Scream,* she thought. *Scream now!* But she couldn't. Her throat wouldn't work. All that came out was a gasp. Blood bubbled up and out the corner of her mouth as a half-smile crept over her face and her eyes fluttered closed. Pain radiated as her face hit the pavement. It was over. Her first love, her heartbreak, her pain. It happened. The boss died, the husband cheated, the heart broke. It's not the truth she would have chosen but she'd take it. It was hers. She would be released from this life and he would walk away. The world went black.

Chapter 49

Annabelle

"I'm the only one in the in the shadows. My heart is fire, my heart is young."
~ Make a Shadow, Meg Myers

"That can't be the end, Jez!" Annabelle yelled. She was gutted, twisted up inside. She reached for her glass of water and chugged the contents trying to stop the rising anger she felt.

"Why the hell not?" Jezebel shot back, arching an eyebrow. Her nose piercing glinted in the light.

"It . . . it just can't. It's so sad." Annabelle's shoulders slumped as she thought about Celeste's story.

"Sometimes, life is sad," Jezebel said. She looked at the woman, shocked at her bluntness. It seemed like such a cold statement, harsh in its honesty, from a woman she'd come to think of as warm. A woman telling a story about a friend, presumably.

"What about Matteo? What about Gabriel?" Annabelle asked.

"What about them?" she answered, nonplussed.

"Ugh! You are killing me here, Jez. It's my last visit. I need answers! There is so much left unfinished!"

"True, kiddo, but not for long," Jezebel stated. Glancing at the clock, Annabelle noticed she was already late for dinner. Her father would be irritated with her.

"Fine, I see what you're doing. I'll come back Friday before I leave for school, but you have to promise to finish the story!" she demanded.

Looking to Jezebel, she excused herself. When she turned to give Jezebel a wave goodbye she noticed that Jezebel wasn't in her chair. *Odd.* Scanning the room she found Jezebel watching her curiously from the bathroom door. Then the room tilted, shifted the wrong way.

"Oh, don't try to move. You won't enjoy that, dear," Jezebel clucked. Her voice sounded far away. Harsh and cold. The room's dance picked up its pace. Annabelle blinked furiously as she started to understand. Fear pummeled her. "What did you . . . do . . . to me?"

"I don't recall what it's called. Almost tasteless, especially in *water*. Your father, Gabriel, really did nail it, didn't he? Well almost. He never did get it to leave the subject able to talk."

Jezebel gave her a dazzling smile. She swaggered over and batted away Annabelle's hand when she made a clumsy grab for the woman. "It took quite a bit of time and money to track you all down. Wouldn't you know it, wishes do come true because I had both at my disposal. By then, I have to admit I'd developed a small infatuation with you all. I wanted to meet your brother and you. Your brother I only saw through the windshield though. I didn't get to know him like you. It was such fun. I hope there are no hard feelings. I wish I could give you my real name, but I have a feeling you've already guessed it." Jezebel kissed her nose, like a snake charmer kissing the head of a cobra. "You were a real treat, you know, kid."

Annabelle's vision blurred. Her arms froze in place, her knees locked up and her neck stiffened. Jezebel pushed an index finger to her shoulder, and she tilted and fell to the floor, unable to move her body.

Epilogue

It seems that insignificant beginnings lead to epic endings. In the beginning she was loved. She was cared for and adored and cherished. In the beginning there was her.

A whole being.

A true sense of self.

A connection with reality and morals.

When the end came, love was twisted into hate, her sense of self destroyed by the select few who had helped create it and had guided her in life. Morals ceased to exist and reality became nothing more than a sparkling memory that hung just out of reach.

Celeste had always preferred collecting moments over things and this particular moment was grand. Annabelle looked at her like she was a monster. Like a cannibal preparing to eat her for lunch. She understood. Celeste rolled Annabelle facedown. It was a shame, but no one left the world unscathed. Wars had casualties. Annabelle was a good girl. But she served a purpose. "Shhh," she told her as Annabelle tried to mumble words into the floor. Celeste had actually grown to like her over the last six months. She was *almost* sad to see her go. She slipped on her sneakers, coat and hat quickly. Pulling a knife from the side table drawer, she plunged it into Annabelle's back, in the exact spot where she had been stabbed so many years ago. Matching scars. She twisted the blade. Annabelle's breath wheezed out. Unlike Celeste, there would be no one in place to rescue the girl in time. She felt lighter.

So much lighter.

Vindicated.

Removing her necklace, she clasped it around Annabelle's neck. The decades-old engagement ring and the gold engraved locket clanked against each other. There would be no doubt left in their minds when Gabriel and Monique — or Gavin and Monica, as they were called, were presented with them later.

As evidence in a murder.

His world has collapsed, he just hasn't realized it yet. Just as he'd destroyed everything Celeste thought was true, she had taken from him all his truths: his marriage, his children, his identity. And it felt amazing.

Celeste left Annabelle Fortin on the floor of Jezebel's room. Briskly walking down the hall, she yanked the fire alarm as she passed. She pushed through the double doors out into the chilled late summer air. It was six thirty p.m. He should be here already. Just as panic began to take root in her chest, a candy-apple-red Porsche pulled up to the curb. Her breath hitched as a grin spread across her face.

Her husband.

She'd missed him these last months. It was difficult being apart for so long. He was her rock. Her truth. Her everything. He smiled, a cigarette dangling from the corner of his mouth as always. She smiled back. Leaning over as she'd approached, he'd pushed the car door open from the inside for her.

"Fiore mio," he cooed, admiring her.

"I missed you," she breathed. His lips found hers. Warmth flooded her. He is so incredibly handsome. So pure. His love, his commitment, saved her and now they were truly free.

"Sei pronta?" *Ready?* he asked. Celeste twined their fingers together and rested their connected hands on her thigh and sighed contentedly. It was over. Matteo put the car in drive and peeled out from the lot as people began to rush out the doors frantically. Her past floated away until it was just a memory of a nightmare from the night before, leaving a new life in its wake.

She is.

She is so ready.

Finally free from all the betrayal.

The End

Stay in touch so you don't miss

Lying in Wait,

the prequel novella to *Jezebel* — it will have the missing years!

Check out the website or **pre-order here:**
http://www.amazon.com/Lying-Wait-Prequel-Novella-Jezebel-ebook/dp/B00WF9KTGE.

Acknowledgments

Before Jezebel, I'd never written in third person. The switch was hard for me until I got into a good pattern of writing. I'll tell you a secret. I went and saw a woman who says she is a soul reader. In the course of our appointment, she told me I would write a book that took place in Paris. I had *no* books in the works that involved Paris at the time. She told me it would be about betrayal and that the first thing I would write would be the last scene. She said once I wrote that page — watch out world, the rest of the book would 'download' into my brain. I was in the thick of finishing up *Target 84* then and had three other ideas vying for attention once that was done. Here's the thing — I finished *Target 84* and then wrote a scene that just 'appeared' in my head. It was the final scene of *Jezebel*. Well, it was Celeste's final scene. Holy hell! She was right. From there, the book literally had its own shape and style and I was just along for the ride. I hope you enjoyed it. I hope you go back and kick yourself because 'Oh! That clue *was* there!'

I have a thousand people I want to thank. Inevitably I will forget someone. Whoever you are: it's not personal. There were oh-so-many people who helped this novel become what it is.

To start, my beta readers . . . without you all I'm not sure I would have finished this book. I kept hitting roadblocks or thinking it was crap and you all kept telling me to push on because it was good. Peggy a.k.a. Mom, Sherry, Reagan, Emma C., Emma A., Raquel, Jesey, Lisa, Trisha, L.A. and Kim and Ella and Sarah. Midian and Yaya and Marisa. I can NOT express enough how valuable your feedback was. Just know that it was. So valuable.

To the bloggers, your endless support of my books is astounding and appreciated and vital. Yes, vital! Without the help from so many of you no one would know who the heck I am. So thank you. Thank you for sharing, promoting, reading, reviewing and being true supporters. It's incredible.

My family. There were lots of times I just zoned out and wrote. No one complained. No one interrupted. No one got pissy. In short-you were all amazing.

And to my readers. It is YOU who carry me along. YOU who motivate me to continue writing. My biggest thanks goes out to you, the reader, for taking a chance on this book. For allowing me to slip into your life and steal your time. It's an honor. Thank you.

Want more of K. Larsen's work?

30 Days ~ FREE
Committed

Bloodlines Series — All can be read as stand-alone books.

Tug of War ~ FREE
Objective
Resistance
Target 84

Stand Alones

Dating Delaney
Saving Caroline

About K. Larsen

K. Larsen is an avid reader, coffee drinker, and chocolate eater who loves writing romantic suspense and thrillers. If *you* love suspense and romance on top of a good plot you've hit the mother-load. She may mess with your head a bit in the process but that's to be expected. She has a weird addiction to goat cheese and chocolate martinis, not together though. She adores her dog. He is the most awesome snuggledoo in the history of dogs.

Seriously.

She detests dirty dishes. She loves sarcasm and funny people and should probably be running right now . . . because of the goat cheese . . . and stuff. Sign up for a chance to win a $5 Gift card every time she sends a newsletter out.

Stalk her — legally
Newsletter
http://klarsenauthor.com/5-gift-card/
Amazon
http://www.amazon.com/K.-Larsen/e/B00AN1BSIE
Goodreads
http://www.goodreads.com/author/show/6871141.K_L arsen
Facebook
https://www.facebook.com/K.LarsenAuthor
Twitter
@Klarsen_author

Author's you don't want to miss . . .

Kim Holden

I'm an indie author (sort of, kind of). I love nice people, music, reading, writing, my dudes (my husband and son), iced coffee, social media, and sarcasm (not necessarily in that order).

I've birthed three books:

All of It, *Bright Side*, and *Gus*.

I love making new friends. Come find me. We'll hang out.

https://facebook.com/KimHoldenAuthor

~***~

R.L. Griffin

She published her first book in 2004. After that she focused on practicing law. A few years ago she began writing the *By A Thread* series, which is out now. Her goal is to keep readers on their toes, whether it's the plot twist or the book itself, her books are outside any box. There is a little bit of grit in most of her books and a ton of cussing. Most books are enjoyed better with a glass of wine, or whiskey, whatever your poison may be.

She lives in Atlanta with her husband, kid and dog. She loves to travel and meeting readers.

~***~

Ella James

Ella is a USA Today bestselling author who writes teen and adult romance. She is happily married to a man who knows how to wield a red pen, and together they are raising two children who will probably grow up believing everyone's parents go to war over the placement of a comma.

Ella's books have been listed on numerous Amazon bestseller lists, including the Movers & Shakers list and the Amazon Top 25 overall; two were listed among Amazon's Top 100 Bestselling Young Adult Ebooks of 2012.

To find out more about Ella's projects and get dates on upcoming releases, follow her on Facebook and follow her blog, www.ellajamesbooks.com. Questions or comments? Tweet her at author_ellaj or e-mail her at ella@ellajamesbooks.com.

Ella is represented by Rebecca Friedman of the Rebecca Friedman Literary Agency.

~***~

Leylah Attar

Leylah writes stories about love — shaken, stirred and served with a twist. When she's not writing, she can be found pursuing her other passions: photography, food, family and travel. Sometimes she disappears into the black hole of the internet, but can usually be enticed out with chocolate.

~***~